To Chris
Enjoy
Much love
Amanda Gn
X

Harry

AMANDA POOLE-GRAHAM

authorHOUSE®

AuthorHouse™ UK
1663 Liberty Drive
Bloomington, IN 47403 USA
www.authorhouse.co.uk
Phone: 0800.197.4150

Published by AuthorHouse 11/07/2018

ISBN: 978-1-5462-9245-6 (sc)
ISBN: 978-1-5462-9246-3 (hc)
ISBN: 978-1-5462-9244-9 (e)

Print information available on the last page.

Front cover and Author photographic image provided by Ashley Poole-Graham.

Dedication

To my dear mother Audrey Poole who I miss very much.
For the wonderful years spent holidaying in S'Agaro I owe her and
my father Michael Poole much love and gratitude.

Acknowledgments

I first felt a passion to write after meeting Jilly Cooper at my aunty Eileen's house having been absorbed by her books as a teenager. She was charming and after telling her I had read all her books she kindly sent me a signed copy of Appassionata. From then I knew that I had a story in me that I just had to tell.

I first started writing this book over 25 years ago when my children Charlotte and Ashley were toddlers. My first attempt was on a Commodore computer back in the late 80's with only floppy discs to store my first draft. I lost focus and inspiration for many years and finally picked up the old floppy discs and tried to transfer the work to my laptop in 2016. Several chapters were missing or irretrievable and I have had to rewrite them recalling the story and updating it.

The main character Harry has always remained in my thoughts. Over the years, we shared many holidays in S'Agaro with my daughter Charlotte, son Ashley, nieces Chloe Venn, Kayleigh Joyce, Gemma Goatley, nephews Sebastian Venn, Ben and Jack England, Ross and Tom Webb, Graeme Wright, Bradley Smith and many of my children's close friends including Kimberly Carter, Emily Bennion, Julie Sheen, Mike Payne, Joel York, Matt Broughton and Thom Hinman, all of whom have enriched our lives and in one way or another inspired some of the characters in this book. Not forgetting those who never came to Spain but have grown up with my children; Rob Hodges, Kate Thomas, Rhiannon West, Tim Williams, Tom Veale. They all helped me create Harry's character as well as her circle of friends.

My daughter Charlotte spent a year at the University of Cadiz, Southern Spain and eventually married a Spanish man she met while she was there, Sergio Coronil Navarro. So yes - English girls do marry Spanish boys! I was reminded during a speech by Richard Robinson at their wedding of how my husband and I embraced their teenage antics giving them the opportunity to enjoy the freedom of our house and the farm and many of these stories have also created a foundation for Harry's experiences.

I would also like to mention my lovely Dutch friends Tago, Yda, Sharon and Mickey who have been life long friends since meeting them on the beach in S'Agaro.

The "Boatmen" also deserve a mention for mooring our various boats over the years. They changed on a regular basis so there have been too many to name. Our holidays would not have been the same without them. They have had to rescue members of my family on numerous occasions from breakdowns of our speedboat in the bay. They are now collectively known as Marina De S'Agaro and they continue to look after us and our boat whenever we are there.

Harry's antics are also based on my own experiences as a teenager exploring the Spanish nightclubs with my sister Jackie Webb and friend Sara Sleight who we met in S'Agaro many years ago. Following our generation my children and Sara's children, Jenny and Jack, have enjoyed nights out together revisiting our old haunts as well as finding new clubs springing up along the coast in and around Playa-D'Aro.

Thanks go to my sister Lesa and brother in-law Laurence for days and nights of congenial holidaying as well as being a daily support to me and my family back here in England. Together we have watched our children grow and blossom. Also, my sister and brother in-law Nicky and Forbes England who have been amazing to my whole family over the years.

Other friends whose company we have been fortunate to enjoy in S'Agaro and have made our holidays special; Steve Pringle, Chris Davies, Richard and Sara Smith, Bobby Hulme and Debbie Miller, Johno and

Lisa Smith, Elaine and Alec Vincent, Alex Duncanson, Joan, Dave and Martin Jones.

My friends Ricky and Jackie Dean who once gave me a book to read "Feel the Fear and Do it Anyway". Well Jackie I finally have!

Mags, Marguerite Oke has made my life so much easier with her love and support over the past few years so a heartfelt thank you to her. Also my sister Pipsy who loved her holidays in S'Agaro.

I also owe a big thank you to my very good friend David Godwin. In the early days of my writing he would correct my spelling and leave me sarcastic comments scribbled in red about the various repetition of words and characters he did not like. This always made me laugh as I continued my journey with Harry's story.

My friends Amanda Whelan and her husband Jim have been fantastic partners in crime for some great nights in S'Agaro. Amanda gave me confidence to finish my book and get it published.

Published Cookery author Fran Warde encouraged me to self-publish which gave me faith in myself and the confidence and drive to continue through to the end.

Finally, a big thank you to my husband Dean for his patience, doing the final check and giving me the green light.

Thank you for buying my book, I hope you enjoy reading it as much as I have enjoyed my journey writing it.

Chapter 1

At 18 years old, and with her braces removed and retainer finally discarded, Harry still lacked confidence. She sat in front of the mirror plucking her eyebrows. Her face had a classical look to it, with thick black eyelashes, deep blue eyes, and a perfectly shaped nose set neatly above a set of rose-coloured lips, all framed by a mass of blond wavy air.

"Harry, dinner time!" Her mother, Anna, shouted up the stairs.

Harry took a last look in the mirror then skipped along the corridor and down the creaking stairs to the large oak farmhouse kitchen. Dinner was a cross between lunch and tea. It was the main meal of the day in the Thomas-Smyth household.

Everyone sat around the old pine kitchen table chattering with excitement. Harry's father, Mark, sat at the head of the table with Anna at the opposite end. The twins, Sophie and Mickey, sat one side of the table, with Harry and Christina occupying the settle opposite. All were eagerly discussing what to pack for their forthcoming holiday.

A record breaking, bumper crop harvested and stored, Mark and Anna were exhausted and looking forward to a break. The children had broken up from College, Harry having completed her first year's secretarial course at Gloucestershire University of Art and Technology, and Christina arriving back from Cardiff University the day before. At last it was time for the family to take a month off and relax at their small villa on the Costa Brava.

No one had started to pack except for Anna, who had been trying to pack for the twins over the previous few weeks, asking them to wear old clothes as she tried to keep on top of the washing, which was an almost impossible task with a family of six.

Mickey, well known for his pranks, was a mischievous little boy. Now eight years old, he was fascinated by nature and was currently fascinated by anything which crept or crawled. His bedroom was like a shrine to every naturalist that ever lived. Photos and posters adorned the walls; books on insects, animals, and birds lined the shelves. An aquarium stood in one corner filled with brightly coloured fish swimming amongst the weeds and diving around a ship-wreck. Entering his room was like entering a miniature version of the Natural History Museum.

Mickey was like his father to look at. With a round face, rosy cheeks, blue eyes, and thick light brown hair, trimmed up to his ears, then cut in a pudding bowl shape around his large head, he resembled a boy from a period drama.

Sophie, Mickey's twin, had blond hair that hung in ringlets around her delicate face. She too had deep blue eyes, a button nose, and beautifully shaped red lips. Sophie had a very dainty little figure and, when in her Sunday best, looked like a little princess. Most of the time Sophie was inseparable from her brother; she dressed in dungarees or long shorts and resembled a rag doll that had been passed down through the generations.

Christina, the oldest of the four children, was a natural beauty with blond hair, big blue eyes, and dimples. She no longer lived at home during term time. She was at university studying. Not only was she born with beauty, but also with brains. Her well-developed figure was the envy of all her friends. She had a string of boyfriends, normally one at university and one at home, a plethora of girlfriends, and a hectic social life. This was about to be rudely interrupted by a month in Spain.

"Your father and I will share a suitcase. I have already packed the big blue case for the twins so, Harry, you can use the other blue case up in the attic, and please get on with your packing. Daddy needs to pack the car tonight if we are to leave at the break of dawn."

At that moment, Sophie started to cry.

"What's the matter now, darling?" Mark asked with a concerned look on his face.

"Mickey has chopped up some dead frogs and put them in the stew," she sobbed.

Everyone looked at him in horror. Mouths were politely emptied around the table.

"I wanted to know what frog tasted like. They eat it in France so I added a bit to the stew. It was only a couple of legs," a sheepish looking Mickey confessed.

Christina and Harry made a hasty retreat to the downstairs bathroom, while Anna set about salvaging the meal. Mark, whilst holding back his laughter, took Mickey out for a quiet word.

Later, after blowing off the dust covering the suitcase she had found in the attic, Harry set about squeezing the entire contents of her summer wardrobe into it. After filling another massive hand luggage bag with makeup, shoes, hairdryer, curling tongs, several books and her camera, Harry set off for the local town with Christina for a last-minute shop. They only had twenty minutes before closing time and spent the time stocking up on suntan lotion factor eight and suntan oil factor zero. In addition they bought body milk, necessary after a day of basking in the sun, hairspray, and finally some chewing gum for the journey. Christina suggested getting a Jiffy lemon for their hair. She'd heard that if you covered your hair in lemon juice it lightened it in the sun. Then, as a last thought for Christina, she bought some cigarettes, lighter, and a bottle of vodka to keep her going on the journey.

"Christina! Daddy will have a fit."

"Don't be so stupid. I'm not going to let him see it. I'll hide it in my luggage."

At that moment, Harry looked up and at the other counter was a tall sun-tanned man with blond, wedge-cut hair. He smiled and said hello before Harry had a chance to look away and pretend she had not noticed him. She blushed.

"Who's that? You are a dark horse." Christina elbowed Harry in the ribs discreetly.

"I don't know; I have seen him in here a few times when I've had to pop down for Mum in the evening. Come on, let's go". Harry quickly packed their purchases away in Christina's large, pale blue, Calvin Klein bag. She could not get to the door quick enough, having visions of Christina introducing them both to the tall, tanned stranger.

Unless Harry had had a few drinks, she felt too shy to talk to people she didn't know, and she did her best to avoid the opposite sex. She had promised herself that she'd make a real effort to make friends and communicate with the Spanish boys and girls this year. She wanted to overcome her shyness before she returned to College in the autumn.

Chapter 2

The next morning they all piled into their parents' navy blue six-seater Range Rover. The twins were very excited, large smiles cracking across their faces from one ear to the other as they climbed in behind Anna and Mark. Christina and Harry, their luggage bulging, squashed into the rear seats. Mark had been up early and had neatly packed the roof-rack holding the display of multi-coloured suitcases in place with rope and bungees.

Three hours later they arrived at the Dover Ferry Terminal. Only twenty minutes queuing and they were parked up in the creaking car deck. They all spilled out and made their way safely up on deck. Anna established a base near the children's play area where they would sit for the journey and everyone could meet in time to disembark. Christina and Harry set off to explore.

Christina spotted the bar and dragged Harry in to join her to drink her way across the Chanel.

"Two vodkas and one orange juice, please." She ordered and paid for their drinks. Together they found themselves a concealed corner, just outside the bar on a sheltered part of the deck, to sit in for the crossing.

"Relax, Harry. Dad and Mum will be eating with the twins for the next hour and then Dad will get a paper and sit and read. They won't come anywhere near the bar."

Harry could feel her cheeks turning pink as the vodka warmed her. She was not used to drinking alcohol, especially during the day, except on Sundays when they hosted family gatherings with a roast or a barbeque, depending on the weather. Then wine was always plentiful to whomsoever wanted to join them, young or old. Having finished her drink, Christina was already scanning around for any talent.

"I'll just go up to the bar and get us another drink." She left Harry to her thoughts. Harry was wishing she had Christina's confidence. She would never get a social life if she didn't try to come out of her shell. Why couldn't she learn to relax and let her hair down from time to time? Well, this holiday, she was going to make a special effort.

She was distracted from her thoughts by the appearance of two boys.

"Hi, I'm Steve and this is Paul. Your sister and I are old friends and she said to come and join you. She'll be back in a moment. She just wanted to get some duty frees."

Harry's face was a picture of shock. The two boys sat down either side of her, one arm each around her shoulders.

"Hi, I'm Harriet." She sat up straight and freed herself by taking a sip of her drink. She choked as it went down the wrong way. In unison Paul and Steve patted her on the back. She hadn't noticed they'd brought her a double vodka and she'd just had a sip of it in its neat state.

"I think you should try a bit of orange juice with that," Paul smiled.

Harry was so embarrassed; she wanted to get up and run. Paul took out a packet of cigarettes and offered one to Harry. Harry took one before she remembered she didn't smoke but couldn't put it back; she would look foolish. After lighting it, she inhaled slowly so as not to choke.

Just as she started to panic because she couldn't think of a thing to say, Christina arrived back with a duty-free bag containing four hundred cigarettes and a litre bottle of vodka.

"I think we should follow you to Spain," said Steve, signalling Paul to the laden bag of duty frees. Christina laughed.

Harry began to relax. They both seemed friendly. Steve was very good looking and Paul seemed very nice. It was breaking up the journey after all, and they were not likely to see Mark, Anna, or the twins if they stayed in the bar.

"I will give you our address in Spain. Then, if you are passing pop in and see us. If you have your sleeping bags with you, you could always camp on the floor for a few days. I'm sure Mum and Dad wouldn't mind." Christina scribbled the address onto a beer mat and handed it to Paul.

Two double vodkas later, having heard how Steve went out with one of Christina's friends at university, she learnt how he had ended up in bed with his tutor. The ferry loud speaker system announced that they would be docking at Calais in ten minutes. Harry and Christina said they should go to meet up with their parents. Feeling very tipsy, Harry got up to leave and found herself starting to blush once again as Paul kissed her on the cheek, then Steve made a grab for her and kissed her full on the lips as they said goodbye.

"I can see I'm going to have to watch you with the boys this year," giggled Christina. "I hope they don't turn up in Spain and cramp my style."

Having popped into the loo to cover themselves in perfume, they had a quick squirt of mouth freshener and a piece of chewing gum as an extra precaution and set off to meet up with the rest of the family. Once the family were reunited they all headed down to the car deck. Within minutes of getting back into the car, Harry and Christina had fallen asleep.

Ten hours later, Harry woke up with a stinking headache and a mouth that tasted awful. The car was in darkness and she could hear Mickey snoring. Sophie was snuggled up under her special blanket (she took this everywhere), and Christina was still fast asleep. Anna was pouring Mark out a drink. The pleasant aroma of coffee filtered through to Harry.

"Could I have a cup of coffee please, Mum?" Harry whispered in case she woke the twins. Anna passed Harry a cup of coffee.

"Where are we now, Mum?" Harry said in the smallest whisper she could muster.

"We are coming up to the French border in the Pyrenees," Anna whispered.

Harry carefully sipped the steaming hot cup of coffee. It tasted wonderful as it slipped down. She placed the empty cup under her seat and drifted back off to sleep, feeling content, knowing the next time she woke they would be nearly at the villa.

"Dad, how long is it till we get there?" A very sleepy Mickey rubbed his bright eyes as he woke. Groans went around the car as everyone began to wake up. With Mickey awake there would be no more rest for anyone else. The light was breaking across the sky, the grey and black clouds of the night being replaced by red and gold as the sun started to climb; morning had arrived.

"In about ten minutes," a shattered, hoarse-sounding Mark answered.

"Now try and remain quiet. Your father is very tired and will really need to concentrate for the rest of the journey," Anna piped up.

As they drove towards the coast the children began to recognise things. They could not help themselves; there was no containing their excitement. It gave Mark a boost. His batteries were totally worn down after the long drive. He loved hearing the twins chatter.

"Is it five Pesetas for the first one to see the sea, Daddy?" Sophie enquired. She remembered the routine from previous years.

"Okay, but the judge's decision will be final," Mark chuckled.

"I can see the sea!" A chorus of shouts echoed around the car. Ahead of them a gap in the line of the hills revealed the Mediterranean coastline. Anna cut the arguing short by saying it was a draw, so everyone could have five Pesetas.

Mark finally left the main road and drove up the hill overlooking S'Agaro bay and turned into the villa.

"Home from home," Anna sighed.

Chapter 3

It was a medium-sized, whitewashed villa in a walled garden, with a pool and a barbecue area to the rear, and a raised patio to the front that overlooked the quaint bay. To the side lay a driveway with a garage attached to the villa. This housed their speed boat and all their beach equipment. On the other side of the villa was a swing, outdoor shower and washing line.

Harry and Christina shared a twin bedroom at the back of the villa. Next to it was a small bathroom with a shower, sink and toilet. The kitchen was situated at the front of the villa with a breakfast bar that opened out into a huge living/dining room. A fireplace, filled with pine cones, stood against one wall with a large family portrait hanging above it. An assortment of armchairs and a sofa surrounded this. The whole villa was quite sparsely decorated with ornaments and pictures the family had collected or brought over to Spain. All the rooms were painted white and contained typical deep oak Spanish furniture. An open plan staircase in the living room led up to the second floor that contained two more bedrooms. The master bedroom had an ensuite. Opposite it was another quite large room with bunk beds and a bathroom. This was the twins' room. On the landing were wall-to-wall shelves containing puzzles, games, and books they had all read, or visiting friends had left behind over the years.

While Anna got to work making everyone a bacon sandwich from food she had brought from England, transported in boxes with other vital supplies such as Marmite and tea, Mark organized the unloading of the car. There was another box of food for the kitchen, suitcases to go to the bedrooms, toys for the twins' room, as well as toiletries and bags full of footwear. A month away from home had taken Anna an awful lot of skilled organization and weeks of planning. After the task was completed and everyone had eaten, Mark and Anna, who were exhausted, went up to their room for a couple of hours sleep. They had a letting agent who took care of the property, garden, and pool, and who had prepared the rooms ready for their arrival.

Christina told the twins they could go and explore, or sort out their beach toys from the garage, while she sneaked into the shower room for a cigarette before doing her own unpacking. Harry set about unpacking her clothes. The wardrobe was full of hangers they had brought out with them on the previous trips. In her usual, orderly way, she hung her dresses on one side, followed by skirts, jeans, and jackets. Between the beds stood a large six drawer dressing table, so she took the bottom three and filled them with underwear, swim-wear, and tops. It didn't take her long to cover half of the top of the dressing table with makeup, jewellery, and hair accessories. When she had finished she left Christina to fill up the other side of the wardrobe and dressing table and went quietly upstairs to unpack the twins' clothes.

An hour later Harry found the twins in the garage sorting through their snorkelling gear. They had already dug out their buckets, spades and fishing nets, and had laid them in neat rows next to the boat. Harry took the battery out of the boat. It was quite heavy and very dusty. She cleaned it off then connected it up to the charger.

"Come on, you two, let's go for a walk up to the park by the Hotel Roca. Mum and Dad will be asleep for hours. In fact, I'd be surprised if they woke up at all, so we might as well make the most of the rest of the day."

Harry took Sophie's tiny hand and led her out to the road. Mickey was already ten yards ahead of them. The road was very quiet. The only traffic that ran along it was the hotel residents, staff, a few visitors, or deliveries for the hotel itself. The road twisted through some pine woods that ran all the way to the cliff tops. There was not a scrap of vegetation on the ground, only layers and layers of pine cones and needles under the trees that had built up over the years. They passed an old man collecting dry needles and cones. This was what the locals used on their barbecues as fuel and it worked very well.

As Harry and Sophie strolled around the last bend, Mickey was already on his way down the tallest slide. It was a huge metal structure. Later in the day you had to be careful your skin did not touch the hot base. It was an unpredictable glide; at times you would not move down the slope as your skin stuck to it, while at other times you would slip so fast you would feel your skin burn with the friction. Mickey knew all the tricks and carefully slid down using his shorts as a mat, protecting his skin as he went. Sophie went next, closely followed by Harry as they climbed the steps to the top of the metal monster.

"Now be careful, you saw how fast Mickey went down."

Sophie pushed off and slid down carefully and slowly holding the sides. Harry was just small enough to fit between the rails and slid down, slowly initially, then picking up speed. She was going so fast when she reached the bottom she flew off the end. Mickey and Sophie laughed so much Harry thought they would burst. With pains in their stomachs from laughing, they decided they would go on the swings next. When they had all had enough (Sophie was feeling sick and dizzy), the thought of a swim in the pool back at the villa seemed inviting.

Mickey raced off ahead shouting, "Last one in the pool is a toad!"

Sophie took no notice and was content to walk at a leisurely pace with Harry.

The next day the whole family awoke refreshed. After finishing the unpacking they went down to the local supermarket to stock up on groceries. It was laid out in a way to suit the locals as well as tourists. There were cash machines at the entrance and a bar next to the checkout with people lined up on stools, sipping their morning coffee. There was also a bakery, with a queue of people collecting their daily croissants, bread, and pastries. The take-away counter was already looking busy, as the chefs were lining up row upon row of fresh chickens on spits, then covering them in herbs. The fruit and vegetable displays were a mass of colour, filled with fresh tomatoes, strawberries, lemons, and other unrecognizable exotic fruits and vegetables. A hairdressing salon, newsagents, as well as the usual rows and rows of groceries filled the massive store, with everything under one roof making shopping easy and quick.

Once back at the villa, Mickey and Sophie sorted out what to take to the beach. Christina and Harry were deciding which bikinis to wear to best conceal their white bodies. Anna, feeling back on the planet after a good night's sleep, was in the kitchen cooking a full English breakfast to set them up for the day. Mark was out in the garage putting the charged battery on the boat ready to test it out.

Christina had decided on a blue halter-necked top with matching high leg bottoms. "This one makes my legs look thinner, but do you think my boobs look too big, Harry?" she questioned, as she looked in the full-length mirror that the girls had both insisted on, three years earlier.

"No, definitely not. The halter-neck top will hold them in place and if you take it off, just lie down before they have time to escape," Harry giggled. "What does this one look like on me?" Harry gently pushed Christina out of the way of the mirror to look at herself. A small, pale blue top, consisting of two triangles with matching triangular bottoms, suited her slim body and long legs.

"You look really nice. You are so slim, you lucky thing. I wish my boobs were not so big. Your legs are naturally long anyway, and look even longer than usual in that one!"

After reassuring themselves several times they were presentable, they went out to join the rest of the family for breakfast.

Mark and Anna were tucking into their bacon, eggs, tomatoes, and French bread. The twins had their Cocoa Pops. Anna had purposely bought a good supply of Cocoa pops because it made the milk taste of chocolate. Spanish milk tended to be very creamy and taste as if it were slightly off. Harry and Christina settled for low fat coconut yoghurts. Everyone had a cup of tea before they all helped to clear up and stack the dishwasher. Anna washed the pans while Harry and Christina dried them while the twins went off to attempt to make the beds.

Christina had a quick cigarette in the bedroom, the window wide open and the door locked. Then Christina and Harry made the final adjustments to their bikinis, convinced they had put on half a stone since eating breakfast.

Christina put her hair on top of her head in a kind of bun, then tied a blue wrap around her waist. Harry tied hers back into low bunches with two little pale blue bands that matched her bikini. She slipped a blue and white striped beach dress over her head. It fitted perfectly around her tiny waist, with a short-flared skirt that hung to an inch below her bottom. They both finished with a little lemon squirted onto their hair, in the hope they would get instant white-blonde streaks. They were at last ready. Grabbing their towels, they went out into the garden to help Mark load the boat up with cool box, sun loungers, and the twins' hoard of toys they had sorted out the day before. The boat was weighed down.

The twins looked sweet, Sophie dressed in a frilly navy and white bikini and straw hat, Mickey in matching swimming shorts and navy cap, and both carrying their navy beach robes.

Mark had some difficulty hitching the boat to the tow bar on the car. At that moment, Anna appeared in a black halter neck costume, a black silk wrap that tied at her waist and went all the way down to the ground. Her beach outfit was finished with a straw hat with a silk scarf wrapped around it that matched her wrap. She looked stunning, always well-groomed, with matching red lipstick and nail vanish to set the whole outfit off.

Mark grabbed his wife proudly. "Not bad for a couple in their late forties, hey, kids?" They all groaned as they jumped into the car and set off for their first day on the beach.

Chapter 4

The old dirt track, a short cut used by the residents of the hill, was as bumpy as ever, full of pot holes gouged out by rain during the stormy weather. The view of the bay was breath-taking with its castle shaped villas, coloured umbrellas littering the sea front, cafes and snack bars fighting for custom from the hordes of Catalans, Germans, Dutch, and the occasional English, all on their annual visit to the land of sea and sun. The clear blue sea was alive with white sails and dancing wind surfers racing from one side of the bay to the other.

Above the granite rocks that framed the bay stood the Hotel Gavina which was one of the most expensive hotels in Spain, its host of flags running along the cliff edge spelling out 'S'AGARO'. The flags flapped frantically on the warm breeze. This meant the turquoise sea was choppy. White horses crashed against the rocks cascading foam into the small pitted rock pools.

Mark pulled up at the boat launch and, after greeting Mercedes, the secretary of the Ski School, and having a brief chat, went back to the car.

"We can drop the boat into the water now; they are not very busy and can run it down the beach on inflated boat rollers," he said as he unhitched the boat and told Anna to drive over to the other end of the beach to their favourite area. Christina stayed with Mark in case there was any trouble starting the boat; it had been unused for twelve months so it was always a worry as to whether it would start for the first time.

Harry jumped into the front of the car and sat next to Anna as she drove the car up to the far end of the beach. They parked just below the Gavina in sight of the beach. This was the narrower end and was separated off from the rest of the beach by the Taverna, a Tapas bar fronting a very up-market fish restaurant. The beach was extremely clean. It was raked every morning and, any rubbish washed up overnight, sorted through and removed. Wooden, pastel-painted towel rails, parasols and sun beds lined the beach. A little old man with a brown, wrinkled, leathery-looking face and white hair, his still bright eyes peeking out from under an equally ancient, battered straw hat, hobbled up and down with his ticket book, waiting to pounce on anyone who so much as glanced at a lounger, and who might be a prospective customer.

To get onto the beach they had to go down a long flight of steps cut out of the ancient red and black granite, with its thin, rusting handrail the only protection from a twenty-foot drop onto the golden sand below. Anna and Harry took the twins by the hand and led them down the steps. Once at the bottom, Mickey took off his shoes and ran ahead, shouting to Daan and Kim, Dutch friends with whom they had been friends for a long time. He had spotted them along the beach. They too had children, Sharon, who was nine, and Arthur, who was ten. Daan and Kim met Mickey with a warm embrace and then made their way to welcome Anna, Harry, and Sophie. They were each greeted in continental style with a kiss on each cheek, followed by the usual interrogation from Kim about their journey and wellbeing.

"Hello, my lovely friends from England. How are you all? You all look so fantastic." Kim looked them up and down as she embraced them all one by one.

"Anna, you have lost weight and, Harry, you are even taller. Look at Sophie! She gets prettier every year. Where are Mark and Christina? Are they bringing the boat?" Kim spoke in perfect English with only a hint of a Dutch accent.

Daan ran a water sports school, which he operated from the beach, during the summer months from June until September. He also had a pub back in Holland which he ran during the winter. Daan made his excuses as he had another pupil booked in for a water-skiing lesson and so left them all to it.

Kim, seeing Anna and Harry had no towels with them, gave them a towel each to sit on. Anna explained that Mark and Christina were on their way with the boat with everything in. Mickey and Sophie had spotted Kim's children over on the rocks and ran off to join them, nets and buckets in hand.

Harry sat listening to Kim and Anna as they caught up on the last year. Kim's English was word perfect. Kim and Daan spoke six different languages fluently, including Hebrew, (when they were younger they spent time at a Kibbutz in Israel). With language no barrier, the conversation flowed.

Soon Harry found herself drifting into a hazy sleep. Still conscious of her surroundings, she listened to the lapping of the sea on the shore and the roar of the ski boat as it went in and out from the shore. A queue of eager skiers were waiting patiently for their turn to try to conquer getting out of the water and up onto two skies, learning to drop a ski, doing a deep-water start, or learning to slalom and eventually mono. The little old man was pacing the beach with his tickets, shouting at a group of young lads now occupying some of his sun loungers and not paying for them. She could hear the laughter of children splashing in the water or building sandcastles on the shore and smell the different fragrances of the suntan lotions wafting passed as people strolled up and down the beach. This was the life she had been longing for.

Mark and Christina arrived safely in the red speed boat, named Rip-Off because, after Mark had bought it, he discovered all the extras were either non-existent or didn't work. So, the little red boat had acquired its name. It had been a good buy all the same. The children had all learned to ski behind it, along with many friends who had joined them for holidays over the years. The family also used it for fishing, diving, and sight-seeing. In all the time they had owned it, it had never had a major breakdown.

The man in charge of the moorings, followed by his helpers, rushed out to meet Mark as he pulled up and tied the boat to a buoy. This section of the beach was rented from the council by the beach men. They made their living out of looking after the boats kept in the bay. Some boats were there for the whole summer while others, like Mark's, only needed looking after for a few weeks a year.

"Mark, you have this." Pedro gestured to his little beer gut and laughed.

Mark immediately replied in his broken Spanish, "You are a fine man to talk, yours is twice as big as mine."

The other three bronzed beach men, with their huge beer-guts, dark hair, and big brown eyes, roared with laughter as they helped Christina and Mark from the boat. Taking out the family's belongings and handing them to Christina and Mark, they pushed the boat out to deeper water where the propeller would not scrape on the seabed, and moored it to a buoy. Once back on the shore, they all hugged and slapped Mark, then kissed Anna who had joined them. Pedro, the oldest of the beach-men, who was also in charge, asked how the rest of the family were. Anna pointed over to the rocks where Mickey and Sophie were still fishing, and then to Harry, who was now fast asleep on the beach.

"She wastes no time," laughed Pedro.

Mark followed Pedro back to his make-shift office to discuss the cost of keeping his boat on the beach. This was a wooden built booth at the entrance of a long cave, cut out of the granite rock. It contained a table, chairs and had electricity running from a generator. The smaller man-made holes around the entrance served as a wine-rack, food store, and wardrobe. A barbecue and cooking utensils were positioned outside the cave to barbecue all their meals on. One of the beach men slept in the cave every night to ensure the boats were permanently guarded from thieves and storms. If a storm whipped up, the boats all had to be moved further up the beach for protection, or out into deeper water to avoid breaking waves.

Christina greeted Kim then went to join Harry who was already turning slightly pink. Christina thought it best to wake her and let her know. There was nothing worse than sunburn to damage your skin. She had seen so many people over the years burn and peel and it looked so unsightly.

"Hey, Harry, you should see the talent running the water sports club at the other end of the beach. I've signed us up for some windsurfing lessons." Harry groaned as she woke feeling hot, groggy, and annoyed at having been disturbed.

"Did you hear what I said?" Christina shook Harry by the shoulder.

"Yes and no. You have signed us up for some wind surfing lessons. I've always told you I don't fancy wind surfing." Harry was quite grumpy.

"You will when you see the teacher. I think he must be Swedish; he's tall, bronzed, blonde hair and has rippling muscles. Very beddable if you ask me! I would definitely give him ten out of ten."

"Christina! Do you ever think of anything else? I was having a lovely sleep then and catching the sun at the same time. Then you have the cheek to wake me up and tell me that!"

"Well, I thought you'd be pleased. Anyway, I'm parched. Shall we go for a drink and a cig?"

"Okay. Let me have a quick dip first. I'm boiling and my head's groggy after that sleep. If you wait, I'll only be a few minutes."

Harry got up and slowly walked into the clear blue sea. The water felt icy cold as it crept up to the top of her long legs and reached her tummy button. It took her breath away as it engulfed her. Having had enough of messing around, she dipped down up to her neck and swam a few strokes before she stood up. With cupped hands filled with water, she splashed her face several times, trying not to wet her hair.

Feeling quite refreshed, but self-conscious, she walked back to the beach. With her body slightly pink and dripping with water, she knew her nipples were sticking out. So that Christina could not comment she grabbed her dress and put it on before she wiped the drips from her legs and face. Sun glasses in place, she picked up her blue bag.

They walked up to the Taverna together, conscious of men eyeing them up as they passed, wondering if it were because they thought they were good looking, or because they were both so pale and obviously English. The Taverna was very quiet, so they made their way up to the sun terrace on the roof. Here, they had an unobstructed view of the bay. They could see their parents sitting, reading, under an umbrella. Sophie and Mickey had come back from the rocks and were now playing in the sea. It was a good lookout post. They could keep an eye on their parents and would know if they started to pack up for lunch. For the moment they all seemed relaxed doing their own thing on the beach. Christina thought it was a good time to have a cigarette.

The waitress arrived, dressed in a white, trim, fitted dress, white plimsolls and a white cap. They ordered two Tri-Naranjas. These were very refreshing and quite watery compared with the thick orange juice they bought in England.

"Would you like a ciggy, Harry?" Christina offered the packet to Harry.

Harry declined. "I couldn't possibly face one in this heat."

Before their drinks arrived, a group of people around their age, arrived on the terraces and took the adjoining table. Harry could watch them quite casually in her dark sunglasses without any of them noticing where she was looking. She noticed how tanned and good looking the boys were; obviously Spanish by their complexions and dark hair. The two girls with them were equally as attractive. Both girls had long, shining black hair, brown eyes, and beautifully tanned skin. They looked very alike. They were all deep in conversation. Suddenly Harry realised how long she had been watching them. Thinking she might appear stupid just sitting there, Harry started racking her brain for things to say to Christina. "When do you start your wind surfing lessons?"

Christina, who was having a job keeping her eyes off the Spaniards too, took out another cigarette, got up then, leaning over the boy nearest, said, "Have you got a light?"

The boy nearest to her had a tan leather man bag (not unusual for men on the continent). He opened it up and took out a packet of Marlborough and a silver Zippo. Christina took a light off him then offered him one of her cigarettes.

"Thank you," he said in perfect English and took one.

She offered them to the two girls and the other boy. The others declined. At that moment, the waitress arrived back with Harry and Christina's drinks.

Christina sat back down and, under her breath, she started whispering. "What a couple of hunks! Do you think the girls are their girlfriends?"

Harry was pleased the waitress left and had not heard Christina's question.

The boy who had given Christina the light turned around and said, with a huge Colgate grin on his face, "Let me introduce my friends to you. This is Pablo, a very good friend." Pablo bowed his head.

"These are Pablo's sisters Rosa and Maria". The two girls smiled. "I am called Manolo. What do you call yourselves?"

"My name is Christina, and this is my little sister, Harry."

Harry blushed wondering if they knew that Harry was a boy's name. Pablo gestured to them to join his table and started making room for them to slot in. Harry was about to decline when Christina moved and sat in the empty chair between the boys. Harry got up and started to drag her chair over but Pablo jumped up and carried it for her, placing it in the space he had created between him and Maria.

Christina was well away, telling them they were here on holiday and pointing out the villa they were staying in on the hill. Then she asked them how old they were, where they lived, and whether they were students or worked. Before the waitress returned with their drinks, she'd found out all she needed to know. The two boys were both students and had just completed university. They also worked part time in their family's businesses. The two girls, who did look the same age even if one was a year older than the other, were still in senior college.

Harry just played with the ice cubes in her glass and listened to the conversation, turning pink every time Christina mentioned her name. After they had all had another drink, which Pablo insisted went on his bill, Rosa got up and said it was time for her and Maria to go. She explained they were having a party that night and had a lot to do. Pablo and Manolo said they would not be too long. As the two girls left, Manolo called to the waitress and ordered another drink. It was so hot on the terrace, the drinks were not lasting very long. Christina was in her element and it wasn't long before Harry noticed how much she was giving Manolo the eye. He seemed to be enjoying it and responded with an invitation for Christina and Harry to go to the party. This was their party to celebrate finishing their exams and it sounded like it was going to be a big affair. After getting directions and the address from the boys written on a beer mat, everyone had finished their drinks so decided it was time they all made a move. Manolo and Pablo stood up as the girls got up and kissed them both on each cheek. Christina and Harry thanked them for their drinks and said they would see them later.

"Hello, girls. We were just going to send out a search party!" Mark winked as he told them they were heading back to the villa for a siesta. "Do you want to come back or are you staying down for the afternoon?" The girls both said they would stay on the beach. They then covered themselves in factor eight suntan lotion and stretched out in the sun.

It was only half an hour later when Harry heard the roar of a large speed boat with a very powerful engine. She sat up slowly, searching for her bikini top. Putting it on she looked out to sea where she could see a huge, wooden-panelled, Fifties-style boat pulling out of the buoys. "Good grief, Christina, I wonder who owns that? How can they possibly hear themselves talk or even think over that engine?"

The boat circled once around the bay then roared off towards Playa-de-Aro.

"Wow! What an exit!" Christina gasped.

Excitement over, Harry and Christina made for the sea. The water was beginning to get even more choppy. The flags around the pool at the Gavina were blowing inland. This meant the wind was now coming in off the sea. Harry found herself standing on tiptoes keeping the water away from her flat stomach for as long as possible. Soon the water was too high and, with her usual gasp, she dived headfirst into the approaching wave. Christina was wet all over and was floating on her back with her feet facing directly up to the sky. Harry suggested they swim out to the large red buoy that held the ropes for the ski lane. They swam out, doing breaststroke at a leisurely pace, discussing what to wear that evening to the party. Christina confessed that she had the hots for Manolo and hoped he didn't have a partner. Once they had reached the buoy they rested, just treading water for a while. Then Christina challenged Harry to a race back to shore. "Okay, ready, steady, go!" she shrieked as she pushed herself off from the buoy.

Harry plunged forward doing crawl. Christina started off quite fast, swimming breaststroke (which was her best stroke). It didn't take Harry long to catch up, sliding through the water as gracefully as a dolphin. She reached the shore several yards ahead of Christina.

"I've done a lot of swimming at uni this year, and I thought I would be able to beat you." Christina panted, as she staggered onto the beach.

"Never mind, Christina, I think your boobs probably slow you down." Harry laughed as she dried the water from her body.

They sunbathed until they were sweltering and then went back into the sea for another cool off. Repeating this ritual all afternoon in the baking sun, they finally collected up their things and headed back along the beach towards the villa. It was a good fifteen minutes walk, and hard going walking on the gritty sand at the far end of the beach. Putting their shoes on they made their way up onto the boardwalk that ran through the dunes. This stretched the entire length of the beach joining one side of the bay to the other. It was the easier option until they could cut up through the woods and onto the old dirt track.

"Hi, everyone, I'm just off for a shower. Harry and I have been invited to a party tonight so I'll have a nap after my shower. It doesn't start until nine," Christina said excitedly and went off to her bedroom while Harry made a cup of tea for everyone. The twins were doing a puzzle, so Harry took her cup of tea over to help them.

"Harry, can I have a word with you?"

"Okay, Dad, what's wrong?"

"It's about this party tonight. Whose is it? Where is it? And what time will you be home? If, and only if, we agree, you can go."

Harry sat down opposite her father and explained about the boys and girls they had met up at the Taverna. She showed him the map they had drawn on the back of the beer mat. Mark instantly recognised the area and thought he knew the villa.

"It's very nice up on Mass Nou. Well you girls have been up there enough with us. I should think if they live there, they must have nice parents."

"Oh, Dad, you're such a snob. It doesn't matter where they live as to what their parents are like! I know if you have never met them it does give a good impression. So, can we go?"

"You can go, but as we don't know them from Adam, I want you home by two."

"Thanks, Dad you're great!" Harry jumped up and kissed her father.

Christina shouted that the shower was now free, so Harry grabbed a towel and went in. She took her bikini off and stepped into the shower. Still quite hot and sticky after the walk home, she turned the shower on running lukewarm, then slowly soaped her body down. Covered in bubbles, she then started on her hair. It needed a good massage all over with shampoo to get the salty water and lemon from her hair. It was so refreshing, just standing there. The soap ran down from her head over her small firm breasts and down to her toes, the water leaving her clean and refreshed. The mirror was completely steamed up. Harry tried to wipe it but still she could not see if she was red. Wrapping a towel around her body, she headed for the bedroom. There was a cloud of smoke above Christina's bed, where she had just had a cigarette before falling asleep. Harry gently patted her body dry all over with the big soft towel. She hoped she hadn't overdone the sun as her skin was feeling quite tight.

The body milk after-sun was on the side and she plastered it all over herself. She looked in the mirror at how coloured she already was. A definite line separated her bottom from her lower back where her bikini had been. Having rubbed the cream in as much as she could, she leapt into bed and closed her eyes. It was hard work, sunbathing all day, and within minutes she too fell asleep.

Chapter 5

Three hours later the alarm woke Harry. She turned it off and slowly tried to shake the sleep from her body. It amazed her how tired she had been. Yawning and stretching like a little dormouse, she slowly came to. It was quite tempting to give the party a miss and just stay in her bed until the morning.

Christina was out of bed like a shot. "Come on, Harry, move yourself. We don't want to be late, it's half seven already." Christina raced around, applying her make-up, and eating a dried French stick whilst getting dressed. Christina could always do several things at once. "Mum and Dad have gone out for something to eat. They left a note pinned to the fridge for us. Dad said we have to be home by two."

Harry made her way to the kitchen. She was terrible at waking up. She was happy enough, just so dozy. It took her a good fifteen minutes to find her feet. Like a squirrel coming out of hibernation, her first thought was food and drink. She grabbed a hand full of butter biscuits and a glass of strawberry yoghurt drink. Soon she was feeling a lot better and went back to the bedroom and began to apply some eyeliner and mascara, and a touch of rouge to emphasise her high cheek bones, with a slight dab on her jaw line and nose. Then she set to work on her hair. It was still damp and all over the place. It was going to be quite a task to sort it out. It went quite curly if left, so it needed a lot of frizz ease and a long session with a hair brush and hair-dryer.

Christina was now ready, looking stunning, in a long, pale pink dress and sandals. "I'll pour myself a vodka to get me going. Would you like me to get you a drink while I'm in the kitchen?"

"Just an orange juice. I can't face any alcohol after just waking up. I've just got to get dressed and put some lippy on, then I'll be ready."

"Put the blinds down and lock the window before you come out then."

Harry put her halter-neck dress and some sandals on. She tied her hair up with a band and applied a pale pink lip pencil, to emphasise the line of her full lips, filled in with a pink lipstick. Finally, after a good soaking of Lou Lou all over, she joined Christina out on the patio.

"I'll just have a ciggy to calm my nerves now and then we can go."

Christina handed Harry her drink and a cigarette.

Harry took a small puff of the cigarette and then had a sip of her orange. "This tastes funny. Here, taste it." Harry handed the drink back.

Christina had a quick sip and gave it back to Harry, knowing she had put a splash of vodka in it to help Harry to chill. "It's fine. It must be the cigarette and the orange together that taste funny. Drink it up so we can go."

Harry finished her drink and had a few puffs on her cigarette. Christina locked the door and they set off to the bus stop at the bottom of the track. Buses ran every fifteen minutes along the coast road during the season, so they just stood and waited. They assumed one wouldn't be long as there were other people waiting: people who had only just come off the beach, an old woman with empty bags going to do some shopping, another younger looking, well-dressed woman with some children, off to the bright lights, and a couple of young lads, who were eyeing Harry and Christina up.

Harry did feel a bit over-dressed, standing at the bus stop, all made up while it was still light. Luckily, having only waited five minutes, the bus arrived. After a few people got off, Harry and Christina followed the small queue on and found a seat.

The bus was very basic, with no air conditioning. All the windows were wide open so, once the bus started moving, a welcome breeze rushed through, cooling them. It only took twenty minutes to reach the centre of Playa-de-Aro. Here, they took a taxi up to Mas-Nou, and to where the party was being held. The drive was quite breath-taking, with a sheer drop on one side of the road overlooking the town, and the distant sea and luxurious gated villas on the other. Each villa had its own pool and tennis court; it was a very wealthy area.

The taxi pulled into a driveway. Soft-topped Mercedes, Porsches, BMWs, and Jeeps were neatly parked in rows. The taxi driver stopped, letting the girls know they had reached their destination. Getting out he opened the door for the girls. Then he asked them for 1000 Pesetas. Knowing they were being ripped off Christina gave him the exact money.

Harry slipped her arm into Christina's. "God, I'm so nervous. I wish we hadn't come."

"Don't be so silly, we will have a fun time, even if we just dance on our own all night. Let's face it, we don't know anyone, so there will be no one to make fools of ourselves in front of, will there? Now, let's follow the sound of the music and, for goodness sake smile and relax. You look far too nervous. Take it in your stride. Let's go and enjoy!" Christina, full of confidence as usual, led the way.

Just as they went through an opened arched gate, in the direction of the music, a waiter greeted them, holding a tray of Champagne filled glasses.

"Buenos tardes, Senorita." They were both offered a glass.

"Muchas gracias," they replied thankfully, in unison. Taking their drinks, they strolled towards the gathering of people, who were dressed in a complete mixture, from jeans to cocktail dresses, dancing away to music on the patio. It was a large, whitewashed, two storey villa with a grapevine growing all along the front, laden with fruit.

"Obviously no dress code tonight, hey, Harry." Christina signalled over to the patio; Harry followed her direction. There was a huge balcony running around the first floor of the villa, beneath which stood the patio. Just down from the patio lay a swimming pool, separated from a smaller pool by ivy shaped stepping stones. Surrounding this were sun loungers, positioned at random, draped in thick yellow towels. To the left was an outdoor shower and some changing rooms. To the right of the villa a lawn stretched out towards flood-lit tennis courts. The gardens were very mature, full of colour and very well kept. Harry was admiring her surroundings as she sipped her drink.

"Hello, girls! I am honoured you have come." Pablo appeared, wearing jeans and a white polo shirt. He leant forward and kissed Harry on both cheeks, then turned to Christina and greeted her in the same way. He seemed even darker than he'd looked earlier at the Taverna. His wavy dark hair was gelled in a spiky sort of style. His teeth looked whiter than white and his big brown eyes sparkled. He had obviously had quite a lot to drink already. He stood for a few minutes, smiling as he looked the girls up and down.

Christina was the first to break the ice. "It's a very nice house, I mean villa. Is this where you live?"

"Only for the holidays. It is good for the beach in the summer and only a few hours from the Pyrenees where we go to ski in the winter. The rest of the year we live in an apartment in Barcelona. Let me show you round, so you know where everything is."

He gestured to the various points in the gardens, most of which the girls had already discovered for themselves. Then he led them through the crowd of people and into a huge living room.

As in most Spanish villas, the floor was not carpeted. Instead, it was tiled, with a huge zebra skin rug in front of a fire place that dominated the room. An oak bar stood on one side of the room with a rosewood grand piano on the other. A huge brown, leather sofa lay around the centre of the room. A scattering of occasional tables, with object d'art carefully arranged on them, stood around the seating area. Lamps, throwing out soft lighting, were situated all around the room, giving it a warmer, more welcoming feeling.

"Christina, Harry!" A voice boomed from behind the bar. "You are here! Come and let me get you a drink."

"That would be lovely, Manolo." Christina headed off towards the bar.

Harry went to follow but Pablo grabbed her by the arm. Harry turned around. "I think I would like another drink too, please, Pablo".

"Okay, we can get a drink, but not in here. I think my friend would like to keep your sister to himself."

Harry was feeling almost panic stricken, not knowing anyone, and now on her own with a stranger. She'd kill Christina when she got her on her own.

Pablo took her hand and led her into the hall-way, pointing to other rooms as he spoke. "The kitchen is in here, this is the dining room, over there is a bathroom and shower."

Harry could not take it all in; it was spacious and so beautifully decorated. Each room had its own colour scheme with the walls stencilled in the most elaborate designs in keeping with the style of the room. Distraction over, Harry wished the floor would open and swallow her. Pablo led her towards the stairs. Harry hesitated momentarily.

"It's okay. I am only taking you to see the view from my bedroom. I will be very good." He crossed his heart and smiled at Harry. "I can tell Christina likes the boys, but you I'm not so sure about. You are very innocent. A typical English rose, I think. Am I right?"

For the umpteenth time that night Harry was wishing she hadn't come but still followed him up the stairs.

"Here, this is my bedroom. You will like the view from here very much."

She walked ahead of him through the oak panelled door into the bedroom. She could feel his eyes were on her looking her up and down as she hurried through, straight passed the four-poster bed and out onto the balcony, without looking around. The hum of the party drifted up to meet her and she began to relax as she could see all his friends were just below.

Pablo arrived out of his bedroom with a bottle of Champagne and two glasses. Again, panic set in. Harry must have shot him a look that he understood.

He casually sat down, trying to make Harry feel more relaxed. He gently patted the chair next to him. "Sit down. I have already had a lot to drink and spoken to most of my friends, so I can excuse myself and talk to you. It has been a very busy evening so far, and I am feeling a little tired now."

Harry sat down and took a glass. God, she needed a drink. She downed it in one and, as she placed it back on the table, he filled it back up. Sliding back in a comfortable position in his seat, he began to study her.

Christina was now on her fourth glass of Champagne and was enjoying the male company. Manolo had introduced her to all his friends.

Most of them could speak perfect English. They were all seeking her attention and she was lapping it up. All the same, she only had eyes for Manolo; he was such a hunk. The music outside was turned up and out boomed Wham's 'Club Tropicana'.

"I love this song. Shall we have a dance, Manolo?"

"Oh yes, I think I would like to dance to this. I have already had too much to drink. Some air will do me good."

Pushing their way through his friends, they headed out to the patio and found a gap amongst the dancers. They were soon moving in time with the beat. Christina loved the way he moved his body and mirrored his dancing. After a few up-beat tracks, the music slowed right down. Manolo pulled Christina towards him and she wrapped her arms around his shoulders as he pulled her tightly into him. She could feel his body pulsing against hers.

"You have a nice perfume." He spoke gently into her ear, nibbling it slightly at the same time before kissing her neck slowly, making his way towards her mouth. At first they kissed gently, then hungrily, tongues touching, exploring each other's mouths as their bodies moved in time to the music.

A roar of laughter came from the pool area. The dancing couples all looked up as two adventurous girls stripped down to their G-strings and jumped into the pool. Other people followed suit. Christina and Manolo looked at each other, then nodding, ran hand in hand towards the pool. Stripping down to their underwear, Manolo ran and dived into the pool and Christina followed. The cool water was very sobering. Christina was feeling quite hot and clammy from the dancing and the Champagne had gone to her head. Manolo dived down and caught hold of her legs, pulling her down. Christina took a huge gulp of air, as she disappeared under the water. Seeking her mouth, Manolo kissed her passionately, before they both rose to the surface gasping for breath. They chased each other around in the water for several minutes, Manolo kissing Christina every time he caught her. A large inflatable ball was thrown into the water. Teams were organised and a game of water volley ball started.

Pablo was very sure of himself. Harry wondered what he would do if he failed his exams. It all seemed a little premature, having a party as he had just finished his exams, rather than waiting until he had his results back. Picking her drink up, she walked over to the edge of the balcony.

"What a lovely view you have from here". Harry did not turn around when she spoke to him. If she had done she would have caught him with his eyes roaming up and down her youthful body, admiring her small, firm breasts, slim hips, and long legs.

"Yes, the view is beautiful."

"Look, is that Christina and Manolo in the pool? I think she has already had too much to drink. Perhaps we should go and check if she is okay." Harry turned to move back towards the table. Not realising Pablo was now standing right behind her, she nearly bumped straight into him.

He encircled her with his arms. He did not want her going anywhere for a while. She was so gorgeous. He had never met anyone in his entire life he felt more attracted to. Pablo breathed in her perfume. With his strong arms around her slender waist he felt powerful and in control of her every move. Pablo pulled Harry in closer. He rubbed her cheek with his nose. God, she did smell good. He could feel himself harden as his hands glided down her back and over her slender hips before they rested on her small, pert bottom. For a moment, she felt too weak to resist him and enjoyed the attention. Then she came to her senses, panicked and struggled to get away. Pablo held her tighter, letting her feel his strength before he released her from his grip.

Still holding her by one hand, Pablo gazed into her sky blue, sparkling eyes; his big brown eyes were pleading with her.

"Look, I hardly know you. In my book, you should get to know someone before you get too close. Do you understand what I am saying, Pablo? It's too early yet."

"I understand what you are saying. Few girls would turn me down. I must have a kiss; I am burning up here wanting you."

Harry was embarrassed. Why did Spanish boys have to be so passionate? She couldn't imagine one of her friends from her old college saying that. She wasn't sure if she liked it or not. Was this what he said to all the girls he fancied?

"Okay then, just one little kiss won't hurt, I suppose."

He wrapped his arms around her slender waist while she gently raised her hands around his shoulders. Oh, he did feel nice. He was so strong and yet gentle at the same time. She glanced into his puppy dog eyes. He was going to be difficult to resist.

His eyes met hers and held her gaze for a moment; they both shared the same wanting but he would have to wait. She was too lovely to frighten off.

Closing her eyes, their warm lips met and locked together for a long passionate kiss. Harry did not want it to end and neither did Pablo.

Never had he felt such soft, warm, tender lips before. Slowly the kiss ended.

Harry opened her eyes; Pablo's were already open. Had he been watching her while they kissed? Once again they stared into each other's eyes.

Pablo was holding her tight. He did not want the moment to end. He was falling for this girl he had only just met in a big way.

Running her hands down Pablo's back, Harry was feeling emotions she had never experienced before. What was wrong with her? She felt so strange, almost weak.

"Come on then, my little English Rose, if we must go down to find your crazy sister. I will wait until you are ready. But I will not let you get away."

Pablo's now husky voice sent delightful shivers down Harry's back. He took her by the hand and led her back through his bedroom and down the stairs.

As they walked back through the lounge, a group of boys looked up and spoke to Pablo. It sounded as though they were having a joke with him. They all laughed at his reply. Harry, convinced they were asking him if he'd scored, was angry and, as she glanced back, she thought they had made a gesture. Pablo quickly pulled her away.

"Well, what did they say?" she demanded.

"Oh, nothing. Boys! You know what they are like." He looked a little sheepish and raised his shoulders.

"Well, I'm not some kind of idiot. I have feelings and I do not think you should speak in Spanish like that when I'm with you."

He kissed her hand before apologizing. How could she resist him? He said in future he would only answer his friends using English if she were with him.

He was so sweet again; how could she possible remain angry with him?

They went outside. The air was now very humid. The music had slowed right down. Couples were pairing off and kissing. Pablo grabbed her and said he wanted to dance with her before they found her sister. He wanted everyone to see she was with him. He was so proud of being with such a good looking English girl. Blushing, Harry agreed to the dance.

Slowly, he rocked her from side to side, trying to push his body closer and closer to hers. They both felt the same passion, sweeping across their bodies, as they had felt upstairs. Christina and Manolo appeared and pounced on them, breaking up the closeness they were sharing.

"I think it is time I took my little sister home. Can we get a taxi from here?"

"Yes, I will call one for you." Pablo looked around and signalled to a waiter to come over. He whispered something to him. "It will take about ten possibly fifteen minutes to get here from Playa. Christina, I would like to talk to your sister for one moment, please."

Christina went off with Manolo to say goodbye. Harry looked down at her feet wandering what Pablo wanted to talk to her about.

Pablo put his hands on her shoulders. "I want to see you again tomorrow."

Harry looked up into his eyes. "I think I will be with my family all day tomorrow on the beach". God, she didn't want him turning up at the beach just yet.

"Tomorrow night. I think I know where your villa is. I will pick you up at around eight. Then I shall take you for something to eat. We can talk and get to know each other a little better."

"I don't know if my father will let me out two nights running." Harry thought for a moment it was too soon to see him for a second night running. She'd be tired after tonight although she could sleep all day on the beach. It wasn't as though she had college or anything.

"Maybe I should come and speak to your father. Do you think that would help?"

"Oh, it will be all right." Horrified at the prospect of introducing Pablo to Mark just yet, Harry thought it would be better just to agree. "Shall I speak to Christina? Maybe she would like to come with Manolo."

Harry spotted Christina and Manolo; they were kissing passionately. Christina looked like she was eating Manolo alive.

"No, I think Manolo can make his own arrangements. Just you and me would be nice." Before she had time to argue with him the waiter came to find them and inform them their taxi had arrived and was waiting in the car park. They all walked out to the taxi together, Christina and Manolo deep in conversation making their arrangements as to when they would see each other again, before they kissed each other goodnight and Christina got into the taxi.

Harry climbed in on the other side. "Thank you for the party, it was very nice."

Pablo reached in after her, took her chin in his hands, and gave her a long lingering kiss on the lips. Tingles ran down Harry's spine.

"Until tomorrow night." He shut the door and waved to them as they pulled out of the car park.

Pablo and Manolo returned to their friends. Pablo was instantly sought out and grabbed by a girl.

"Pablo! Where have you been? I have been looking for you all night." The Spanish girl wrapped her arms around his waist and looked longingly into his eyes.

"Some friends of my parents are visiting from England. I had to entertain one of the daughters whilst Manolo entertained the other. In fact, I have had a very boring night so far." He lied just to keep the peace. "Now you have found me, Conchitta, let's party." With that he grabbed her, his frustration taking over at not being able to have the girl he wanted. He gave her a quick, hard, peck on the lips and then started to dance with her. Manolo, now with another friend, joined them and the four of them danced the night away.

Harry sat silently, deep in thought. She liked Pablo. Did he really like her or was she just another holiday challenge for him?

Christina bubbled with excitement; her eyes were sparkling and her face flushed. "Manolo is so fantastic. He makes me feel so horny. Did you see the way he danced?" Not waiting for an answer, she carried on. "Is he not just the sexiest thing you ever saw? How did you get on with Pablo?"

"Okay. Pablo is taking me out tomorrow night. Do you think Dad will object?"

"No, it will be fine. I'm going out with Manolo anyway. He said he would pick me up at eight, so we'll just get ready and go out together. If we leave at the same time Dad will never know."

The taxi pulled into the road outside their villa and the girls clambered out. Christina went to pay. The driver shook his head and said something in Spanish.

"It looks like they have already paid, Harry. Quite a cheap night in the end!"

Chapter 6

The next morning Harry woke to the sound of Alka Seltzer fizzing in a glass that her mother had just placed by her bed.

"Did you have a good night, darling? You were very late you know. Christina said you may have a headache."

"Er, thanks, Mum, yes it was really great."

Anna left her to come around; she knew how dozy Harry was first thing in the morning.

Harry rolled over and stretched. She felt drowsy and knew the best cure for a hangover was a good ski. "Christina, I am going to the beach today, are you coming too?" Harry sleepily announced.

"I think I will stay up at the villa, I have some studying to do while I'm here so I might as well get on with it while I have the chance."

After a fresh croissant and a strong cup of coffee Harry felt much better. She quickly packed her rucksack and helped the twins into their jelly beans. Once she'd found their towels and sun block, Mark and Anna appeared; they were also ready.

Mark took the main road to the beach as they had to stop at the garage to fill the tank with petrol for the boat. "Do you fancy a ski this morning, Harry?" he shouted as he struggled down the slope and onto the beach with heavy tanks.

Harry looked across the bay. It looked perfect; there were no white horses breaking on any of the rocks. The flags up at the Gavina were motionless. The sea was like a mirror.

"Yes, please, Dad. I'm really in the mood to attempt my first ski of the season."

The twins were hot on their father's heels. "Dad, you promised us a ski today. You haven't forgotten, have you?" they protested.

"Everyone can ski this morning. Look at the bay, it is like a lake. Harry and I will go out first and you two can sit in the boat and be the look outs. Then, when we have found the best route to take, you can both take a turn."

Although the water was flat, quite a few boats had dropped anchor overnight, so it would take a while to pick the route that would be safest towing a skier.

Harry unpacked her towel and laid it out next to her mother's sun bed. She called the twins over and covered them in a factor fifty sun lotion. That ritual over, she then had to cover herself in a factor eight. Nicely creamed up, she headed towards the cave to get the twins' nets and buckets out. The cave was manmade and an outlet for the road water during the rainy season. However, during the summer, it dried out and was used by the boat men for storage. It was just the same as it had been the previous year. It was usually dark, smelly, and full of mosquitoes, and this year was no exception. Rushing to the back of the cave as her shiny blues eyes adjusted to the light, Harry found all their equipment. Mark had stored it all in there the day before. She retrieved what they would need for the day and dashed in and out quickly as she was trying not to breathe. She was convinced the beach men went to the loo in there by the urine smell wafting around.

The rows of coloured beach huts running from the west end of the beach up to the Taverna and then continuing, past the Taverna to the East end of the beach, were owned or rented by wealthy people for the season. Their main use was storage and changing facilities for people who frequented the beach, usually for the extended season from June to October. Sometimes families, grandparents and cousins, all crammed their possessions into these cabins. Once you acquired a beach hut you hung onto it and passed it from generation to generation. It was very difficult to buy a hut these days, so the boatmen kindly let the people paying for their services use their cave for storage.

Harry returned with the twins' large beach bag full of fading toys and dumped it on the sand next to their towels, then waded out towards the boat and to where Mark was waiting, and the twins were bobbing up and down in the water. She begged Mark to bring the boat in closer, so she didn't have to get wet just yet. The sea felt very chilly; the sun was still very low and first thing in the morning half the beach was still in the shade of the towing granite wall. Mark pushed the boat in a little further and Harry climbed the steps and into the boat. Leaning over the side she pulled the twins out of the water and into the boat. Once in, they both scrabbled into the seat next to where Harry was standing. Anna climbed into the front and sat next to Mark. Mark turned the engine on, put the boat into gear, and off they went, carefully picking their way in and out of the boats dotted along the shore line. Once they had reached the end of the ski lane the boats disappeared and the flat blue virgin waters lay before them. The engine roared and the front of the boat lifted out of the water as they picked up speed and flattened out as it started to plane across the bay.

Chapter 7

Up at the villa on Mass Nou, Pablo woke with a thumping headache. As the reality of the night before sank in, he realised someone was in bed with him. The dark, naked body, lying with her back towards him, started to stir. It took him a few minutes to comprehend it was Conchitta. She was his ex and she was in his bed. Although they were no longer going out, they always seemed to end up together at the end of an evening out. She found it difficult accepting they were no longer in a relationship and had managed to worm her way into his bed recently whenever she got the opportunity. Pablo gingerly crept out of bed and went into his en-suite for a shower. A cold shower would wake and refresh him. He would soon be functioning normally. He did his teeth and shaved, all the time trying to piece together the previous night's events. As he thought about the earlier part of the evening, he remembered being with Harry, the English Rose; a smile filled his face and a warm glow filled his body briefly. He tiptoed back into his bedroom so as not to wake the woman in his bed.

How could he have been so stupid? She always managed to get off with him when he was under the influence of alcohol. He grabbed the first clothes he could find, dressed in haste, then quietly left the room. Once out of ear shot of Conchitta, and any possible chance of waking her, he ran down stairs to see who was still about.

Juan, the butler who had been with the family since before Pablo was born, appeared.

"Good morning, Juan, has everyone gone?"

"Good morning, Pablo, there is no one around here. Your sisters went back to Barcelona early this morning. Manolo said he had to sort his father's boat out and left at about ten. There is still someone in your room. Did you notice?" he said with raised eyebrows.

"Yes, it is only an old girlfriend. Will you take her up some juice?" he replied, trying to cover his embarrassment.

The maid appeared from the kitchen, tutting and shaking her head as she raced around polishing and dusting, trying to get the house back in some sort of order before Pablo's parents returned from Barcelona.

Pablo gave Conchitta a good half hour hoping she would be up and dressed before he returned to his room. Conchitta was standing naked on the balcony examining the two glasses left from the night before. She ran her finger around the rim of the glass with the pink lipstick on.

"Please get some clothes on, Conchitta, I have a lot to do today." At the back of his mind he was remembering the date he had arranged with Harry.

"Yes, I know, what is her name?"

"She is a friend of my parents, I told you last night. I am just showing her the sights as a favour." Luckily, he remembered what he had told her last night and decided it would be better if he stuck to the same story.

"Well, I would like to meet her. Any friend of yours is always a friend of mine." She smiled in the sweetest way she could. Conchitta walked back into the bedroom, opened a draw, and pulled out a Nike T- shirt and some baggy shorts. "Is it okay if I borrow these? I was not expecting to stay," she teased as she began to get dressed in front of him.

He swung around and headed for the door. He had been so stupid. Why had he let her stay? He could not remember anything about the end of the evening, only up to the point when he put Harry and her sister into a taxi and then danced with Conchitta. He must see Manolo and find out what had happened.

Conchitta scooped up her bag, placed her dress into it, and followed Pablo downstairs.

Once he had called a taxi and put her almost physically into it, he returned to the villa and went into the office. Sitting at his father's desk, he started leafing through the huge pile of mail that had arrived that morning. Although his family was wealthy his father did not believe in just handing out money. Instead, each of his children had a responsible job they had to do if they were to receive their allowance. Pablo's involved the running of the villa, the house in the Pyrenees, as well as marketing their sportswear products and dealing with the personal house staff, all of whom adored Pablo and would do anything for him. He gave them respect and, in return, they treated him with both respect and love. Juan had, on occasions, even given Pablo a good hiding if justified when he was growing up. Pablo thought of him as an uncle and the housekeeper as an aunt. He had never known life when they had not been around to watch over him in his parent's absence, and he loved them both dearly.

His two sisters who were still at College, had to help run one of the family boutiques during the holidays. Pablo's family had their own chain of boutiques and sports shops. The girls found this no chore; they attended fashion shows, advised buyers of what would be "in" during the season, and basically had a good time. It was every girl's dream.

Chapter 8

Mark drove alongside the smaller yellow buoys. These were positioned in a floating line from one side of the bay to the other. This was to prevent the public swimming into the dangerous area of the sea where the yachts moored up and the water sports took place. Then he turned along the east side of the bay facing out to sea towards the flattest waters sheltered by the rocks. Finally he accelerated along the open mouth of the bay, the front of the boat lifting right out of the water. Harry could feel the salty breeze on her face followed by the occasional splash as the boat crashed down on a small swell. Harry's body came alive, adrenaline pumping; she couldn't wait to get out of the boat and into the water.

Mickey was leaning right over the side of the boat, his hand cupped in the water. He was trying to splash Sophie. At last he succeeded. Anna heard Sophie squeal and spotted what he was up to, so she told him off. Mark brought the boat slowly to a halt. It sank slowly down into the water; they were in position for some sporting action.

"Right, Harry, you first."

Harry tried her foot in one of the skies to check it for size, then put the life jacket on and climbed down into the dark, cold, water. Mickey passed the skies down to her. She bobbed about trying to keep herself upright until she found the boot of the ski with her foot. Then, with a further struggle, she managed to get her left foot balanced into the drop ski. "I'll ski around on two first and then, if I feel confident enough and not too rusty, I'll drop a ski," Harry shouted over the roar of the engine.

Harry held the rope with one hand, with her body leaning back and in a crouching position she managed to keep her balance with the other hand.

Mark put the boat in gear and the rope tightened.

"Hit it!" Harry shouted, and the boat lurched forward. Within seconds Harry gracefully lifted out of the water. Mark headed the boat back along the rocks and towards the beach. It was a fantastic feeling racing through the water but, with only a drop ski on her one foot, she did not try to venture over the wake. Her adrenaline pumping, she decided it was time to drop a ski.

She lifted her one foot out of the drop ski. Feeling with her big toe she found the back of the mono ski and slipped her foot into the back strap. She turned the triangle holding the rope upright and adjusted her hands so they were now one above the other, then lent back into a perfect mono position. Feeling quite confident, she raised her thumb up to the boat, indicating to Mark that she wanted to go faster. Having changed the position of the bar in her hands she was now going for the wake. She cut through the left-hand wake almost touching the water with her shoulder. Sending a massive amount of spray up over a stationary paddle boat, she changed hands and headed towards the wake on the right. Having not skied for so long, after two laps of the bay, her legs and arms soon began to ache, so she glided in behind the boat and signalled to Mark that she was tired. The boat slowed, then came to a stop. Harry sank slowly into the water. Mark circled back towards Harry and came to a halt as she pulled her ski off, handed it over the back of the boat to Mickey, and climbed back into the boat. Breathing heavily after the exertion, she beamed at her father who winked back as though to say, "That's my girl."

Mark headed back across the bay to pick up the drop ski. Anna, having noted where Harry dropped her ski, soon saw the huge wooden boat with flames down the sides of it, the man on board waving at them, holding up their drop ski.

"Look, that man on the flame thrower has it." She pointed to Mark. Harry, still feeling chuffed with her ski, hadn't even noticed the boat in the bay.

Mark pulled alongside the huge, wooden, fifties-style boat and Mickey reached out and took the ski off the man. With both his hands free the man, who was very dark and had his long, greying hair tied in a ponytail, clapped.

Blushing, Harry did a bow and said, "Thank you very much."

"Mi Papa!" Mark shouted as he began to drive away.

"Shut up, Dad, you can be so embarrassing," said Harry.

Next it was Mickey's turn. He jumped straight into the water with his life jacket on and waited for Harry to throw him the skies and, once he had put them on, the rope. He was straight up. Once he'd sorted out his balance he cut back and forth through the wake like a maniac until Mark slowed the boat down and he dropped into the water.

"Why did you stop, Dad? I was going really well," he panted as he climbed into the boat.

"You have been around the bay twice. That's enough for your first ski. You wait until tonight. Your legs will be really aching. Let's give Sophie a turn."

Sophie was in the water as quick as a flash. Harry passed her down the little skis and she bobbed about like a cork whilst she struggled to get the skis on, then shouted she was ready. Mark glided off slowly. As Sophie was so light she came out of the water with no trouble and, as her brother had done before, she began to cut through the wake. She looked very small and dainty, very much like Harry had done as a little girl. Mark gave her a whole lap of the bay and, as she got half way around the second time, he slowly stopped and let her sink into the water. He had halted by the wooden boat again.

Once more the man on board clapped and shouted, "You have a very talented family, Señor."

Mark shouted a thank you as he helped Sophie back into the boat. He turned to his wife and asked her if she would like a ski.

"Later. I think the children are all a little cold so we should head back to the beach," she replied.

Mark turned the boat in the direction of the beach and headed in. The bay was bursting into life and there had been quite a lot of boats skiing people and towing wake boarders; the water was beginning to chop up.

Once back on the beach Harry headed for the loo up at the Taverna. She was still dripping wet and wanted to change back into her bikini. She looked in the mirror and cursed herself for not bringing a hairbrush with her. She ruffled her hair as best she could with her fingers then went back down to the beach to lie on her towel. She had become quite cold. As the sun warmed her body, slowly she drifted off to sleep.

At the villa, Christina had spent the morning studying by the pool while she soaked up the sun. She was getting quite a tan. She heard the car pull up outside the villa; her family had returned from their morning skiing for lunch. They had a light salad, washed down with a cool, crisp, glass of wine. After a short siesta the family all returned for an afternoon on the beach.

Mark, Anna, Mickey, and Sophie went out on the boat fishing. Harry spent the afternoon lying on her stomach reading the latest Jilly Cooper book. Christina leafed through some magazines. She had had too much to concentrate on in the morning and needed to relax. Later, they discussed the previous night's events and what they would both wear that evening. Harry had already decided on a white short skirt and her gypsy top. The skirt was fitted and her top had quite a low-neck line; it would look nice now she had some colour to her body. Already feeling nervous about the evening ahead alone with Pablo, she wondered if she should cancel altogether. She wished they were just going for a drink; she would have felt a lot more at ease in a pair of shorts or her three-quarter length boyfriend jeans. Christina decided she would wear her red dress. Manolo hadn't said too much about what they were going to do but, as he was picking her up so early, she presumed they would eat something.

Out on the boat the fishing trip was going well. Mark had caught a large mullet. Mickey had landed three small fish. Screaming with excitement Sophie had caught a tiny fish. As she tried to land it, the little fish wriggled free and swam off. Anna had been dozing on the front of the boat, rocking up and down as the boat bobbed over the waves, anchor slowly dragging across the sea floor. It wasn't long before Mickey landed another fish. At the exact same time Sophie managed a catch and, with the help of her father, landed it successfully. Mark woke Anna up to watch Sophie's moment of glory. Her small, pink face lit up.

"Look, Daddy, look, Mummy I've got one. I've got a fish! Is it big enough to eat, Daddy?"

"Yes, dear, it's another little mullet. You can have it for your breakfast."

"But, Daddy, you must gut it for me. I couldn't bear to do that."

Mickey took the fish off the hook. For a small fish it was very strong and took several knocks over the head with the mallet before it finally lay still.

"Well, now we have six fish, thanks to Sophie and Mickey. That is at least one each for breakfast, if we let your big sisters have a taste. I think it's time we headed back to the beach."

Both the children objected. Sophie was so excited it would have been useless to argue.

Anna opened her mouth, before they got too loud, and distracted them with a suggestion they all went back to the beach and had an ice cream. Mickey pulled the anchor in as Mark started the engine. The boat headed slowly towards the shore, dipping up and down as it rode over the small waves.

Mickey and Sophie were eager to get to the shore. Jumping out of the boat and nearly spilling their catch, they ran up the beach. "Look what we've caught," Sophie screeched.

Harry and Christina could hear them coming. Getting to their feet, before they were pounced on, they were presented with six stiff fish, staring up at them.

"There is enough for one fish each for breakfast tomorrow morning. I caught that one." Sophie proudly pointed to her catch.

"Daddy's going to teach me how to gut them myself when we go back to the villa." Mickey grinned proudly with a wicked sparkle in his eyes.

"Anyone for ice cream?" Anna hurried up the beach with six dripping ice creams and they all dived for them.

It was now five o'clock. Everyone felt tired and in need of a cup of tea. They had all had enough of the beach, so they packed everything away, collected up their towels and headed home.

When the shower was free, Harry took her turn. Keeping the water cool enough, so as not to shock her body, but still quite refreshing, Harry washed her hair and rinsed the sun cream from her body. Stepping from the shower she wrapped her hair in a towel, patted her glowing, pink body dry, then smothered herself in after-sun. Leaving the bathroom tidy, with a towel around her body, she went back into her bedroom. Slipping into her nightshirt, she shook her hair down and lay on her bed.

Chapter 9

"Harry, Harry! Wake up! It's half past seven!" Christina was shaking Harry by the shoulder. "How long will it take you to get ready? I thought we were going to leave the villa together at about eight?"

For once Harry dived out of bed. She looked in the mirror. Her hair had half dried and was sticking out in all directions. She brushed it through, as hard as she could, trying to straighten it. Thank God she had brought her straightening tongs with her. Sitting in front of the mirror, she applied a thin line of eyeliner followed with a coat of mascara to separate her already thick lashes. Outlining her thick, well-shaped lips with a deep pink liner, she ran over them with a dusky pink lip gloss, with a brush. Finishing off with a little rouge to highlight her cheekbones, at least her face looked okay. Her hair was now completely dry and a lot straighter than it had been when she woke up.

Christina offered to style it for her. She was ready and looked great in her red dress. She had even painted her nails so she had time to kill.

She lit a cigarette while she waited for Harry to dress. Producing her secret supply of vodka from the wardrobe, she quickly popped out to the kitchen and got some orange juice and ice. Mark and Anna were nowhere to be seen but squeals could be heard from the garden. They were obviously gutting fish. Returning to the bedroom, she expertly mixed the drinks. Handing one to Harry she said "Here, have this for Dutch courage."

For once Harry took it and pinched a puff on Christina's cigarette before she sat back down and let Christina do her hair. Her nerves were beginning to take over. Oh, she wished they were going out together and not separately.

Christina was very good with hair and, in no time at all, she had Harry's hair smooth and falling nicely around her shoulders, the shortest part curving in around her chin.

"There you are, Harry; you do look nice. You must remember to be careful. I expect Pablo will eat you alive when he sees you."

"Thanks, Christina, but I don't think I look that nice. It's you who should watch out with that hot-blooded Manolo." They both laughed. Spraying themselves with perfume, they picked up their bags to leave.

In the kitchen, Mickey and Sophie were proudly lining their gutted fish up on a plate.

"Look, you two, I have gutted that one and that one." Mickey pointed to the fish he had gutted while Sophie squirmed with horror.

"They look really good and we can't wait to help you eat them," Harry and Christina agreed.

Anna looked the girls up and down and said they looked great, while Mark lectured them on what they could and could not do. Kissing their parents goodbye, they decided they would walk down the old dust path a little way to wait for their friends. They did not fancy the prospect of introductions and a once over from their father just yet.

"I haven't brushed my teeth." Harry began to turn back when Christina grabbed her by the arm and swung her back round.

"Here, I've got some chewing gum. Chew on this and Pablo won't notice."

They walked out to the main road and waited. Pablo turned up first in a black BMW convertible. Christina dug Harry in the ribs as she raised her eyebrows. "I'll see you later".

Harry opened the door and stepped into the car. Before she had time to straighten her skirt and put her seatbelt on, a car drew up beside them. It was Manolo. He too had a nice soft top, only it was red. Christina got in next to Manolo and adjusted her hair in the mirror while Pablo and Manolo had a chat.

"Adios, hasta luego." Pablo raised his voice as he pulled away from Manolo and Christina. Pablo drove towards Saint Feliu, an old fishing and market town. "You look lovely, my little English Rose."

Harry could feel her cheeks fill with colour as Pablo's eyes wandered from the road and over her body. She crossed her legs and tried to keep her hands flat on the edge of the seat to stop them sweating. "Thank you," she replied, trying to think of something to say. "Is this your car?"

"Yes, it was a present from my father when I was twenty-one. My father always says if you have a nice car, everywhere you go you command respect. Rosa and Maria have a jeep." As he accelerated along the road, Harry's hair started to blow all over the place. "Would you like me to put the roof back on?"

"No, it's nice, it keeps me cool. Where are we going?" Harry replied as she pulled her hair into a pony tail then tied it into a knot.

"There is a little restaurant on the hill above Saint Feliu that is very quiet during the week. I had to phone to check they would be open. They said for me they would stay open. I told the owner that I had a special guest for the night."

Harry was beginning to relax a little now. She felt good sitting next to Pablo; he was so cool. If only Emily Bunting, her college rival could see her now. He had a khaki pair of chinos and a white shirt on. She could just about see his Italian leather shoes working the accelerator. His aftershave smelt alluring and she could not work out what it was. Every time they pulled up for a red light, or slowed down in a queue, people would automatically stare at them. It made her feel cool and excited.

Pablo put on his cassette player and asked her if she liked Duran Duran. She nodded so he let it blare out as he drove up the hill. He parked the car right on the edge of the cliff overlooking Sant Feliu harbour. The yachts and catamarans were all neatly lined up, bobbing up and down with the swell of the water. Fisherman, settling in for the night along the harbour wall, were setting up their rods.

People were promenading and admiring the boats.

Pablo came around and opened the door for Harry then, taking her hand, helped her out of the car. Harry, not used to this treatment, felt awkward and started to blush as their eyes met briefly.

Pablo tried to hold her gaze; she had such beautiful blue eyes framed with a mass of ebony lashes. Harry looked away quickly and released his hand.

It had once been a charming old farm house that had recently been converted into a restaurant. A middle-aged man with slicked-down, black hair greeted them. He wore a black waiter's outfit with gold trim on the lapels. In his right hand he carried a single red rose which he presented to Harry.

"Buena's tardes, Señor Cruanos." With both hands now free he embraced Pablo and kissed him on both cheeks.

"Buena's tardes, Carlos," Pablo replied, "This is Harry, a friend I have met recently. She is from England." Carlos gave Pablo an approving nod.

Carlos kissed Harry on both cheeks too. "What a beautiful perfume for a beautiful lady." He smiled then gestured for them to follow him.

At first they were taken through an arch in the wall which opened out into a small courtyard. A large fig dominated the facing wall whilst around the arch a climbing Bougainvillea, with deep purple blooms, framed the entrance. A fountain sprang out of an old well in the middle of the courtyard. Carlos continued to beckon them on through the restaurant and out on to the terrace where he led them to a table overlooking the bay, separated only by a small granite wall extended by a row of terracotta pots, filled with deep red geraniums, in the typical Spanish style.

Harry's eyes were sparkling. She looked down over the wall; the drop was dark and took her breath away as she heard the waves crashing against the rocks below. Carols pulled a chair out and Harry sat down. Pablo seated himself opposite.

"Would you like a drink? Maybe a jug of sangria or Tisana?"

"I think we will have a jug of Tisana and two vodkas with ice."

Carlos having taken their order, retreated into the restaurant.

"I shouldn't drink too much, I get drunk very easily."

"It's okay, don't worry, I will look after my English Rose and return you to your family safely," Pablo grinned.

Harry saw his eyes were sparkling too. God he was gorgeous, Harry thought as his mouth, spreading into a wide grin, exposed his perfect white teeth.

Harry did need a drink; she was feeling a little stiff and wanted to relax. When the drinks arrived, Harry downed her vodka and then Pablo poured her a glass of Tisana. It was potent stuff so Harry knew she would have to watch how much she drank.

The menus arrived. Pablo said he was happy to order for them both. Harry, not wanting to make a fool of herself reading the Spanish menu and trying to understand it, was quite happy to go with Pablo's choice as she was not a fussy eater. Nothing would make her squeamish or ill.

Manolo and Christina headed into Playa de Aro looking for a bit of night life. They parked in the central car park and walked through the side streets to the town centre. The promenade was overflowing with culture. Stall holders and artists lined the streets. Playa was buzzing. The shops were magnificent, designer labels everywhere. They headed to the Hit Box. The bouncers on the door knew Manolo and let him straight in. It was a trendy, split-level eating place with a spacious, wall-to-wall bar and music booming out from every corner. There were mirrors wherever they looked and a huge, white, grand piano, with a life-sized Elton John sat playing it, suspended from the ceiling. Over the stairs was a model of Elvis playing a guitar. Manolo headed towards a table where a load of other young people sat. He spoke to them first in Spanish and then introduced Christina to them all in English. There was a lot of kissing then names thrown at her from every angle before everyone shuffled around to make a space so they could sit down.

"We have already ordered just some Tapas. There is enough for you also if it's okay?" A rather pretty girl spoke in perfect English.

"It's okay for me," said Manolo, looking at Christina for her approval.

She nodded. She was in her element. This was her idea of a holiday. Christina was asked if she would like a vodka or what she would like to drink. She said vodka was fine. She looked around the table to see what everyone else was drinking. They all seemed to be drinking vodka or Bacardi; some of the boys had bottled San Miguel's. Then she was away. She could talk to anyone and got on with almost everyone, unlike Harry, who was very cautious and shy at first until she got to know someone well.

Harry was now feeling quite talkative herself. The drinks were having an effect; she was relaxed, and her confidence was growing. She told Pablo about her dog and horse, about the beautiful place she lived at in England and where she went to college.

While she talked Pablo just gazed into her eyes and smiled. She was gorgeous. He'd dreamed of meeting a girl like this. Carlos came with a bottle of wine followed by different courses; first a fish course, then a meat course, all of which were small but deliciously cooked, and finally some strawberries. Pablo insisted on feeding her one by one, teasing her with them before he placed them in her mouth with his fingers, stopping occasionally to wipe the cream from her mouth then licking his finger.

Harry lapped it up. He was lovely.

"Oh! I'm sorry, I have talked too much." She realised how happy she was, how relaxed she felt in Pablo's company.

"It's fine. I love to hear you talk. Your voice is so nice and soft. You are so beautiful to look at." He leant across the table and stroked her hair. She'd taken it out of the knot and shaken it loose.

"Would you like a cognac or coffee?"

"I will have whatever you are drinking." She was beginning to feel a bit tipsy and hoped he would not have anything too strong. The Tisana had gone straight to her head but luckily the food had soaked some of the alcohol up. She had only had one glass of wine with her meal and had kept sipping water all evening.

To finish off they had a small brandy, then Pablo raised his eyes to Carlos who had been hovering near to the table ever since he came out to light the candles, adding to the romance of the atmosphere. Carlos arrived with the bill and, without so much as a glance at it, Pablo handed over a wad of money. Carlos returned with the change on a small silver tray and placed it on the table. Pablo left the change and said goodbye and thank you to Carlos and then they left.

Harry was already home and in bed. She could not sleep; she was bursting with news of her evening with Pablo.

As she was so happy Christina decided it would be a bad idea to tell her about what she had learnt about Conchitta. Instead she relayed her evening out with Manolo, leaving out the details of their trip to the beach where they had walked bare foot on the cool sands and skinny dipped in the sea. She asked Harry if she fancied going to a club with the boys the following evening. Harry said she could not wait then, without another word, they turned the light off and went to sleep.

Chapter 10

The following day everything was slightly damp; there had obviously been a big storm. Everyone seemed to have slept through it. The air was slightly fresher for the moment. All in jovial moods, they listened over breakfast to what they had all done the previous evening.

Mark drove them all to the beach where Daan was waiting to see them. He seemed very excited. Greeting them all with the usual kiss on both cheeks, which took some time to get around the whole family, Dann spoke. "Mark, I have a job for your girls. Is it okay if I ask them?" He winked at the girls.

Mark nodded.

Daan explained how one of the makers of 'Ski Summer', a major water sports clothes manufacture in Spain, wanted two pretty girls who were also good skiers, to be filmed wearing their wet suits for an advertisement. "If you will do this they will pay well and give you the wet suits, towels, and all the other Ski Summer accessories. When the film is ready you will all be invited to a big launch party near the mountains. It will be fun, yes?"

Christina nodded excitedly while Harry was a bit more reserved. She thought she might make a fool of herself. Christina rounded on her. "Oh, come on, Harry, it will be fun. You said the other day you would like a new wet suit. Think of the party! Come on, who's going to know about it anyway?"

Harry agreed. Who would see it anyway? It wouldn't matter if it went well or it was bad; she might as well have a bit of fun doing it.

"They will be here tomorrow at seven thirty when the water is still flat. So, I shall tell them it's a date?"

"Yes, that will be fine, Daan," said Christina.

Harry just smiled.

Mickey ran around making a joke of it and asking the girls for their autographs. Sophie said they had all the fun and she wished she was older so she could do it too.

They spent the morning out in the boat practicing their skiing; Christina was a little shaky at first but soon she was back in the swing of it and slaloming from side to side. Harry practiced her deep water start on one ski until she was so exhausted she was ready to drop. Finally they ran out of petrol and had to row in. Thankfully they were only just outside the buoys when the boat cut out so it was not a big deal.

Sunbathing, sleeping, and swimming took up the rest of the day; it was blissful.

"If only we did not live so far away." Harry was dreaming. "I would do this for the rest of my life given the chance." It was her idea of heaven.

After a day in the sun, Mark and Anna said they were going up to the Taverna for a drink while they waited for Mickey and Sophie to come back from their snorkelling. The twins had set off about half an hour ago in the direction of the rocks that framed the little bay. Harry and Christina joined their parents on the upper terrace overlooking the bay with a mixture of ice cold drinks to rehydrate them. The main topic of conversation was about the ski filming the next day, what they would have to do and where they thought the party might be. Harry was beginning to think perhaps it would be good fun.

One of the waitresses arrived over. "Is there someone in your party name of Harry?"

"Yes, my name is Harry." Shocked she replied, wondering what the problem was.

"Good. I have a message for you to phone this number." The waitress handed Harry a piece of paper.

Harry took the number and asked if there was a phone anywhere she could use.

The waitress asked Harry to follow her into the cool, dark, wooden panelled office and said it would be possible for her to use their phone.

On the piece of paper was just a number and the name "Cruanos." Harry thought it was what Pablo had said his surname was so she dialled the number. A woman answered the phone and Harry asked if she could speak to Pablo.

"No, this is Maria. Pablo is not here. Can I help you?"

"Hello, Maria, this is Harry. I have been asked to phone this number."

"Oh Harry, it was me who left the message. Pablo asked me to say he would pick you and Christina up at your villa at ten tonight. I hope you understand."

"Thank you, Maria, I understand. Goodbye." With that Harry put down the phone and went back to the table where everyone was waiting to see what the phone call was about. She explained about Pablo and his sisters.

"If these hot-blooded boys are becoming an item, I think tonight at ten I shall be around," Mark said under raised eyebrows.

They could hear Mickey and Sophie shouting. They finished their drinks, left the money on the table, and headed back down to the beach.

Once he'd dropped everyone at home and taken a quick shower, Mark went to the supermarket to get them all chicken and chips for their dinner. He could smell the chickens cooking, row upon row of chickens stuffed with herbs and spit roasted. There was nothing like the taste of Spanish chicken, stuffed with Mediterranean herbs, basted in its own fat, and cooked on a spit. Ordering two chickens and three chips, the chef informed him it would be about ten minutes, so Mark strolled off to see if the day's English papers where in the newsagents.

Back at the apartment Anna and the girls prepared a fresh green salad and a large plate of beef tomatoes and onions sliced in oil and vinegar, while the twins took their last dip of the day in the pool. Once the table was prepared, Anna took a slice of lemon, popped some ice chunks into a glass, and poured herself a gin and tonic. After carefully twizzling it she retired to the patio with Christina and Harry to wait for the food to arrive. It was a lovely evening; the sun had set and slowly the lights were twinkling on around the hill side. Christina lit the Citronella candle to keep the mosquitoes away.

"You girls are already looking a lovely colour. Have you decided what swimwear you're going to wear tomorrow morning?"

"Harry's going to wear her pale blue Speedo and I'm going to wear my white."

"Oh, you'll look lovely." Anna marvelled at the thought of her two attractive daughters skiing around the bay. They heard the crunch of tyres on the drive and returned to the table to dish up.

"I've got two chickens so that is a quarter each. Are you all sure you can manage it?"

A chorus of yeses echoed around the kitchen. Once everyone had taken a plate they all headed out to the patio to enjoy their dinner in the cool evening air. After they had all eaten their fill, Anna let the girls go to their room for a sleep while she supervised the twins washing up.

The girls were both tired, so they set the alarm for nine and slept for a couple of hours.

Chapter 11

That night, when the alarm went off, Harry jumped out of bed and dived into the shower for a cool-off, thinking all the time about what she was going to wear.

"Christina, should I wear my short fitted black dress if we are going to a club?"

"I don't know. I think I'm just going to wear my little red one. Your black one would probably be ideal."

Harry tied her hair up into a knot and pulled a few strands loose to hang around her face. Her pale pink lipstick complimented her tan and her eyes were shinning, clear and blue. She looked stunning. Christina slipped into her little red dress and put on matching lipstick. She was also looking good. They each had a squirt of perfume, packed up their bags, and headed into the lounge.

The twins were sent up to bed just as there was a knock at the door.

"Well, Harry, go and bring them in for a few minutes," said Mark.

"Dad, do I have to?" Harry pleaded.

"Well, if you want to go out tonight you do."

Harry went to the door. "Hi, Pablo." She leant forward and kissed him on both cheeks, then turned to Manolo and greeted him in the same way. "Can you come in for a few minutes? Our parents wish to meet you."

"Of course, I understand." Pablo winked at her and followed her through the door and into the lounge.

Harry introduced Pablo and Manolo to their father and mother. They all shook hands.

"You can call me Mark, and this is Anna," Mark chipped in.

"Well, I can see where Harry and Christina get their good looks from. They have such handsome parents."

Harry looked at Christina who was pretending to make a retching motion behind Pablo's back.

"Why, thank you." Mark smiled while Anna blushed. "Now don't let us keep you and don't be late tonight. Early start in the morning, girls."

They all said good night and headed out to the car. Once outside the villa, Pablo grabbed Harry's hand and pulled her in close to him.

Harry, still worried that Mark would be watching, held him back and said, "Wait."

Christina followed Manolo's cue and jumped into the back of the car. It was a bit of a squash but they snuggled in nicely. Harry sat in the front next to Pablo. He looked gorgeous. She could smell his aftershave and the faint smell of toothpaste.

Once down the road Pablo started talking. He told Harry about his busy day and was glad his sister had managed to get a message to them. He glanced in his rear mirror. Christina and Manolo were deep in conversation in the back. He leant over and whispered to Harry, "I have been thinking about you all day, you know. I don't think I have ever been so crazy about anyone before. I could not wait for the night to come so I could see you again. Tomorrow I have the entire day to myself with no work. Maybe you would like me to spend it with you at the beach?"

Harry was beginning to feel a little worried. She'd never spent an entire day with a boy before, a group of mixed friends, yes, but not one to one. Besides which she had the filming to do in the morning. What if she'd gone off him by then? Tonight he seemed adorable and she wanted to throw her arms around his neck and kiss him, but tomorrow? She'd have to think about it.

"Well, what do you say, my little English Rose?"

She explained about the advertisement for Ski Summer and said she would prefer if he did not come to the beach until later. Manolo and Christina joined in the conversation and they decided they would take a boat out for the afternoon with a picnic. Manolo and Pablo said they would take care of the picnic so all the girls had to do was to be ready for them.

The sky had darkened and the night life in Playa was waking up with lights flashing and music blaring. The market traders and artists lined the streets creating organised chaos as people crammed to see what they were selling or painting. The pace was fast and the excitement bubbled into the car. They all seemed very excited as they pulled into the entrance of Camel night-club. A parking attendant appeared from nowhere so they all got out. Pablo had a chat with him as he handed over his keys. Then he took Harry by the hand and they followed Manolo and Christina towards the door.

The club was like a large pyramid or rather two small pyramids joined onto one large pyramid. Two bouncers frisked them and signalled to Christina to open her bag. Harry opened hers ready. Once they had all been checked they went into the club.

Inside the club a woman dressed as an Egyptian goddess greeted them. Pablo produced a card from his wallet. Her coal-painted eyes glanced at it then she led them to a table overlooking a dance floor. Each table had its own triangular shaped canopy over it and tall wooden stools covered with leopard print cushions. The round table tops were ceramic; each had a picture telling a different story. Palm trees lined the walkways that were set out on various levels between tables, bars, and dance floors. The bars were circular and covered by a canopy. It gave the impression of a camp set up in the desert. They seated themselves at the high round table with four stools. Pablo sat next to Harry, Christina to Harry's right, and Manolo to the left of Pablo. It was very cosy. Another Egyptian goddess appeared at the table carrying a gold notepad and matching pen. She took the order for their drinks and disappeared. The music was loud and mainly English and American, although Harry and Christina were not familiar with all the soundtracks. The drinks arrived; four vodka and Cokes. Typical club style, the glasses were filled to the rim with vodka and ice with not much room to put the Coke in. Harry downed her first vodka and Coke quickly. She was thirsty and needed a bit of a confidence boost before she could start to relax or have a dance.

Christina and Manolo were straight off to the nearest dance area. They moved well together.

Harry wondered what it would be like to dance with Pablo. She'd danced briefly with him at his party. That now seemed ages ago.

Pablo ran his finger down her arm. "You look very lovely tonight. I like the dress; it fits you very well and shows your nice body." He moved his stool a little closer to Harry's and slipped his hand around her waist. "You tan very well."

Harry began to get embarrassed. She couldn't bear people giving her compliments; she never knew how to respond. Once again, she found herself wondering if this was another of the chat up lines he used on all his girlfriends. He took her chin in his hand and gave her a lingering kiss on her lips. That sent a shiver down her spine. She needed another drink. She felt so tense and she knew he could sense it.

"Hey, Harry, would you help me find the ladies room?" Christina interrupted them and Harry was quick to her feet and set off to find the toilets.

"Thanks, Christina. I have not had enough to drink yet. Let's have a quickie over there and take it with us." They popped behind a bamboo screen and headed to one of the little bars on their way. Christina ordered two Tequilas. "I have never had a Tequila before," Harry smiled.

"Copy what I do." Christina licked her hand, poured salt on the damp patch, then downed the Tequila before biting into the lemon and licking the salt off her hand.

Harry copied her then wrinkled her nose and shook her head in disgust. "Oh my god, that was ghastly!" Harry felt the Tequila hit the back of her throat and burn as it went down. She just managed to stop herself from choking as they made their way into the ladies' toilets.

There was a row of shallow basins made of marble on one wall surrounded by ceramic tiles in keeping with the rest of the club decor. Above each sink was a mirror set in a gold frame. The toilets were set out along the opposite wall in bamboo cubicles. It was very different to the clubs Harry had been in before. On the facing wall was a huge mirror, necessary for any girl who wanted to check herself from top to toe. The lights hung like little suns over each mirror. The lighting overall was quite dim; this was a good thing for Harry as she checked her flushed face in the mirror and re-did her lipstick. She did not want to see all her blemishes.

Christina headed for a toilet. "Oh, I think Manolo is lovely. He moves so well and I felt like everyone was watching us when we were dancing. It was great".

"I'm too embarrassed to dance. I always feel like people are watching me because I look so stupid."

"Oh, Harry, you look great when you dance. You have really good rhythm and your figure is so lovely, I do not know what you worry about."

"Well if I dance you must tell me or distract me if I look silly."

"Of course I will." With that they checked their hair, had a good look at themselves in the large mirror from the front, sideways on, and from behind, then headed back to join the boys.

"Pablo, I think I should tell you I saw Conchitta up on the other dance floor when I was dancing with Christina. You know she still thinks you can get back together. It has only been two months since you split up and the way you were dancing with her the other night at your party she probably thinks she has a really good chance!"

"Manolo, do you not think if she sees me with someone else she will get the message? It's over and has been for months. I never realised until I met Harry how much Conchitta is getting on my nerves."

"Be careful then. Conchitta will cause trouble and I don't think Harry will take any messing around, from what Christina has told me. She's young but she has very strong values."

"I like Harry very much and I would not do anything to hurt her. She makes me feel like I want to protect her. Do you know what I mean?" Before Manolo could answer, Christina and Harry arrived back. Manolo took Christina by the hand and headed towards the dance floor.

Pablo grabbed Harry by the hand and followed, heading for the centre of the dance floor. She looked so beautiful he wanted everyone to see she was with him.

Luckily, just as they got to the dance floor, Oasis came on. Some music they both knew and it was an easy beat Harry could feel straight away and was able to dance to. The Tequila was also beginning to take effect and she was relaxing. This showed in her dancing. As she looked around she noticed quite a few people watching them and did not mind. She felt safe and protected with Pablo; being with him gave her confidence. Christina and Manolo joined them and they all danced together for quite some time. They all seemed to be having such fun dancing, but it was a very humid night; the heat was beginning to affect them. Christina was in her element; she loved the attention they were getting as people stopped and watched them. They did look a very handsome foursome.

After a few tracks they returned to their table and sat down. They were all gasping for another drink. Christina took out a cigarette, gave one to Manolo, and then offered one to Harry.

As Harry went to take one, Pablo pushed her hand away and told her not to smoke. She was a bit annoyed but she didn't smoke or want one anyway. It was just something to do. Christina and Manolo headed out for some fresh air whilst Harry took another sip of her drink. There were large ceiling fans all around the room and the air conditioning was coming up through vents in the floor too, so it wasn't long before Harry began to cool down.

Christina and Manolo arrived back just as another goddess appeared at the table with a bottle of Champagne on ice and four glasses. "This is from the girl on the balcony. She hopes you all enjoy your evening."

Pablo and Harry looked towards the balcony bar. A very pretty, Spanish girl held a glass up to toast them. Harry lent over to Christina and asked if she knew who the girl was. Before Christina had time to reply, Pablo popped the Champagne cork and began filling their glasses.

"Happy life and happy holidays," he toasted. They all clinked glasses then Pablo turned to the balcony and raised his glass to the girl. He sat back down and pulled Harry's stool close to him. At last Conchitta had accepted it was over and was showing him that she was happy for him.

The Champagne went straight to Harry's head; she was feeling very relaxed and quite confident.

"Let's go and have another dance, Pablo." She took hold of his hand and pulled him up off his stool. Pablo held her close and gazed into her sparkling eyes. "You are so beautiful; I find it hard to resist you. Are you sure you are okay?" He bent his arm around her back, holding her tightly. He lent down, kissed her gently on the lips then, releasing her, led her back to the dance floor.

The music had changed now to a slow beat. Couples hurried to the dance floor for a more intimate dance. Pablo found a space and put his arms around Harry's waist.

Gently Harry reached up and placed her arms around his neck.

She could smell his aftershave and was convinced he was wearing Paco Rabanne.

Pablo ran his hands up and down her back resting them on her bottom. He squeezed it gently, pulling her closer to his body. He whispered into her ear, "I think I am falling in love."

A thrilling shiver ran down Harry's spine; she felt all weak.

He said it again then kissed her neck. He moved his hands up to her face. "Do you understand what I am saying? I want you so much."

Harry looked up into his eyes. He was so gorgeous. She put her lips to his; they kissed. Gently at first, then with passion. His tongue was in her mouth, feeling her teeth and seeking her tongue. Harry responded and put her tongue inside his mouth, searching every inch, feeling his teeth and teasing his tongue with hers. He pulled her closer. She could feel how hard he was against her.

Someone caught her arm roughly from behind and swung her around, catching them both unaware. Pablo let her go.

A man grabbed her and held her close to him. She struggled and shouted for Pablo. For a moment she was distracted as she thought she saw him dragging another girl by the hand through the crowd and out of sight. The man who had grabbed her was holding her too tightly for her to struggle free. She tried to scream but he just put his lips on hers and started kissing her. He stank of spirits and stale sweat. What could she do? She held her lips tightly closed and struggled to free herself. When he loosened his grip slightly and Harry took the chance and brought her knee up hard between his legs and, as he gasped in pain, he released his grip and she was free. She searched around quickly for their table but could not see it anywhere; she was completely disorientated. Someone else grabbed her arm. She was ready for this. She swung her right hand around as hard as she could and was blocked. Thank God it was Manolo.

"Quick, come with me. We have to go."

She followed him through the crowded dance floor towards the exit. Christina was waiting for them outside. She had hailed a cab and the three of them jumped in.

"Wait! What about Pablo? Where has he gone?"

"He will be all right. We will go back to S'Agaro and wait for him there."

Harry felt shocked and sick. She had sobered up very quickly. "What happened, and who was that girl Pablo went off with?"

Manolo told Harry what he had told Christina before. "When she sent the Champagne over Pablo hoped she would be okay. Seeing him with another girl may be the cure for her to see that it is all over. She is mad, and she has three mad brothers. I hope Pablo will be okay."

They reached the Bar Maria and Manolo paid the taxi. They went in and took the table out on the balcony overlooking the bay. Manolo ordered three brandies knowing they could all do with one.

Christina took a packet of cigarettes from her bag and they all took one.

Harry, not caring she didn't smoke, lit hers, drawing hard on the filter. The smoke hit the back of her throat as she inhaled.

They sat in silence looking out to sea and sipping their brandy.

All sorts of thoughts were going through Harry's mind. *"What if he does like her and just used me to make her jealous? For all I know he could be kissing her right now. He just wanted me out of the way so probably arranged for Manolo to take me home. So much for telling me he loved me. I expect Manolo feels awful. He obviously likes Christina. Poor Manolo. It must be hard for him."* Harry finished her brandy and stood up. "If you two don't mind I will walk home. It's getting late and I want to get a good sleep." She stood up and leant over to Manolo. "Thanks for getting me out of there. I feel such a fool." She gave him a kiss on both cheeks and then kissed Christina too. "See you later, Good night, Manolo."

Harry stopped in the bar to get a packet of cigarettes out of the machine. She looked at the choice: Marlboro, Winston, or B and H. She put her money in and pressed the button below the B and H. The machine clanked around and out dropped a packed of Marlboro Lights. She could not be bothered to go to the bar and get them changed. Placing the packet into her bag, she headed out of the door. A nice walk along the sea front would clear her head and make her feel better.

She took off her shoes and walked down onto the sand. It felt quite cold. The big orange moon was bouncing off the dark sea. Little fishing boats twinkled on the horizon, bobbing up and down with the motion of the water. Children ran up and down the beach hiding from their parents who were calling them from a parked car. Laughter rang out from a group of teenagers having a barbeque further along the beach. Some young lovers stopped for a kiss in front of Harry. This was all too much. Her heart was breaking. She picked up her shoes and ran towards the sea. Stopping by an overturned boat she sat down then, taking a cigarette out of her bag, rummaged for a light. After pulling out some lipstick, a tampon, and a packet of chewing gum, she finally found a lighter. The shock of the evening was beginning to set in. She started shaking, a lump appeared in her throat and the tears welled up in her eyes.

"Is this seat taken?"

She looked up. Pablo was looking down at her. Harry burst into tears. Pablo knelt next to her and cradled her in his arms as she sobbed and sobbed uncontrollably.

Pablo spoke softly. "I told you this evening that I think I am falling in love with you. My heart, when I am with you, is just so full, overflowing. These last few days, when I am not with you, I think about you all the time. When I go to sleep I dream of you. It is you I want, only you. Manolo, told you about Conchitta. She is mad. Tomorrow I will go and see her father. I will speak to him. He will understand." He took her limp arms and placed them around his body then he tilted her face towards his. His lips traced the lines of her tears until he reached her mouth. He started kissing her mouth. At first, she did not respond. He pulled her body closer to his and held her tightly, kissing her harder and harder.

The world was spinning around in her head. Her lips began to respond. She could not help herself, she kissed him back passionately.

He was biting her lips. He pushed her slowly back onto the sand and lowered himself onto her. His hand ran up and down her dress tracing the outline of her body. Once again, he whispered into her ear how much he wanted her. His hands ran down to her bottom he squeezed it, pulling it firmly towards him.

She could feel how hard he was and she wanted him. Their passion got hotter and stronger, his hands working up and down her body. He started undoing the buttons on her dress and slipped a hand inside her bra. Her bosom was small and firm. He moved his lips down to her nipple and started to kiss it. Her nipples were now erect. She responded, kissing the top of his head, feeling his firm, muscular back. Her body ached for him. His hand slipped inside her pants and he traced his fingers over the baby smooth skin of her bottom. He pushed himself away, not looking at her.

She spoke for the first time. "What's wrong?"

His voice was low and husky. "I think you are still a virgin. Am I right?"

Embarrassed now, in a whisper she said, "Yes, I am."

"Well then, this is not right."

"But you told me you were falling in love with me. I think I am in love with you, so what is wrong?"

"You are falling in love me too? While that is fantastic, it is more reason why this is wrong."

"But how can it be wrong? I really need you now. Please, Pablo, it will be all right."

He took her in his arms and kissed her gently, stroking her hair back from her face. "No, it's not the right place. You are very young and it is your first time. It will be wrong. We must wait until the time is right and you are sure. You are my English Rose." He could not believe what he was saying but he knew he was right. He stood and pulled her up from the sand. He dusted her down and did her buttons back up. His hands were gentle but firm.

She looked in his eyes, understanding why they should wait.

"Your body is wonderful and, one day, I hope you will love me enough and I will love you, but not tonight. It's not right and I know that. I respect you." He held her tight in his arms and kissed her long and hard. Then he bent down and picked her bag and shoes up. He noticed the packet of cigarettes lying on the floor and bent down picked them up and threw them into the sea. "You do not need these." Taking her by the hand they strolled back up the beach to where he had parked his car. He opened the door and she sat in. He knelt down and gently dusted her feet off, studying them as he did. "Even your feet are beautiful." He kissed her feet then put her shoes on. "I will take you home now. It has been a long night and you need your sleep." Pablo got in the car next to her and drove back up the old dirt track to her parents' villa. The car stopped and he leant over and held her firmly for a moment. Then he kissed her on the lips.

She got out of the car, still a little shell shocked but, once again, completely in love with Pablo, and walked to the door. She turned and waved.

He blew her a kiss as drove off into the night, his mind working on what he could do to sort Conchitta out.

Chapter 12

The next morning the Thomas-Smyths breakfasted early and headed for the beach. Mickey and Sophie were very excited. They had never watched a film crew in action before. As they drove along the wall overlooking the bay to park they could see there was already a crowd of people gathering to see what was going on. Christina felt like a celebrity as she made her way down to the waiting film crew. Harry was feeling nervous; her stomach was doing somersaults. She wished she could send everyone away and ski without an audience.

Mark could sense her nerves. He squeezed her hand gently. "Just go out and ski as if it was just another ski on an ordinary day. Forget about everyone else and just enjoy yourself."

Harry smiled, grateful for the encouragement and reassurance. After last night, her nerves did feel in tatters. Still, time to relax and concentrate on the job in hand she thought to herself.

Daan and Kim were waiting for them. "Harry, Christina, this is Armando, he will give you your instructions."

Armando greeted the girls with a kiss on both cheeks then he led them away to sort out their wet suits.

Up at the Taverna the beach huts had been taken over by the crew; makeup artists in one hut, racks of different Ski-Summer wet suits in another. Leaning up against the wall were several water skies in various sizes and colours. Armando introduced them to a makeup artist who was to do their makeup. She ushered them into the makeshift makeup hut and told them to sit down. Two girls appeared with pots, pencils and brushes and got to work on their faces applying dark eyeliner around their eyes with a small amount of blue on their inner lids to match their eyes. They were asked if they would mind having blue eye drops as well.

Christina looked in the mirror. She was looking quite stunning, even if she thought so herself.

Harry felt a bit over made-up to be on the beach and ski. It felt quite strange. She wondered if it were all waterproof. The makeup artist applied a brush over their faces with some rouge to highlight their features, then finally a rainbow selection of lipsticks to see which colour would be best for each of them. It was settled. A fluorescent pink for Christina and a soft fluorescent rose for Harry. Once the makeup artists had finished with them they were ushered out into the sun where the costume designer decided which colour and size wetsuits would be suitable. For Christina it was a quick decision; they decided on the pink. It was almost the same colour as her lipstick. Next it was Harry's turn. First, they tried the white but it was too sophisticated for the sporty look they were trying to achieve. The red was too bold. Possibly the cornflower blue? She started to slip into it but it was obviously too large, so they swapped the size for a smaller one. It would be the cornflower blue suit. With an overall nodding of approval, the decision was made. Christina wore pink and Harry, cornflower blue.

Once again they were moved into another beach hut where two hairdressers waited to do their hair. They didn't have a great deal done because it was to flow out naturally behind them as they skied. At last they were ready. Someone led them over to a full-length mirror to look at themselves. Christina couldn't help breaking out into a big grin. She looked amazing. The pink was the perfect colour for her. The curves of her body set the wetsuit off. It had a white stripe that ran down from the underside of her arms to her tiny waist then on down her legs. Harry looked stunning too, having been given a smaller sized wetsuit, it hugged her body beautifully. Everyone agreed she looked good, leggy and slim, although she, personally, was not convinced. She did not like all the attention and found it difficult to enjoy herself and relax.

There was a bit of a commotion and a man appeared through the crew. They grovelled and scattered, making a pathway through to the girls for him.

Christina looked up and said, "Hello."

Harry looked up when she heard the man speak. It was the man from the Flame thrower.

He came over and kissed them both on each cheek. "Señor Cruanos." He introduced himself to them. "I hope my crew are looking after you?"

"Oh, yes! Is this your company?" Christina asked.

Well, yes, it is my family business. My brother and I are the owner stroke directors. The advertisement is for one of our companies, Ski-Summer. Have you ever heard of it in England?"

"No, I'm sorry, but I have never heard of it in England have you, Harry?"

Harry shook her head. She smiled. At least it was someone who had already seen her ski. This made her feel much more relaxed. She now knew she had nothing to prove. This man had seen her ski before. He had even given her a standing ovation last time she skied.

"Well, we are in most of Europe now, but I'm hoping to launch into England and America before the end of the year. Good! Are you ready ladies?" He clapped his hands and Armando appeared to explain about a few still shots he wanted first with them just on the beach.

Three large white umbrellas were set up by the shore. There were two camera men, one taking colour shots and one taking black and white.

First Christina went under the lights. They tested her skin for light then took shot after shot: Christina looking out to sea, Christina sitting on a deck chair, Christina pretending to put Ski-summer block on her lips. The photographers clicked and clicked. The crowd above the beach looking over the wall was growing, everyone craning their necks to see what was going on below. Christina loved every minute.

"Okay, that is enough now. Harry, can we have you doing the same shots?"

Harry felt herself turning pink. It was a good-job she had so much make up on so no-one could tell.

After Harry had repeated the poses she had seen Christina do Armando said, "Now, I want some pictures of you holding the skis together. That's great. Let me see some more of those white teeth. That's great. Now can you pretend you are going out to ski. I want to see you enthusiastically running into the water carrying a ski each."

The crew handed the girls a ski each. Several times on the count of three they ran to the water where the cameras had been repositioned. Harry felt much more relaxed moving around than she had felt when just standing in poses. She was even beginning to enjoy herself. The skis were very much lighter than the ones Harry was used to and she could not wait to try them out.

A black BMW convertible pulled up by the wall above the beach. Pablo got out. He had been to see Conchitta's family and thought he had convinced them that it was all over. It had been easier than he first thought. Conchitta's father was away but her mother had been very apologetic and said she would talk to Conchitta. She seemed almost embarrassed at her daughter's behaviour. After being reassured that she would also speak to Conchitta's brothers, Pablo had left for the beach.

Pablo tried to find a place to watch from the granite wall that stood above the beach. There were too many people for him to get anywhere near to see what was going on. He headed up along the boardwalk to the Taverna and onto the sun terrace. It was deserted. Everyone was down below on the lower terrace or on the beach. He found a position that gave him the perfect view of the bay and all the action. He was wearing a white T-shirt, faded Levi jeans and, on his feet, he wore a pair of Lacoste sandals. He placed a pair of Gucci sunglasses on his head and put his feet up on the wall in front of him. In seconds a waitress arrived to serve him. He ordered a coffee. The girls who worked at the Taverna knew Pablo and all fancied him. He also tipped well so there was always a bit of a row over who would serve him. His little English Rose would never know he had been there. He was still a little worried about telling her it was his uncle and father who owned the Ski Summer logo. He was not sure how she would react.

Harry was with Christina having their makeup touched up after sipping a cool Ski-Summer fruit-type drink, while having yet more photos. Then it was time to do the water skiing shots. Three different film crews were sitting in Ski-Summer speed boats out in the bay waiting to have their turn to film the action.

The skis had been chosen and set ready to use. Harry's being cornflower blue and Christina's fluorescent pink, they were checked for size. They were going to do one round on two skies side by side then they were to have their makeup touched up yet again before they returned to do another round each on mono.

Harry was quite relived when she saw Mark climb into the boat with the film crew and driver that was going to tow them. The girls waded into the water and stopped when it was up to their waists. Two triangles and ropes were attached to the boat and handed to the girls. Although they were both very confident skiers, neither had ever skied at the same time behind a boat.

Butterflies started fluttering around in Harry's stomach as the engine started and the boat began to edge slowly forward. They both sat back and stuck their feet up either side of the triangles. The boat accelerated, pulling the girls out of the water and to the end of the ski lane.

Harry heard a cheer from the beach and began to relax. This was more like it. She glanced across at Christina who was grinning back at her. "Are you okay?" she shouted.

"Yes," Christina laughed.

They followed the boat for 100 yards around the buoys out into the open bay. After several whistles from the boat they soon got the idea of what was required. There was some sort of choreographer on the boat who pointed in different directions when the boat was about to change its direction. He clapped when he wanted them to look straight ahead. After doing a complete circle of the bay he signalled they would return to the shore. As they came back along the buoys he signalled again that they should sink into the water at the same time as the boat slowed down, both looking straight ahead. The other boats circled in close to them and Armando held out his hand to lift Harry, then Christina, into the boat. Beginning to get a little tired, the girls were pleased of a break.

"I'm feeling quite tired," Christina whispered into Harry's ear as they were wrapped in Ski Summer towels.

Armando addressed the girls "Now, I would like to film you on one ski before the sun gets too bright. Is it possible to continue or are you too tired?"

Harry got her breath back and said she didn't mind going straight back out and doing it then. A makeup artist jumped across from another boat and dried, then dusted, Harry's face over with a brush and re-did her lipstick. Her hair was dry as she had managed to avoid putting her head under the water.

"Tell me, can you do a jump start?"

Harry said she could, so they headed back to the shore to start again. She jumped out of the boat and was quickly ushered up the beach where the costume department were waiting with the white wet suit for her to slip into for her next session. Harry dried herself down with the aid of half a dozen other hands then back into a beach hut to slip the new wetsuit on.

As she reappeared something make her glance up to the Taverna where, on the top terrace, a figure she recognised was watching in dark shades. *Shit*, she thought to herself. *Why did he have to come and watch? Now I am bound to make a fool of myself.*

Luckily Mark appeared and distracted her. "Now, Harry, remember all the trouble we had teaching you how to do a jump start? Just go through in your mind what you did when you managed to get it right."

Harry was deep in thought and concentrating on her skiing. A white ski had been produced to match the wetsuit. They adjusted it to fit her right foot and then she waded into the sea and stopped when the water reached just below her knees. Determined to get it right and not to make a fool of herself in front of Pablo, she concentrated on the sound of the engine. The crowd no longer visible, she coiled the rope up into her left hand and held the triangle with her right. Slowly she raised her right foot so the ski was just above the water. "Hit it!" she shouted as she threw the coiled rope out and the boat roared off. Harry's right foot shot forward. For a second she thought she was not going to make. It was just like riding a bike; as she jumped her left foot found the back of the ski and slipped into its slot. She straightened herself up as she heard cheers vanishing into the distance. The water was still very flat. There was no wind and the flags at the hotel overlooking the beach were motionless. Harry turned the triangle so the bar was parallel with her body and pulled her arms in close to her body. Everything set she made for the wake, cutting through it like a knife, then leaning so far over her shoulder nearly touched the water. Passing the bar to the other hand, she cut back across the wake to the other side. She felt great. Mark and Armando were both clapping her from the towing speed boat, while the film crews following darted alongside her, taking snaps and filming then dropping back so as not to cause any waves or interfere with the wake Harry was tracing.

Pablo watched from the Taverna, he was standing up now. He never realised Harry was this good. His love welled inside him. "One day you will be all mine," he smiled to himself.

After her second lap of the bay Harry signalled to Mark she wanted to go in. She was tired. They must have enough film now for their advert, she thought to herself. The boat turned for the shore. As a happy, smiling Harry skied in, everyone on the beach, and the audience along the wall above the beach, clapped. The boat came to a standstill and Harry, still completely dry, skied past the boat over the ski lane and nearly made it to the shore. She stood in the water, only wet up to her knees, feeling completely exhilarated.

Señor Cruanos rushed up and kissed her on both cheeks. "That was fantastic. I would personally like to give you a contract for all my ski products. You are a princess."

Where had she heard that before? Suddenly the name dawned on her. It was the same name as Pablo's. She wondered if they were related. Before she had time for any more thought on the matter, she was surrounded by children, all waving pens and paper at her.

"Autograph, autograph?"

She took her time and signed them all. Someone wrapped a towel around her and led her back to the hut to change. She sat on the stool in the hut, suddenly feeling extremely tired. There was a knock on the door. "Come in." She looked up.

Pablo stood in the doorway. He looked gorgeous. He closed the door, locked it, and walked over to her. He pulled the towel up over her shoulders and hugged her. The warmth flooded through her body.

"You were fantastic." He lifted her face up to his and kissed her gently on the lips. "I must go before someone comes, but I could not resist coming in to see you. It's too late to go for a picnic so why don't I come and get you later, maybe do something together. I can take you for something to eat when you have finished here. Shall I come to your parents' villa and pick you up this afternoon?"

"That will be great." Harry's energy briefly returned.

Pablo kissed her again then slowly opened the door, checking the coast was clear before he left.

Chapter 13

Harry was sleeping on a sun bed by the pool when there was a crunch of tyres on the drive. Mark put his paper down and got up and looked over the garden wall.

Pablo got out of his car and waved to him. "Good afternoon, sir,"

"Good afternoon, Pablo, have you come to see Harry?"

"Yes, I thought she would like to come for a drive with me. It's a lovely day and I was going to take her up Mas Nou to my parents' villa."

"Now? She is asleep but come around and I'll wake her up for you."

Mark signalled the way around the villa to the pool.

Having heard the conversation, Anna was already on her feet, and making her way to where Harry was sleeping. "Harry, Harry, wake up." Anna softly placed a hand on Harry's arm and shook it. "There is someone here to see you. I think it is Pablo."

Harry opened her eyes in horror. "Oh goodness! I said I would go out with him, maybe for something to eat. What time is it?"

At that moment Pablo arrived by the pool. The twins pounced on him. "Are you Harry's new boyfriend?" Mickey grinned.

"Well, yes, I suppose I am a boy, and a friend, if that is what you mean. You must be Sophie and you must be Mickey."

Sophie blushed as Pablo took her little dainty hand in his and kissed it. Mickey put his grubby hand out and shook Pablo's.

Harry wrapped a towel around her waist and headed over to Pablo. "I am so sorry, I lost track of the time and fell asleep." How embarrassing, she thought to herself. I must get him out of here, quickly.

Pablo leant forward and kissed her on both cheeks. "It's okay, no rush, we still have the rest of the day. Would you like to come back to the villa? We could play tennis, or swim, before we eat."

"I would love to. Can I just go and grab some clothes? I will only be a few minutes?" Not waiting for an answer, Harry disappeared into the villa leaving Pablo being entertained by Sophie and Mickey.

Mark offered Pablo a seat and Anna rushed off to get him a cool drink.

Harry was rushing around her bedroom when Christina arrived back from a walk.

"Come on, Harry, get yourself organised. You will need a bikini. You have already got one on. Slip some shorts on over the top."

Harry found her white shorts and slipped them on, sprayed herself with deodorant, and then pulled a little blue top on. "What shall I take with me to wear if we go out later?"

"Put in your little black top and your cropped black trousers. Then, if you go anywhere casual, you will look fine and if you go somewhere posh you will still look fine."

Harry grabbed her bag, folded her clothes into it whilst Christina found her black underwear and toiletries, and packed them too. Harry grabbed her handbag and stuffed her hairbrush, make up and perfume into it. Slipping into her trainers and stuffing her black heels into her bag, she checked herself in the mirror and headed back out to rescue Pablo from the rest of the family.

I'm ready," she shouted as she came out of the villa, hoping to stop the conversation before Pablo was interrogated to death.

Pablo got up, thanked Anna and Mark for the drink, and headed over to Harry. He took her bag from her, waved to Anna and Mark, and headed out towards the car.

"Bye, Mum, bye, Dad, see you later."

Chapter 14

Pablo had the top down on the BMW, so he threw Harry's bag onto the back seat as he opened the door for Harry. Then he went around to the driver's side of the car and got in. He started the car and headed down the track and back out to the main road. As he stopped at the junction to wait for the traffic, he glanced at Harry, then reached over and took Harry's hand. He squeezed it affectionately in his and laid it on his thigh. Pulling out into the road, he headed off at quite a speed. Harry felt happy and safe sitting next to Pablo, the wind blowing in her hair and the music blaring out. The previous night had been forgotten. She had not been so happy in a long time.

Pablo turned into the villa and skidded the car to a halt.

Harry suddenly had an awful thought. What if his parents were there? She didn't want to meet them yet. She was not prepared. She felt such a wreck; no makeup on, her hair all over the place from the journey.

Pablo jumped out taking her bag off the back seat. "Come on, my English Rose, we have the place to ourselves."

Relief flooded through Harry's body as she scrambled out of the car and ran to catch up with Pablo.

Firstly, they went up to his bedroom to leave her bags. The house seemed very cool; fans were humming, everywhere.

"Have you eaten, or would you like something to eat now?"

"I ate when I got back from the beach, but you go ahead and eat if you are hungry."

"I am only hungry for you." Pablo took Harry in his arms and gave her a long, lingering, kiss. Shivers ran down Harry's spine and she kissed him gently back.

Pablo stared into her sky-blue eyes, held her sparkling gaze, and smiled. He loved her so much; his body ached for hers, but he had not brought her home to the villa for that. He just needed to be with her. When he was not with her she took up all his thoughts. He never wanted her out of his sight again. She was someone who had come along and had such an effect on him. He was unsure of how to handle himself. He did not want to push her. He was afraid he might frighten her off, a risk he did not want to take. "Come on, you look tired. Shall we go out to the pool and you can sleep some more in the sun?"

Harry nodded.

Pablo took her hand, led her down the stairs, and out of the Villa. They went down to the pool area where Pablo positioned two sun loungers next to each other, then laid two large fluffy, yellow towels over them. "Here, we can lie. I will read my book while you sleep."

Harry settled herself down on a lounger.

Pablo leant over and kissed her briefly on her rose-red lips. "Would you like a bottle of water to drink?"

"Oh, yes please! That would be nice."

Pablo headed to an outdoor kitchen and barbecue area near the pool and took two bottles of water from the fridge then joined Harry. Harry was already asleep. He placed a table at the side of her sun bed and set her drink down. He took his jeans and T-shirt off. Underneath he was wearing a navy-blue pair of crew swimming shorts. Lying on the lounger next to Harry, he could not resist leaning over and kissing her gently on the forehead, on her nose and then very gently on her lips. She was dead to the world. She didn't stir. Then, lying on his stomach, he wrapped his arm over Harry and began to doze off whilst watching her breathing.

Harry started to stir. She opened her eyes only to see Pablo gazing at her. For a moment she had to think where she was and then it came back. In her usual dormouse way, she stretched and rubbed her eyes.

Pablo leant over and kissed her on the lips. "Did you have a good rest, my sleepy little English Rose?"

Harry nodded as Pablo took her in his arms and kissed her eyes, nose and then her mouth. She kissed him back. Opening her eyes again, she stared into his. He had been watching her while they kissed. His eyes were warm and loving. She felt she could stay in his arms forever. He made her feel so safe and wanted.

Pablo thought she was perfect. He never wanted to let her go. "What are we going to do now?" he whispered as he brushed her soft cheek then her small, dainty ear with his lips.

"What time is it?"

Pablo looked at his watch. "It is quarter past six. Would you like to go up to the villa for a drink? This water has got quite hot." He pointed at the bottles he had carried out earlier.

Harry nodded and they headed up to the villa, hand in hand.

Pablo led the way to the lounge and gestured Harry to sit at the bar. "How about a little vodka to help wake you up?"

"No, thank you. I could really do with a long drink of water. I do not want to become dehydrated."

Pablo took two long glasses from behind the bar and filled them with ice. He filled them with bottled water and handed one to Harry. "Do you want to have a shower? Then we can go out. Maybe we could go into Playa and have a walk around, look at the shops, see the street crafts and get something to eat?"

Harry drank her water and said she would like that.

After finishing his drink, Pablo took Harry back upstairs to his room. He handed her a bathrobe and left her to shower.

Pablo's bath room was compact and very well designed. It was tiled from floor to ceiling in navy. The sink was white and had chrome taps; a chrome shaving mirror pulled out to the right of a larger central mirror. Matching the toothbrush holder, the mug and soap dispenser were also chrome. Next to the sink stood a white ceramic toilet with chrome flush and mahogany seat. In the corner of the room was a walk-in pressure shower. Harry took off her bikini and looked around for somewhere to place it. On the back of the door was a line of chrome hooks and fresh white fluffy towels. Harry placed her bikini on a hook and stepped into the shower. After fiddling with the dial for a few seconds, she finally had the water at an even temperature. Finding her shampoo in her bag, she washed and conditioned her hair, then lathered her shower gel over her body whilst her conditioner worked its magic. Standing for a while under the warm massaging pressure, the water flowed over her body washing the bubbles away. Once out of the shower she put the bathrobe on and went out into the bedroom.

Pablo was lying on his bed. "Come here." He reached out and pulled her down onto the bed next to him. The bathrobe fell open. He reached across and wrapped it back around her and just held her in his arms, kissing her dripping hair and wet forehead. "I don't know what I am going to do with you. I want you so much, but it is not right. We must wait." He rolled over on top of her.

Harry could feel him harden as he kissed her and she kissed him back. She too knew it was too soon and they should wait until they both felt it was right and they were both ready. Everything was so nice; she was afraid something would go wrong. If she did make love with him he might go off her. She was still uncertain as to whether he did love her, or was it just a game to him? She had never felt this close to anyone before. They kissed and cuddled for ages. They could not get as close to each other as they wanted. Their bodies were aching and hungry. Eventually, Harry pulled away. "I had better get some clothes on if we are going to Playa this evening.

Pablo groaned as he sat up on the side of the bed. "Okay. I will have a shower. A cold one, I think." Harry laughed and pushed him towards the shower. Harry quickly dressed then brushed her hair out. It was a mess. Luckily, she had a scrunchy with her and tied it up into a bun. Hearing Pablo still in the shower, she put some perfume on and a little make up. Bag packed, she headed out to the balcony and sat leafing through a Spanish copy of "Hello" magazine, left on the table, while she waited for Pablo.

Pablo slipped into some black jeans and a black cotton shirt. He splashed some aftershave over his newly shaved chin and throat before he joined Harry on the balcony. "Is my English Rose ready for a little drink before we go into town?"

Harry got to her feet. He looked as handsome as ever and she just wanted to throw her arms around him and say, "I surrender."

"Yes, I think I would like a little drink before we go. I feel a little nervous."

Downstairs, at the bar, Pablo fixed them a couple of gin and tonics. He told Harry where he thought they could go and eat. They could not keep their hands off each other. In between kissing and touching they somehow managed to finish their drinks and headed off to Playa.

Chapter 15

It was getting dark and the night air was humid. They drove down the winding mountain road. Lights were twinkling all over the valley. Playa was alive and vibrant. The big wheel at the Magic Park stood out like a giant Catherine wheel. In the distance, towers of sixties style apartments lined the coast, blocking the sea from view. The mountain road joined the main coast road into Playa and Pablo started looking for somewhere to park. It was already very busy and the main car park was full. Pablo drove around and round until he spotted someone leaving and took their space. He put the roof up on the car and locked it. Taking Harry's hand, they headed for the maze of designer shops.

Harry loved Playa. It smelt of leather, perfume, and cigar smoke. Heads turned as the couple wandered in and out of the shops. Both dressed all in black, they were a stunning looking couple. Pablo could not ignore the envious looks he was getting as he paraded Harry up and down. He paused at a jewellery shop. "Show me what type of things you like."

Harry pointed to the white gold necklace, earrings, and bracelets. "I always think white gold looks nice, don't you?"

Pablo grinned. "I think, with your tan, white gold would look lovely. Let me buy you something?"

"Oh no, Pablo, I don't want you to buy me anything. It's not my birthday. Come on, let's go and look in the leather shop. We can pick a set of luggage out for when you come to England to stay with me," Harry laughed teasingly.

"I don't want to think about you going back to England. I want you to stay in Spain, with me."

They stepped out right into the path of a photographer who took their picture. "Are you the girl from the Ski-Summer pictures?"

Harry was quite flattered at being recognised and nodded. It was the wrong thing to do because, the next moment, they were surrounded by people wanting autographs. Harry started to sign a few as the photographer flashed around them snapping away.

"Come on, Harry, that is enough now, we must go." Pablo grabbed her hand quite roughly and pulled her out of the crowd and into a shop. He spoke to the owner in Spanish and they were quickly ushered through a back door. Pablo pulled Harry down an alley and into another street. "Come on, we are safe here if we move fast." He led the way, back into the main street, and headed for the Piano bar. Bouncers on the door let them straight in and they were greeted by a waiter and taken to a concealed table, in the back corner, where they sat down. "Harry, you must not encourage them. Now your picture is everywhere people will want you wherever you go. You will lose your privacy. Promise me, if someone asks you if you are the Ski-Summer girl again, you will say no." Pablo spoke quite sternly.

"Gosh, I'm sorry, Pablo. I didn't think people would recognise me and it was quite flattering when they did. I can see what you mean though. From now on I will keep a low profile." Harry was shocked at how angry Pablo had been but she could see what he meant.

Pablo took her by the hand. "I'm sorry I was so rough with you. Did I hurt you?"

"No, I'm fine. A bit stunned, I must admit."

"Well, from now on we must be very discreet. Your pictures from the skiing must already be in papers and maybe on a poster already." Pablo waved his hand in the air and a waiter appeared.

"Champagne and the menu please."

The waiter was back in minutes. He placed the glasses on the smoked glass table top and opened the Champagne.

Pablo handed Harry a glass and, lifting his to his mouth, said, "To my little, Ski-Summer Rose."

The first bottle went down very quickly and Pablo ordered another. Pablo, at last, began to relax. He translated the menu to Harry and they both agreed they would just have a Catalan salad followed by a simple steak.

The piano bar was at the front of a very spacious restaurant. The tables were all secluded and separated by palms. A pianist sat at a huge, white, grand piano, playing a melody. The waiters glided around on the chequered floor, white napkin neatly folded over their starched, black, suit sleeves, discreetly taking orders then disappearing through a swing door and returning with trays of drinks and plates of food.

"I don't think I'm dressed correctly to be in here," Harry whispered to Pablo.

"You are the most stunning women here. Look how they keep glancing over to admire you. Do not worry, they would not have let us in if they thought we were under-dressed. The bouncers are on the door to keep the place respectable."

Pablo was squeezing Harry's knee under the table to reassure her when the waiter arrived with a plate full of appetisers. As they tucked into their appetisers, a wine waiter appeared and showed Pablo the wine list. He ordered a full-bodied Rioja. Pouring the last drop of Champagne into their glasses, Pablo gazed into Harry's eyes, took her hand in his, and asked what was going to happen to their relationship when she returned to England?

Harry had not thought that far ahead until that night. It had started as a holiday romance and now, suddenly, it was getting serious. The waiter arrived with the Catalan salad. Harry looked at Pablo. He suddenly looked so sad.

"I have to go back and finish college. Maybe you could come over to England and spend some time with me?"

"I wish I could. My exam results will be back tomorrow and my parents will return from Barcelona. I should see if I have passed my exams and then have a long chat with my parents about my future and the business. You know I will want you to meet my parents. It is very important to me that you like them."

"Pablo, don't you think it is a bit soon for that?"

"Why will it be too soon? I have met your parents and I like them."

"Oh, I am just nervous; they will wonder what I have done to you. I think it will be a bit of a shock to them."

"No, it will not. I have spoken to my father every day and told him all about you. He says my mother is very excited to meet you."

"Oh, Pablo, now you have made me really nervous. What have you told him exactly?"

"I told him that I have met a very nice English girl. She is very beautiful, charming and a great skier and, most of all, I have fallen in love with her."

"God! You have really told your father all that?" Harry blushed through her beautifully tanned skin. That made her look even more radiant.

"Now I am going to disappoint them." Harry frowned.

"My mother was only sixteen when she met my father. My father was five years older than her. They were married as soon as my mother reached eighteen. My father understands exactly how I feel. What about your parents, Mark and Anna? What have you told them about us?"

"Not a lot. I told my mother I like you a lot, and my father obviously approves of you or he would not let me go out with you, but I think, to them, this may be a holiday romance, I don't know."

"Well, I must come and talk to them, with you, and explain my feelings."

"Pablo, you want to do that? English men generally don't express their feelings like that."

"I understand, but I am a Spanish man, I like to make my feelings clear. I will have a talk with your father when I get the chance." Pablo was quite adamant. "Then we will talk about what I am going to do, after I have seen my parents. Is this okay with you?"

At that moment, the wine waiter interrupted them and asked Pablo to sample, and approve, the wine. Pablo had a taste and nodded so the waiter poured them a glass each. With the arrival of their steaks they tucked in. Harry had not realised how hungry she was.

The wine waiter interrupted them again and said, "The Señor on the table over there sent this wine for you with a note." Harry and Pablo followed the direction he pointed. A sturdy, greying, middle-aged man, with a very glamorous young partner, waved. They both waved back. Pablo said to thank the man very much. He opened the note and read it.

"What does it say, Pablo?"

Pablo handed the note to Harry. "It is for you".

Harry scanned the note. It was written in Spanish and she could not understand a word of it. "What does it say, Pablo? I cannot read it."

"It says you are the most beautiful girl he has ever seen, and could we join him and his wife for a drink at the bar after our meal?"

"Well, that was very nice of him, but why does he want us to join him for a drink?"

"I don't know, but I do not like the look of him. His wife looks like she could be his daughter. What do you think?"

"I think you are right, but we must not be rude. We will join them for just one drink. You can hold my hand and protect me in case he wants to whisk me away to his harem." Harry laughed.

"Okay, I will always protect you, and we will have a drink with them. Why not? It's only a drink."

Harry was too full to eat another thing however Pablo ordered the Crème Catalan and insisted on spoon feeding some to Harry. She giggled and made him catch the corner of her mouth with the spoon. A small amount of caramel dripped down her chin. Pablo wiped it back to her mouth with his finger and gently pushed the tip of his finger into her mouth. Harry sucked the caramel off it.

"Come on, let's go to the bar and get that drink over with so I can get you out of here"

As they approached the bar, the stocky man came over to them and introduced himself. His wife followed and, after the introductions, he ordered them all Champagne. He was the owner of a model agency, "Costa Brava Beach Babes". He thought Harry had a classic look that would suit his autumn collection and wondered if she would be interested in a spot of modelling, for him. Harry said she was very flattered but she was going back to England, to college, in a few weeks.

Unable to take 'no' for an answer, Pablo thought he should get Harry away. This man was trying to be very persuasive. Pablo ordered a taxi and they managed to make their getaway with the promise that Harry would think it over and let him know. A business card pressed firmly into Harry's hand, she was kissed on both cheeks by both the husband and wife partnership. Pablo settled the bill and they left.

It was only eleven thirty and Harry was buzzing. She could not believe all this attention she was getting. How could the pictures of her skiing have been seen so early? There must have been something in the local evening paper. She knew she was to see the proofs before they were printed. These must have been photos taken by other photographers that had been attracted by the crowd that gathered and watched.

Harry was glowing all over and started giggling in the taxi. Pablo sensed she was a little drunk and suggested they should get dropped off by the beach in S'Agaro. They could walk along the sea front and have some fresh air and a coffee before he took her home. He didn't want her father thinking he could not take care of his daughter.

Pablo stopped the taxi by the boardwalk. He paid the driver and they got out, starting along the trail of sleepers that formed the boardwalk. Slipping their shoes off, they stepped onto the cool sand. The night breeze was coming in off the sea. A few lights dotted around from fishing boats bobbed out in the bay. They walked for a while hand in hand and then they sat on the steps below the Taverna and dipped their feet into the sea. A shiver engulfed Harry. Pablo wrapped an arm around her.

Pablo was deep in his own thoughts. He was thinking about all the attention Harry had received. He felt proud that she was his girl. At the same time he was worried. He felt threatened; worried that something would tempt her away. She was so lovely and innocent now. It just felt right that she should remain in Spain with him by her side and as her protector. What could he do? How could he persuade Harry and her parents he would take care of her? Pablo urged Harry up from the step; she was getting cold. He pulled her away from the sea and they strolled along the beach, Pablo with his one arm around Harry and the other carrying his shoes.

Heading back toward the road at the far end of the beach, Pablo led Harry into a little beach fronted bar. It was timber framed with a terrace running right down onto the beach. There was a free table on the terrace. They made their way towards it. Sitting themselves down, Pablo ordered two hot chocolates. He had gone off the idea of a coffee and somehow hot chocolate seemed appropriate. These arrived in tall glasses, each with a straw.

Harry sipped on hers; it was just what she needed. Coffee would have sent her higher and she would never have been able to get to sleep.

"What are you going to do tomorrow?"

"We normally go to the beach every day. I think I will have a long sleep in the morning and then go to the beach with my family in the afternoon."

"I have some work to do before my parents arrive back. I will come and pick you up in the evening and you must come to the villa and meet my father and mother."

The cool evening air was beginning to sober Harry up. The thought of meeting Pablo's parents terrified her. She changed the subject and talked about her horse and dog back in England. She told him about the farm and how beautiful it was. She knew he would love it, if only there were some way he could come back and stay with her family.

After finishing their drinks and paying, they strolled back up the old dirt track, and back to her parent's villa. The villa was in darkness, all but a light coming from the pool area from where they could hear the whisper of voices. Harry and Pablo tiptoed up the drive and towards the light. To their surprise, Christina and Manolo were sitting having a night cap.

"Hi, what have you been doing?" Harry greeted her sister and then kissed Manolo on each cheek. Pablo kissed Christina and sat down next to Manolo. They talked about their evening and what they had all been up to.

Christina could not believe all the fuss Harry had received in Playa. Studying the business card Harry had been given, said she would be mad not to go along and see about the modelling job.

The chatter began to die down as the night drew in. Finally, Pablo said he should call a taxi and go. Manolo offered his friend a lift home. Clearing their glasses away, Christina and Manolo popped into the villa.

Harry walked to the car with Pablo. They had a long, lingering, kiss goodnight, and when Manolo arrived at the car the boys left.

Harry and Christina disappeared into their bedroom and updated each other on the gaps that could not be spoken in front of their boyfriends. It wasn't long before their whispered chatter went quiet and they both fell to sleep.

Chapter 16

Harry's relaxing day on the beach didn't last very long. The twins begged and begged her to take them rock pool fishing. Anna plastered the children in sun protector while Harry put on her plimsolls and wrapped her tasselled, blue, tie-dyed skirt, around her waist.

Mickey and Sophie, well protected from the harsh rays of the mid-morning sun, wearing hats and their beach jelly shoes, were ready, having sorted out of couple of buckets, one for the crabs and one for the fish they were hoping to catch. A net each in their hands, they headed for the rocks. Having stopped at the end of the beach, where the granite rocks began to rear out of the water, they began fishing.

Harry was quite the expert and knew where to find all the different types of fish. Firstly, she wanted to catch them some horse pins. She knew from years of experience and her own childhood fishing expeditions, the end of the first rock, where the water was still quite warm and shallow, was the ideal place to find them. Waist high, skirt now dripping in water, she waded around and spotted what looked like a little shoal of sea horses. Creeping slowly through the water, the twins were hot on her trail. They knew better than to talk when Harry had something in her sight. In a very slow motion, Harry signalled to them what she was stalking. Having cornered the shoal, almost against the rocks, Harry made a quick sweeping motion with her net and scooped them up. Mickey and Sophie pounced on the end of her net and peered in. There, in the bottom of the net, was a dark spaghetti mixture of several little horse pins. Mickey turned the net inside out, over the bucket, and in they dropped. Several, perfect little horse pins glided gracefully around the bucket. Sophie climbed out onto a flat part of the rock and Mickey handed her the bucket. Sophie sat and contentedly arranged seaweed, shells, and stones, making a perfect little sea garden for them to hide in. Mickey spotted a shoal of very tiny sardines, about a centimetre in length. Copying Harry's movements, he scooped them up in his net and pulled it in sharply. He had caught quite a few so he quickly paddled over to the rock and handed his catch to Sophie. Sophie tipped them into the bucket.

Harry was chasing a bright red, rock pool fish. It had disappeared under a rock on the sea floor. She held her net against one side of the rock and, with her free hand, carefully lifted the rock, tilting it in the direction of the net. The fish fell for her trap and swam straight into the net. The bucket was now looking like an aquarium. It was filling up with all sorts of pretty fish. Having caught as many little fish as they could, they moved on over the big rock, towards a flatter bed, full of smaller pools. These, freshly filled by the waves that had roughed up from the sea overnight and hurled them in. Here, Harry and Mickey caught many crabs of all different species, colours and sizes. Sophie sat on a dry, flat rock, arranging a home for them in the other bucket. From past experience they knew not to put the crabs in with the fish or they would eat the smaller fish. A few hermit crabs were added to the collection. Finally, with a small, spindly-looking starfish, caught by a very excited Sophie, they decided they had caught enough.

It would not have been safe, trying to climb back over the big rock with the full buckets and nets, so they headed up towards the coastal path that ran around the headland and onto the next bay. This was quite a climb but safer and easier than returning the way they had come.

Back at the beach, Pablo had joined Harry's parents. He'd finished his work earlier than expected so he thought he would pop along and spend a few hours with Harry. On discovering she was not there, he was invited to join Anna and Mark, so he set himself down and chatted to them. He told them how much he liked Harry and that he wanted them to be assured he thought the world of her and had her best interests at heart. At first, Mark and Anna were quite shocked at this frank, smooth talking individual. They soon realised he was genuine and the initial shock vanished as they all relaxed and got to know each other.

Harry and the twins made their way back along the path. As the beach got closer, and the little specks became clearer, the people in their stretched-out huddles were now more visible. Harry could not believe her eyes.

"Who is that sat talking with Mum and Dad?"

The twins looked down at the beach. It was Sophie who spoke first. "I think it's your boyfriend, Harry."

"Yes, it's the man who keeps coming to the villa to pick you up," Mickey agreed.

All sorts of thing were going through Harry's mind. *Oh, no, what are they talking about? Is this the chat he said he was going to have with her parents?* Her heart started pounding. She was excited to see Pablo so unexpectedly, but she had thought she would try to avoid ever giving Pablo the chance to talk to her father.

Mickey and Sophie shouted down to their parents. Mark heard them first and waved as he looked around in the direction the sound had come from.

Pablo looked up and saw them approaching. His heart leapt as he saw Harry walking along with her little brother and sister. She looked so young and sweet, carrying the nets while Mickey and Sophie struggled with a bucket each. Pablo felt he just wanted to melt. The more he saw of Harry, the deeper his love and desire grew.

He excused himself from Mark and Anna and went to meet them. At the bottom of the steps Mickey and Sophie stopped and put their catch down. Pablo squatted on the sand and listened as Mickey proudly told him who had caught what. Sophie giggled away as she explained how she had made them a beautiful home to live in. Pablo admired their catch and asked them all sorts of interesting questions. Finally, Pablo got to his feet. Mickey and Sophie raced off to show Anna and Mark their catch.

Pablo glanced back to see if they were being watched. They were so he had to restrain himself from grabbing Harry and kissing her passionately. Instead, he leaned forward and kissed her on both cheeks. Then, taking the nets out of her hand, he carried them back for her.

"I didn't have much to do so I thought I would come and join you for a few hours. Are you disappointed I am here?" Now it was his turn to tease. He could see how happy she was to see him. They slowly strolled back and joined the family.

They all had a great afternoon. Harry, at last, felt she could relax with Pablo in front of her parents, who seemed to like him. The twins adored him and played endless games, in the sea and on the sand, with Pablo. Harry sunbathed, joined in some of the games, and slept during others.

After helping the twins give the fish and crabs back their freedom, over by the rocks where they had been caught, Pablo said he should get back. His parents would be back soon and they would expect him to be at the villa when they arrived. Having already said goodbye to Mark and Anna, he said goodbye to the twins. Harry sent them back over to Anna and Mark and walked with Pablo up to his car. Pablo told Harry he would pick her up at eight; they would have dinner at the villa with his family and she could meet his parents. Pablo leant against his car and slipped his arms loosely around Harry's waist.

Harry asked, "What should I wear tonight?"

Pablo told her it didn't matter what she wore, she looked great.

Playfully punching his chest with her fists, she said, "You know what I mean. Should I wear something dressy or just casual?"

"Just a dress. That will be fine." Pablo pulled Harry forward and kissed her on the lips.

She still had her hands on his chest, and gently pushed him back. "Oh no," she laughed, "You know in England we have a saying. They say too much of a good thing is bad for you."

Pablo grinned, looking Harry up and down. He took her hands and pulled them apart. Harry struggled to keep him at arm's length. He was far too strong for her and he pulled her in close, now holding her hands behind his back so her face was very close to his. He kissed her again.

This time she kissed him back, a short, quick, peck. "That's all you are getting."

Just as he relaxed his grasp, Harry pulled away and ran back towards the top of the steps. Laughing as she made her escape, she turned back and waved. Pablo was still leaning on his car, arms crossed, his wide, flashing, smile following her.

She blew him a kiss and shouted, "See you later!" Pablo tapped his chest and Harry smiled then disappeared down the steps.

Chapter 17

"Harriet, what are you going to wear tonight? Pablo told us he was going to introduce you to his parents and you were all going to have a meal together up at their villa. He seems very keen."

"Oh, I don't know, Mum. Do you really think so? Oh, I am really nervous."

"Just wear your little black dress and your black sandals with the thick strap around your ankles. You have such a lovely figure and legs you should show them off." Anna stood in the doorway of the bedroom smiling at her beautiful daughter as Harry covered herself in after sun.

"What do you think she should wear, Christina?"

"Well, let's see what you look like in what Mum suggested, Harry." Christina and Anna fussed around as Harry got dressed.

"Oh yes, that looks very nice. Now Christina, are you going to do Harry's hair for her? You can put it up so well."

Harry sat on the old wicker chair at the dressing table while Christina swept her hair up into a simple bun on the top of her head. Anna found her earrings and necklace and helped her put them on. A squirt of perfume and she was ready.

As Anna left the room, Christina produced a bottle of vodka and poured a slurp into Harry's orange juice. "Here you are; a drop of Dutch courage to help your nerves."

"Thanks, Christina. For once I'm glad you've got this!"

Harry's heart jumped as she heard a car draw up outside.

Mark knocked on the bedroom door. "Harry, Pablo's here. Are you ready?"

"Wish me luck."

Christina wished her luck and said she wanted to hear all about it when she got back.

Harry picked up her bag and made for the door. Pablo was waiting in the lounge with Mark and Anna. Harry blushed as she walked into the room to her awaiting audience. Even Mickey and Sophie were sitting on the stairs, watching all the goings-on and waiting for Harry's appearance.

Pablo walked over and kissed Harry on both cheeks. "You look very nice," he whispered.

As they turned to walk towards the door, Anna said they made a very handsome couple and said she hoped it would be a lovely evening.

"Thanks, Mum." Harry kissed her parents goodbye and headed for the door with Pablo. Pablo put the roof up on his car so Harry's hair wouldn't blow out of place.

"You look great, Harry". Pablo put his hand on her knee and gave it a little squeeze.

"Are you sure? I feel so nervous."

"I have told my father and mother all about you and they are very excited to meet you."

Harry was feeling sick. Perhaps the vodka Christina had given her had not been such a clever idea. She just wished it was all over and they were on their way home instead of just going.

Pablo put some music on and kept patting Harry on her knee, trying to give her confidence and reassure her.

It was not long before they pulled onto the driveway of the villa. Pablo jumped out of the car and held the door for Harry. Before she had a chance to get out of the car, Pablo's parents arrived in an excited commotion through the gate.

"Buenos noches. I am Isabel, Pablo's mother. I am so excited to meet you." She greeted Harry with a kiss on each cheek and then she turned to her husband. "This is Pablo's father. You must call him Jordi."

Harry turned to greet Jordi and he too kissed her on both cheeks.

"You are far lovelier than Pablo said. Come, Juan is waiting." He took Harry by the arm and led the way up the path to the villa. Pablo took his mother's arm and followed.

They were not at all what Harry had expected. His mother had lovely olive skin, quite a round face, and thick, black hair rolled up onto her head and held in place by a massive black bow which matched her loose fitting black dress. Despite her size, she was very attractive. Jordi was tall, well built with a very distinguished head of grey hair. As he smiled down at Harry she could see where Pablo got his dark eyes and wide grin from.

They joined his sisters, Maria and Rosa, who were sitting on the terrace. The greeting kisses started again. They all sat around a large, marble-topped table and Juan appeared with a tray of drinks. Harry listened as they all chatted away in broken English, obviously for her benefit. Occasionally someone would ask her a question and she would reply.

Pablo sat to the right of her. Every now and then he managed to catch her gaze and would throw her an encouraging wink. The sherry was beginning to have an effect and Harry was, at last, beginning to relax. Unless she was spoken to she sat quietly while the family caught up on the past few weeks they'd spent apart. Juan appeared again and said that the first course was ready. Pablo jumped up and slid Harry's chair back so she could get up. He then did the same for his sisters. His father had held his mother's chair out and led her by the arm. Pablo, Harry, and his sisters followed through to the dining room.

The room was air conditioned and very spacious with white vases of fresh lilies placed around on the dark wooden side tables and sideboard. Their perfume filled the room. Harry waited to be shown where to sit, relieved when Pablo's mother and father took the head of the table. His sisters sat on one side, leaving the other two laid places for Harry and Pablo. For the first course, they had gazpacho. Harry was pleased it was something simple and nothing that would prove messy to eat. Cutlets of lamb followed this, with fresh roasted peppers and a sort of sautéed potato. As they ate, the wine flowed. Harry did her best not to drink too much and sipped slowly, remembering to have a glass of water now and again. Finally, the dessert was brought out. Much to Harry's delight, this was just a very extravagant tropical fruit salad, topped with the thickest of cream.

When the dessert was finished they moved back out onto the terrace. Juan appeared with a rather large bottle of Champagne.

When everyone had received a glass, Jordi stood up and toasted Pablo. "My son, Pablo, who has received the news that he has passed all his exams."

They all raised their glasses for Pablo, who stood up. "Thank you, Papa. I would also like to say how happy I am that Harry is here tonight, to meet my family and celebrate my hard-work." He turned and raised his glass to Harry.

Harry was extremely embarrassed. "Thank you. You must be so pleased you have passed your exams." She blushed.

It was very late, by the time they had all finished their coffee. Pablo suggested it was time to take Harry home. At first his family protested that they'd hardly had time to talk to Harry, but Jordi and Isabel agreed it was late, he was right, and he should get Harry home. After walking them to the car, Jordi kissed Harry on both cheeks and said it was a pleasure meeting her.

Isabel too was very sweet and embraced Harry as she kissed her goodbye. "You must come again, very soon. We still have a lot to learn about you, and you must have questions for us. Next time, it would be nice if you would bring your family. We should all get to know each other."

Harry got into the car next to Pablo. His parents stood and waved, until the car had disappeared out of sight.

Harry was relieved everything had gone well. She had liked his mother and father, and they had really gone out of their way to welcome her and make her feel at home. His sisters were very nice and made her feel like a friend. It could not have gone any better; she'd thoroughly enjoyed herself.

"Harry, you are wonderful. My parents and sisters really liked you." Pablo slid his hand down Harry's arm until he found her hand. He lifted it up to his mouth and kissed it gently, then held it to his cheek until he had to release it to change gear. Instead of taking Harry straight home, he continued past the villa and drove to the top of the hill overlooking S'Agaro bay, and parked.

"I thought it would be nice to be alone with you and just to sit for a little time, before I take you home."

"That will be nice. I feel we've hardly had any time together, even if it was only yesterday that we spent the whole afternoon and evening together."

Pablo got out of the car and went around to Harry's side. He opened the door and Harry got out. They walked around to the front of the car and sat against the bonnet, admiring the view of the bay. Pablo slipped his arm around Harry's shoulder. On the opposite hill the lights from the Gavina Hotel blazed out across the bay. The bay, separating the two hills, looked very black other than a few odd twinkling lights dotted around, where night fisherman were trying their luck. Waves were crashing angrily on the rocks below. Harry started shivering as the cool sea breeze enveloped her body.

"Come here, you are cold." Pablo pulled Harry in front of him and wrapped his jacket around them both. She was still looking out into the bay, dreamily thinking about how lucky she was to have met Pablo.

He leant down and spoke quietly in Harry's left ear. This sent a thrilling shiver down Harry's spine.

"What are you thinking about, my English Rose?" As he finished his sentence, he kissed the top of her ear and snuggled his head onto her shoulder.

"I'm thinking the same as you." Harry twisted round, staying inside his jacket, and looked up into his eyes. They always seemed to be twinkling. She reached up and kissed him firmly on the lips. He kissed her back and his tongue went straight inside her mouth, feeling her perfectly shaped, smooth teeth and playing with her tongue. He pulled her closer to him so she could feel his firm body against hers, his hands gently pulling her small, firm, buttocks in towards him. Harry ran her hands up and down his back, feeling his muscular physique then resting them on his shoulders. The kiss went on forever, neither wanting to stop. They were both feeling aroused. Harry knew she could surrender to him, here and now.

Pablo slipped his hand up inside Harry's top. Her soft, warm skin felt like silk. He desired her so badly. He had to control himself and stop. He gently kissed her face and then, in a low, husky whisper said, "We must talk about what we are going to do. I want you so badly, I'm hurting." He traced a finger down her cheek. "I can't bear the thought of you leaving me."

A few tears appeared from nowhere and ran down her cheek. "I don't want to leave you, but I have to go back to England, to finish college."

"Don't cry. We will work something out. Now I have finished my exams and passed them all it makes life a little easier. I will talk to my father and see if he can help in anyway." Pablo kissed away Harry's tears.

"I love you, my little English Rose."

"I love you too."

Pablo picked Harry up and swung her around and, at the top of his voice, shouted, "She loves me! Harry loves me!" At last he put her down, both laughing and feeling their mutual love.

Pablo took Harry by the hand and led her back around the car. He stole one last kiss then he opened the door and Harry got in. Both were smiling like Cheshire cats as Pablo drove Harry back to her parents' villa. They arranged that the following day Pablo would pick her up and they would go to church and then have a walk around the market in Sant Feliu. Pablo kissed Harry good night and then drove off.

Chapter 18

The next morning, when Harry awoke, everyone was already up. She slipped into a long T-shirt and went out for breakfast. Her family were all waiting to hear how the evening had gone. Harry told them all about Pablo's family and the lovely meal they had given her. She told them that his parents wanted to meet them all and had suggested they all went up to the villa for an evening. She told them that Pablo had passed his exams and how his father had made a toast.

Anna could tell Harry was in love. She was glowing and full of her evening with Pablo. She was pleased Harry was happy but, at the same time, worried about the time when Harry would have to say goodbye and return to England.

Christina had been out with Manolo and his friends again. She told everyone about her evening and that all his friends kept asking why they hadn't seen much of Pablo all week, and who was this girl he'd been seen out with? They had all said he must be in love if he'd taken her back to meet his parents. Apparently, the only other girl he'd ever taken back was Conchitta, and that was because she wouldn't let him out of her sight.

Harry wasn't very hungry. After a glass of fruit juice and a quick nibble on a croissant, she excused herself and told her family that Pablo was going to take her to Church and to the market, so she needed to get ready.

Getting into a floral sun dress, putting on just some lip gloss, twisting her hair into a loose bun and grabbing her straw sun hat and sun glasses, Harry was ready. Pablo arrived on cue. He came into the villa to say hello to Mark, Anna, Christina, and the twins, before he took Harry off to Sant Feliu.

It was extremely busy, cars queuing into the town centre from all directions, battling for a parking spot near the market and church. After fifteen minutes of curb crawling, Pablo found a parking space. They walked through the dusty streets and across the old, sandy courtyard to the gigantic, fortified church. They stepped out of the heat into the old 11th century cool, stone church. Harry removed her glasses and Pablo pushed his up on his head as their eyes adjusted to the darkness. Harry and Pablo both crossed themselves with Holy water from the marble font and slid into a pew. The Priest was speaking through a microphone. His voice echoed around the huge, stone building. The church was packed full of people from all the different generations that came to worship and cleanse their souls. Stone pillars rose from every angle forming a huge arch that ran from the high alter to the small, dark, confessional boxes at the back of the church. Little alters spread out from the backbone of the church. These were beautifully decorated with flowers and lit by a mass of glowing, flickering candles in memory of departed loved ones, or to boost a prayer for a sick family member or friend. Widows dressed in black and ladies in their Sunday best sat fanning themselves with their heads bowed. Men, children, and people from all levels of society wandered in, genuflected, prayed, and left, their Godly duty over, consciences clear, ready to start a new week. Some stayed deep in prayer for the whole duration of the Mass. Harry could just about keep up with the Mass. She stood when everyone else stood. She sat when they sat and knelt when they knelt. She could follow some of the prayers and said them quietly to herself in English.

When it was time for Holy Communion, Pablo asked if Harry was going to take it. Harry nodded and followed him out of the pew and up to the altar. When it was Pablo's turn, he took the Eucharist in his hand, so Harry did the same. Returning to their pew, after saying a few prayers, Harry and Pablo rose, slid out of the pew, genuflected facing the altar, and headed towards the door. On leaving, once again they crossed themselves with Holy water from the large marble font and departed.

Sitting in the entrance of the huge wooden doorway was a beggar rolling a cigarette. He put out his hand and Harry placed some change out of her purse into it. Pablo took his wallet out and handed the old man a note. It was now quite hot and as they stepped out of the cold, dark, church, the heat and glare of the sun hit them. Harry pulled out her sunglasses and put them back on. Pablo slid his down and back onto the bridge of his nose. Hand in hand they crossed the road and headed down some steps and into an alley heading towards the market square.

Looking at nothing in-particular they strolled up and down the rows of clothes, jewellery, and crockery. Pablo wanted to look at the fish, so they headed to the indoor section and wandered around, looking at the vast stalls of fresh fish. The smell was overwhelming. Luckily Harry did not have a weak stomach so it did not bother her. Pablo bragged about being an expert cook and told Harry about his specialty that was a sort of fish stew. After being extremely choosy about what he would put in it, he finally bought what he needed and said he would cook a meal for Harry that evening.

Returning to the square, they decided to head for the main Rambla and have a coffee. The main Rambla was lined with trees which housed hundreds of chirping birds and sheltered the tables and chairs from the burning sun. Cafes ran into each other up and down the promenade. Sitting down, Pablo spotted a newsagent with racks of postcards and Sunday papers outside its open doors. He told Harry to order him an espresso and said he was just going to pick up a paper.

He arrived back flustered. "Look, Harry."

Harry went to remove her sun glasses.

"No, don't take them off, leave them on."

Puzzled, Harry did as Pablo said then looked down to where Pablo was pointing on the front page of the paper. It was the photo of Harry and Pablo leaving the jewellery shop in Playa.

"The caption reads, 'Ski-Summer girl to wed?' It then goes on to say, 'This is the new Ski-Summer girl. It hasn't taken Harriet Thomas-Smyth long to find her Spanish Romeo. Seen coming out of a jewellery shop in

Playa de Aro with Pablo Cruanos, son of Jordi Cruanos and Nephew of Julian Cruanos, joint owners of the Ski-Sports empire. Is this the future Señora Cruanos? Or, has she just skied him off his feet?'"

Harry could not believe what she was hearing.

"Keep your sunglasses on, Harry, and maybe no one will recognise you or me."

At that moment the waiter arrived with their coffee. He glanced at the paper so Harry slid her bag onto the photo to hide it.

"How did they get all this information? It is not even true. People are going to think I'm just after you so I can be the Ski-Summer girl. I did not know your father was related and in partnership with Julian!"

"Yes, I did not think it was worth mentioning. My father is a silent partner and runs another part of the business, so he is unaware of what my uncle Julian is doing."

Harry was livid, her heart pounding. What would her parents think if they saw this? She would have to find them, and explain, before they saw it.

"Come on then, Harry. Just drink your coffee and we will go and find your parents and show them the paper. Do you want to try and ring them at their villa and find out if they are there?"

"No, they will be going to Church and wandering around the market. I will catch them when they are back at the villa."

"It is a Spanish paper so they may not have seen it. So, don't worry, Harry. We will find them before they see it or hear about it."

A few people started slowing down as they walked past the table where Harry and Pablo sat. They both kept their heads down, just continued talking and pretended not to notice. When the waiter arrived with the bill, Pablo handed the money straight over to him. The waiter handed Harry the bill and asked her to sign it. Harry looked up at him in amazement, not knowing whether to take it or not. Harry quickly signed it. Collecting up her things ready to move, Pablo was already standing. Some more of the waiters gathered around the table. Harry handed the signed bill back to the waiter.

Pablo ushered her through the gathering crowd that was growing by the second, and they made a dash for the market. Once they were back amongst the crowded stalls they felt quite camouflaged and safe. Making their way straight through the vegetable stalls, they headed for the alley on the far side of the square. Pablo held Harry's hand tightly so he wouldn't lose her. They raced down the alley, as quickly as they could, then back out into the court yard by the Church. So far, so good. No-one was following them.

As they neared their parking spot, Pablo came to an abrupt halt. "Look, someone is hanging around my car, and he has a camera." Pablo pointed to another street nearby.

"You go down that street as far as you can. Just keep walking and I will go and get the car and find you.

Harry kept walking and suddenly felt very alone and frightened. She did not dare to look back. After five minutes she began to panic. What if Pablo didn't come? Her fears were soon forgotten as a horn sounded and Pablo pulled up alongside her. Harry jumped in the car and Pablo sped off.

"It was another reporter. We must go and warn your family and then we must drive up to see my parents and warn them."

Harry clutched the paper tightly in her hand. By the time they reached her parents' villa it was a crumpled heap. Outside the gate were another load of reporters.

"We can't stop, Harry, they will surround us. Come on, let's drive up to my parents' villa." Half way up Mas Now, Pablo pulled the car into a verge and to a halt.

"Pass me my phone. It is in the glove compartment, Harry. I will phone my parents and see if it is safe to go on."

Harry opened the glove compartment, found Pablo's mobile brick, and handed it to him. He quickly keyed in his parents' number. He spoke in Spanish and Harry could not understand what he was saying.

He handed the phone back to Harry. "Too late! They are already at the gates of my parents' villa. My father said he will get hold of my uncle and see what is going to happen about the launch. He will ask him to issue the press with a statement. In the meantime, my sister is going to get me some clothes together and then she will go with my mother to meet your parents and speak to them. My parents think it would be good if we went to stay at my grandfather's house in the country for a few days until this whole thing dies down. I said we could meet my sister in a couple of hours, up at the restaurant above Sant Feliu. Carlos will take care of us until then. My father has already spoken to him and he is expecting us."

Harry was very worried. What would her parents think? "Pablo, I am worried. What do you think my parents will think when they see the paper? It asked if I am going to marry you."

"Don't worry. My mother will explain it all to them. I told her why we were outside the jewellers and my mother thought it was very funny. Don't forget, I have already spoken to your father and he understands how I feel about you. He knows I will take care of you. When we get to the restaurant you can phone them, and speak to them. Would that make you feel any better?" Pablo squeezed Harry's knee to comfort her.

"Yes, thank you, Pablo." Harry was too alarmed about the whole situation to chat, so Pablo put on some music. He tuned the radio to radio Costa Brava. Wham were singing. Harry sat back and briefly enjoyed the familiar music.

They soon arrived at the restaurant. Carlos had been looking out for them. Pablo leant over and took his phone from the glove compartment and jumped out of the car whilst Carlos ran around and opened the door for Harry.

"Come out to the terrace. There is no one out there!" They followed Carlos, under the archway and through the restaurant, to the terrace. He seated them at a table and snapped his fingers at one of the waiters, who arrived with some fresh coffee and three small brandies. He joined them, sitting between Pablo and Harry. He placed his hand over Harry's.

"Now, my beautiful little friend, you must not worry. Señor Cruanos will sort everything out for you. Come into the office and make your phone call. You will have some privacy." Harry followed Carlos back through the restaurant and into his office. Guiding Harry to a seat, he handed her the phone and left her in private to ring her parents. Harry dialled in the number of her parents' villa. Mark was quick to answer.

"Hello, Dad, it's Harry." As Harry spoke she burst into tears.

Mark assured her everything would be all right. He told her to be strong and that Pablo was a very nice young man and he would take diligent care of her until the press got fed up with the story. He said he had already spoken to Pablo's parents and, when his sister, Maria, and mother arrived, they would get Papa's address and try and arrange to visit them. He told her Christina had packed her a bag and all her toiletries. He handed the phone to Anna. Anna again reassured Harry and said they were going to try to go and see them when they were settled, and not to worry.

Harry asked her mother to make a note of Pablo's mobile number then she could phone whenever she wanted. Having said goodbye, she spoke to the twins and finally Christina.

"Hi, Harry. Great picture of you and Pablo outside the jewellers. You look like a real celebrity couple. Anyway, I have packed everything I think you will need, and your hair dryer. I'll put my curling tongs in as well. I think you will use them more than I will. Make the most of the next few days. It could be such fun. Someone has just arrived. I think it is Pablo's sister so I had better go. Take care and enjoy."

"Okay. Thanks, Christina, look after the twins. Bye". Harry wiped her eyes and took a minute to compose herself before she re-joined Pablo and Carlos.

Pablo could see she had been crying. He stood up and gave her a quick hug.

Having spoken to her family, Harry felt a lot better.

Carlos said that he should get some food ready for them and that it would do them both good to eat. They had a good few hours driving ahead of them. Leaving them alone, he headed for the kitchen to see what he could rustle up.

Pablo and Harry began to relax as the brandy ran through their bodies. Pablo patted Harry's hand.

"Can you remember what a lovely night we had here?"

Harry's sad eyes sparkled at the memory. "Yes, it was a lovely night, and now it's all been spoilt. Why did I ever agree to do that dammed skiing?"

"Harry, you did it because you are good at skiing and, if this is just something we have to go through, let's make the most of it. Also it will give us some time together, to get to know each other better."

Harry smiled at Pablo; he was right. She did, once upon a time, have a dream about being an actress and famous. She should make the most of it and turn it to her advantage and it was going to be great spending time with Pablo. She leant across the table and gave Pablo a kiss.

Carlos arrived; he coughed to announce his entrance.

Harry sat back in her seat. He had made them a Spanish omelette and salad. A waiter quickly arranged the table, leaving some scented, fresh flowers and home baked bread which he placed in a basket in the centre of the table. Carlos, who had quickly disappeared, arrived back with a bottle of wine and jug of water. Harry and Pablo tucked in. They had not realized how hungry they were. Pablo poured Harry a glass of wine and water for himself.

Just as they put their knives and forks down there was a commotion at the door. Pablo's mother and sister had arrived. Isabel bustled through the restaurant, followed by Maria and Juan carrying their bags. Juan sat himself discreetly at the bar while Isabel and Maria went out onto the terrace and embraced Harry.

"You poor little thing. I am sorry all this has happened to you. Never mind. You must go to the country and stay for a few days while my husband sorts everything out." She then turned to Pablo.

"You must take very good care of this lovely girl. She is very precious."

Pablo kissed his mother and said they would be fine. Maria gave them a kiss and said they had to get back; there was a lot to do. She and Rosa were going to help organise the launch. The sooner it was done, the sooner everything would be back to normal. After an emotional goodbye from Isabel and Maria, Juan stepped forward. They'd not noticed he was there. Juan embraced Pablo and kissed Harry on both cheeks. A man of few words, they both realized how much he cared about them. He was like a second father to Pablo and felt extremely protective towards him.

"I must get the Senora and Senorita back to the villa. Good luck, I will see you both soon."

Carlos returned from his office. He was very sweet and would not take anything for the food, or phone call. He helped Pablo carry the bags out to the car. He made them promise to come and see him when everything had blown over. He saw them out to the car, helped Pablo load it up, and waved them off.

Chapter 19

"Come on, Harry, let's look at this as another holiday, rather than going to hide." He turned the music up, put his foot down, and the car roared off.

Harry slept most of the way. Pablo woke her up, tapping her gently on the arm, just as he pulled into the gateway of his grandfather's country house. He had to stop the car to open the huge, rusted, wrought iron gates. Harry roused herself and got out to help him. Pablo drove the car through the gate and then helped Harry drag the gates back across the entrance.

"Well, what do you think?" The driveway twisted through a vineyard. The long, neat rows of vines were heavy with fruit. Doubling back on themselves, the car finally stopped outside a large, old, stone farmhouse. It was lovely. Vines crept over the entire front of the house, trimmed neatly, to expose the square windows framed with pale-grey painted shutters, some of which were closed, and others open, letting in the daylight. Pablo pulled the car up to the bottom of the stone steps at the front of the house. At the top of the steps, the old wooden double doors creaked open and out came a very old man. He had white, wispy hair and leathery looking tanned skin. His soft brown, piercing eyes twinkled.

Pablo jumped out of the car and ran up the steps, two at a time. He wrapped his arms around the old man and kissed him on both cheeks. Harry got out of the car and made her way up the steps. Pablo introduced Harry to his grandfather, who insisted on Harry calling him Papa. They greeted each other with a kiss on both cheeks. Harry thought he was charming.

After looking her up and down and making her do a turn, he smiled with an approving nod. "You are a good-looking girl," he said, taking her by the hand and leading the way into a vast hallway, panelled in oak. A stone fireplace dominated the facing wall; a portrait of a beautiful women hung over the mantelpiece.

Pablo's grandfather noticed Harry staring up at the picture and said, "That is a picture of my wife. She was very beautiful, huh?"

Harry nodded.

"Pablo, take Harry up to the guest room and show her where she will be sleeping, while I go and prepare us a drink. You have fifteen minutes. Then I want to hear all about what has happened."

Pablo led the way up the oak stairway, coiling up to the second floor.

Harry glanced up. There was a balcony running along the second floor, overlooking the hall. As they passed various doors, Pablo explained what the different rooms were. Halting outside the fourth door along, Pablo explained to Harry that this was the guest room. He opened the door. A huge, rosewood four poster bed lay in the centre of the room. The floor was not carpeted. The polished boards were just scattered with rugs. A fireplace, filled with jasmine that fragranced the room, stood facing the bed. A wardrobe and a chest of drawers filled one wall, whilst on the other side of the room, a large window with a cushioned window seat, overlooking the garden, invited Harry to sit on it. She sat down next to an old, tattered, teddy, propped up on a floral cushion, and looked out of the window to the back of the house. Harry saw a brightly coloured, whitewashed, walled garden, draped with pots full of geraniums. A fountain had been positioned at the centre as a focal point.

"It's lovely, Pablo. I'm so glad we came here."

Pablo pulled Harry to her feet. "This is the best bit, Harry, look." Taking her across the floor to a door in the corner of the room, Pablo pushed the door open. A quaint, white-marbled bathroom with plump, white towels stood the other side of the door. At the opposite end of the bathroom was another door; this opened into another bedroom.

"This is my bedroom. Ever since I can remember, I have slept in this room. It is full of things I have collected over the years. Wasn't that thoughtful of Papa, to put us next door to each other? I will be just here when you go to bed and when you wake." Pulling Harry into his arms, he kissed her gently on the lips.

Harry kissed him back feeling safe at last. Pablo's room was the same size as Harry's only, instead of a four-poster bed, it had a metal framed bed, a tall-boy, chest of drawers, blanket boxes at the foot of the bed and bedside cabinets to each side of the bed. Pablo's room was cluttered with books, games, stones, minerals, and pictures of wildlife. It was very like Mickey's at home. No wonder he got on so well with Mickey; he must have had the same interests when he was a boy. Harry suddenly thought of home and the secure feeling of being surrounded by familiar things and the love of all her family.

Soon Pablo was tugging at Harry's hand. "Come on Harry, we must go and join Papa for a drink."

On the way down the landing Pablo pointed out his grandfather's room, right at the end of the landing and off to the right. It too must have been overlooking the walled garden. There were only two rooms on the left. The rest of the space was taken up by the hall which reared up to the full height of the house to a tiled roof held up by aged beams. Its grand, antique chandeliers hung level with the landing.

Downstairs, they made their way across the hall, into the kitchen, a typical farmhouse kitchen with years of clutter scattered around its granite tops. A long, worn, rectangular, oak table, scarred with burns, indentations, and years of bleaching, ran the length of the room, surrounded by an assortment of chairs. An old Aga puffed away under an arched stone chimney breast. A kettle whistling away, stood on one of the hot plates. Linen scattered along an airer above, socks dancing in the steam. Boots and shoes lined up either side of an open door leading out to the garden. Pablo rushed forward and took the kettle off the heat.

Harry noticed Papa was seated at a table under a flowering Bougainvillea that twisted and weaved its way around the pergola standing outside the door.

Hearing them approach, Papa forced his old bones to stand. "Here, come and join me." He patted the chair next to his. Pablo pulled it out for Harry to sit on. "I have some fresh orange juice for you." He poured them some juice from a cut crystal jug. "Pablo, your father phoned and told me what happened. You are both welcome to stay as long as you wish. You know that, don't you, Pablo?"

"Yes, thank you, Papa. It's great to be here. I don't know why I do not come here more often. It's so beautiful and peaceful." Pablo spoke to his grandfather in very slow English so Harry could understand, rather than in Spanish which would have excluded her. Papa could once speak fluent English but, over the years, he used it less and less and was now a little rusty, to say the least.

Pablo left Harry with Papa, who wanted to show Harry around the garden. He proudly took her to see his vegetable garden. Neatly laid out in weed-free rows, it was his pride and joy. Tomatoes, courgettes, and peppers in bright colours were climbing up canes towards the sunlight. Harry told Papa about her grandmother, back in England, and how she too enjoyed tending a garden and growing all sorts of vegetables. She told him about their farm and how beautiful it was. She spoke of her horse, Bounty, and their old dog, Smudge. Papa said they had a couple of old horses, kept stabled down the road. He said they were still quite highly spirited and suggested Pablo could take her out for a ride. There were some lovely rides around the vineyards and citrus orchards.

Pablo had taken their bags up to their rooms. When Harry joined him he had already unpacked his bags and neatly placed everything in its appropriate place, his toiletries lined up in the bathroom and his toothbrush in a glass on the shelf above the sink. Pablo offered to help Harry unpack.

"I can manage. Why don't you just sit and watch me. You must be exhausted."

Pablo kicked his shoes off and lay back on the four-poster bed. His eyes followed Harry around the room as she self-consciously hung the few garments Christina had packed for her, and quickly placed her underwear, T-shirts, and shorts into the empty drawers. After arranging her makeup and perfume on the dressing table she had not noticed earlier, in the corner of the room, she finally took her toothbrush, shampoo, conditioner, and toothpaste into the bathroom, placing her toothbrush into the glass next to Pablo's. Suddenly she felt very grown up, realising that she would be sleeping near Pablo and sharing a bathroom with him.

"Oh, my God! I have left the fish in the car that we bought at the market this morning." Pablo leapt to his feet and raced out of the room, leaving Harry to finish off in peace and to make a better job of arranging her clothes.

Bags unpacked, shoes away and bedroom left neatly, Harry went downstairs to find Pablo. He was in the kitchen with Papa. They were chatting away in Spanish whilst they chopped vegetables and added them to a bubbling pan placed on the Aga. It smelt delicious.

"Come, my dear." Papa noticed Harry standing in the doorway.

"Pablo has bought some fish from the market and we are making it into a wonderful Spanish stew."

"Papa is my teacher. I told you I could cook."

Harry sat in a chair at the table and watched as grandfather and grandson prepared a delicious meal. Pablo poured them all a glass of chilled, white wine from their own vineyard.

After a lovely meal, eaten in the comfort of the cosy, cluttered, kitchen, Harry and Pablo insisted on doing the washing up, while Papa sat telling stories about Pablo as a boy. He used to spend every summer and most Christmases in the country house with his grandparents, until his parents bought their villa up on Mas Nou. His childhood sounded very familiar to the way Harry had spent hers. Pablo had the freedom to roam and explore the surrounding countryside. He'd had many an adventure staying here with his sisters and friends from the village.

Papa kissed them goodnight then went upstairs to his room.

Pablo asked Harry if she would like a walk before they went up to bed. It was dark outside however the moon was full and bright, lighting the garden. They wandered round the scented paths, hand in hand, still talking of the things they had done as children. Crickets whistled in the long grass, while frogs croaked around the pond; the noise was overwhelming. The fountain flowed and sparked, like a spectacular Catherine wheel spitting its sparks in the moonlight. It seemed as though they walked and talked for hours. Ending up back at the kitchen, Pablo made sure he'd bolted the door securely. Sitting in the cosy window seat, looking out at the stars, they sipped on hot chocolate laced with brandy. Neither wanted to mention the day's events in case they broke the magic of the closeness they were sharing. Once they'd finished their chocolate, Harry went upstairs, while Pablo checked the front door had been locked, and all the shutters were closed. It wasn't a big job, as most of the rooms were closed off these days and only opened for use on special occasions. Papa spent his days mainly in the kitchen, his study, and a small living room, with a little television in.

Harry had a quick shower and slipped into her soft, cotton pyjama shorts and top. After brushing her teeth, she got into the four-poster with a book. Luckily for Harry, Christina had remembered to put the book Harry was reading as well as a few others for extra reading material should she need it. The bed seemed enormous and very soft. Harry sank right into it. With the duck down duvet tucked around her she felt very relaxed and sleepy.

When Pablo came up, he went straight into his room from the landing in case his grandfather was still awake. Pablo slipped his jeans off, leaving just his boxer shorts on, and went into the bathroom to wash, and brush his teeth. As quietly as he could he pushed the door open into Harry's room. He tiptoed across the floor to Harry's bed. She was fast asleep. The book had fallen onto the pillow by her head. Pablo took the book from the pillow and placed it on the table next to her bed. Very cautiously, he climbed into the bed next to Harry and turned the light off.

Harry felt the warmth of his body next to hers. It felt like she was dreaming. Lifting her head, she moved it on onto his shoulder.

Pablo slipped his arm under her pillow and around her shoulders.

Harry snuggled into Pablo's neck, and slept like a baby, feeling safe, comforted, and warm.

Pablo could not get to sleep. He turned the events of the day over and over in his mind. He could not think of a solution as to how they could live normally if Harry was going to be in the spotlight. He knew this was just the start of things to come. Harry was a beautiful girl. She was also very stylish and talented in everything he had seen her do. The smell of her hair tormented him. The thought and touch of her soft, warm body next to his was eating him up. He had to control himself. This was the girl he wanted to spend the rest of his life with. Eventually, Pablo too drifted off to sleep.

Chapter 20

Back in Playa, Christina was enjoying a night out with Manolo. They had a great time with all her new-found friends, eating, drinking, and sharing stories. The group was very jovial. As the end of the evening approached, Conchitta arrived in the entrance to the bar with her brothers, one on each arm like her own personal bodyguards.

"Where is Pablo?" The whole bar went silent focusing their attention on Conchitta. She had clearly seen the paper and was furious. She'd have taken every word literally. Aiming her fury directly at Manolo she spat her words out again. "Where is Pablo?"

Manolo's grin disappeared as he responded, "I have no idea. All I know is that he has gone away for a few days."

"You tell that English bitch that Pablo belongs with me."

Christina was horrified. How could this girl be so jealous? Did she not realize it was over between the two of them?

"Just leave them alone, Conchitta. You know it's all over between you and Pablo." Manolo tried speaking quietly and calmly.

Conchitta's brothers just stood there like a couple of knuckleheads, waiting for instructions.

"Just you wait until the papers come out tomorrow. We will see if it is all over." With that she turned and was escorted out of the bar by her brothers.

As soon as they had disappeared everyone in the bar fell about laughing.

Manolo decided he and Christina should go too. On the way back to his car he started to worry about what Conchitta had done. "What do you think she meant by 'wait until you see the papers.' What has she done?" His mind working overtime, Manolo suddenly realized she had sold a story to the papers. Checking his watch, it was now the early hours of the morning. He quickly realized they may be able to get hold of a first issue if they could find an all-night news agent or tobacconist that sold papers. Sharing his thoughts with Christina, they decided to cruise around looking for a newsstand. Having driven to every place in Playa Manolo could think of with no luck, they headed back towards S'Agaro.

"There! Look, Manolo, an open garage. Try in there."

Manolo pulled off the road and stopped on the garage forecourt. Just as Manolo went through the door a newspaper delivery van pulled up. Christina jumped out of the car and ran across to let Manolo know. They brought a coffee and stood around waiting while the forecourt attendant took the previous day's bundles of unsold papers out to the van and swapped them for the fresh delivery. At a snail's pace he worked his way through them. When he had finally sorted through them he laid them out in neat rows onto the racks. Manolo and Christina were on their feet, pacing the racks and scanning the front pages. Christina was the first to spot Conchitta. Tapping the picture, she quickly pointed it out to Manolo. On the front page of the Costa Brava Fun was a very attractive, forlorn-looking Conchitta. Manolo snatched the paper up and placed a few pesetas on the counter and marched out across the forecourt to the car. Christina followed. When they got in the car Manolo scanned the headline then translated what he had read to Christina.

"Ski Summer Girl Stole the Father of my Baby, Pablo Cruanos. Full story page five." Quickly licking his index finger, Manolo turned the pages and continued reading. "Pablo has left me and our love child for an English college girl." The story went on to say how Conchitta was carrying Pablo's child and how he and Conchitta had been childhood sweethearts and very happy together. She had fallen pregnant and at the time Pablo had been over the moon, before this English college girl came along and turned him against her. There were photos of Conchitta and Pablo at College, a photo of a group of teenagers at Conchitta's 13th birthday, then a more recent one. Looking closer Christina realized that the photo, where Pablo's arm was wrapped around Conchitta, must have been taken at the party they went to, when they had first arrived in Spain. Pablo and Manolo were celebrating finishing their exams. It must have been taken after Harry and Christina left. The article finished by saying that this last photo was taken before they spent a romantic night together at the Villa Cruanos on Mas Nou.

"What are we going to do, Manolo? We must warn Pablo and his parents, as well as my parents."

Manolo agreed and headed straight up the mountain to see Isabel and Jordi Cruanos. He told Christina it would be better if they drove up to see them, rather than phoning them that late in the night.

When they arrived at the villa there was one light on by the gate. Manolo and Christina rang the bell and waited. At first no one came so Manolo tried the bell again. After a further five minutes Juan appeared.

"Buenos noches, Manolo, Buenos noches, Christina." Juan did not seem alarmed by the late visit and never forgot a name or face. Manolo explained briefly why they were there at such a late hour. Juan did not need any further explanation. He opened the gate and showed them into the lounge where they waited for Jordi.

Jordi appeared with Isabel hot on his heels, both dressed in long, silk, burgundy and black dressing gowns and wearing slippers. They greeted Manolo, who re-introduced Christina to them.

Turning their attention to the article in the Costa Brava Fun, Manolo handed Señor Cruanos the paper and let him read it himself. Reading the article, his face blackened and the lines on his brow deepened. He was not happy. He passed the paper to his wife and beckoned Manolo to his office. Christina sat with her arm around Isabel, who was now very upset herself, trying to comfort her. Manolo had the hard task of recounting the events of the evening when they had held their party. He explained how he thought Conchitta had climbed into Pablo's bed. He was convinced nothing had happened and how he thought it was all a last attempt by Conchitta to hold on to Pablo. Jordi remained very calm as he listened. As a very old friend of the family, Jordi was pleased with Manolo for waking them. He was glad to have been informed of the news before more journalists woke them. He said he needed some time to think about the accusations before he went to see Pablo and decide what his reaction would be. Manolo said that he would take Christina home and let her inform her family of the latest bad news. Shaking Jordi's hand as he left the study, he found Christina sitting with Isabel drinking a huge brandy. Telling Isabel he thought there was no truth in any of it, Manolo and Christina both embraced Isabel then left.

Back at the Smyth-Thomas's villa everybody was still asleep. Christina thought it would be better if Manolo went home. He'd already done enough and she was very grateful for his help. After seeing him out of the door, Christina made herself a hot chocolate and curled up on her bed to wait for her parents to wake.

Jordi and Isabel decided they should waste no time. Jordi washed and dressed before he headed off in his black Mercedes to see his son. When Jordi arrived, the main gates to the house were shut. Rather than opening them, he drove on around the village. It was an extra three kilometres to the trade entrance into the vineyard. Here, deliveries and supplies arrived. He drove through the back way, leaving his car by the labelling factory. Making his way to the back of the house, he entered the walled garden. The aromas of the jasmine engulfed him and triggered many memories, most happy and some sad. Afraid of alarming anyone if he banged on the door, he seated himself at the garden table and decided to wait for a sign of someone stirring in the old house. He knew his father was an early riser and it would not be long before he appeared. He was right. He had only been sitting for a few minutes when the kitchen light went on.

Making his way to the window he peered in. To his surprise he saw it was not his father but his son, Pablo. Placing his hand on the glass he quietly tapped. Pablo, in a world of his own, at first did not hear him. Then, with a second tap, this time slightly louder, he caught Pablo's attention.

Pablo, wrapped in a bath robe, went straight to the kitchen door, unbolted it, and let his father in.

Greeting each other with the usual kiss, his father said he had some very bad news. He insisted on making himself a cup of coffee before he sat at the table facing his son, clutching the paper in one hand, his eyes running over Pablo's face. His son seemed so young. He did not want him saddled with the burden of a baby at his age, or married to a girl he did not love.

"Where is Harry?"

"Harry is still sleeping, Father. She was very tired. What has happened? Please tell me."

Still lost for words and shaking his head, he handed his son the paper. Pablo's face dropped as he saw the picture. He quickly turned the pages and read the article, all the time shaking his head and tutting. By the time he had finished, tears had welled up in his eyes.

His father wrapped an arm around his shoulder. After several minutes, when Pablo had composed himself, his father gently spoke. "Do you think she is having your baby, my grandchild?"

"No, Father, I do not." Pablo confirmed Manolo's story about the events of the evening of their party and, prior to that it had been months ago that they had had any kind of sexual relationship.

"We have to find out if she is truly having a baby, Father. I am sure she is not. If she is, it is not mine." Lifting his hands to the heavens he pleaded, "How do I prove it?"

"There are ways of testing the blood group or DNA of an unborn baby. It will be necessary to get Conchitta to agree with this. Do you think she will if you ask her?"

"I do not know. She is so crazy, Father, but I should try. I will speak to her mother if not and she will persuade her."

"It must be done today, my son. We must stop these rumours. Your mother is very upset, and so will Harry and her family be when they find out. Manolo and Christina came and woke us late last night to inform us. Manolo and Christina then left to let Harry's parents know. What will you tell Harry?"

Pablo thought very deeply, before he replied. He decided it would be better to speak to Conchitta first and see if he could find out what she was playing at. Jordi agreed. Pablo would arrange to take Harry riding that morning and later leave her with Papa while he went to see Conchitta. Jordi would drive back and arrange for Conchitta to come to the villa where they would have some privacy to speak. The arrangements for the Ski-Summer launch had also been finalized. It was taking place on Saturday at the Boating Club on Lake Banyoles. There would be drinks first followed by the film of the girls in action, and photo shots, finishing with more drinks and Tapas. Hopefully the Conchitta issue would be over by then as the press had been invited for a second showing should the girls agree.

Jordi looked at his watch and decided he should head back. Pablo would be at the villa later and hopefully so would Conchitta. They would speak again soon. Pablo embraced his father and said goodbye.

Chapter 21

Pablo's mind was in overdrive. He struggled but managed to make a tray up with fresh orange juice, coffee, and croissants with a little dish of the farm's strawberry preserve. Adding a rose from the garden, he mounted the stairs and headed for Harry's room. Knocking, he waited for a response. As Harry did not answer Pablo turned the handle and entered. Harry was showering so he placed the tray on the bed and waited for her.

Harry appeared, flushed, hair up in a band, and wrapped in a white bathrobe. Thrilled to see Pablo sitting on her bed she rushed over. Throwing her arms out she greeted him with a warm, wet, kiss. Pablo breathed in; she smelt soapy, fresh, and irresistible. Pablo lifted her into his arms and responded to her kiss. Putting Harry down, he seated himself back on the bed. "Look, I have made your breakfast."

Harry looked down at the tray. Pablo was so sweet and thoughtful. "I had a really good sleep last night and I feel so much better today. I think everything will be fine. What does it matter what the papers say and do? We know what the truth is and, if we remain strong and always remember the truth, we will cope."

At that moment Pablo wanted to tell her everything. "Do you mean that, my little English Rose?"

"Yes, I do. Now come on and help me eat my croissant." Harry sat cross legged on the bed opposite Pablo with the tray between them. Breaking the croissants open she lavishly smothered them in jam and began eating. Holding a piece to Pablo's lips he took a small bite. "Come on, Pablo, you must help me eat them. I will never manage three croissants on my own."

Pablo was still feeling all churned up. He didn't have much of an appetite. He was worrying about his meeting with Conchitta.

"What is wrong, Pablo? You look like you are worried. Did you have a bad night?" Harry's eyes sparkled as she remembered Pablo climbing into bed and snuggling up to her. "It was really sweet of you to look after me last night. I felt safe and I want that feeling to stay with me for the rest of my life."

Pablo leant over the tray and traced his hand around Harry's face, his face serious as he longed for the rest of the world to vanish and leave them alone. Wondering if he should tell her about Conchitta, running his finger over her lip he spoke. "I want you to stay with me for the rest of your life. I will always keep you safe."

"What shall we do today, Pablo?"

"I thought we could go riding this morning."

Harry couldn't contain her excitement. Diving off the bed she hurried over to the chest of drawers. Rummaging through her clothes, unable to find anything to wear, she turned to Pablo. "I haven't got anything suitable to ride in other than a pair of jeans and they are far too stiff." Pablo managed a laugh as she held them against her legs. They were boyfriend jeans, turned up at the bottoms, not ideal for riding in. Seeing the look of horror on Harry's face, Pablo took her by the hand and down the landing and into his sister's room. It was a clearly a girl's room. Beautiful dolls, in traditional Spanish costume, lined the window seat. A dressing table was covered in makeup and jewel boxes. An old dolls house sat on a chest of drawers; it was fully furnished and had been left open as if someone had just finished playing with it. Two beds situated side by side with lavender print duvets took up the centre of the room. An old rocking horse stood in front of the fire place.

"Here, you can borrow some of my sister's riding britches, I think they are all kept in this chest." Opening the drawer and rooting through it, he found several pairs of jodhpurs and handed them to Harry. "There are many pairs of boots downstairs by the kitchen door. There will be a pair that will fit you."

Harry held the jodhpurs against her and decided to take two pairs back to her room to try. Carefully folding the others and placing them back in the chest of drawers, they left the room as they had found it and headed back to Harry's room.

Pablo said he was going to get ready himself and would see Harry down in the kitchen when she was ready.

The first pair Harry could hardly get into so she awkwardly peeled them off and tried the second pair. These fitted perfectly round the waist but were too short in the legs. Still, they were all she had. Once completely dressed, with her own white polo shirt on and her hair tied back, she glanced in the mirror and decided the beige jodhpurs, although a little short, would do.

Entering the kitchen Harry found Pablo sitting talking with his grandfather. He sprang up telling Harry she looked great.

Papa greeted Harry with a kiss. "Did you sleep well, my dear?"

"Yes, thank you, I had a very good night. My room is so lovely and the bed was very comfortable." Pablo winked over Papa's shoulder at Harry who started blushing. Luckily Papa didn't notice. He beckoned Harry to the door and pointed to all the boots. Pablo, dressed in his dark-brown jodhpurs, with a white cotton baggy shirt on with the first three buttons undone, looked very handsome. His brown leather boots were slightly battered but shined up until you could see your face in them. Harry found some boots to fit and off they went through the walled garden and down the back road.

It was quite early; the air was still fresh and the sun still lay low in the sky. It was a perfect morning for riding. After entering the yard, Harry could see the stables, set out in rows, all immaculately whitewashed. A groom approached. He introduced himself to Pablo and Harry and explained Jose had been called away, but he was expecting them. Harry and Pablo followed him into the first row of stables where two horses, one black and the other palomino, were tacked-up, ready for them. They looked very proud, with their coats shining and their tack gleaming. Pablo thanked the groom and took Harry up to the palomino, which was slightly smaller in build than the black one.

"This horse is called Crème. She is very good girl and very nice to ride. I think she will be good for you." Pablo patted Crème before untying her and handing the reins to Harry.

"She is lovely, Pablo. How old is she?"

"She is sixteen now. I rode her when I was younger. Now I am too heavy so I shall be riding The Professor. He was named The Professor because he always thinks he has to teach you a lesson, don't you, old boy?"

Pablo patted the old Professor and ran his hand down the horse's front legs. He checked the girth, before untying him.

Harry followed Pablo as he led the way to the corral and a mounting block, where they both mounted. Harry checked her girth once she had mounted. It needed tightening up a notch so Pablo steered The Professor in front of Crème and leant down to hold Crème's reins while Harry adjusted the girth. Standing in the stirrups, Harry altered her girth too. The saddle felt strange at first. Harry was used to an English saddle; these were just like the saddles the cowboys used in the old westerns, with big box stirrups and pommels on the saddles.

Once they were both comfortable, Pablo told Harry to follow him down the road, until they reached the citrus orchards.

Crème arched her neck proudly as they stepped out onto the road. She had a lovely smooth stride that suited Harry.

Pablo tried to slow The Professor's pace down by turning him in circles. Not having much luck, he sat firmly in the saddle as The Professor trotted, bounced and side-stepped down the road. They had not gone far and Pablo was already leaving Harry behind. Pablo turned around and shouted back, "This is where we enter the Orchards. Once we are off the road come and ride next to me."

Harry saw him disappear up a path and squeezed Crème into a trot to catch up. The path was quite narrow to begin with and then opened into acres upon acres of lemon trees. Harry could see Pablo, up ahead, waiting for her. She continued in a rising trot, keeping in perfect time with Crème, until she caught up with Pablo.

Pawing at the ground with his front hoof, The Professor was itching to go. "How do you find Crème?"

"She is lovely. I am fine." Harry looked ahead. The orchard ran on for miles and miles, the smell of lemon wafting all around, and the path ahead clear.

"Come on, Pablo." Harry loosened her reins, clicked her tongue, and Crème was off.

Pablo took up the challenge. The Professor was ready to go. Like a coiled spring he leapt into action. Galloping along next to Crème, Pablo urged his horse on. The trees whipped past as they made their way up through the orchards.

"There is an irrigation ditch up ahead, Harry. Be careful!"

Harry sailed over the ditch and carried on through the arched fruit tunnels. Standing in her stirrups, leaning forward, the wind whistling past her head, for the first time in ages, Harry felt free. Pablo was now in line with Harry. They reached the end of the orchard together. Pulling their horses in, they slowed them down to a trot. The horses were panting and puffing. Harry felt quite breathless; she loved a good gallop. Pablo took the lead again and Harry followed. They went out of the bright, citrus-scented orchard and into some woodland. The landscape slowly reared up ahead of them. The smell of pine needles took over from the citrus fragrance as the landscape dramatically changed. The path vanished so they carefully picked their way through the trees to a clearing. A stream had sprung up in front of them and ran down into a deep pool.

"We can stop here and give the horses a drink." Pablo dismounted and led The Professor down to the cool clear water. Crème followed. Once they had both had a good drink, Pablo tied them to a fallen tree.

Harry followed him down to the pool and sat on a protruding rock. Pablo started to strip, taking his shirt off. "What are you doing, Pablo?" Harry screamed.

"Come on, the water will be lovely."

Harry shook her head. "No thank you, but please, you carry on."

Pablo laughed as he tore his jodhpurs off, balancing on one leg and trying not to fall as he revealed his white boxers. His body was glimmering with sweat. Harry thought to herself, *"what a hunk."* Having tossed his clothes over a branch, Pablo climbed onto a rock; throwing his arms over his head, he dived straight down into the clear water and disappeared.

Harry leant forward looking for him but there was no sign. Just as she was about to panic, up he came, inches away from where Harry had been looking.

He soaked her. "Come on in, you are all wet now anyway!"

"You meany!" Harry was quite mad. Her top was absolutely soaking. Stripping down to her bra and pants, she carefully placed her top over a branch where the sun could dry it, then stretched out on the smooth, flat rock, to sunbathe.

Pablo was not going to give up. He crept out of the water, around the back of the rock, and scooped Harry up into his arms. "You are coming in the water with me for a swim. I think you need to cool off."

Harry screamed and punched at his chest in protest but he was too strong for her.

He ran to the water's edge and jumped in with Harry in his arms. Throwing Harry clear of him as he hit the water, he didn't want to be near when she came up; he knew she would be very angry.

As Harry surfaced she looked around for Pablo who was swimming as fast as he could towards the other side of the pool. Harry broke into her best crawl and raced after him. Just as he tried to grab an overhanging branch from a tree to pull himself out of the water, Harry grabbed his shorts. Reaching round to free himself, the branch broke and he fell back, almost landing on top of Harry.

Resting on a rock, Pablo grabbed Harry by the arm and then, with all his strength, while she struggled to get away, he dragged her onto the rock. Harry could just about stand, so Pablo wrapped his arms around her and held her tightly until she stopped wriggling. Forcing his lips onto hers, he kissed her passionately. Harry's struggling slowly ceased as she melted to his kiss. His hands slid down her cool, wet body. Her nipples were firm and erect. He could feel them through her bra, rubbing against his chest. Pablo's tongue toyed with Harry's.

His body felt solid, strong, and muscular as Harry ran her hands over his shoulders and down his back.

Pablo held Harry by her shoulders and separated her body from his. "I want you so much. I cannot wait much longer."

"I want you too, Pablo, I have never felt this way about anyone before."

"Come on, we had better get back." Pablo sobered up as he remembered what he had to do later that day. They swam back across the pool to where the horses stood patiently waiting.

Once they had dressed, they mounted their horses and made their way back down through the woods, towards the orchards. This time, working their way around the outside of the orchard, they made their descent. The view of the village was spectacular. Pablo pointed out the village, the church, and the square where the men played boule and the women sat and gossiped. Small grocery shops surrounded the square; it even had a little restaurant, bar and coffee shop that spilled out onto the square.

It was just like a postcard. Harry could see the vineyard and farmhouse she was staying in. She wished she had her camera with her to take some photos to show her family and her friend, Julie, when she got back to England. She caught up with Pablo who had been very quiet for the past fifteen minutes. "What are you thinking about?"

"I was just thinking how I could keep you here, with me, forever."

"Me too. We must sit down and talk about the future. I don't want to, but we must."

Pablo nodded and pushed The Professor into a trot. Having a lot on his mind, he didn't want to even think about their future until he had sorted Conchitta out for the last time. Why did everything have to be so complicated?

As they got back to the stables, the groom appeared and held the horses while Harry and Pablo dismounted. Harry said she would like to un-tack Crème and put her away, and Pablo agreed. Having collected the grooming kit from the tack room, Harry rubbed and brushed Crème all over. Harry led her into her stable. She had a clean bed of shavings, a full hay net and a fresh bucket of water. Harry untied her halter, patted her on her neck, and made her way out of the stable door.

Pablo had gone to put the tack away. As he placed the saddles on a rack, he spotted a newspaper on a stool. It was the Costa Brava Fun and was lying open on the article about Conchitta. Hoping Harry had not spotted it when she had gone in to get the grooming kit, he quickly closed the paper and turned it over. As he turned around to leave, the groom stood in the doorway with a smirk on his face. He had obviously been reading it. Pablo pulled a few crumpled, damp notes out of his top pocket and handed it to the groom and, without a word, placed his finger over his lips, thus indicating the boy was not to say anything.

Harry was talking to The Professor over his stable door when Pablo returned. She looked up and smiled at him.

Good, Pablo thought to himself, she hadn't noticed the paper. Pablo took Harry by the hand and led her away as quickly as he could. He did not know how many other grooms had seen the paper. As they left the yard a few girls entered and starred, quizzically, at Pablo and Harry. Pablo stepped up their walking pace; he would not feel safe until they were back up at the farmhouse again.

Papa had laid on a nice assortment of cold meats; chorizo, ham, pork, as well as cheese and a fresh baguette. He had already eaten and had left them a note to say he had gone to the village for some groceries. He said he may be a few hours as he was also going to pop in on an old friend. Pablo and Harry, although quite damp from their swim, had built up quite an appetite and demolished everything in sight. Once they had eaten, Pablo explained he had to go out for a few hours; he had some business he had to sort out.

Harry said she would be fine and would find something to do. While she washed, and put away the dishes, Pablo showered and changed. He returned, smelling fresh, cleanly shaved, and wearing a pair of khaki jeans and a white T shirt, jacket, and sand boots. He said he would be as quick as he could. Just as he was about to leave, having kissed Harry goodbye, he remembered there had been a message left by Harry's door. Harry's mother had phoned and she would call back later. Once again he kissed Harry goodbye, then left.

Harry finished tidying up the kitchen and then headed up for a shower herself. She was still damp and beginning to feel very uncomfortable. Her wet underwear had dried to her body and she couldn't wait to get it all off and dress in something clean.

After showering, she looked out of the window in her bedroom. The sun was high in the sky. Putting on her bikini, she grabbed her book, sunglasses and a towel, and headed out to the garden to find a nice sun trap.

Chapter 22

Pablo arrived at his parents' villa. Conchitta's car was parked outside. He made his way through the locked gate. Luckily he kept a key for it with his car keys. The press must have bothered his parents again if they were having to keep everywhere locked up.

Conchitta sat on the terrace with Pablo's father and mother. As Pablo approached she sprang to her feet and threw her arms around him. "Pablo, my darling! Isn't it good news? You are going to be a father."

Pablo peeled her off, glancing at his father who had raised his eyes to the skies. Jordi turned to Isabel and suggested they left Pablo and Conchitta to their discussions.

Once they were alone, Pablo lost his temper. "What do you think you are playing at, Conchitta. You know very well we have not slept together for months."

Conchitta smiled sweetly. "Pablo, I seem to remember the night of your party. It was only a couple of weeks ago; we had a fantastic night together, when everyone had left. It was very late, you asked me to stay over, and we both fell asleep in each-other's arms."

"Conchitta, you know we never had sex. We had a few dances. I had far too much to drink and staggered up to bed and fell asleep. You just got into my bed, uninvited, and slept next to me." He was beginning to calm down a bit now.

Conchitta was not at all fazed by his outburst. Always as cool as a cucumber, she just sat playing with a straw in a glass of iced water. "Pablo, we had sex and, when I was a week overdue, I had a pregnancy test and it was positive. My parents are very happy and will remain so. I have told them you have just had a fling with a little college girl, a tart from England, and it meant nothing to you. We are going to get engaged."

"Don't you ever speak about Harry like that! You know she is the one I love. Why are you so cruel?"

"At the moment, Pablo, you are clearly quite infatuated with her! I am the one carrying your child. I am the one that has loved you ever since we were children. I am the one you know you want to marry."

"Listen, Conchitta, I do not want to marry you and I don't believe for a minute you are pregnant. If you are, where is the note from the doctor with the result of your pregnancy test?"

Conchitta reached down and picked up her handbag. Opening the zip, she pulled out a note and slid it across the table to Pablo.

Snatching the note from Conchitta's hand and glancing over the note, Pablo could not believe his eyes. It clearly stated Conchitta was pregnant. Screwing the note up, he threw it back at Conchitta.

"I want to speak to your doctor. I do not believe for one moment this is a legitimate note. Once I have spoken to your doctor, if, and only if, you are pregnant, I will want a test done, proving that the baby is mine. Only then will I consider what to do about the child. But you, you can go take a running jump. I will never want anything to do with you. You are nothing but a manipulative, screwed-up girl. Make the arrangements and let me know when I can speak to your doctor, or would it be better if I phoned him myself to make the arrangements?" He was hoping, if she were lying, he would frighten her into a confession at this point with his outburst.

Conchitta was not giving in that easily. Pablo's parents' money was all she wanted. "Okay, I will phone and make an appointment for you to see my doctor, and then we must discuss what is to be done, when we will get engaged, and where we will live. There is so much to sort out. Let me go and phone my doctor now."

Was Conchitta calling Pablo's bluff? There was only one way to find out. Taking the phone from the stand in the lounge, he spoke in a calmer voice. "Here, you can use the house phone. You must know your own doctor's number." Pablo handed the phone to Conchitta.

Her long, bright red nails, tapped the number in and waited. "Hello. Could I make an appointment for Conchitta Causape and Pablo Cruanos to see Doctor Carmen? Next week, on Monday, at ten." Pablo nodded.

"Yes, that will be fine, I'm sure he knows what it's all about. Thank you". Conchitta triumphantly handed the phone back to Pablo.

"Right, I will pick you up next week on Monday at nine, and we shall see who's telling the truth, then."

Conchitta collected her bag up from the table and turned to leave. Pablo watched as she strutted down the path to the gate that he had left open. As she went through the gate, she turned to see if he was watching her, then blew him a kiss.

Pablo got to his feet, and went into the villa, to find his parents. His father handed him a small brandy to calm him down. He explained to them that she was not prepared to retract her statement and so he had made an appointment with her doctor to find out the truth.

His father said it was the only way.

Once Pablo had got it all off his chest he calmed down.

His father told him all the arrangements for the launch for Ski-Summer were set for Saturday, and Harry's parents were going to meet them there with Christina and the twins. Isabel had seen quite a lot of Anna and they had become quite good friends, in the last twenty four hours.

Chapter 23

Pablo arrived back at the farmhouse late in the afternoon. He entered through the front door and shouted around for Harry. There was not a reply anywhere in the house so he headed through the kitchen and out into the garden. Spotting Harry in a secluded area, where she was reading a book, he quietly crept over. Harry was so engrossed in her book, with her headphones on and her CD player pumping away, that she never heard a thing.

Pablo slipped his hands over Harry's eyes. "Guess who it is?"

"Is it someone with dark eyes, black hair, and very kissable lips?" Harry swung her feet to the ground and, dropping her book, put her arms up to embrace Pablo.

Leaning down, he kissed her soft, full lips, and then sat down beside her. "Good news. The Ski-Summer launch is to go ahead next Saturday. We have to arrive at two thirty p.m. for drinks."

"Oh, that's brilliant news. What should I wear? I don't think I have anything suitable."

"How do you fancy a day shopping in Barcelona, and then we could stay the night at my parents' apartment or a hotel, so we can take our time?"

"Oh yes, I would love that, but I only have a little money with me and in the hurry to leave I left my bankcard in the villa. I should go back to S'agaro, to get it."

"Don't worry about that. I have plenty of money. It will be my treat. I will phone and organise something for tomorrow night. Is that okay?"

"Yes, that will be great, I'm so excited!"

Standing up, Pablo took off his jacket. "I must go and shower again, I am really hot".

Pablo headed back towards the house and Harry stayed in the sun until she had finished the chapter she was reading. Her tan nicely topped up after an afternoon in the sun, she too was hot and went up for another cooling shower.

Once she heard Pablo leave the bathroom, Harry entered and showered. No wonder the Spanish stopped work for the afternoon and started again in the evening. While Harry was soaping herself down in the shower, she heard the door open. Pablo came back into the bathroom wearing nothing but a towel. Harry was still in the shower so he asked if she minded if he had a shave while she was showering.

Harry said she didn't mind so Pablo got his razor out, wiped the steam from the mirror then, filling the sink up with hot water, he lathered his face and, with a cut-throat blade, began scraping his stubble away. While he was shaving, he could not help glancing sideways at the shower. He could see Harry's silhouette through the translucent screen. The steaming water was cascading down her firm, tanned body. As the bubbles washed away, her body became more visible. Feeling himself begin to harden, Pablo tried to concentrate on his shaving. His towel was riding up and he wanted to leave the bathroom before Harry saw him. Just as Harry turned the shower off, Pablo frantically splashed his face with fresh water, rinsed the sink, and hurried back into his bedroom.

Harry heard the door shut, and stepped from the shower.

Once he had dried and dressed, Pablo joined Harry in her room. She had not even had the chance to get dressed. Sitting at the mirror in her robe, she was applying some moisturizer to her arms and legs. Pablo sat on the window seat, studying her every move. He was smiling.

"What are you smiling at, Pablo? Why are you looking so happy?"

"I just like to watch you. You are so beautiful. I feel so lucky, that I met you".

Harry stood up, saying she wanted to put some clothes on, and asked Pablo to turn away while she dressed. Pablo stood up, and turned around. Facing the window he stared out at his grandfather's garden. Harry, dropping her robe, found a thong in the drawer and put it on. Pablo was just wearing jeans and a T-shirt, so Harry slipped into her three-quarter-length jeans and a white, fitted T-shirt. When she swung round to tell Pablo he could now look, he turned around laughing. He had been standing in front of the window and had caught Harry's reflection as she dressed.

"You are awful." Harry collapsed on the bed, laughing.

Pablo dived on top of her. Pinning her down by her arms, legs straddling her body, he leant forward and kissed her. "Papa is still not back yet. Why don't I make love to you now?"

Harry kissed him back, passionately. "No, Pablo, not yet. I would be too nervous and worried Papa may arrive at any moment. You must wait."

Pablo released Harry from his grip, and got off her. "You are such a tease. Come, let's go down and I will make a phone call. Did you phone your mother?"

"Yes, I rang her earlier from the kitchen. I waited until I knew they would be back at the villa having lunch. My Mum said she has met your mother and she likes her very much. I think they are becoming good friends."

Pablo was relieved Harry had spoken to her mother. Anna knew what was going on with the press and Conchitta. She obviously had not said anything to Harry and was giving Pablo a chance to sort things out. He just hoped they would survive the trip to Barcelona without being spotted. Still, now they knew the press were on to them, it would be a lot easier to go in disguise. He made the phone call, booking them into a hotel. He thought this best as the press might be camped outside his parents' apartment in Barcelona, and Harry had agreed. He booked a room with twin queen-sized beds. Although his body was aching with love and he wanted Harry so much, he still thought it best not to push her, but to wait until she was ready.

Pablo cut some fruit up and made a jug of Tisana which they took out to the garden, and sat at the table. They had a laugh, talking about their ride earlier in the day and about Harry's skiing. Pablo confessed he had watched her for some time that day, and how impressed he had been with her skiing. Halfway through their second jug of Tisana, Papa arrived back, quite merry after a visit with his friend. He was carrying an iron dish of piping hot paella which he had picked up from the restaurant for their dinner. Pablo and Harry ran into the house for some plates, cutlery, serviettes, and another glass. The paella looked and smelt delicious. Pablo dished it up while Harry filled their glasses. The rice was full of shellfish, octopus, prawns, and mussels. Harry carefully took the shells off her fish and spooned the feast into her mouth, savouring the assortment of flavours. Pablo and Papa tucked in and ate, systematically shelling their fish, and finished long before Harry had broken and consumed her last king prawn.

Wiping her mouth and hands with a serviette, she had finished. "That was lovely Papa. It's the first paella I've had this year and it was delicious."

Papa agreed it was good, but not one of the best paella's he had eaten from the local restaurant.

Papa stood up, saying he was tired after an afternoon with his friend, and he was going to have an early night.

Pablo could see he was a little unsteady on his feet and walked back to the house with him.

Once they had gone, Harry placed all the plates into the empty paella dish and carried them into the kitchen to wash up. The Tisana was beginning to influence her too.

When Pablo came down he said he had put Papa to bed. Papa had been playing dominoes with his friend and they had consumed quite a lot of local wine.

Taking a coffee back to the garden, and sitting themselves down, they decided it was time they talked about the future. They both agreed that when they were in Barcelona they would have some fun. Pablo asked Harry if she had thought about going back to England.

Harry had thought a lot about it. She was still quite young and should go back to finish her course, but she loved Pablo so much she did not know if she would be able to leave him.

Pablo desperately wanted to ask Harry to get engaged, but something held him back. At the back of his mind he needed to get rid of Conchitta first. It made him feel like a two-timer, even though he was not doing anything wrong. He was only protecting Harry from a lot of unnecessary upset. He was now beginning to hate Conchitta. Until she was out of the way, there was nothing he could do to get rid of the uneasy feeling he had.

After a lot of discussion they had not been able to reach an agreement. Pablo could not persuade Harry to stay until he knew there was not a baby and he could offer her the security she would need.

Harry felt that Pablo did not want her to stay that much or he would have asked her. He kept saying he loved her. All he had to do was ask but, if he could not do this, maybe it would be best if she just went back to England.

That night when they went to bed, Pablo kissed Harry goodnight and went down the corridor to his own room. Harry curled up in bed with her book. This time she did not fall straight to sleep but read for ages. Finally, just as she turned the light out, the bathroom door opened. In walked Pablo.

"Harry, are you asleep yet?"

Harry leant over and turned on the light. Pulling the quilt back, she beckoned to Pablo who walked over to the bed and, taking his robe off, slid in next to Harry. Harry turned the light out and snuggled into Pablo's arms.

Pablo kissed her gently on the forehead and wrapped his arms around her before he was overtaken with sleep. He'd had a long, hard, day and was shattered.

Pablo woke early and crept out of bed. He showered, got dressed, then went down to the kitchen. He greeted Papa who was already sitting eating breakfast. Having made himself a cup of coffee, Pablo seated himself at the kitchen table. Papa listened while Pablo relayed the previous day's events. He told Papa the big Ski-Summer launch was going to be on Saturday and how he was worried about the press tracking them down at the farm after some people at the stables recognised them yesterday. He knew Papa deserved the whole story, so he also filled him in on what was happening with Conchitta. Papa had already seen a copy of the paper with Conchitta's story in. He also thought it was time they moved on again. Pablo said they were booked into a hotel in Barcelona and would spend the next couple of days there. On Saturday they would travel straight to Banyoles from the Hotel. This way he hoped they would stay ahead of the press. Papa wrote the name and number of the hotel down so he would be able to contact them if the need arose. Pablo also made him write down his mobile number. Papa insisted he already had it but Pablo did not want to take any chances.

Having made up a tray for Harry, Pablo went up to wake her. He wanted to get an early start so as not to be stuck on the road, bumper to bumper with tourists in the middle of the day. His little English Rose was still fast asleep. Her face was perfect. Leaning over the bed, Pablo kissed Harry's tempting, soft lips. Harry's eyes flickered open as she woke. She sleepily rubbed them and stretched her arms over her head.

"Hello, my little English Rose. Did you sleep well?"

Harry smiled up at him. He smelt of freshly made coffee. Struggling to sit up, as she was not properly awake, she propped her pillow up behind her back.

Pablo placed the tray in front of her and explained he would like to get away as quickly as possible. Pablo sat and watched Harry eat some fresh bread with strawberry jam and poured her a rich cup of coffee. He then left while she got up to get dressed. Returning to his own bedroom he packed a bag with enough clothes to last him a few days.

Harry showered and dressed quickly. By the time Pablo appeared she had nearly finished packing. "Shall I take everything or just a few items of clothing to last me the next few days?"

"Just put a few things in. The weather is good; you don't need many clothes. We can always buy anything you need if you don't have it." Harry threw the last few bits in she wanted to take and was ready to go.

While Pablo took the bags to the car, Harry went out and found Papa out in the garden. He was pruning the dead heads off his prize roses. Harry gave him a big cuddle and thanked him for letting her stay. She hoped he would make it to the Ski-Summer launch on Saturday as she would like him to meet her family. He said he wasn't sure; it wasn't really his sort of thing and insisted she must come back to stay. They were just having a farewell cuddle when Pablo arrived. Papa embraced his grandson then followed them through the kitchen and out to the front of the house where he waved them off. As the car pulled away both Pablo and Harry felt very sad. Harry looked back and waved. She could see Papa wiping the tears from his eyes. He was a lovely old man and she truly hoped she would be back to see him soon.

Chapter 24

The drive to Barcelona was very smooth and quick. Within two hours of leaving the farm they were winding their way through the old back streets of the magnificent city with its tall yellowed apartment blocks towering over the dusty narrow streets. Pablo explained this was a short cut to the hotel to cut out the one-way system that he did not want to get stuck on.

At last they had reached the Hotel Grande, a magnificent modern structure made entirely of granite and glass. Although a modern building it didn't look out of place in the old city. Pablo suggested they both put on their sunglasses before they got out of the car. Harry rummaged in her bag and found hers and placed them on her head. A porter arrived and opened the door for Harry while Pablo went around to the back of the car and took out the bags. Once the porter had escorted Harry up the steps to the rotating glass doors, he took the car keys from Pablo.

He then beckoned another porter over to take their luggage in while he parked the car.

The foyer was extremely cool and spacious with black and white marble flooring, large green palms everywhere and a large seating area with black leather sofas and chairs. There were chequered coffee tables littered with daily papers and copies of Hello. The ceiling was very high. Glass chandeliers and rotating fans hung amongst the crisscross Spanish architrave. The porter took their bags to a service lift. Pablo confirmed their booking and collected the room key. Another porter was summoned and led the way to a glass lift in the corner of the foyer. The view from the lift was spectacular. It slid smoothly up the outside of the Hotel displaying a panoramic view. By the time they reached the twentieth floor Harry could see right across the city.

The porter ushered them down the lavishly decorated corridor and stopped outside room 220. He unlocked the door and led the way in. Pablo thought there must be a mistake. They stepped into the large sitting room with a maroon leather suite surrounding a smoked-glass topped coffee table. Double glazed doors lead out onto a balcony. From the lounge another set of double doors lead into a huge bedroom with a king-sized bed and wall to wall mirror fronted wardrobes. There was Champagne chilling in an ice bucket set out on a side table in the lounge, and a large flower arrangement on the coffee table.

Pablo plucked a card protruding from the arrangement and opened it. "To Harry and Pablo, relax and enjoy the city, all my love, Papa."

Harry took the note from Pablo and read it again to herself. "That was sweet of him, Pablo. He's so thoughtful."

Pablo nodded and suggested they brought him a present when they went shopping. The porter was waiting by the door and, once he was satisfied they were happy he took his leave, but not before Pablo tipped him generously.

Pablo opened the mini bar and asked Harry if she would like a drink before they started unpacking. Harry had a bottle of water while she nosed around the rooms. The bathroom was richly decorated in maroon tiles with gold trim. There was a sunken bath with a built- in Jacuzzi; all the taps were gold plated. Fat maroon towels lay draped over the warming rail. New soaps, creams and shower hats filled a basket placed on the counter between the his-and-hers sinks.

Harry went back into the bedroom and started to unpack, placing her underwear in the chest of drawers next to the bed and hanging what few garments she had brought with her in part of the wardrobe.

Pablo called her back into the lounge. He had opened double doors onto the balcony, beckoning for Harry to follow him out. In one corner were two wicker chairs and a table. At the other end were two wicker sun loungers with maroon cushions. Pablo pulled Harry into his arms. "It's just perfect. Don't you think so?"

Harry, delighted with the hotel, kissed him appreciatively on the lips before replying. "It's fantastic, Pablo. Come and unpack and then we can go out to see the sights and get some lunch."

Pablo placed his clothes in the chest of drawers on the other side of the bed and hung a few garments in the wardrobe.

Harry tied her hair up in a baseball cap and put on her sunglasses, determined she would not be recognised. Pablo wore a black bandanna and a pair of sunglasses. They both laughed as they looked at each other. Harry looked very young and a little innocent with her hair twisted up in the navy cap. Pablo looked like a rock star as they headed out of the hotel and into the street.

Before long they had made their way onto the ramp that connected Maremaghum, the shopping and free time area, with La Rambla. Pablo thought La Rambla would be a good place to go to find something to eat. As they crossed the ramp Pablo pointed out the Columbus monument and told Harry how it was pointing in the wrong direction because it pointed to the Mediterranean Sea and not to America. Next they went to look at the Place Reial. This was next to La Rambla. It was a very popular square with many bars, restaurants, and discos. Harry and Pablo weaved their way in and out of the palm trees and headed for the Glaciar bar. This was a famous bar and very popular, so they decided not to stop there and headed for La Rambla.

All the time they walked Pablo acted as Harry's tour guide, keeping up a commentary of where they were and places of interest to look at. "This is one of the most famous streets in Barcelona. It is La Rambla."

Harry looked down the crowded tree-lined Rambla with its central sidewalk littered with kiosks, flowers, and birds shading in the trees and chirping overhead. There were people of every nationality buzzing around. They wandered up and down, hand in hand, looking at the tall, old buildings until they reached the Sant Pau. Pablo said there was a little restaurant in this street he thought they could eat in.

The Romesco was nearly always full but Pablo managed to find them a little table for two tucked away in the corner. Pablo knew what he was going to order. It was a place he had been to on several occasions with his friends. The waiter appeared. Ordering the house specialty and a bottle of wine for them both, Pablo assured Harry she was in for a treat. They sat amongst young foreigners and locals alike enjoying the noisy and exciting atmosphere. The waiter arrived with the wine and a basket of bread. Pablo offered Harry some bread to eat.

Taking a piece Harry broke some off and popped it into her mouth. The Spanish wine was very cold, light, and drinkable. Harry thought she would go steady as it was only lunch time and she wanted to see quite a lot of the city that day.

The house specialty arrived. Pablo explained it was a Spanish-Caribbean dish that consisted of black beans, mince, rice, and fried banana.

Harry said it sounded revolting, then she tasted it. Finding it delicious, she asked Pablo what it was called.

"It is a dish called Frijoles." While they ate their lunch, using only forks, Pablo told Harry about the sites of Barcelona. They decided to head for the Cathedral. Harry had seen it many years ago with her parents but the memory had faded and she had not appreciated its splendour as a child.

The cathedral looked like a huge cluster of stalagmites from a distance. As they neared it, the sculptures became visible.

"This is the Cathedral. It was designed by Antoni Gaudi; the construction began in 1884. It is still being built and will not be finished until the twenty second century. To carry on building it they rely on money from donations. Antoni Gaudi was a very religious man. He lived in the Sagra Familia. Another artist now lives in the building. Subirachs. He is the sculptor who is now doing the rest of the other facade's sculptures. Some people believe it should not be finished but should be left as it is."

Harry and Pablo wandered around the outside of the cathedral in silence, admiring its many wonders. They climbed up to the platform tower and took a closer look at the sculptures that formed the arch over the entrance. Harry could see now why her parents raved about it when she was a child. She also understood how, for a child, it was not much fun.

Ending their afternoon at the Olympic Village Neighborhood, with Pablo doing his tour guide bit again, he explained how it had been built in 1992 for the Olympic Games next to the harbour. Pablo threw his hands out. "This was where the Olympic sportsmen lived. Barcelona rediscovered the Mediterranean Sea and transformed the old industrial neighbourhood into a modern marine village."

Harry and Pablo walked along the narrow paths separating the marina from the mainland, admiring the old yachts and the modern power boats. For a while they walked around playing a game, each picking out their very own favourite. They fantasised about escaping on one and sailing around the world together.

The marine village held many little bars and restaurants. Choosing one right on the waterfront, Pablo and Harry seated themselves. Ordering a glass of iced tea, they sat and reminisced about the sites they had seen that day. The iced tea arrived and vanished in no time. It had been a hot sticky afternoon and Harry felt quite dehydrated. Pablo ordered them another iced tea that they sipped down slowly this time, before they hailed a cab and made their way back to the hotel.

Chapter 25

Harry, totally exhausted, decided to take a relaxing bath. While Harry was undressing in the bedroom, Pablo filled the bath up, poured some oils in, and switched the Jacuzzi on. Harry arrived wearing only the plush maroon bathrobe that she found folded up in one of the drawers. Pablo left the room while Harry slipped out of her robe and got into the Jacuzzi. The water was warm but not hot. Harry slid down onto a ledge making the water lap over her shoulders, her whole body submerged in the bubbling water. It was a real tonic; she was feeling really relaxed. The bubbles fizzed against her skin leaving it tingling and refreshed. Some music boomed out of the walls. Pablo had turned the CD player on and music seeped out of the bathroom speakers hidden amongst the tiles. Pablo adjusted the volume a little and arrived into the bathroom wearing a matching complimentary hotel robe and carrying the chilled bottle of Champagne and two crystal flutes. Placing them on the edge of the bath he leant over and kissed Harry on the lips. "Is it okay if I join you?"

Harry suddenly felt very embarrassed as she was naked. "Okay," she stammered. Closing her eyes she slipped deeper into the Jacuzzi while Pablo slipped his robe off and climbed in.

Pouring them a drink, he handed one to Harry and sat down in the bubbling water on the ledge opposite. Then, raising his glass, he said, "Cheers, I think you say in England. Here is to a nice stay in Barcelona."

Harry raised her glass to touch his. "Salut!"

Pablo sat with a grin on his face studying Harry's face. He could tell she was slightly embarrassed. He liked that. It made him love her more and made him want to protect her. She was so innocent. He was desperate for her now. Finishing his glass, he beckoned Harry to drink hers up so he could refill both of their glasses.

Harry emptied hers and handed it to Pablo. Once Pablo had finished his second glass he leaned towards Harry, taking her half- filled glass from her hand and placing it on the side of the bath. Taking her hands, he pulled her into his arms. Feeling her warm, smooth, naked body against his, he quickly became aroused. Her nipples were now erect on her small firm breasts as they brushed against his brown chest.

Harry felt nervous. She had been waiting for this to happen ever since she met Pablo and had fallen deeply in love with him. It felt right but, even so, she still felt nervous. Pablo kissed Harry gently on the lips, and she kissed him back. All the time his hands were running over her body, exploring every part of it. Their kissing became increasingly passionate and frenzied as they explored each other's mouths with their tongues.

"Let us go to the bedroom," Pablo whispered in a husky voice. Climbing out of the bath, Pablo placed a towel around his waist, and handed Harry her robe.

Harry, still embarrassed about Pablo seeing her naked, took the robe and put it on quickly as she climbed out of the bath.

Pablo led the way into the bedroom. The bedside lights were dimmed and the bedcovers had been turned back. Once they reached the bed Pablo untied Harry's robe and stood for a moment looking at her. Her body was beautiful. There was one little white triangle surrounding her heart-shaped black, fluffy, down. Pablo slid his hands inside Harry's robe and dropped it to the ground, leaving her completely naked. He lifted her into his arms and kissed her lips as he gently lowered her onto the bed.

Removing his towel he lay on the bed, propped up on one elbow, whilst he traced a finger down her body.

Harry looked up into his dark brown, eyes and whispered the words, "I love you".

Pablo kissed her face as his hands gently roamed over her breasts, stopping now and again to play with her nipples. Harry's kiss was getting increasingly responsive as Pablo pushed his tongue in and out of her mouth. Gliding down her body, slowly, his mouth paused when it reached her breast. His lips surrounded a nipple and he gently sucked on it.

Harry's hands were running through Pablo's hair and down his firm muscular back. He did have a fantastic body.

Pablo moved his lips back to meet hers as he slipped his hand down to her thigh, gently massaging the inside of her leg until he found his way in. His finger probed gently into the warm, moist opening, working its way in deeper and deeper. Harry's breathing was getting stronger and louder as Pablo gently moved to concentrate on her G spot and gently teased it with the tip of his finger. Finally, Pablo moved on top of Harry and parted her legs. He could not wait a moment longer. His whole body aching and about to burst, he pushed his hard, firm penis inside her.

Harry gasped as she felt a slight pain and then relaxed as Pablo gently pulled himself back out, before pushing back into her, this time deeper. He presumed she was a virgin but, up until this point, he was not sure.

Harry was losing control as her pelvis moved in time with Pablo's. The rhythm quickened as every second passed. Harry could feel her body tingle all over and let out a cry as Pablo had one last hard thrust into her.

Lowering himself gently on top of Harry, Pablo remained motionless for a moment before propping himself up, on his elbows. He gazed into Harry's deep blue eyes. "I love you", he whispered, before kissing Harry's forehead, nose, and lips.

Once again, she kissed him.

Gently he pulled himself out of her and wrapped his arm around her shoulder as he lay on his back next to her. He pulled the bed clothes up to his waist. "Your body is wonderful. It is the most beautiful body I have ever seen, and now it will always be mine."

Harry snuggled her head into Pablo's shoulder and placed her arm over his broad chest, and there they slept, exhausted, finally fulfilled and feeling deeply content and in love.

Having slept late, Pablo phoned down to order room service. Donning their robes, they took their breakfast out onto the balcony, feasting on croissants, fresh fruit juice and coffee. The sun was already high in the sky and the street below was busy with black and yellow cabs cruising up and down the road, businessmen hurrying to meetings, people shopping, and the whole of the city was wide awake. Harry and Pablo were in no hurry to go anywhere. They took pleasure in breaking the fresh doughy pastry, smothering it in fruit jellies and then slowly eating, watching each other's every move and holding each other's gaze. Once they had finished, they decided they ought to go shopping at some point in the day to get Harry something to wear for the Ski-Summer launch.

Pablo showered while Harry busied herself by tidying up their room. After Pablo had finished Harry stepped into the shower. Floating on cloud nine, she felt relaxed and happy. Covering herself in gel, and lathering it up with a sea sponge, she rinsed the rich lather off under the powerful jets. Wrapping herself in a towel, she headed back to the bedroom.

Pablo dressed, wearing beige chinos and a navy Polo shirt. When Harry appeared, dripping wet and wearing only a towel, Pablo couldn't resist her. Grabbing the towel, he tried to pull it off. Harry struggled, and playfully fought him off. Finally, unable to keep up the fight, they fell on the bed together laughing.

"Come on, Harry, please. I want you now." Pablo kissed her gently on the lips, as he tugged at her towel. She smelt of expensive soap and her mouth tasted of toothpaste. Her body felt irresistible. Harry surrendered as she pulled Pablo's polo shirt up and hoisted it over his head.

Undoing his chinos, Pablo jumped up and ripped them off, boxers and all. With one swipe he removed Harry's towel. Massaging his hand down over her flat stomach and down to her little mass of dark hair, he slid his finger inside her; she was hot, moist, and ready for him. He slipped his firm, erect, penis inside her and brought her slowly to ecstasy, holding back himself; like a pot about to explode, they came together. Lying back on the bed next to Harry, he asked her when they could get married.

Harry kissed him and jumped up. "I will marry you when you get down on one knee and ask me like a gentleman." Scooping up her towel and tossing her wet hair over her shoulders, she strutted back into the bathroom.

Chapter 26

Pablo had ordered a cab from their room and, as soon as they had seen one pull up outside the hotel, they made their descent. The hotel foyer was bustling with the day's activities as they discreetly made their way to the entrance. The heat of the day engulfed them as they stepped out into the midday sun. The porter had spotted them; he pointed out to the cab. Pablo nodded so he hurried out ahead of them holding the cab door open.

Harry jumped in and slid across the black, leather seat, closely followed by Pablo.

Pablo asked the cab driver to take them to El Groc. On their way, Pablo explained to Harry it was a very good shop that did both men's and women's clothing, and that his sisters shopped there regularly.

El Groc was the boutique they had passed when they had been in the Rambla. Pablo had pointed it out to Harry. She had liked the look of the beautifully designed dresses in the window.

"Toni Miro is the designer at the shop, and he is one of the most admired Catalan designers. His clothes are designed with a very distinctive flair. I think we will find you something there."

The driver pulled up as near to the Rambla as he could get. The traffic was heavy so they decided it would be quicker to make the final part of the journey on foot, cutting through an alleyway which took them out on to the Rambla near the shop.

Pablo held the door for Harry who led the way into the shop. It was a richly designed, spacious shop separated into two sections by a seating area, with sofas and a coffee table littered with glossy magazines. A wealthy looking woman, with golden accessories, was being served by the smartly-dressed female assistant. Harry glanced around the room, at the rails of dresses, suits, and lingerie. Expensive shoes were dotted intermittently on small display shelves. Hats and tiaras sprang out above the clothes rails. Harry did not know where to start. In the middle of the room a cabinet, housing costume jewellery, caught Harry's eye, and she peered into it. There was a beautiful silver necklace, with matching tear-drop earrings, bracelet, and ring.

"Look, Pablo, aren't they just beautiful?"

Just as Pablo glanced into the cabinet the assistant came over, introduced herself, and offered her services. Pablo explained they had a big function to go to and Harry needed something nice to wear. It was a daytime function that would probably run into the early evening.

The assistant took Harry off to the changing room which was situated near the sofas. Beckoning Harry to take her clothes off, she handed Harry a robe and left her to it.

While Harry was getting undressed, the assistant brought Pablo a fresh cup of coffee and asked him to sit down, whilst she brought some dresses out to show him. Pablo sat down and leafed through some magazines and the assistant went back into the changing room with a tape measure.

Harry undid the front of her robe and the assistant complimented her slim figure whilst taking her measurements.

The first dress she appeared with was a purple, off-the-shoulder, silk dress. Pablo had said it was quite elegant, so the assistant took it into Harry and helped her into it. Harry considered her outfit in the mirror; it was a very pretty dress but she was not over keen. The assistant found some purple shoes for Harry to try with the dress; it looked better with the heels on.

Harry went out and showed Pablo. Pretending to be a catwalk model, she turned this way and that. Pablo agreed it was an appropriate choice, but not the dress he would have chosen for her; he did not think the colour was right.

Harry was relieved; she had never been keen on purple. Next came a short black dress. Helping Harry into the dress, the assistant gave Harry the correct shoes to complement it, and sent Harry back into the shop to show Pablo. Pablo shook his head straight away. It was the sort of dress that flattered Harry, as it clung to her, but was not what he had in mind.

"This is one of my favourite dresses. It is one of Toni Miro's most recent designs, and the material is irresistible." The assistant held up a long, white dress. It looked just the sort of thing Pablo had imagined. The assistant took the dress into Harry and helped her into it. It fitted like a glove. The neckline was beautifully cut. Little silver straps held the dress in place over Harry's slender shoulders, leaving her back exposed and sitting seductively over the top of her bottom. From there it clung loosely down to her knees, before it splayed out to the floor. At the front it emphasized her firm breasts, fitting closely to her flat stomach and kicking out below her knees. Slipping her feet into the little, white, strappy sandals, also designed by Miro, Harry glided out of the changing rooms to where Pablo was sitting patiently.

As soon as he saw Harry he stood up, holding his arms out. His English Rose glided towards him. He was speechless; the dress was perfect. She looked both sophisticated and innocent. "You look fantastic." Taking her hand, he turned her round. He hadn't noticed the back. It was so seductive; he loved the whole effect.

"Yes, I like this one." Harry agreed. She was excited. The dress felt wonderful. She knew the minute she put it on she wanted it. "How much is it Pablo? Ask the assistant."

Pablo shook his head. "Does it matter how much it will cost? We both agree this is the one. You go back and get dressed. I will sort out the bill."

The assistant was obviously very pleased with her sale. She had just sold one of the most expensive dresses in the shop. After she had helped Harry out of the dress, she returned to Pablo with the garment and shoes, and wrapped them carefully, the dress in tissue-paper and the shoes in their box. Pablo asked if he could see some costume jewellery, to match the dress. The assistant took him over to the cabinet and pointed to a simple pair of silver, twisted earrings, with a matching necklace, bangle, and ring.

"This is a very nice set, designed by Chelo Sastre. She would not be able to wear the necklace, because of the neckline of the dress; it is too high. She looks so innocent in the dress, I think it would be vulgar to put anything heavy on her."

Pablo agreed and asked the assistant to wrap it up separately and give it to him. He wanted the jewellery as a surprise for Harry. Before he settled the bill, he headed into the men's section, still unsure of what he should wear.

The male assistant introduced himself, before taking Pablo around the various racks of Miro's designer menswear. He had been busying himself but secretly watching Harry trying on the various garments, and listening to their conversations. "Can I ask you what function it is you will be going to?"

Pablo, not wanting to give anything away, said it was his grandfather's birthday.

While Pablo tried a few suits on, the female assistant took care of Harry, bringing her a cup of coffee and offering her some biscuits. These were customers that they would want back again.

Before Pablo made his final choice, he asked Harry if she liked what he had picked out. The assistant gave Harry a gift and said it was not to be opened, until she got home.

Pablo settled on a light-coloured, linen suit, with a white shirt.

Harry said he looked fantastic. She felt so proud that she would be arriving with him. She was getting very excited now that they had both found something to wear.

By the time Pablo had settled the final bill it was getting late. An assistant called them a cab and chatted away about the party until the cab arrived. They had ordered it to come to the back entrance. This would avoid Harry and Pablo having to carry their shopping back down the Ramblas. The assistant had offered to deliver their bags but Pablo declined the offer, not wanting to let them know where they were staying. They had been a little too nosey for his liking.

As soon as they were seated safely in the cab, the assistant returned to the shop to phone the manager and ask if he knew who they were. The manager recognised Pablo's name from his credit card. His family had many sports boutiques and shops. He soon put two and two together and realised who they were, from the recent press reports. His mind began working. What function could they possibly be going to? It dawned on him; the young lady must be the new Ski-Summer girl. They were a very hot couple for the moment. He felt flattered that they had been in his shop and told his staff to be very discreet and not to tell anyone that they had been there until he'd had time to think about it.

Once all their parcels had been unpacked and neatly hung away, Pablo ordered them a baguette each for lunch. Sitting on the balcony, giggling about their mornings shopping like a couple of naughty school children, they tucked into tortilla baguettes.

Harry decided she should phone her parents later and fill them in, on what they had been up to. Pablo too said he would phone his father and check everything was still okay for Saturday. With only one day left, it was agreed they would go to the beach after lunch. Harry wanted to top up her tan. The redness had faded and she was now a lovely shade of bronze, but she did not want to lose that.

Chapter 27

Slipping into their swimwear, Harry into a sun dress and Pablo shorts and T-shirt, Harry kept Pablo at arm's length, determined not to give in to his flattery. Finally defeated, Pablo put on his disguise of bandanna, and sunglasses, grabbed a couple of towels, and followed Harry out to the lift. Once outside, he hailed a cab, directing it to the Platja de Boatell. This was the beach built for the Olympic Games. Before the beach had been rebuilt, the people of Barcelona only had the old Barceloneta, but this was neither clean, nor beautiful, so they all used to travel to the villages along the coast near Barcelona.

The cab stopped. Pablo paid the driver and they headed discreetly along the golden sand that stretched before them. A volleyball game was taking place; people were darting around everywhere. They strolled on, looking for somewhere quiet, away from all the crowds. Setting their towels out, side-by-side, they stripped off.

Pablo sat back, leaning on one elbow, watching Harry rubbing her sun-cream on. Glancing round, he noticed a group of boys a few meters away, studying Harry as she protected her skin from the harsh rays. She did have a fantastic body. She kept her hair tucked up in her navy cap and only removed her glasses when she lay down. Pablo glanced around once more; he noticed all the boys nudging each other. "Harry, do you think it is a good, idea to sunbathe here?"

Without opening her eyes, Harry told Pablo to look at all the other girls on the beach. There were plenty of much prettier girls around.

"There are pretty girls but, Harry, you are the most beautiful and have the best body; everyone is looking at you."

Harry told Pablo not to be so silly and paranoid.

Pablo gave the boys a dirty look then lay back. Feeling for Harry's hand, he placed his over the top of it protectively, then began to relax. Harry dozed off while Pablo lay getting fidgety and bored. He was very active and was not keen on sunbathing. Normally if he went to the beach, he would sit at the bar with friends and chat, or he'd be joining in the volleyball, playing football, or skiing. He had not even taken a book with him to read. Noticing Harry's book sticking out of her bag, he leaned over and carefully removed it. Harry didn't stir. His spoken English was very good but, when it came to reading English, he was quite slow and it took him some time to get going.

After a while Harry woke up feeling overheated. Sitting up, she decided to take a dip in the sea. Pablo worried about the group of boys who had been ogling her earlier and decided he would go too. The water was beautifully clear and very refreshing. Swimming out as far as they could, Pablo challenged Harry to a race back to shore. Harry broke into crawl. It was the first time she'd raced with Pablo over any distance. Pablo could not believe how fast she was and had difficulty keeping ahead of her. Determined not to be beaten by his girlfriend, Pablo stepped up a gear. When the water was too shallow to continue he jumped up, proclaiming himself as the winner.

Harry just smiled at him as she walked from the water onto the sand. "You only just beat me," she mocked as they walked back to their towels.

"I was not trying very hard." Laughing, they kissed briefly before settling themselves back down on the sand.

Harry rolled onto her stomach, and gave her back a top-up, before they re-dressed and headed back up the beach towards the road. The taxi was waiting where he had dropped them off. Pablo had been worried about getting a cab back from the beach. It was a place they tended to avoid, not liking their cabs covered in sand. Pablo had already arranged for the cab driver who dropped them off to come back. Dusting the sand from their feet, they placed their shoes on and climbed in. The cab driver had a good look at them, to make sure they were sand-free, before heading back to the hotel.

After a bite to eat, Harry phoned her family, who were all very well and had been for a barbeque at the Cruanos villa. Singing Pablo's parents praises, they'd had an enjoyable day. Mark had played tennis with Jodi and the twins had played in the pool all day. Christina had not gone. Some friends had turned up, travelling from England, the ones they had met on the ferry, and she had gone off to spend some time with them.

After Pablo had phoned his parents, he and Harry spent the evening sitting on the balcony talking, sharing a bottle of wine, and admiring the view of the city as darkness fell and the lights of the night sparkled around them.

Chapter 28

Sitting closely, enjoying being alone, every now and then their eyes meeting, their love deepened. Pablo took Harry's hand and led her back in through the lounge and back to the bedroom. He took her tenderly in his arms and looked into her shining blue eyes. His lips brushed her nose then locked onto her lips. They kissed, Pablo's hands tracing a route down Harry's back and down to her bottom. Cupping both cheeks he pulled her body in close to his. They kissed passionately, removing their clothes as their lips dared to briefly part. Falling onto the bed in each-other's arms, Pablo ran his hands slowly down Harry's arms, gently turning her over and kissing her shapely back from the top of her elegant shaped neck, slowly making his way down to her soft buttocks.

Harry was tingling all over with pleasure, enjoying Pablo's soft, light touch exploring her body. Pablo turned Harry onto her back, seeking out her lips and kissing her passionately.

Each at the point where they needed to be as close as they could,

Pablo continued to explore Harry's body as she ran her hands up and down his back, over his firm bottom and back up to run her fingers through his thick dark hair.

Pablo parted Harry's legs and gently slid a hand between them, his fingers probing her tight, warm, wet opening. Pablo's lips tightly held against Harry's; his tongue was dancing and playing with hers. Finally, Pablo entered her, thrusting hard into her.

Harry gasped with pleasure, scraping her fingers across Pablo's back, digging her nails into his skin as he thrust into her until they could hold back no longer and climaxed together.

Pablo remained on top of Harry breathless with pleasure.

Harry, tingling all over, basked in the aftermath, feeling love and pleasure.

At last Pablo propped himself up on his elbow and gently ran his finger down Harry's nose and over her lips then, leaning forward he softly kissed Harry and told her he loved her more than he ever imagined he could love anyone.

Harry kissed him back and told him she felt the same way. Closing their eyes and wrapped in each-other's arms they slept, contented, and at one.

The next day, waking early, they headed for the beach. Pablo was armed this time with a book, his CD player, and headphones. Harry had settled and, after a couple of hours, Pablo popped up to a kiosk to get a couple of bottles of water for them. Whilst waiting to be served his eyes scanned the rack of daily papers. On the front of the Daily Fun there was a photo of him and Harry; it was one of them kissing on the beach the day before, with the title, 'Playboy can't make up his mind, Papa or Casanova!'

He quickly paid for the water and headed back to the beach to check on Harry. Luckily the beach was still quite deserted. Harry was dozing in the sun. She always looked so perfect, her face beautiful, body gorgeous and completely relaxed. Few people were around and it was very early. Pablo thought to himself that he had better get Harry back to the hotel before anyone spotted them and made the connection.

Waking Harry, Pablo suggested it might be a better idea not to overdo it today. They could spend the rest of the day at the hotel getting ready for the launch. Thank Goodness! Pablo found Harry was ready to go so he didn't have to think of an excuse to get her away.

Back at the Hotel, Harry busied herself packing. The next day they would be leaving and she didn't want to be packing when she was all dressed up. Pablo packed then showered, slipped into his jeans, and said he needed to pop out for a while. He wanted to go to his parents' apartment to sort some jobs out for his father.

While Pablo was away, Harry soaked in the Jacuzzi and then put her short black dress on. As Pablo was not there, Harry made the most of her luxurious hotel suite. She took her time getting ready. That night she wanted everything to be perfect so was going to make a real effort. This gave her a perfect opportunity to do her hair and put some makeup on. She hadn't worn any all week and although she had enjoyed just putting her sunglasses on and not bothering, it felt nice to be doing herself up. That night would be their last night together for a while. Pablo had booked a table in the hotel restaurant and they were going to have special meal.

When Pablo returned, Harry was sitting out on the balcony, reading her book. She had ordered a bottle of champagne from room service and was waiting for Pablo to return to surprise him.

Pablo thought she looked beautiful. He made her stand up and turn around for him before he kissed her softly on the lips. "I'll only be a minute." Disappearing into the bedroom, he changed out of his jeans and into some trousers, a shirt and jacket, and splashed on some aftershave. On his return Pablo took Harry back out to the balcony where he got down on one knee. Taking Harry's hand, he looked up at her bemused face, radiant in the evening light and, with a very serious expression on his face said, "Harry, would you please be my wife, and stay with me for always?"

"Oh, Pablo, of course I will."

Pablo pulled a little box out of his jacket and opened it. A large solitary diamond sparkled up at Harry on a white gold band. Getting to his feet, Pablo slipped the ring onto Harry's engagement finger, then kissed her hand. Taking Harry in his arms, he again told her how much he loved her.

"I love you too, Pablo and I want to stay with you forever."

Pablo pulled Harry into his arms and kissed her.

Opening the champagne, the cork popped off and flew over the balcony and towards the night sky, Pablo filled their glasses. "To you, my English Rose."

Harry clinked his glass before taking a sip. After finishing their drinks they took the glass lift down to the restaurant.

The restaurant was very quiet. The sound of their footsteps echoed around the room as they followed the waiter across the marble, chequered floor and through the low-lit room. He led them to a table, hidden behind a palm and in front of a large window, overlooking the street. The green palms gave each table its own privacy. Hanging from the ceiling, large fans whirled round. Their table was laid with a fresh, crisp, white linen cloth and silver cutlery. The waiter lit a candle and placed it in the centre of the small round table as he seated them. He handed Pablo the wine list, which Pablo waved away and ordered more champagne. Tonight, he was going to make the most of his freedom and time alone with Harry, before he delivered her to the waiting press and her parents the next day.

The evening flew by. Pablo and Harry returned to their room bursting with happiness.

Harry kept glancing at her ring. She could not get used to wearing it. If she was not looking at it, she was feeling it with her thumb. Pablo put some slow music on. Holding each other tightly, they danced closely, afraid of losing the magical feeling they'd found. After a while they undressed and got into bed to spend their last night together, possibly for some time.

Waking early, still wrapped in each other's arms, they realised their freedom was over. There had been a storm in the night. The dust had been dampened down and everywhere had been refreshed and washed clean. Ordering room service, they stayed in bed, while breakfasting on freshly squeezed orange juice, croissants, and coffee.

Getting up at a leisurely pace, they finished their packing wearing just the hotel robes. Harry tidied around, leaving the rooms just as they had found them, while Pablo ran them a bath. Pablo said they would need to be away by twelve thirty to be on the safe side. He wanted to get there in plenty of time in case the press surrounded the entrance of the venue.

Harry finished what she was doing and joined Pablo in the bath. The Jacuzzi turned off and the bath overflowed with bubbles. Pablo gently massaged some shampoo into Harry's hair, then poured fresh, clean water on it from the shower, rubbing gently with his spare hand until all the soap had vanished.

Harry insisted on doing Pablo's for him. Tenderly she worked the soap into his scalp while he relaxed. They refrained from making love and decided they would wait now until they got the launch over with and they had told their parents about their engagement.

Pablo thought it best to ask Mark for Harry's hand before their announcement. He also knew he had something else that needed sorting out. This he was not looking forward to. He longed to confide in Harry, but he was afraid she would reject him and his love. He could not face the thought of losing her. Everything had to be sorted out before he sat Harry down and explained the events she knew nothing about. He shuddered at the thought.

Harry kissed Pablo then climbed from the bath and brushed her teeth, leaving Pablo deep in thought. Back in the bedroom, Harry dried her body before applying moisturizer to her soft brown, glowing skin. Slipping into the white G-String she had bought, she wrapped the robe back around her. Sitting at the dressing table, she brushed her hair through before carefully applying some eye-liner and mascara. Harry always liked to look as natural as possible and used very little make up. Next she dried her hair, then carefully pinned it up leaving a few strands hanging. Before slipping into her dress, she painted her fingernails and toenails to mimic a French manicure.

Pablo came out of the bathroom cleanly shaven and smelling of aftershave. He had a job keeping to his vow of no sex when he saw Harry standing in just a thong, but managed to control himself and helped Harry do her dress up.

Harry sat on the bed and placed her shoes on. Checking her make-up, she applied a pale lip-liner and some natural gloss to her rosy, full lips. Checking her hair, she sprayed a little Channel around her neck and on her wrists before declaring she was ready.

Pablo got dressed in seconds. His linen suit looked great. Calling room service, he told them they wanted to check out, so asked them to send up his bill; he wanted to settle it and get their bags taken down to his car ready for them to leave.

The manager arrived in person and thanked them for staying at his hotel. He knew who they were and had made the staff be very discreet during their stay. Pablo was very grateful for his kindness. Before leaving the manager complimented Harry on how beautiful she looked. Taking Harry by the hand, he kissed it gently, wishing her good luck and happiness. A porter arrived and carried their bags out and the manager followed, leaving Pablo and Harry alone. Pablo produced a package from the drawer by his bed, and handed it to Harry.

"Oh, Pablo, what have you brought me now?" Harry took the small package and opened it. Inside was a small, flat, leather box. Harry took the lid off. It was some jewellery.

"I brought this for you to wear with your dress. You should take your engagement ring off now and wear this ring until we have asked your father if I can marry you."

Harry looked in the box. A set of silver jewellery sparkled up at her; a piece of metal twisted into the shape of a ring, matching twists linked together to form a bangle, and little individual twists hanging from zircons to form earrings. Harry took the silver twisted ring from the box and Pablo removed her engagement ring and replaced it with the dress ring. Harry placed the matching twisted silver bracelet over her hand and moved it up her arm.

Pablo carefully removed the little silver loops Harry was wearing in her ears and inserted the twisted drop earrings in their place. Harry was thrilled. The jewellery set her outfit off. Pablo pulled Harry towards him, and kissed her rosy, glossy lips. "I love you."

Harry looked up into Pablo's dark, sincere eyes. "I love you too". They held each other for ages. Harry did not want Pablo to let her go.

"We must go now." He gently tilted her face up to his.

Harry's eyes filled with tears. "I wish we didn't have to go".

Pablo took Harry's hand and led her to the door.

Taking one last look around, Harry suddenly remembered the present the nice shop assistant had given her when they went shopping. She had placed it in the top of the wardrobe. Running back to the bedroom, she opened the wardrobe door and slid her hand around the top self until she could feel it. Pablo watched as she opened the parcel. Inside was a white pashmina. It matched her dress perfectly. Pablo helped Harry drape it around her shoulders.

As they waited for the lift, Pablo took hold of Harry's hand and gripped it tightly. He could tell she was feeling nervous. Harry smiled back at him. The empty lift arrived. As it glided down the side of the building, Harry took one last look across the city she had enjoyed so much. Arriving on the ground floor, the doors opened. The busy foyer almost fell silent as Harry and Pablo stepped out. The manager was waiting. He ushered them through the main doors and down the steps to Pablo's shining car. The manager had instructed that it should be polished and given a full valet. He liked to please his customer and had recognised his important guests. He handed Pablo the keys then he rushed around and opened the door for Harry. Taking her hand, he helped her into the car.

Harry sat down and arranged her dress so it wouldn't crease. They thanked the hotel manager before he shut the car door and Pablo sped away.

Chapter 29

Arriving at Banyoles, Pablo took the road on the far side of the vast lake to the Marine Club. Pablo wanted to check it out before he drove anywhere near. He could see the press packed around the entrance to the Private Marine Club, hovering with their cameras.

"Look, Harry, there are loads of reporters waiting for you. Pass me my mobile out of the glove compartment." Harry handed the phone to Pablo, who quickly phoned his father to say they had arrived. He wanted to find out if there was any other way to get into the Club without the press hassling them. His father asked him where he was exactly and told him to wait where they were; he would send a van over to collect them.

Sitting listening to Radio Costa Brava, "Time of my Life" came on. Harry could relate to the music; she sat and smiled at Pablo. Pablo was lost for words; Harry thought he looked worried, but he smiled back.

A black van pulled up, Pablo leaned over and kissed Harry on the lips careful not to smudge her lipstick. Knowing they would not get a chance to speak again in private that day he said, "Just remember, I love you, no matter what happens today."

"I love you too, Pablo, and always will, so stop being so serious, you are making me nervous."

Pablo got out and ran around to open the door for Harry. He helped her out of the car and into the van and jumped in next to her. The van was, in fact, quite a plush minibus with no back windows. The only window they could see through was the front windscreen and this had smoked glass with one-way viewing. Harry and Pablo sat in the back of the mini bus. The doors were closed, locking out the hungry press-pack.

Taking Harry by the hand, Pablo wished her good luck and told her she looked beautiful and would be amazing, as the van drove around the lake then through the startled press, and parked with back doors opening against the Marina club doors. Pablo jumped to his feet and helped Harry down the steps. A group of suited men surrounded the pair, blocking them from the press. The reporters spotted them and started shouting questions in Spanish which Harry could not understand. The doors to the entrance closed; the noise from the eager pack was shut out.

The men in suits dispersed and Pablo's uncle, 'Senor Cruanos, stepped forward with his arms outstretched, welcoming them.

The Marine Club had been decked out like the inside of a yacht, all the walls panelled, polished and varnished. There were port holes positioned high up in the panelling, allowing light into the building, and plush, blue velvet upholstery covering all the furnishings.

"Harry, how lovely you look." Greeting her with a kiss on both cheeks, then taking her by the arm, he nodded to Pablo and led her into the reception, leaving Pablo to follow.

Harry glanced back to check Pablo was still there.

Christina was waiting just inside the door with Armando. When she saw Harry, they ran into each other's arms and embraced. "Harry, you look fantastic. Where did you get your dress from?"

"Pablo bought it for me in Barcelona. I'll tell you about it later. You look great yourself. Where have you been shopping?" Christina was wearing a long, black, halter-neck, satin dress and black sandals.

Before Christina had time to answer, Senor Cruanos clapped his hands together to gain everyone's attention and started his announcement. Speaking in Spanish first, then translating into English for the sake of Harry and her family.

"Welcome to the Ski-Summer Launch."

Everyone clapped as waiters and waitresses, dressed in traditional Spanish sailor suits, arrived with silver trays displaying rows of glasses filled with Champagne, and immediately started serving the gathering.

Harry was pounced on, people trying to ask her questions from all directions, and then slowly everyone parted to make a space for Mark and Anna to greet their daughter.

"Dad, Mum." Harry threw her arms around her parents and they hugged her.

"We'll have a good chat later, darling. You are looking very well." Anna whispered in Harry's ear, as she kissed her cheeks.

Mickey and Sophie were next. "Where have you been, Harry?" Sophie was the first to speak.

"We have all missed you." Mickey grinned up at Harry.

Harry crouched down, and gave them a big cuddle. "Well, I'm back now and looking forward to having some fun with the pair of you tomorrow."

Pablo's parents came over and greeted Harry and both agreed how fantastic she looked. They asked her if Pablo had looked after her well.

At that moment, Harry suddenly remembered Pablo and looked around for him. He was deep in conversation with Mark. All eyes were on Harry as she crossed the floor to join Pablo.

Pablo smiled down at her and gently squeezed her hand. "I've just been telling Mark about our trip to Barcelona."

Harry didn't have the chance to join their conversation. Señor Cruanos was hot on her tail and said he would personally escort her around the room and show her the photos. Harry was very impressed as she studied the photos; she found it difficult to believe that they were of her and Christina. Once she had viewed them all, Señor Cruanos took her into an office and asked her if she was prepared to take up a contract with him. He would pay Christina handsomely for her part in the promotion, but he had further work he would like to discuss with Harry. He would be launching the winter Ski-wear in the next few months as soon at the Pyrenees had the first snow fall, and wanted Harry to model that too. It would entail a skiing trip to the Pyrenees, lots of stills in different ski wear, and some action shots for adverts. He liked to have most of his promotional work done around Spain using well known beauty spots; this played a huge part in marketing the products.

Harry read the contract. It would mean coming over when the snow started to fall to take the shots. In all, Señor Cruanos thought it would take a week, or two, at the most. Señor Cruanos was being very persuasive, however Harry said she would think about it and would prefer if her parents and Pablo could read the contract before she signed it. A five-figure sum was mentioned for the winter Skiing promotion on top of which, she too was being paid handsomely for the Ski-Summer wear she had already modelled.

Harry joined her family, only to find Christina fluttering her eyelashes at one of the waiters while being chatted up by another.

Señor Cruanos had no time to lose. He wanted that contract signed that day. He rounded up Mark, Anna, and Pablo, and took them into the office. After taking them through the contract that had been translated into English, Mark and Pablo agreed it was a very good deal, and a great opportunity for Harry. She could continue at college, in England, until it snowed, and then it would only take a few days, two weeks at the most.

Harry was summoned back to the office and, after a brief discussion with her father and Pablo, she agreed to sign the contract. The rest of her family were invited in for a photo. A photographer and a lawyer both appeared, the lawyer to witness the contract, and the photographer to take photos of Harry signing the contract, for a press release. Once this had been done, Harry had to pose for a few photos with Señor Cruanos.

Armando entered the room carrying a giant bottle of Champagne, which was handed to Harry; more photos were taken. Once the waiter had popped the cork, the Champagne was passed around, and group photos of Harry with her family were taken.

Harry looked around the room for Pablo. She wanted him in the photos too.

Pablo was standing by himself, with a glass in his hand, in the corner of the room. He was smiling proudly at Harry. At least now he knew whatever happened, Harry would be coming back. Harry caught his eye and he raised his glass.

Señor Cruanos followed her gaze and beckoned Pablo over. "Come on, Pablo, let's have a couple of pictures of you and Harry together for the papers tomorrow."

Pablo shook his head as he stepped forward. "No, not for the papers, but it would be nice to have one for our private collection."

Harry agreed as Pablo slipped his arm around her waist. Smiling at each other they chinked glasses. Pablo leant down and gave Harry a kiss; click, click, click, the photographers continued. One look from Pablo and the photographers then shuffled off; they had what they wanted.

After joining the rest of the guests the film-show took place. Harry and Christina sat at the front with their parents, with Mickey and Sophie on either side. Pablo and his family sat in the row behind. The film was beautiful. All the colours had been enhanced; the water turquoise, the sails on passing yachts snow white, the sky a pale blue, and the granite rocks surrounding the bay dark and menacing in the background. Harry and Christina had clearly been airbrushed. The girl's skiing was stylish and perfect, both looking highly professional and not like two girls on their summer holidays. Music had been composed to complement the scene. This was about to be released in Europe for the public to see and hopefully for the music to be available to buy. There were two separate films to watch. The second began with Harry's jumpstart, this timed to perfection, followed by her mono around the bay, throwing spray up at the cameras as she touched the water on a sharp turn, and finishing with Harry skiing almost onto the beach. A still of Harry standing with her skies in her hand, on the beach, ended the film.

The lights came on and everyone applauded as Señor Cruanos took centre stage, clapping the girls himself. Once the noise had died down, Señor Cruanos introduced Harry as his new Ski-Winter model.

Christina dug Harry in the ribs and made her go and join Señor Cruanos to more applause. Harry stood and smiled as Señor Cruanos raised Harry's hand into the air. Once he had released Harry's hand she sat back with her family.

At the end of the afternoon, when everyone else had departed, Señor Cruanos said he would make the press release on behalf of the girls, and they could all leave when they wanted.

Pablo found Harry. Strangers had surrounded her all afternoon, interrogating her about what she did and which college she was at, how long she had known Pablo, and were they in love. The occasional waiter had asked for an autograph or photo with her.

Some of the questions Harry answered; others she avoided. She hadn't had much of a chat with her own family yet; she needed some space and time and was desperate to get away from the pack.

At last Señor Cruanos started showing people out.

Pablo spoke to Harry and suggested they drove back to S'Agaro together; he would drop her off at her parents' villa.

Harry told Mark and Anna, who were both ready to go, that she would see them later. Christina had already vanished; Manolo had arrived a little earlier and had driven her away. Mark said he thought it would be an excellent idea for Pablo to take Harry home. They didn't want to mess around getting bags and cases out of Pablo's car and swapping them to his car; the press could still be lurking.

Pablo took Harry into the office to pick up her copy of the contract before they left. Señor Cruanos, Jordi and Armando were sitting around the desk talking when they entered.

"A press release has been issued so be prepared to make the front pages tomorrow, Harry! We have said you have been taken off to another location for some filming so, with any luck, all the press will have dispersed now. But just to be on the safe side, the van will take you back to Pablo's car." He followed Pablo and Harry out to the van. There was no one in sight.

Having been dropped back at the car, Pablo and Harry drove back along the coast towards S'Agaro.

It was getting late. Harry had not eaten a thing during the afternoon so Pablo tried to stop in Figures to get her something to eat. Harry protested; she was so tired she just wanted to get back. Now she had seen her parents she couldn't wait to spend some time with them and tell them about their trip to the farm, and then Barcelona.

Once back in S'Agaro, Pablo carried Harry's bags into the villa. It all seemed very strange to Harry. It felt she had gone away a girl and arrived back a woman. The villa suddenly seemed very small compared with the hotel.

Mark and Anna were pleased to have their daughter home. They thanked Pablo for all he had done and insisted he sat and had a drink with them by the pool before he headed off. The twins couldn't leave Harry alone. Finally, Anna made them kiss Harry and Pablo goodnight and took them up to bed. Pablo said it was time he went too. Harry walked with him to his car. Pablo produced Harry's engagement ring and said he would rather she kept it. He would come over tomorrow afternoon and find them either on the beach or at the villa, and then he would ask Mark if he could marry her. Harry was so happy. She was pleased Pablo had such respect for her father and was going to ask his permission. Happily, she placed her arms on Pablo's shoulders. "Everything has worked out well, hasn't it? We can get engaged. I'll go back to England and carry on at college. You can come over and stay as soon as you get the chance, and I will be back in a couple of months to do the filming for the winter skiing range."

Pablo held Harry very tight; he didn't want to let her go. He knew in a couple of days he would know, one way or another, if he would be able to keep her, or whether he would lose her forever. They kissed and said goodnight. Releasing her, he got in his car and drove off.

Harry went back into the villa, kissed her parents goodnight and went to bed with her ring safely tucked under her pillow.

Mark and Anna were very relieved everything had gone well. Harry had been protected from the press that day; they had both been very proud of their two daughters. Harry was back, looking very well and was obviously happy. They too would only be able to relax once they knew the paternity result of Conchitta's baby. Knowing how happy Harry was, they knew this could crush her.

Chapter 30

The following morning Harry woke early. Christina was already awake and dying to hear about Harry's trip to the farm and Barcelona. They talked until Anna appeared at the door and asked if they were ready for breakfast. Everyone was so happy. The twins stayed constantly by Harry's side. She promised she would take them fishing at some point and, if Pablo was there, that he would come too.

After breakfast they all left the villa and headed to San Feliu to go to Church. Harry wore a sun dress and tied her hair up, put her sunglasses on and a straw hat. She did not want to take any chances at being recognised. Christina too wore sunglasses and a cap. She wanted to be noticed but she knew the consequences would be too disastrous for Harry. They all set off with Mark driving. It was the first time they had all been together as a family for quite some time.

The old Church was cool and crowded, full of Sunday worshippers. The Smyth-Thomas's squeezed into a pew and prayed. Not staying for the whole service and having said some private prayers, they crossed themselves with holy water and left. The old beggar was waiting by the door; he seemed to recognise Harry and smiled up at her as she tipped all the change out of her purse into his cap. Heading off for the market, Mark and Anna took the two younger children, leaving Christina and Harry to wander around on their own. They arranged to meet back at the car a little later. Christina wanted to go and check out the newspapers to see if there were any pictures of her in them. Harry managed to convince her to wait until they were on their way back to the car, just in case anyone around the paper stands spotted them.

Harry bought a short, wrap-around lacy skirt to wear to the beach, and some hair accessories. Christina had taken a fancy to Harry's hat and was on a mission to buy one for herself. Having walked the length of the market they gave up hope. Just as they set off for the car, Harry spotted a jeweller's shop. She wanted to buy Pablo something for their engagement and told Christina she wanted to get him a thank you gift. They went inside to study the vast presentation cases of rings. Nothing seemed suitable so they gave up. On their way back to the car, Harry noticed an artist displaying his paintings along the street. As she admired the pictures she saw a familiar scene. It was the view of the bay painted from the spot she and Pablo had stopped at one night. This was just the sort of thing she was looking for. It would always remind Pablo of that magical evening they had spent together. Harry asked the artist how much it was.

"Eleven thousand, two hundred and fifty pesetas," he replied.

Christina said, "Leave this to me." After five minutes of haggling, Christina had got him down to half the price.

Harry agreed and the artist wrapped the picture in some crisp brown paper and tied it up with string to make it easier for her to carry.

On their way back to the car, Christina went into newsagents and came out armed with papers. "I have not looked at any of them yet; I just grabbed them off the shelf and paid for them. We'll look at them when we get home," she giggled.

Mark and the twins were waiting at the car, and said he had arranged to pick Anna up outside the supermarket. Mickey and Sophie had both bought new fishing nets, ready for their next expedition. By the time they arrived at the supermarket, Anna was waiting outside the entrance looking out for them with a loaded trolley. "We thought it would be nice if we had a barbeque tonight. I think we could all do with a night in."

Harry and Christina helped a harassed-looking Anna load the bags into the back of the car and they set off back to S'Agaro.

Chapter 31

The beach was deserted. According to the beach men it had been crowded all morning then, at about two, everyone had vanished leaving behind their sandcastles and empty water bottles. It was always the same on a Sunday. People flocked down to the beach early in the morning and then disappeared as quickly as they had arrived. Siestas were needed before huge meals were prepared and consumed on a Sunday evening.

There was no sign of Pablo, so Harry took the twins over to the rocks, with their new nets, to fish. The twins had been practicing and were keen to show Harry how productive they had become. Harry was very impressed. They insisted she sat down with the bucket whilst they caught everything. Mickey caught something every time he dipped his net in the water. He was very quick and seemed to be able to work out which way the fish would dart when startled, and trap them. The recent rain had freshened the pools; they looked green and full of life again. The swollen sea had tossed angry waves, refilling every crevasse with fish.

Sophie was doing very well. She had managed to catch a small, red, rock pool fish, some little herrings, and she had found a perfect specimen of a star fish. The bucket was teeming with life. Harry said they shouldn't overfill it or the fish would die in no time. Collecting up their nets, they headed back to the shore to show off their latest catch.

Christina was basking in the sun. Manolo had joined her. Luckily her two friends from England had only stopped for one night and were now heading down towards the South of Spain. They were both hoping to meet some rich Spanish girls, living in Marbella, and spend some time there living off them before continuing down to Tarifa and windsurfing territory.

Harry could not work out whether Manolo and Christina were just good friends with benefits, or whether Manolo thought they were going out together. At times she thought they were very close and inseparable, whilst there were times when she thought they had a very casual relationship.

Pablo had still not arrived so Harry went for a swim with Mickey and Sophie. Mickey said they could both swim to the buoy and back without stopping now and wanted to show Harry. The water was lovely and refreshing. The rocks had been a sun trap and Harry wanted to cool off, so a slow swim to the buoy was just what she needed. Mickey swam ahead doing his dolphin impression, always having to be faster and better than Sophie. Sophie was very sensible and took her time. It was a long way and she knew if she went too fast she would never make it. Harry swam slowly behind Sophie, keeping one eye on her and the other on Mickey. Triumphantly, Mickey reached the buoy first. He was gasping and out of breath as he clung to the algae covered rope attached to the buoy and declared himself to be the winner. Harry swam alongside Sophie and they both arrived at the buoy at the same time.

Harry praised and congratulated the pair of them on how well they had done. Mickey and Sophie floated around the buoy for a few minutes, getting their breath and strength back, while Harry trod water until they were ready for their journey back. The swim back to shore was a lot quicker than it had been swimming out. The incoming waves helped drive them shoreward. Again Harry hung back, staying behind and taking her time, making sure she was working every muscle in her body as she pulled herself through the water, as well as making sure Mickey and Sophie were not struggling. Glancing up towards her parents she noticed an extra figure sitting with them. As she got closer she realized it was Pablo. Excited at seeing him, Harry had a job not to leave the twins and race into the shore. Instead she waited patiently for the twins to reach a depth where they would be able to stand.

"Look, Pablo has arrived." The twins raced towards the beach, half swimming and half running in the water, both dying to show Pablo their bucket of fish.

As they ran up to Pablo he jumped to his feet. Winking at Harry, he lifted Sophie up over his head. It was really Harry he wanted to grab and lift.

He was so relaxed with her siblings Harry wondered what he would be like as a father if they, one day, had children of their own. It was far too early in their relationship to talk about children yet and it would be years until they got married.

Once Pablo had placed Sophie safely back on the sand, Pablo threw Mickey a few playful punches. Turning to Harry, he gave her a greeting kiss on each cheek and a quick one on the lips. He apologized for not making the fishing trip. He studied all the fish with the twins whilst Mickey talked him through each catch. He then told them what the correct name of each fish was in Spanish. Walking back towards the rocks with the bucket, he encouraged Mickey and Sophie to release their crowded catch back into the sea. The water in the bucket was warming up despite having been kept in the shade; he could tell the twins would have been devastated if they had harmed a fish.

The afternoon was over. Christina and Manolo had already gone back to the villa. Christina had not had time to look at the papers yet and was desperate to see if she was in print.

Harry and Pablo helped Mark and Anna pack everything away before they took the children home. Harry said they would give them an hour to sort themselves out before she and Pablo went back, or there would be a queue for the bathrooms. Pablo had brought some fresh clothes with him and was shortly going to shower and change up at the beach huts, while Harry sat and read her book. He would then drive her back to the villa. He was quite looking forward to an evening with Harry's family.

Chapter 32

Back at the villa, Christina had been through all the papers and the only one with any pictures in was the Costa Brava Fun. On the front cover was a flattering, colour picture of Harry signing the contract with Señor Cruanos. Harry looked stunning and Christina thought she no longer looked like a girl but a beautiful woman. The headline read, "New Ski Girl, it's official. Full story and more pictures on page five." Christina quickly turned to page five. Here was another colourful picture of Harry and Christina standing on S'Agaro beach holding their skis. The story line read, "Sisters, Harry and Christina Smyth-Thomas, currently on a summer break from England, have been been spotted for their skiing ability and good looks, and have been signed by the Cruanos empire to launch their Ski-Summer wear. Christina, currently at University in England, is due to leave at the end of the week to pursue her vocation. Younger sister Harry has been offered a five-figure sum to stay and become the new Ski-Winter babe that is due to be launched later in the year." It then went on to say Harry had been romantically linked with playboy Pablo Cruanos, who was also linked with an ex-girlfriend who was claiming to be carrying his baby.

Christina cut the article out, making sure she had left the line off where it said Harry had been romantically linked etc. She joined her parents and Manolo, already showered, changed, and sorting the barbeque out. Anna and Mark thought the pictures were very good and said the article was acceptable too.

Christina waited until the twins had gone off to explore the surrounding woods before she explained about the part she had cut out of the article. Manolo helped Mark prepare the barbeque, filling the base with pine needles and sticks the twins had collected from the woods earlier, to get it started. A car crunched to a halt on the old dirt track outside the villa; Harry and Pablo had arrived back. Christina got the paper clipping out while Harry went in to shower and change. Manolo disappeared off to the kitchen to collect a jug of Tisana he had made for them all. Mark and Anna had never tried Tisana before; Christina warned Manolo to go steady with the brandy. Whilst it was quiet and only the five of them, Christina quizzed Pablo and asked if he had seen the paper. Pablo said that Juan had rushed out first thing to get all the papers so they could check them out. He too had been worried about the article and thanked Christina for cutting out the part saying he was a play-boy and his connection with Conchitta. They talked about the test Pablo was insisting Conchitta had; it was going ahead the following day.

Anna asked if he knew how long it would take them to get the results.

Pablo said he thought the results would be back within twenty four hours; they had already had a DNA swab from him when he booked the clinic. He would be straight up to let them know as soon as he received it.

Christina followed Anna into the villa to prepare a salad while Manolo, who was given a nudge by Pablo, went off to look for the twins, leaving Mark and Pablo alone.

Now was Pablo's chance to ask Mark if he could marry Harry. Not normally the type to feel nervous, Pablo had butterflies in his stomach. He realized it was not ideal with his current situation but decided he should get it over with. "Mark, I have something to ask you."

Mark put down the poker he had been prodding and turning the coals with, sat down opposite Pablo, and responded, "Come on then, Pablo, let's hear it."

"Mark, I would like to marry your daughter, Harry, and I would like to have your consent."

Mark was not shocked; he could tell Pablo was smitten with his beautiful daughter. "Have you already discussed this with Harry?"

"Yes, we have talked about it a great deal. We are both in love and want to get married. We realize we should wait and have a long engagement. Harry is so young. This does not matter; we are happy to do this. We would like to get engaged now, and then marry in a few years when Harry is perhaps twenty one, if you agree?"

Mark moved his chair closer to Pablo then, looking directly into Pablo's eyes, spoke. "Firstly, Pablo, what about this Conchitta girl? What if she is pregnant? What then?"

"I know that she is pregnant, but I also know the baby could not possibly be mine. I will have the proof after tomorrow."

"Well, Pablo, you are a nice young man. You have shown me over the past week that you can take care of Harry and make her happy. I can tell that Harry is very much in love with you. Providing you are right about Conchitta and the baby is nothing to do with you, and this is what Harry wants, the answer is yes. I would be very happy to have you as my future son-in-law."

Pablo jumped to his feet and embraced a very embarrassed Mark. His British maleness was not used to this type of behaviour. "I will wait until after the results of Conchitta's tests before we make the announcement, so would you please keep it to yourself until then?"

"I will definitely keep it to myself until we know the results."

At that moment the girls arrived out of the villa carrying salads, bread, and the steaks for cooking, just as Manolo came back with the twins and a lizard Mickey had tracked down and caught. The little lizard was placed in a big cardboard box. Mark agreed Mickey could keep it to study for the evening, and then it had to be released.

Manolo and Pablo took over the barbeque with Mark's agreement and began cooking. Seasoning the steaks with salt and pepper, then dipping them into whisky, they laid them over the barbeque, its grill blackened with age, and they soon began to sizzle. The meat was delicious and the salads fresh and crisp. Manolo and Pablo kept everyone entertained with stories about their childhood in Spain, and of all the antics they got up to together as they were growing up.

Mickey spent the whole evening making his lizard a home. He had arranged rocks, sticks, and pieces of greenery he had gathered from around the villa in the box, replicating a vivarium; its temporary home was complete. The lizard, Mickey had named T-Rex, had nearly escaped twice, so the box was covered with one of Anna's scarves, held down with some stones.

It had been a perfect evening and was getting late; the dark night sky had replaced the evening sunset. Mark stood up and told Mickey he had to let the lizard go. Mickey started to protest that T-Rex had just begun to settle. Pablo suggested he went with Mickey to release the lizard where he had found it. Mickey was happy with this suggestion and transferred the lizard into a jar with a sock over the top of it so the lizard could breathe but not escape just yet. Pablo had not realized quite how far Mickey and Sophie had strayed when they found the lizard. No wonder Manolo had knowingly nearly choked on his drink when Pablo had offered to help Mickey take it back and release it where he had found it.

It was dark now as they moved away from the lights of the villa, left the dirt track, and entered the woods. The canopy of the pine trees had cut out the moonlight. Pablo was grateful he had his car keys with a mini torch key ring with him. As they clambered through the woods, trying to stick to the worn path, Mickey surprised Pablo by asking Pablo if he loved Harry. Pablo was quite taken aback and said he did very much, and one day he hoped they would marry. Mickey asked Pablo if he would take Harry away from them. Pablo said he would never take Harry away from them. He hoped, when they got married, he would be part of their family too and Mickey would be a real brother to him and not just a friend. This pleased Mickey. He had grown very fond of Pablo in the short time he had known him and looked up to him.

"This is where we found him. I left two sticks in the shape of a cross to mark the spot." Mickey pointed down to his marker. "Shall I let him go now?"

They had reached the far side of the wood and stopped by the walled boundary of another villa. Pablo nodded to Mickey.

Mickey carefully placed his hand onto the top of the jar and removed the sock. Gently he slid his hand down the inside the jar and cupped it around the lizard. Pablo shone the torch for him.

Lifting the lizard up to his face Mickey said, "Goodbye T-Rex," then slowly lowered it to the ground. The lizard jumped out of Mickey's hand and headed for a crack in the wall. Pablo and Mickey stood in silence, watching until the tip of the lizard's tail vanished from view. T-Rex was free.

"Come on, Mickey. It is very late. We must go back now." Pablo broke the silence. On their way back through the wood, Mickey walked very close to Pablo. Suddenly realising how dark it was, he was a little afraid. Pablo placed his hand on Mickey's shoulder and kept it there guiding him back along the path and giving him some reassurance until they were out of the woods. The moonlight lit up the old dirt track that led them back to the villa.

When they arrived back, they heard the quiet mumble of the family still sitting around the table talking quietly. The barbeque embers were still glowing, the plates cleared away, and the washing up done. Sophie was asleep on Mark's knee. When Mickey and Pablo returned, Mickey relayed their adventure back through the dark woods to release T-Rex.

Mark carried Sophie into the villa and up the stairs. Without waking her, he gently laid her onto her bed, removed her shoes and laid her duvet over the top of her.

Mickey begged Anna to let him stay up and, much to his disappointment, was not allowed. Mark returned and took a protesting Mickey up to his room, where he made sure he had a good wash after handling the lizard, before tucking him up in his bed.

Manolo and Pablo thought they should call it a night too. Anna announced they would like the girls to accompany her and Mark to see some old friends staying in a hotel just up the coast the next day. Agreeing they should go, Harry and Christina arranged to meet back up with Pablo and Manolo in Playa de Aro the following evening. Mark and Anna said they would drop the girls off on their way back from San Antonio at around eight. This seemed to suit everyone, especially Pablo. He was pleased Anna had thought of a distraction for Harry; he had been worried about the next day. It would be nice to know Harry was well away from the area as Conchitta was bound to cause a stir.

Thanking Anna and Mark for a lovely evening, Pablo and Manolo made their exit. Harry walked out to the car with Pablo. Pablo had been trying to get her on her own all evening; he was dying to tell her that he had asked Mark if they could get married, and that Mark had agreed. Leaning against the car, holding Harry with both hands around her waist, Pablo told Harry the good news.

Harry was over the moon. She had noticed Mark and Pablo talking alone when she had been helping prepare the salads and had tried to work out what was being said by examining the expressions on their faces and what they meant. Typically, while she had not been looking, Mark had given Pablo his consent and they had embraced. Mark had agreed, and Harry was elated.

Pablo asked Harry if she would go back to his parents' villa the following evening and stay the night as they had already committed themselves to going into Playa with Christian and Manolo. Pablo wanted Harry by his side so he could break the news to his parents.

Harry said no one could stop her; she was so excited.

After a long embrace, a soft gentle kiss that Harry did not want to end, Pablo said goodnight. As he drove off he glanced back in his mirror getting one last view of the girl he loved.

Harry followed Christina into the villa and went to bed. She was exhausted. The last few days had been demanding and were creeping up on her. She did not know how she was going to cope next week when the time came that she had to say goodbye to Pablo; it would seem like an eternity returning to England and to college, and the waiting that she would have to endure until they could be together again. The days were flying by far too quickly. Checking under her pillow she found her ring, kissed it, and then slipped it on her finger. It would not hurt to sleep with it on. She would just wear it for one night and then take it off again in the morning. Closing her eyes, she drifted off to sleep with the image of Pablo smiling at her; content and happy she dozed off feeling blessed and in love.

Chapter 33

It was another sweltering day in S'Agaro. Harry ran her fingers over her ring and took it off, hiding it back under her pillow as soon as she woke. Once out of bed, Harry slipped into her blue halter-neck bikini, a crop top, and pair of jeans. She wanted to dress casually and blend in when she was in San Antonio.

Christina followed Harry's choice and also placed a pair of jeans and a T-shirt on. The twins were both dressed, Mickey in long denim shorts and a white T-shirt, Sophie in her denim sundress, both with their swim wear underneath.

The drive to San Antonio did not take very long on the new road that had been built to improve the coastal commute in time for the Spanish Olympics. It was now a much quicker route and there was no longer the need to wind in and out of the coastal villages. On their way into San Antonio, Mickey spotted a billboard with a picture of Harry posing, holding her water skis. It turned out they had been placed everywhere along the coastal route. Each direction they glanced there was an advertising poster or print of some description, with Harry on some and others with Christina on, all with the big Ski-Summer logo, slashed across the centre. Mickey and Sophie got very excited and it soon became a game. Who would be the next person to spot the next poster?

Arriving at the Palm Beach Hotel, Mark parked the car and they all climbed out and waited for their friends to arrive. They had not seen the Blake's for five years. Mickey and Sophie had been toddlers the last time they had all met up. Even though Mickey and Sophie could not remember what they looked like, or who they were, they shared in Mark and Anna's excitement.

Neither Harry or Christina were very happy at the prospect of spending a day in San Antonio. However, they both realised how excited the twins and their parents were to have a family day out and see their old friends, so had agreed to go along and make the most of it.

David came striding across the car park. He had put on even more weight since they had last seen him. Mark and Anna ushered the children over to greet him. Hugs and good wishes were exchanged. David said Carol, his wife, was waiting by the pool for them all. The twins both whooped with joy when they saw the arrangement of slides and boards arranged around the deep-end of the large pool. At the shallow end was a paddling pool and a couple of Jacuzzis bubbling away. Carol was very slim and took great care of herself. Having greeted the family one by one, she paused when she reached Harry. "You look very familiar even though it's five years since we last saw you," she said with a wink to Anna. Harry blushed.

Mark was quick to cover Harry's embarrassment and said, "It's a long story, but you have probably seen both Harry and Christina on the Ski-Summer billboards and posters all around the town."

"Come on then, pull up a sun-lounger, and tell us all about it."

The twins were frantic to get into the water so, as Mark and Anna settled down to reminisce and catch up with their friends, Harry and Christina helped the twins take their clothes off. After excusing themselves, they headed off to the lure of the deep end where all the slides were situated. Harry suggested starting on the three little slides, building up Mickey and Sophie's confidence. Harry was beginning to enjoy herself. She was going to have some fun today with the twins. Christina was fed up and in no time went back to join her parents.

All the slides had a continuous flow of water trickling down them, making them faster and easier to glide down. Having tried out the three gentler looking slides and having adapted to the temperature of the pool water, Mickey wanted to go down the larger, taller slide. Sophie said she was not ready to go on it just yet, but said she would stand at the bottom of the steps and watch Harry and Mickey go down it first. Harry followed Mickey up the steps and waited while he whizzed down, screaming with excitement the whole way. He splashed into the water and had to hold his breath as he went under. As soon as he surfaced he swam back to the side, holding onto the steps and waited for Harry to set off. It was fast. Initially she had quite a shock. By the time she reached the bottom, Mickey was already half-way back up the steps and ready for his next go. Sophie decided she would like to go down with them this time, so Harry shouted up and made Mickey wait for them on the platform at the top of the slide. Sophie climbed the steps gingerly. When they reached the top Mickey told her to watch him; if she wanted to slow down she had to sit up, and if she wanted to go faster, then she had to lie down. Mickey sped down, lying flat on his back. Once reaching the water, he swam out of the way and waited near the steps for Sophie. Sophie set off, sitting bolt upright and screaming the whole way down. Harry was a little worried as Sophie disappeared under the water at the base of the slide. Finally, like a cork, she popped back up and, with a big grin on her face, waved up to Harry. Relieved, Harry pushed herself off, lying down this time to see how fast she would go. It gave her quite a thrill. It was nice to have a different adrenalin rush and she revelled in the fun of being childish.

The next slide to try was a spiral one that was undercover all the way down. Shaped like the helter-skelter at the fair, it twisted and turned before it ejected you into the water. Mickey went first. His voice echoed all the way down the spiral pipe. Landing feet first in the water, he made a huge splash. "That was great. It's the fastest one of them all," he shouted back up to his sisters.

Sophie, feeling more confident now, went next. Taking off at such a speed she again screamed all the way down. Gasping for air, she surfaced. Harry held her breath for a second until, once again, Sophie waved up to her letting her know she was fine. Harry gripped the roof of the pipe entrance and, once Sophie had cleared the area, she swung into the slide, throwing her feet and body forward. She flew down, swishing along the pipe from one side to the other until she plunged off the end and into the pool. Mickey and Sophie were both waiting for her by the edge of the pool. When she emerged from the water her hair flopped all over her face and they both killed themselves laughing.

"You little toads! That was very fast. You could have warned me."

After a couple of hours taking it in turns to go down the slide, Harry noticed Mickey and Sophie were looking rather red. Their skin had turned quite dark already, but the sun had caught them, intensified by the reflection of the water. She took them back to find their parents.

Mark and Dave had gone off for a game of golf and had left Anna and Carol gossiping by the pool. Christina had disappeared to find the toilet. Once Harry had deposited the twins with Anna she headed off to find Christina and the loo. Christina was just coming out as Harry went in.

"Do you fancy a drink, Harry?"

"To be honest with you, Christina, I am feeling quite cold now so I would rather just get a soft drink and go back outside to sunbathe."

Christina went to the bar and bought them a couple of drinks. She also chose the twins an ice cream each. Harry found her struggling to carry the drinks and dripping ice creams back to the pool, and took the ice creams from her. The twins were huddled together, sitting shivering in their robes by the pool. When they saw the ice creams arrive they forgot how cold they were and got stuck into them.

Harry set her drink on the table next to her sun lounger and lay down on her stomach. Christina pulled her lounger up to Harry's so she could chat to her whilst Harry sunbathed.

Harry picked up her orange and took a swig. Almost choking, she tried not to spit it out. Once she had managed to swallow it, eyes watering, she turned to Christina who was killing herself laughing. In a low whisper, Harry accused Christina; "You've put vodka in this."

"Oh, come on, Harry, I thought you looked cold and needed a little warming up."

"You are awful. I'll never last the day out if I start drinking vodka now." Harry told Christina she could finish the drink off, and then lay down to sunbathe, relax, and have a sleep.

Half an hour later, Carol took Anna and the twins off to have some lunch in the Hotel Restaurant. Harry and Christina said they would just get a baguette from the pool bar and eat it where they were. After Christina had interrogated Harry about her relationship with Pablo,

Harry finally confessed she had been swept off her feet by Pablo. She was deeply in love with him and wanted to spend the rest of her life with him.

Christina said she had thought as much. Harry didn't seem the type to have loads of relationships, whereas she and Manolo were going out together, but neither of them wanted to make a commitment. They both liked their freedom and accepted the fact that it was just a bit of fun and Christina was going back to England and back to her life there; they might never see each other again.

Harry said she was dreading going back to England; she did not want to leave Pablo. She could not imagine how she would feel knowing he was so far away and that she would not be able to see him every day. Now at least, with this contract she had signed, she knew it would only be a couple of months before she would be coming back again. Then, when she had finished college, she didn't know what they would do. Pablo's family were hoping to branch out further into Europe. Maybe Cheltenham would be a good place to have a Ski-Summer/Winter sports fashion shop. Snow-boarding was getting very popular amongst her friends, and wake boarding was starting to take off in the summer. Loads of their friends headed off to the Three Valleys or Alpes d'huez annually, and none of them were able to buy their equipment locally. They generally had to drive to London to find the specialist sports clothes and equipment they needed. Cotswold Water Park, with its many wake boarders and water-skiers, was also close and would have quite a rich clientele that would use the shop. Cheltenham was a very wealthy area in the Cotswolds and could be ideal.

As the morning drifted into the afternoon, the pool was getting increasingly crowded. A group of boys had taken a fancy to Harry and Christina and had settled themselves down on the vacant loungers near to them. Harry turned and faced the other way as Christina, quick off the mark, started to introduce herself to them.

Having slept for most of the afternoon, Harry woke to the sound of Mark's deep voice. "We are all going up to Carol and Dave's suite for a drink, so if you girls want to come and get yourselves showered off and dressed, Carol said you can use her bathroom and bedroom."

The hotel was beautifully designed. With elegant floral displays everywhere, it all looked ultra-modern and very clean. The walls and furniture were covered in beige leather and very stylish. The lounging sofas in the lobby were shaped like half-moons, the bar circular. Even the stairs circled around the lobby in a large, spiral, coil leading to the other floors.

The rooms David and Carol occupied were also decorated in creams, beiges and neutral colours. Carol took Harry and Christina through to her bedroom. "Help yourselves to a shower, deodorant, makeup or anything else you want, girls. There are two clean towels hanging behind the door, in the bathroom."

"Thank you, Carol," Harry and Christina responded as Carol shut the door behind her and left them to it.

"Can I have the first shower, Harry?" Christina begged as she headed for the door to the shower room and, before waiting for a reply, she had locked the door and the shower was running.

Harry sat at Carol's dressing table and looked at the range of makeup Carol owned while she waited.

Chapter 34

After a restless night Pablo got up early. Trying to make himself feel a little more human, he had a long, cold shower and got dressed. He was not looking forward to seeing Conchitta at all. Any feelings he once had for her were long gone. If anything, all he felt for her now was a loathing pity. He had already changed his plans and would now meet her at the clinic. He did not want her near him. It would be hard enough having to face her at the clinic. His father came into his room and offered to go to the clinic with him. Pablo declined the offer saying he would rather go alone. Manolo was going to meet him at the Canary bar for a coffee when he had finished.

Pablo went downstairs to the kitchen and sat on a stool at the breakfast bar. Isabel offered him some breakfast. Pablo had a knot in his stomach; he felt so depressed and worried that he could not face anything.

"Come on, please, Pablo. You cannot last the day without having anything to eat or drink. At least have a drink." His mother tried to coax him with iced tea and fruit juice.

Pablo said he would have a coffee, just to please her.

Handing him a strong cup of coffee, Isabel continued to fuss around whilst trying to hide her despair. She felt his pain and anguish.

Drinking the hot, steaming black coffee as quickly as he could, Pablo felt claustrophobic with his mother's annoying fussing and decided to go into town to escape from everyone.

Kissing him goodbye, Isabel and Jordi wished him luck and tried to reassure him he was doing the right thing.

Sporting his dark glasses and a cap he got in his BMW. He loved the smell of the leather and the feel of the sporty steering wheel in his hands. Turning the ignition on, he flipped a button and the top slowly went down. He drove along the main road into Saint Feliu. Pablo was lucky and managed to find a parking space along the beach front. Locking the car up, he headed for the Marina. Wandering along the quay, he noticed the fishing boats had just arrived in with the previous night's catch. Pablo ambled over to watch the unloading of the boats. The air was thick with the smell of fish. Men, covered in sweat and slime, frantically off -loaded crates of flapping, gasping fish onto trolleys. They were then wheeled into the huge auction room where they were sorted into species, size, and weight, and covered in ice to protect them from the rising temperature before being auctioned. The auction room was like an empty warehouse, slowing being filled with trolley loads of fish. Some of the fishermen's wives set up stalls at one end of the auction room. Here they sold some of their catch, neatly displayed in size and species order.

The auction started and one trolley load after another was wheeled in front of the auctioneer and sold. These were snapped up by restaurants and fishmongers alike, both bidding against each other for the best deal, making the price climb and climb until the gavel hit the desk.

Pablo fought his way back through the hordes of tradesmen and out into the sunshine. As he strolled along, past the empty fishing vessels, the day was not yet over for the fishermen. Nets were being unravelled along the concrete. Old and young women, some working together and others alone, sat on little stools, laughing and gossiping while repairing torn nets, mending all the holes that had appeared overnight. The odd dead fish lay discarded and like vultures the seagulls circled waiting for their chance to breakfast.

The fishy smell faded as Pablo walked out onto the main Marina. Yachts of all shapes and sizes were moored up in neat rows, bobbing from side to side in the sheltered waters. Walking along the quay that separated the bay from the Mediterranean, protecting the town from the harsh, winter seas, he tried not to think about Conchitta. How could she do this to him?

Stopping briefly, he admired a small modern yacht being cleaned. Temporarily distracted, he watched as the white fibreglass was scrubbed clean of algae, but then his mind wandered back to Harry. What was she doing at that precise moment? A smile cracked across his face at the thought of his lovely English Rose. Once tomorrow was over, he hoped he would be free. He and Harry could get engaged and they could enjoy the rest of her holiday without having to worry about the press hounding him, or about Conchitta.

Having reached the end of the pier, Pablo climbed up the steps to the top of the wall, looking out across the huge, manmade barrier, filled with giant granite boulders, securing the marina, and gazed out to sea. The deep, black waters were quite rough. White horses tossed their manes as they raced in on the waves. No little boat would have been stupid enough to venture out of the bay in such waters. Only a huge tanker, right out at sea, was visible.

Having passed some of the time, Pablo headed back towards the town. If he left his car where it was and walked to the hospital he would be just on time. The park and gardens that ran along the beach front were quite deserted; everyone was down on the beach. The carousel and bumper cars stood motionless. Covered up for the day, they would come to life later that afternoon, just in time to catch the tourists leaving the beach.

Turning into the Ramblas, Pablo stopped and bought a magazine to read; it would be a distraction in case he had to kill any time at the hospital. The cafes were filling up and the sun was by now high in the sky. Pablo was feeling hot, nervous, and quite sick. He still had knots in his stomach as he made his way through the back streets and towards the clinic. Head down, feeling low, he walked along slowly, dragging his feet. He even said a silent prayer. Never, in his whole life, had he felt that alone. As he turned into the next narrow, dusty street, he could see the green fluorescent cross marking the hospital entrance.

Having arrived at the hospital slightly early, he asked at the main reception for directions to the clinic. As he was about to head off down the corridor he heard a commotion outside. Conchitta had arrived flanked by her two brothers, dressed in matching suits, and a horde of reporters. Pablo rushed down the corridor before they could spot him.

Conchitta stopped at the entrance and addressed the press. "You are all probably wondering, what I'm doing here. I will explain. I am meeting Pablo Cruanos, whom I believe is the father of my baby. Today I am going to undergo a procedure which will determine whether he is the father of my baby. I don't need any proof but, unfortunately, my future husband does." With that Conchitta, who was dressed to kill in a tight-fitting, little black dress and high heeled shoes, turned on her heels, clicked her fingers for her brothers to follow her, and entered the hospital. Some of the press tried to follow her in but her brothers blocked the door until hospital security arrived.

Conchitta was taken down the corridor to where Pablo was waiting. "Hello, darling." She rushed up to him, placed her arms around his neck, and gave him a kiss on both cheeks.

Pablo backed away, peeling her hands from his neck. "Come on, Conchitta, let's get it over with."

Having been shown into the waiting room, a female doctor appeared in white overalls to explain the procedure to them. Once told of all the risks, Conchitta signed a consent form. A nurse, neatly dressed in loose cut, cotton, dark blue trousers and tunic, with her hair scooped up into a little white hat, took them into a clinically scrubbed room where Pablo was to have his blood taken. They were happy with his DNA results but, in case of any further evidence being required, they had advised the blood test.

The room smelt of disinfectant, the bare walls painted white, with blue gloss skirting. All the grey marbled table tops were neatly covered with rows of sterile instruments. An operating table occupied the centre of the room with a huge light looming above it. In the corner of the room a door opened and a cabinet full of needles, syringes, and test tubes, was wheeled in by the nurse.

Conchitta was taken to a changing room and asked to undress and come back in when she had put a surgical robe on.

Pablo was asked to roll up his shirt sleeve and a tourniquet was placed around his upper arm to get the vein up. It didn't take long before his veins had risen nicely under his skin. The nurse used an antiseptic wipe and cleaned the area before she pushed the needle into his vein; Pablo didn't even flinch. As the nurse released the tourniquet, the dark red blood flowed from his arm, filling the syringe.

Conchitta arrived back into the room, trying to look as sexy as possible, with her robe hanging open to her chest, revealing her large cleavage. She was told to climb onto the operating table and lie flat.

Pablo turned to leave.

Conchitta pleaded with him, "Don't go, Pablo, I'm quite nervous. Can you just stay and hold my hand, while it's done?"

Conchitta's brothers would be waiting in reception and Pablo didn't want to spend any time with them. Whilst Pablo was looking towards the door, hoping to escape, Conchitta managed to blink until she had forced some tears into her eyes. Pablo suddenly felt sorry for her and went to stand by her side. She held her hand out for him. The nurse smiled at him.

Feeling guilty, he took her hand. The Nurse placed a green, sterile sheet over Conchitta's legs and pulled the robe up over her stomach, leaving a gap around her abdomen. Another sterile sheet with a small hole in it was placed over her lower stomach. The Doctor appeared, having been scrubbed down and wearing a navy gown and matching hat. Placing gloves on, she took a large needle from the trolley.

Pablo looked away.

The needle was inserted through Conchitta's abdominal wall. Conchitta flinched; she tightened her grip on Pablo's hand. Once this was in place a malleable catheter was guided by real-time ultrasound through the needle into the chorion villi of the placenta.

The doctor carried on explaining to Conchitta what she was doing as she continued with the procedures. "Five to twenty milligrams of tissue is aspirated. This is dissected from maternal tissue. We will be able to check if your baby has any abnormalities, and its blood group. We can let you know the blood group tomorrow, but the rest of the test results will take a week."

The whole procedure took less than half an hour. Conchitta was then told to go home, put her feet up, and rest for twenty four hours.

Pablo felt obliged to wait while Conchitta got dressed. He thanked all the staff and walked Conchitta back to the main reception area where her brothers were anxiously waiting. Stepping out in front of Pablo and Conchitta, they cleared a path through the waiting journalists.

"Pablo, over here!" a voice bellowed across the crowd.

Pablo looked up and saw Manolo waiting in his car with the engine running and the top down. Checking Conchitta was all right, he could see she was consumed in manipulating the journalists. He made his break and rushed for the car, jumping over the door and landing feet first on the seat.

Pablo made himself comfortable as Manolo put his foot down and they sped off.

"I drove in this way and saw all the press so I thought you would need rescuing. I drove around a couple of times and then thought I would just wait until you appeared."

"Thanks, Manolo. I owe you a big favour. I dread to think what would have happened if you had not been there. I would have probably have had to get in the car with Conchitta to make my escape. I cannot believe she alerted the press and told them to be there."

"I think she is making some money out of this; she's got some sort of deal with them. Okay, where to now then? I bet you could do with a drink."

"Yes, I could. I am so relieved that it's all over. I only must wait until tomorrow for the results."

Manolo drove out of town and up to the old farmhouse on the hill. Carlos would give them sanctuary for the rest of the day until it was time to meet the girls.

Chapter 35

Harry and Christina had both showered and changed; they emerged feeling fresh and ready to hit the town. Saying goodbye to Carol and David was emotional.

"We must make sure we do not leave it so long until we see you again. Give us a ring when you get back to England at Christmas." Anna kissed Carol goodbye as everyone climbed back into the car.

It took just twenty minutes to drive up the coast road into Playa. Mark dropped the girls by the roundabout and headed back out towards the bypass to avoid queuing through the centre of the town.

Harry and Christina headed along, gazing into the shop windows and at the street stalls, and towards where they had arranged to meet the boys. Harry had her dark glasses on and her hair in a ponytail, flowing down her back, her cap neatly finishing off her casual look. Christina had put her dark glasses on too to avoid being recognised. Their pictures were now everywhere they looked. As they discreetly weaved their way in and out of the evening shoppers, street artists, and pavement cafes, a car horn tooted at them.

"Just ignore it, Christina. Don't even look, just keep going." The horn tooted again, followed by a loud whistle, very close to them. This time Harry and Christina both looked around. It was Manolo and Pablo. The girls both laughed and climbed into the back of the convertible.

"We thought it would be nice if we headed back to the Taverna and had a meal there tonight. You girls have not eaten there this year, have you? We can sit inside by a window and admire the sea view while we are eating. What do you think?"

Harry leant over the seat and kissed Pablo on his cheek. "That sounds great, Pablo, but will we be allowed in? We've both got jeans on."

"I will go in ahead of you all and ask them if it's possible for us to sit in the restaurant." Pablo parked outside the Taverna and ran in to enquire. They were extremely apologetic and said the restaurant was already full to bursting point. Would they mind sitting up on the roof terrace? It was a lovely warm evening. Pablo relayed the message back to his friends. They all nodded so Pablo went back in and confirmed. Manolo pressed the automatic button and the roof slowly closed. Safely locked, Manolo handed his keys to Christina and she placed them in her bag. Manolo took Christina's hand and followed Harry and Pablo in through the double-doors and into the large, arched entrance hall.

The restaurant walls were whitewashed and covered in pictures of old S'agaro. A high shelf, a meter below the roof, was covered in fishing paraphernalia. Lobster baskets, nets, anchors, bells, and lanterns, cluttered the shelves. A large fishing net, with an assortment of empty shells, star fish and stuffed fish, completely covered one wall. At the other end, an old bar ran out from the restaurant and onto the terrace. A pretty, young, dark-haired waitress, dressed in a white tunic, plimsolls and cap, appeared.

"Señor Cruanos." The little waitress recognised Pablo straight away. "I thought it was you I could hear at the bar but I was not sure. Oh, you have the Ski-Summer girls with you. Look, we have had one cancellation and I have managed to squeeze a table into the corner, over by that window, for you. I have put a screen across, separating you from the other diners, because of your casual clothes. We are not really allowed to let anyone in, unless they are in formal dress."

"That will be fine, thank you very much. Oh, one more thing, if anyone phones to speak to me, or arrives here looking for any of us, will you tell them you have not seen us?" Pablo slipped the waitress some money.

Harry and Christina led the way across the cool, stone-flagged floor, through the crowded restaurant, to the beautifully dressed table, followed by Pablo and Manolo. The two girls sat by the window; Pablo sat next to Harry and Manolo next to Christina.

The waitress took out her notepad and asked them what they wanted to drink. Once drinks were ordered, a basket of bread was placed on the table and was instantly passed around by Manolo. They all appeared to be very hungry, except Pablo, who slipped his hand under the table and on to Harry's knee. He longed to hold her and make all his troubles vanish.

Harry was looking out across the bay. The sun had vanished down behind the hills and the moon was rising slowly up from the dark, night sea. The wind had changed direction and the water had calmed down. It was almost flat. The fishermen were out in force, their bells ringing and lanterns swinging gently from side to side. Harry placed her delicate hand on top of Pablo's, and rubbed it gently. She could sense he was very anxious about something and she would ask him later what was wrong.

Christina was in a chatty mood and relayed the story of their boring day in Sant Antonio.

Chapter 36

Mark and Anna had stopped to pick some chicken and chips up on their way back from dropping the girls off. The twins were starving. Once they were back at their cosy little villa, Mark divided the chicken amongst them and dished up the chips whilst Anna tried to set the table around them. They had not been back very long and had just finished eating when the villa phone rang. It was his sister. Anna watched as his happy face turned ashen.

Mark placed the phone back on the side. "It's my mother."

Anna jumped up and sent the twins up to their room to play. "What's wrong, Mark?" Anna moved to where Mark was standing.

He crumpled into her arms. "She's had a stroke. Mum's had a stroke and they don't know how bad it is yet."

"Oh, Mark, I'm so sorry".

Mark rocked backwards and forwards in Anna's arms then, snapping out of his grief, he started thinking. "There's nothing we can do, but

I must get home. We'll have to leave tonight. We'll be home by the morning."

"Okay, Darling. I'll go and pack while you try to find Harry and Christina.

Mark rang Pablo's mobile. The answer phone clicked on. He left a message for them to get back to the villa urgently. Then he tried every restaurant he could think of in Playa. He was feeling stronger now. His adrenalin had kicked in; he had to concentrate and think. Finally he phoned Pablo's parents. Isabel answered the phone but, her English not being very good, she went and found Jordi.

Mark explained to Jordi that his mother had been taken ill and that they would have to leave for England straight away. He could not find Harry and Christina and he wondered if Jordi had any idea where they were.

Jordi said he had not heard from them since Pablo had phoned after his visit to the clinic to say he would be home later that night. He too would phone round and try to find them. His two daughters were in Playa; he would contact them and see if they could spot them in any of the bars or cafés.

Mark had loaded all the luggage into the car and the girls were still nowhere to be seen. Anna wrote them a note, explaining what had happened and not to worry. Mark had paid for two plane tickets with his credit card. The girls might as well stay the rest of the week; there was nothing they could do. Anna would phone them once they had seen Grandma and let them know how she was. They could get a lift or taxi to Girona airport, where they would fly from, and catch a coach back to Gloucestershire once they had landed.

The twins did not realise the seriousness of the situation; they loved sleeping in the car and thought it was exciting. Anna had made them both nice, cosy beds and put them into their pyjamas. Chatting away to each other happily, they were really looking forward to seeing Smudge the dog and all their other animals again; they did not mind leaving the villa.

As they were about to leave, Jordi phoned to say he had tried everywhere, even the Taverna. Nobody he had spoken to had seen them. Isabel asked him to send her love, and asked them to phone, once they were back in England. Jordi promised to keep an eye on the girls for the rest of the week and said he would make sure they made their plane on Saturday. He wished Mark a safe and speedy journey.

Having filled the car up with fuel, they were off. Anna felt a little apprehensive, leaving her daughters in Spain, and thanked God they had met the Cruanos, who would look after them, and help them, if needed.

Chapter 37

The meal was fantastic. Harry had eaten lobster for the first time in her life and thoroughly enjoyed it, not noticing Pablo had hardly touched his. For dessert, Harry, Christina, and Manolo indulged in fresh strawberries and cream. Pablo asked for the bill and, while he and Manolo settled-up, Harry and Christina headed for the loo.

"Don't you think Pablo is very quiet tonight?" Harry whispered loudly, over the top of the loo door, to Christina, as she retouched her lip gloss and checked her hair.

Christina had noticed how quiet Pablo was, probably worrying about his test results. She would find out from Manolo how it had gone when they were alone. In the meantime she could not let on to Harry what she thought. "He seemed all right to me. It must be your imagination."

"No, there is definitely something wrong with him. He seems very distant."

Manolo was waiting by the door for the girls. Christina fished in her bag and pulled out the car keys which she handed to Manolo. Pablo was leaning against the car waiting for them all. Once Manolo had unlocked the car, Christina climbed into the back next to Harry, letting Pablo take the front seat again. Manolo put some music on to distract them all from Pablo's obvious low mood. Then he drove Pablo into Saint Feliu to pick his car up; it was still where he had left it earlier, by the harbour.

"Why did you leave it in Sant Feliu?" Harry questioned Pablo as she climbed out of Manolo's car and waited by the passenger door of the BMW.

"Oh, I had arranged to meet Manolo here earlier. We both had some time to kill so we went for a coffee in the Ramblas. There seemed no point in taking two cars so we left mine here. Hold on, I do not have my phone. Pablo ran after Manolo and caught him, just as he was about to pull out of the car park. Laughing, Christina looked in the glove compartment and found the mobile brick. Handing it to Pablo, she noticed he had three missed calls.

He listened to his messages as he walked back towards his own car. One was from Conchitta saying she would like to meet up with him tomorrow, after he had got the results of the tests. There was an urgent one from his father saying, "Please phone me when you get this message," and one from Mark saying, "Take the girls home as soon as possible."

"Important?" Harry nodded at the phone.

"Yes. Your father wants you home. Why, I don't know. And there's one from my father asking me to phone him. Pablo pressed his automatic unlock and the hazards flashed twice as the car unlocked. Harry climbed into the passenger seat. "You had better phone your father before we set off."

Pablo called up his home phone number. It was quite late and Juan answered the phone. Pablo asked him if his father was still up. Juan said yes, his father had been waiting for Pablo to call; he would take the phone to him.

"Papa." Pablo spoke quietly, and for some time, with his father. His face looking grave, he turned to Harry who had been fiddling with her seat, trying to adjust it. Sliding his arm around Harry's shoulder, he moved closer towards her. He explained about her grandmother. He waited for a reaction before he continued.

Harry started to shake and the tears rolled down her cheeks. At first she cried silently whilst picturing her grandmother; the only picture she could muster was of her grandmother out in the garden doing what she loved most. What if she was so bad she could no longer speak or move? What if she was so bad she would never recover? What if she had already died and she would never see her again? The silent tears turned to sobs.

Pablo leaned right across and held Harry with both arms. "I'm sure she will be fine. You are always telling me what a strong woman she is."

Harry sobbed and sobbed, her head nestling on his shoulder. She rocked back and forth cradled in Pablo's strong arms. Pablo kissed the tears from her cheeks. It made him very sad to see Harry so upset. He knew he would feel the same if it was his grandfather. Now he had to be strong for Harry. She needed him; her parents had gone back to England. He once again felt very responsible for Harry. It was up to him.

Once Harry had calmed down Pablo started the car up. As he drove her back to the villa he told Harry her parents had already left. Mark had left them plane tickets to be picked up at Girona airport and they would be leaving on Saturday.

Manolo and Christina had reached the villa. All the lights were on but there was no sign of Anna or Mark through the windows. Christina tried to open the door but it was locked. She knocked and called out but still no one came. Shrugging her shoulders at Manolo she wandered around to the garage to find the spare key. Opening the side door, the garage was in darkness. She felt for the light. The car had gone. Where was everyone? Picking a red plastic bucket off the shelf she took the spare key out.

Turning the lights off and shutting the door Christina headed back around to where Manolo was waiting. At last they had got in. There was an envelope on the table with her and Harry's names on it. "I wonder where they've gone at this late time of night. At least they've left us a note. Do you want to get us both a drink, Manolo while I read this note?"

Manolo, pleased at having the place to themselves, skipped off to the kitchen to make drinks. When he returned Christina was slumped over the table. Manolo had never seen Christina looking upset; she was always laughing and smiling. He spotted the note screwed up on the table. "What is wrong?" Manolo was by her side in seconds and placed his arm around her shoulder.

Christina pushed the note towards him, afraid that if she opened her mouth and said the words, "my grandmother has had a stroke," she would break down.

Manolo took a few minutes to read and translate the note. Squatting on the floor next to Christina he took her hands in his. "I am very sorry about your grandmother." Standing, he pulled Christina towards him and held her tightly for a while.

When she finally broke away she picked up the drink he had placed on the table and drank it back in one. Then she lit a cigarette and calmly sat back down. "How will I tell Harry? She will be heartbroken."

At that moment a car pulled up. Manolo glanced out of the window and nodded, letting Christina know it was Harry and Pablo.

Harry was walking very slowly with her head down. Pablo had his arm around her shoulder, leading her towards the door.

"I don't think you have to tell her. I think she already knows." Manolo went to open the door as Christina got up from the table, stubbing her cigarette out, and crossed the room to meet her little sister. Throwing her arms around Harry she cuddled her for a few minutes before leading her to a chair and sitting her down.

Pablo went to the kitchen with Manolo and got them some glasses and the bottle of brandy. "Come on, let's all have a drink. It will help you to relax and brandy is good for a shock."

An hour and a half later they were all reminiscing about their grandparents and relaying stories of their childhood.

At last Harry said she was tired. Christina asked Pablo and Manolo if they would like to stay as it was so late and they had all drunk rather a lot. They were both grateful for the offer. It had been a very long evening. Christina got her things out of her room and told Pablo he could sleep in her bed then he would be near Harry.

Manolo and Christina said goodnight and disappeared upstairs to sleep in the twin's room.

Harry went into the bathroom to wash and change, leaving Pablo undressing in her bedroom.

Pablo was sitting in Christina's bed reading one of Harry's books when she returned.

Having kissed Pablo, Harry said goodnight and got into bed.

Pablo turned the light off and lay back on the pillow with his hands behind his head. Staring into the blackness he thought how awful it would be for them all if the test proved positive. He would never be able to face Harry and tell her. Would she be understanding and still love him? Would she hate him? How would he feel about being a dad? His mind was racing. He heard a quiet sob. Quickly distracted he whispered, "Harry is that you?" There was no reply. Getting out of bed he crossed the floor to where Harry lay. Sitting on the side of the bed he felt for the light switch. Harry was in floods of tears again. Pablo pulled the covers back and, gently pushing her over, got into the single bed. Turning the light back off he scooped her up in his arms and kissed and cuddled her until at last, all cried out, Harry fell to sleep. Pablo remained where he was holding the girl he loved, his little English Rose. Eventually sleep took a hold of him.

Chapter 38

Mark drove right through the night arriving at Calais fifteen hours later. Exhausted and desperate, he tried to convince the ticket attendant to let them on to the ferry that day instead of the date on the ticket. He was told he would have to wait until all the other vehicles booked on had boarded. Luckily, after sitting at the back of the queue for half an hour watching all the other cars loading, they were waved through. They had been allowed onto the ferry that was about to depart.

The twins were awake, bursting with energy and dying to get into the playroom on the ferry. Anna handed them their clothes and they struggled to dress in their sleeping bags. Once up on deck they all headed to the washroom to do their teeth and freshen up. Mickey went into the men's toilet with his father while Sophie followed Anna into the ladies. Anna had a wash and applied some make up. Feeling much better, Mark led the way to the dining area; a full English breakfast and he would be as right as rain again. He had phoned his sister earlier whilst they were lining up to board the ferry, and she had assured him their mother was stable. Once they had finished their breakfast Anna took the twins off to find the play area and Mark went to buy a paper. He would find a nice seat with Anna near the play area and have a little read and doze if he could until it was time to disembark. The duty-free shop was crowded; marching past the rows of cigarettes, perfumes, aftershaves, and gadgets he found a separate counter selling papers. Waiting patiently in line to be served, he scanned the headlines and photos on the front of the other papers.

There, on the front of the Costa Brave Fun, was a picture of Pablo with Conchitta outside the clinic. Snatching it up he took it back to show Anna and to read it. This was all Harry would need after the shock she'd had last night. With any luck, Pablo would have his results and Harry would know all about it before she'd seen a copy.

Harry woke still snuggled warmly in Pablo's arms, her head thumping. It must have been all the brandy she had drunk the previous evening. She must get up and take some paracetamol. As she stirred, Pablo woke.

It took him a few minutes to remember where he was.

Harry ran her hand over his chest and kissed him gently on the lips. "I love you," she whispered as she rolled over the top of him and got out of bed. Grabbing some underwear from the drawer she headed off to the bathroom to shower.

When she got back Pablo was dressed.

He eyed her up and down; she looked so sexy in her underwear. Still, they had the villa to themselves for the whole week. With any luck they would be celebrating their engagement later. Then he would take her to bed and make mad passionate love to her. "How are you feeling today?"

"A lot better. I don't think I could cry another tear. I will phone home later when I am sure my mum and dad have arrived back and see how my grandmother is."

"Good. I'm going to have to race off. I want to shower and change. I have a few jobs to do and then I'll be back later. What are you going to do today?"

"I'll tidy up the villa. I want to pop down to the little shop at the bottom of the road and get some bread and then spend the rest of the day by the pool, so come and find me when you're free."

Pablo pulled Harry into his arms. Running his hands down her smooth, bare back, he rested them on her small, firm bottom. Squeezing her bottom, he pulled it hard against his body. "I love you and don't you forget it, my little English Rose. Get that ring out ready to wear."

Their lips met and they kissed. As the kiss ended Harry opened her eyes. Pablo was watching her. They held each other's gaze for a few moments before Pablo released Harry and left.

Harry slipped into her three-quarter length black jeans and a black T-shirt. Having tidied her bedroom she set about the kitchen, throwing all the perishable food away and cleaning out the fridge. She and Christina would not be doing any cooking. The rest the maid would take when she gave the place a once over at the end of the week. Christina and Manolo were still sleeping so Harry tiptoed round whilst she cleaned the lounge.

There was a sound from upstairs. She decided to leave Christina a note saying she'd just popped to the shops. She didn't want to be around when Manolo appeared. Tucking her hair up into her black cap, she put her sunglasses on, picked up her purse, and headed off down the road. It was another beautiful day. The air was still quite fresh and the sun was still low in the sky.

Harry pushed her way through the beaded curtain. The little shop was quite dark and very cool inside. Harry removed her dark glasses so she could see better. The walls were racked from floor to ceiling, shelves filled with tins, pasta, bottles, and sauces. Every available space was used. Harry glanced around for the bread basket. Two ladies stood gossiping to the shop keeper as they pawed their way through the daily papers. The bread and rolls were all lined up in baskets behind the counter.

Harry went up to the counter and stood patiently waiting to be served. Eventually the shopkeeper dragged herself over to Harry and asked her what she wanted. Harry asked for a couple of baguettes. The shopkeeper just stood mouth open. Harry wondered what the matter was. The shopkeeper spoke to the other two ladies, who handed her a paper. The women placed the paper on the counter and pointed to a picture of Harry at the bottom of the front page.

Harry glanced down at the picture and laughed. "Yes, it's me." As she looked down again she noticed that the larger picture above it was a picture of Pablo with Conchitta. Harry could not believe her eyes. Trying to stop her hand from shaking she took a note out of her purse, handed it to the shopkeeper, and left without her bread, clutching the paper. Placing her glasses back on, she walked away as quickly as she could. She could sense the three ladies staring after her. Once she had rounded the corner she broke into a jog. When she was a safe distance away she looked around making sure she was alone. She leant against the wall and tried to translate the article. The picture had been taken yesterday. Pablo had been to the clinic with his future fiancée for some tests. She could not work it out. She had to get back to the Villa and get Manolo to translate it for her. Arriving back hot, flushed, and confused, she threw the paper onto the table where Christina and Manolo were sitting eating breakfast.

"Oh, Harry." Christina jumped up and placed her arm around Harry's shaking shoulders.

"Tell me, Manolo? What does it say?"

Christina managed to coax Harry onto a chair and rubbed her shoulders while Manolo explained what had been going on.

"You mean to tell me Pablo may be the father of Conchitta's child, yet he still thinks he can marry me? All this time he's been lying to me! All of you have!" Harry was too angry for tears. Running into the bedroom and pulling her suitcase out, she began to throw her clothes in it.

"Harry, what are you doing?" Christina was behind her trying to take the clothes out of the case but, as quickly as she did, Harry threw them back in.

Manolo hovered in the doorway not knowing quite what to do.

"Look, Christina, I'm leaving. I'll get a taxi to the airport. I'm going home. You do what you like. Manolo, can you take me down to the taxi rank?"

"At least wait and talk to Pablo. He gets the results today. He's convinced it's not his baby." Christina pleaded.

Harry just carried on packing, tears now stinging down her cheeks.

"Manolo, I'm going to have to go with her. I can't let her fly home on her own in this state. You take us to the taxi rank and then go and find Pablo. Meet us at the airport. Maybe if she sees him, he will be able to make her change her mind."

Christina started packing everything into her suitcase. By the time she had finished, Harry was already waiting by the car.

Manolo tried once more to convince her to wait and hear what Pablo had to say.

Harry was having none of it. She'd trusted Pablo; she'd given him everything. She'd given him her heart. He had just been carrying on with two separate lives. "Can you give this back to Pablo for me?" Harry gulped back the tears as she handed her engagement ring to Manolo.

"Keep it, Harry. Pablo would want you to keep it." Harry shook her head. Manolo loaded their bags into the boot of the car, Harry climbed into the back, and Christina sat in the front, next to a very worried and anxious Manolo.

They sat in silence as Manolo drove to Gerona airport. He pulled up outside the departure area and went to find a luggage-trolley, while Harry threw the cases out of the boot and onto the pavement. Not waiting for Manolo to return, Harry was through the automatic doors, dragging her suitcase with her back pack thrown over her shoulder, and heading towards enquires.

Christina waited for Manolo to return before placing her case onto the trolley. She could take her time now. Harry might not even be able to get them onto a flight.

"Manolo, I'm so sorry about all this. Can you go and find Pablo and bring him here, as quickly as you can?"

Manolo kissed Christina reassuringly on the lips and left.

Christina caught up with Harry at the enquiry desk. Children were sliding up and down on the polished, slippery floor. Lines of people, with trolleys loaded with luggage, stood patiently in front of check-in desks waiting to dispose of their luggage.

Tearfully Harry explained to Christina that they had located the tickets their father had booked for the Saturday flight. They were now checking if there were any places left on that day's flights. Harry drummed her nails impatiently on the counter while they scanned the computer.

"You are very lucky, Señorita. We have two seats left on the next flight for Birmingham."

At last something was going right. The quicker she got away from this place the better. She could not face Pablo or any more deceit. Their tickets were altered and handed to Harry. The check-in desk for their flight had just opened and a small queue was just forming.

Christina took Harry's suitcase from her and placed it on the trolley. Harry was looking a complete mess. Christina gently spoke to Harry as if she were speaking to a small child. "I'll stay in the queue, you go to the loo and wash your face."

Harry glanced into the mirror. She could not focus. Filling the sink with cold-water she splashed her face. Turning the hand dryer onto her face, she waited for a few moments while the hot stuffy air dried the water dripping down her blotchy face. Rummaging in her bag, she found some moisturising cream. Her face felt taut. Gently she worked the cream into her skin. Two little English speaking girls were whispering in the doorway, trying to decide if Harry was the girl off some poster they had seen, or not. Harry was on auto pilot, brushing her hair and tucking it back up into her cap; she just ignored them, walked straight past them, and went back out to join Christina.

"Is this all your luggage?"

"Oh, yes," Christina replied as she handed the tickets over. "Window or aisle seat?"

"Please can we have one window seat?" They were handed their boarding passes and told to make their way upstairs to the departure lounge.

Christina checked the time. "God," she thought, "this plane is leaving in two hours, I hope Manolo makes it back with Pablo."

Before entering the departure lounge their hand luggage had to be placed in a tray. Harry had to remove all her creams and carry them through in a clear, plastic bag. She was asked to remove her cap and shoes and again placed them on the tray on a conveyer belt to be checked, while she waited her turn to show her passport and boarding pass.

Once they were clear, Christina suggested they made for the bar. Harry, still on auto pilot and feeling numb, followed Christina past the duty-free shops and to the outdoor bar. Christina ordered them a double vodka each and handed Harry a cigarette. Harry took it. It was the first one she'd had in ages. Pablo disapproved of her smoking. Well, now she didn't care.

Manolo drove back towards Mas Nou like a bat out of hell. He'd try Pablo's parents' villa first. Why didn't he have his mobile charged up? He was useless.

Back at the villa, Pablo's parents had been very anxious to hear how Harry was. After giving them a quick update, Pablo had showered and changed. He paced up and down in the kitchen with his mother and father, who were drinking coffee and waiting for the phone to ring. His father had phoned the clinic last night and called in a favour from an old friend who was a doctor at the hospital. His friend was going to get the results of the tests as soon as they had been completed and was to phone them through to Señor Cruanos. He would let them know before anyone else. It would give them time if they needed any. Pablo drank one coffee after another while watching the phone. His father sat and read the paper while his mother busied herself preparing a meal.

Juan entered the kitchen. "I don't want to alarm you, Pablo, but have you seen today's Costa Brava Fun?"

Pablo shook his head.

Juan handed the paper over to Pablo. His father and mother both joined him as they looked at the photos and read the article.

"Oh God, I hope Harry has not seen this. This could ruin everything."

At that moment, the phone rang. Jordi answered it then, nodding to Pablo, handed him the phone. His father's friend was very nice. "You are a free man, Pablo. Your blood group does not match that of the foetus. You are not the father of Conchitta's baby."

Isabel started dancing around the kitchen. She could tell by the relieved expression on Pablo's face it was all over. Pablo handed the phone back to Juan who congratulated him.

His father hugged him. "You have had a terrible experience, my son. Now learn from it. Go and find Harry and tell her the whole story."

Pablo left his overjoyed parents after promising he would bring Harry over for dinner that night. Kicking his heels in the air he ran out to his car. He could not wait to see Harry. Everything was going to be all right. By the end of the day they would be engaged.

Manolo pulled into the parking area in front of the Cruanos villa, almost knocking Juan over as he stormed the house shouting, "Pablo! Where is Pablo?"

Isabel and Jordi heard the commotion. They met Manolo talking to Juan in the hall. After explaining quickly what had happened, Manolo was ushered back out of the door. He had no time to lose.

Pablo had driven to Harry's parents' villa and was surprised to find it all locked up. As he got back in his car, wondering where to go next, Manolo came speeding around the corner. Flashing his lights, he managed to flag Pablo down.

Abandoning his car, Manolo jumped in the BMW; it was the faster of the two cars. "As quickly as you can, Pablo, Gerona Airport." The wheels span as Pablo put his foot down. Manolo told Pablo exactly what had happened. Pablo's happy expression changed to one of anxiety as the story unfolded.

"This is the last call for flight B2407." Christina had got Harry drunk and was trying to go as slowly as possible with her to the departure lounge, hoping they would miss the plane. A steward spotted them and hurried them along. Christina had to support Harry on the conveyor belt that took them to the awaiting train. It was no good; the boys were not going to make it. Christina led Harry to the back of the shuttle and sat her down on the window seat. Looking back at the windows of the departure lounge, she hoped to see a familiar face. The train pulled away at some speed. Harry nearly fell off her seat.

Christina helped Harry out of the train and onto the baking tarmac.

"This way please." Another flight attendant pointed towards the steps of the waiting plane. Once on the plane, Christina gave Harry the window seat. Leaning across her, she scanned the second-floor windows of the airport, still searching for Pablo.

Pablo screeched the car to a halt, leapt out, and ran for the departure lounge. He was stopped and frisked and scanned up and down with a portable hand scanner. Just his luck it bleeped. Ripping his belt off he handed it to the security guard who scanned him again. He was clear. The security guard handed him back his belt. Taking the stairs three at a time he reached the top and burst through the double doors, his eyes searching the flight departure's board. The flight for Birmingham was flashing; "Flight B2407 for Birmingham now departing at gate 19." With no time to lose he ran to gate nineteen. The gate had closed. He pleaded with a security guard to let him through, but the guard was adamant he was not allowed to cross the line; his time had run out. He looked through the huge glass window and watched, with tears stinging his cheeks, as the plane taxied down the runway.

Chapter 39

The plane touched down in England.

"Wake up, Harry. Come on, wake up. We are back in England."

Harry's head was foggy. Lifting her hand up to her brow she rubbed it gently; it was thumping.

"Look, Harry, the weather is really nice."

Harry glanced out of the little airplane window. The sun was high in the sky. With her head aching from too much alcohol, lack of sleep, and endless crying, it was far too bright for Harry. Delicately, rummaging in her bag, she found her sunglasses and put them on and checked her cap was still securely in place on her head.

Christina had made a point of hogging the plane toilet for the last hour while she did her hair and make-up. She was ready to face the world with her usual confidence.

Harry thought they would slip away quietly and hoped no one would recognise her.

"This is your Captain speaking. Before you depart the sun is shining and the temperature outside is a very warm twenty two degrees. I hope you have enjoyed your flight with Skyline, and let me thank you on behalf of the cabin crew and myself for being such good passengers." The captain switched off the humming fans, and the doors opened.

The air stewardess handed Harry a note just as she was about to descend the steps. Safely placing her feet on the black sticky tarmac, she walked across to the main airport terminal.

Christina was anxious to read what the note had to say and urged Harry to read it. Harry threw her backpack over her shoulder and opened the note. It was from the captain. It read, "Very impressed with your skiing. Any chance of a coffee? Will be in the coffee bar in the airport lounge in about 30 mins. P.S. Watch out for reporters waiting for you in Airport."

"Oh God, that's all I need," Harry moaned as she crumpled the note up and stuffed it in her pocket and pulled her cap peak down lower over her eyes.

Having read the note over Harry's shoulder Christina was very enthusiastic. "Come on, Harry, he may be very good looking. Why don't we just go along and see."

Harry did not need to reply. The look she gave Christina was enough to shut her up. "Please, Christina, just keep your eyes open for the reporters. I thought I'd left them behind. I really couldn't face any today."

The luggage collection was a nightmare. People pushing to get an unobstructed view of the conveyor belt, hands ready to pluck their bags off, hoping theirs would be the first to appear. Harry sat on the trolley with her head resting in her hands, away from the crowd, and waited for everyone to disperse. Christina disappeared off to the smoking area for a quick cigarette. When she returned the conveyor belt was empty but for their two suitcases and a buggy with a broken wheel that no one wanted to claim.

Arriving at customs they followed the arrows to the Nothing to Declare section. They were the last two people through. All the customs officers, already occupied, didn't give them so much as a second glance.

Christina led the way and Harry followed pushing the trolley loaded with suitcases and backpacks.

"Now first we have to go to enquiries and find a coach back to Gloucestershire. This should be fun." The airport entrance was packed.

They followed the queuing ropes that formed a path leading to the airport exit. As they turned the next corner a bank of journalists and photographers met them. Pointing their notepads and cameras directly at Harry, flashes exploding like a synchronized firework display, a hungry pack of reporters started firing questions. Harry just looked straight ahead and ignored their questions.

"Harry, this way please? Harry, look over here? Harry, can we have a smile? Harry what happened between you and Mr Cruanos? Where is Pablo now? What do you think of his fiancée? Did you ever meet her?" As the questions came thick and fast, Harry just kept walking. Where she was going, she had no idea.

Christina just kept shouting back at them, "No comment!"

As the rope forming a barrier between Harry and the press started running out, Harry felt a hand on her shoulder. Glancing back, she saw a tall, tanned, fair-haired man dressed in a captain's uniform. For a split second, she thought she recognised him.

"Harry, wait, let me help you. Do you need a lift somewhere?"

Christina jumped in. "Oh, yes please, we need to get back to Gloucestershire."

Taking the trolley from Harry he was quick to respond. "Follow me." Swinging the trolley around, he headed for a door with a notice above saying "staff only."

Christina grabbed Harry's arm and steered her to follow him.

He led them through a series of long, poorly lit corridors and into a large lift. The lift descended then clanked to a halt. The doors opened onto a car park. "Come on, this is the staff car park. My car is parked over there."

Harry and Christina followed him over to a racing-green Audi.

He unlocked the doors and told them to get in as he loaded their suitcases into the boot.

Christina jumped into the front and Harry slumped onto the back seat.

As the handsome knight-in-shining-armour, dressed as a pilot, glided into the front seat, he held out his hand to Christina. In a typical public-school voice, he spoke. "Hello, nice to meet you, I'm John."

"Hi, John, thanks for this. I'm Christina and this is my sister whom I believe you already know; Harry."

John turned around to face Harry who was staring out of the window in the back of the car. He offered her his hand. Harry shook it. It felt warm and very firm compared to Harry's soft limp hand.

"Oh yes, thank you for the lift." Harry sat back. She didn't want to have to make conversation but felt she should be polite. After all, if he had not appeared, what the hell would they be doing now?

John started the car up and turned it around. Pointing it in the direction of the exit, he explained he had had time to kill whilst waiting in Girona, and had seen the Spanish papers. He was pleasantly surprised when he had seen the revised passenger list and thought he had recognised the names. His parents lived in Gloucestershire in a little village called Dymock. He had a few days off so was heading out to stay with them. He needed a break and it was the only place he knew to get some peace and quiet.

Christina was over the moon. "What a coincidence," she exclaimed. "We live in a little village not far from you."

Harry ignored the chatter, stacked her backpack against the door and used it as a pillow. She would pretend to be asleep all the way back and then she would not have to talk.

John drove smoothly and quickly. Christina chatted away to him, finding out as much as she could about his family and whether he had a girlfriend. He was very polite and sweet. He answered all Christina's questions. As he drove he kept glancing at Harry's beautiful, innocent face in his rear mirror. She was so attractive. They both were. What a stroke of luck to have met them and be able to help and offer them a lift. Harry looked very sad and depressed. Thinking she was asleep, he questioned Christina about Harry's relationship with Pablo. He was surprised to find out the truth about what a rat Conchitta had been. Poor Harry, Poor Pablo, he thought. Fancy letting her slip from his grasp; he must be heartbroken.

He insisted on taking them all the way home. Christina gave him instructions once they had arrived in Newent. He followed the narrowing road back out of the town towards May Hill. He slowed down once he'd reached the chestnut trees, a landmark Christina had told him to watch out for. This was where he was to turn. He pulled into the farm. The car crunched slowly up the stony drive and stopped outside the door of the Georgian farmhouse.

Harry pretended to wake up when he switched the engine off. She'd kept her glasses and cap on so it had been quite easy to keep up the pretence of sleeping. Sitting up slowly, looking around at the familiar buildings, relief swept through her.

The front door burst open and out came the twins, shouting in excitement, followed by a surprised looking Anna. "Girls, you're back!"

Christina introduced John to her mother and the twins, explaining how he'd rescued Harry from the waiting press and the prospect of a nightmarish journey home.

Harry got out and stood by the door, gripping her back pack and praying Christina would not invite John in for a coffee. He took their cases from the boot and placed them carefully on the flagstone floor of the entrance hall.

"Would you like to come in for a coffee, John?"

John looked at Harry. He could tell she was not in the mood for socialising. He'd learnt a lot from Christina on the way back from the airport and decided she was a nice girl, but he was not sure if she would be his type. Harry, he would like to get to know better. He'd give it a few days and then give her a ring, offer to take her out and cheer her up. "Thanks very much but I really should be getting home myself. My parents will be expecting me." John put out his hand to Harry. "Nice meeting you."

Harry gently shook his hand and thanked him for rescuing them. He then shook Christina's hand, wished her luck when she went back to university, and left.

Sitting around the cluttered, pine kitchen table, Anna told the girls that their Grandma had been very lucky. She had some paralysis down the one side and her speech was very slurred, but the doctors were quite sure, with physio and speech therapy, there was no reason she should not make a good recovery. It had been a warning; she had to slow down and take things a little easier when she recovered.

Harry and Christina were both very relieved. The twins sat patiently listening as Christina and Harry explained the events of their mad day and rush to get home. It seemed like weeks ago since they had all been altogether at the farm. The twins had had enough; they had been sitting like coiled springs. Having only been home for a few hours themselves, they had been for a nose around the farm. They were eager to go out to explore and play. Desperate to find out what was new and what been going on in their absence, they asked their mother if they could go out and play. Leaving the table, they sorted out their wellington boots from the large old chest by the back door, and headed off to find Smudge, their dog.

Christina headed off to phone her friends. She had so much to tell them and she needed to catch up on all their gossip.

Anna sat herself down next to Harry. Placing her arm around Harry's shoulder she asked Harry how she was feeling. Harry said she was feeling awful. Everything felt numb. She loved Pablo so much, but she had felt so betrayed. She was feeling empty, had a knot in her stomach, a lump in her throat and wanted to scream. Half of her had wanted to stay in Spain. She wanted to give Pablo the chance to explain, hold her and tell her he still loved her. The other half of her was too angry, her pride so strong it prevented her. Instead she had just run; she couldn't think straight and needed to get back to the farm. Anna said that they all knew about Conchitta. They were all to blame, not just Pablo. It had been pretty much a mutual decision to keep her in the dark. Now she could see it would have been better to have told Harry everything right from the start and not to have tried protecting her. After shedding more tears and receiving a big hug from her mother, Harry went upstairs for a long bath. Anna said she would feel much better after a long soak in the bath, a homely meal, and a good night's sleep.

Chapter 40

Even though Pablo was feeling devastated, his world had fallen apart and his English Rose was on a plane flying back to England, he had insisted he would be fine to drive, and drove them back to the coast. Manolo tried his best to console Pablo, reminding him that Harry would be back in a month or two for the Ski-Winter filming and promotion.

They spent the night at the Canary bar drowning Pablo's sorrows with the owner. At the end of the evening, feeling very sorry for Pablo, he stuck them in a taxi and sent them home. The taxi arrived at the villa on Mass Nou. Pablo struggled to get out of the taxi. He had no control over his own body as the alcohol overwhelmed every limb. At that moment, trusty Juan appeared in his dressing gown. He'd insisted he had wanted to stay up and wait for Pablo's return. With no contact from Pablo, and as the night had gone on, he had been getting worried.

Isabel and Jordi had passed the time eating with their daughters, although no-one had much of an appetite. Juan paid the taxi driver and helped Manolo, who was in a slightly better state than Pablo, into the villa. Pablo had been left propped against the gate until Juan returned with Jordi to carry him in.

Taking him straight up to his room, Juan took his clothes off him and got him into his bed. Jordi kissed his son on his forehead and told him to try to get a good night's sleep. They would talk in the morning. Manolo was to stay the night and was made comfortable in the spare room. After telling him what a good friend he was to Pablo, and how grateful they were to him for looking after Pablo, they left him to sleep it off. That evening Anna phoned Isabel to say she was so sorry how everything had worked out. Isabel was not very good at speaking English so had repeatedly sobbed and said sorry to Anna until Jordi took the phone from her. Anna said she thought Harry was in shock, very jet lagged and tired. She had gone to bed now and Anna would try to persuade her to phone Pablo in the morning. She asked how Pablo was. At that point in the evening Pablo had not arrived home and Jordi was concerned about him. Anna said she hoped everything would be all right and she would phone Pablo herself if she could not convince Harry to do so.

Chapter 41

Harry woke early having gone to bed at eight. Her head was no longer thumping, just feeling fuzzy. Her first thoughts were of Pablo. What did he do last night? Was he okay? Was he relieved she had gone? He'd probably forgotten all about her and spent the night with Manolo in hot pursuit of another innocent victim. He might have even gone back to Conchitta. Well, it was probably better if she forgot all about him. She pushed him to the back of her mind.

The house was silent; the rest of the family were still sleeping. Harry slipped into her jodhpurs and tiptoed along the landing, avoiding the floorboards she knew creaked, and down the stairs to the kitchen. Smudge's ears pricked up as the doorknob turned. Seeing Harry he dragged himself out of his chewed, wicker basket, lined with old jumpers. Staggering across the floor, his tail thumping from right to left, he placed his head on Harry's knee, as Harry crouched down. Wrapping her arms around his thick, shaggy neck, she hugged him and rubbed his tummy.

"Why can't people be as loyal as you are?" Getting back to her feet she placed the kettle on the hot plate of the Aga and started making a cup of tea. "You couldn't beat a good cup of tea with English milk," she thought. It was one of the things she had missed when she had been in Spain. She was going to try to be positive from then on. Today was the first day of the rest of her life.

The fridge was empty save for a mouldy piece of cheese and a shrivelled lettuce leaf. Anna had not had time to shop or stock up since arriving home. There was no milk in the fridge so Harry popped out to see if the milkman had been. Unbolting the heavy, oak back door, it creaked open. Letting Smudge out first, as he'd sat patiently waiting whilst banging his long bushy tail against the quarry tiled floor, Harry followed and went around the side of the house, through the kitchen garden and along the warn cobbled path to the gate. The honeysuckle climbing up the side of the house was in full bloom; Harry breathed in its sweet scent. The milkman left milk and papers for everyone living at the farm in a little weather proof wooden chest by the gate.

Harry picked up the pile of papers and sorted through them; a tabloid for Mark and a copy of The Sun for Fred.

Something familiar caught Harry's eye. "Oh, my God!" On the front page of The Sun was a picture of Harry pushing her trolley through the airport. Head down, she looked pissed off and angry. Now all her friends at college would read all about her holiday affair. How would she be able to face them?

Just at that moment Fred appeared. Ignoring the shocked expression on her face, he approached in his usual friendly manner. "Hi, Harry. Welcome back, I wasn't expecting you till next week." He leaned forward and kissed Harry on her cheek. "My goodness, you look brown. Was it a good holiday?"

Harry could not speak. He obviously had not heard about the holiday yet. Leaving a very puzzled looking Fred, Harry, unable to speak for fear of bursting into tears, thrust the papers at him. Taking a pint of milk from the crate, she rushed back to the kitchen and shut the door. The kettle was cheerfully whistling away on the Aga. Harry was shaking as she poured the hot steaming water onto a tea bag in her mug, stirred it up, discarded the tea bag and poured a spot of milk in to the cup.

Having drunk her boiling tea, she placed the empty cup on the cluttered draining board and set off, out of the back door and down the farm, to find her old friend Bounty.

The chestnut trees were laden with conkers, ready to fall. The verges along the drive were all overgrown having not been mown for several weeks. At least Bounty wouldn't ask questions. Bounty came galloping up to the gate the minute she heard Harry's voice calling her. Harry patted her faithful old friend and placed her head collar on. Back at the tack room, she brushed the dust from Bounty's short summer coat and placed her tack on. Leading her into the yard she climbed onto the stone block and mounted. Hearing Fred around the corner playing with Smudge, she turned Bounty in the opposite direction and towards the road, and squeezed her into a trot. Bounty knew exactly where they were going. She could sense from Harry's leg movement which direction they were going. Trotting up through the village, Harry was beginning to feel better. It was still quite early and no one seemed to be about yet. It was nice to be alone with no-one to pester or question her. She would phone Julie later and invite her over. Julie would be just the tonic she needed. She might even get a bottle of wine in.

The sloping road cut through the village and rose ahead of them. The steeper it became, the more Bounty puffed and blew, and the slower she walked. Ambling up the road and through the gate to the side of the cattle grid, Harry urged Bounty on. At last they'd reached the open National Trust land. Reaching the ditch that surrounded May Hill, Harry picked a shallow spot to cross at. With new found strength gained from the excitement of reaching the vast area of green, Bounty pricked her ears forward, took a huge leap over the dried-up ditch, and broke into a gallop. Harry made her way through the bracken which had now turned brown after the summer heat wave. Once out into the open the wind raced through Harry's hair as she pushed Bounty on. She charged around the hill, jumping the flowering gorse bushes and dodging the grazing sheep.

When she reached the top of the hill Bounty's nostrils were flaring. Panting and sweating she slowed down to a trot. Harry picked her path, moving in and out of the ninety-nine conifers that capped the peak, planted in 1887 to commemorate the golden jubilee of Queen Victoria. She tried to place the twelve different counties she could see from the summit on a clear day, which reached nearly a thousand feet. Only able to spot five, she turned and took the short cut home through the woods, slowly making her way back down to the waking village. The paths were tricky for Bounty with their deep crevices made by the forestry machinery, edged with a dried-up crust of mud, baked by the summer sun. Nothing grew beneath the thick conifers that carpeted the floor with their needles and pine cones making the soil extremely acidic. Crossing the main road she headed back to the farm along a track that skirted the outside of the village and ended by the stream at the bottom of the farm. More people would be up and about now, and she didn't feel like meeting anyone she might be forced to make pleasantries with.

By the time she had reached the yard Bounty was flagging. She was getting old and Harry knew she'd worked her too hard. She was fat and unfit after a summer of gorging herself with no exercise for a few weeks. Sweated up with a foaming lather running down her neck and between her legs, she was pleased to be home. Removing Bounty's tack, Harry gave her a thorough rub down and a well-earned meal before returning her to the paddock.

On her way back to the house Harry decided it was time to phone Julie. She really needed to talk to her and she didn't want to risk missing her if she had already made plans. Julie had not been expecting her back until the weekend. They had arranged to meet for a catch up and go out on Saturday night when she was due back.

Anna was just clearing the breakfast things away when Harry entered the kitchen. The smell of freshly cooked toast filled the air. "Hi Harry, you were up early. Did you have a good ride?"

"Yes, great thanks, Mum and, before you ask, yes, I am feeling a lot better. "Harry plonked herself down on the wooden settle by the back door and started tugging at her boots.

"Harry, Pablo was terribly upset over the whole ordeal. He has been through a lot, you know. Don't you think it would be nice if you phoned him and sorted this mess out?"

Harry's smiling face turned to thunder at the mention of Pablo. "Look, Mum, I really don't think I could face talking to him. Not yet anyway."

Before Anna had time to respond Harry had crossed the kitchen, almost knocking Mark over as he entered the room. She crashed through the doorway and ran down the hall and up the stairs to her room, slamming the door behind her.

Mark and Anna heard the bang. The kitchen windows rattled in their frames. "What did you say to her?"

"I tried to persuade her to phone Pablo. I promised his parents last night I would."

"Well, she's very hurt. She thinks we've all betrayed her, and I feel we have in a way. It was wrong of us to keep her in the dark. She is a grown up now. We should have told her the truth and let her handle it in her own way."

"You are right, Mark. I'll leave her alone now. I'll phone them myself and say she's not feeling well."

Harry tore her suitcase open and started to unpack, stuffing things away as quickly as she could. She'd had enough. She wanted every trace of her holiday to disappear. Each item of clothing held a different memory of the time she had spent with Pablo. At the bottom of the case was her dress, the one she had worn on their last night in Barcelona. Hugging it to herself she could still smell Pablo's aftershave. Harry burst into tears. Lying on her bed she cried and cried until she could cry no more.

Chapter 42

Pablo woke with a terrible hangover.

Manolo had risen early, helped himself to some stationary out of Jordi's office, and written a note for Pablo that he'd placed on the breakfast bar downstairs before leaving. Isabel had found the envelope and was fretting. She'd picked the envelope up to move it and felt a ring inside. Was this the ring he'd brought for Harry? Would he be terribly distressed when he opened it? Placing it back where she'd found it she jumped, feeling guilty as the door opened and Pablo entered wearing his comfortable robe. His hair was ruffled, his eyes still heavy with sleep. He stood swaying like a lost little boy, looking at it. Isabel handed it to him and left the room. He would probably want to read it in private.

Manolo had only written a brief note saying Harry had left him with the engagement ring Pablo had brought for her, and how sorry he was. He would be around if Pablo wanted to talk or just for company. Pablo looked at the ring. It was the perfect ring for a beautiful girl, his English

Rose. He would not give up hope. Somehow he would try to get her back. Undoing the chain around his neck he threaded the ring onto it. Kissing the ring he placed the chain back around his neck. Firstly, he would go and have a swim to clear his head, then he would sit and write Harry a letter. He knew she wouldn't phone, and she wouldn't speak to him if he phoned her. He needed to give her time. He would get her back if it took forever.

Chapter 43

Julie arrived in her beat up, old, red mini. She was looking very well, her long blond hair bleached almost white in the summer sunshine. Her pale skin had turned golden and her green eyes were sparkling. She looked a picture of health. Opening the front door, she shouted down the hallway.

"Hello, anyone around?"

Anna responded from the kitchen, greeting Julie and saying how well she looked. She told her to go upstairs, saying, "Harry is very fragile. See if you can cheer her up, and do excuse the state of the house, we are still unpacking and in chaos."

Everywhere was in a mess, cases half unpacked, piles of washing, toys, and muddle everywhere. Julie picked her way through the pandemonium and went upstairs. She found Harry sitting in her bedroom, reading. It was the only thing she could do to distract herself from the pain in her heart. Harry jumped up off the bed, and hugged her friend. "My goodness, you are looking good. You obviously had a good holiday."

"You do too. Look at the colour of you. I feel pale compared to you." Julie opened her rucksack and produced a bottle of Chardonnay.

"It's nice and cold. I stopped at the shops on my way and bought it. I took it straight from the fridge. Do you have a corkscrew?"

Harry popped downstairs to the dining room and returned with a corkscrew and two glasses. Making themselves comfortable, sitting cross-legged opposite each other on Harry's bed, Harry poured them a good, chilled glass each, which they sipped as Julie filled Harry in on her summer holiday. She'd had a great time; the weather had been excellent and the resort had been teaming with activities all through the days, and the nights had been amazing.

Once Harry had heard all about Julie's holiday, Julie was anxious to hear what had happened in Spain. She'd kept all the cuttings about Harry that had appeared in The Sun. Harry was keen to read the English version of events. Julie said she thought Pablo was good looking and extremely fit, as they leafed through the scraps of paper. She'd been quite jealous of Harry when she'd seen the first article. In fact it took a while for it to sink in; her best friend in love, suddenly famous, and being hounded by the press. Harry was quite the talk of Newent, and would be the talk of the college when they went back.

Harry was dreading going back to college. Julie assured her that, after the first day, things would return to normal and the fact she was now a celebrity would all be forgotten.

It wasn't long before they'd polished off the wine so Harry went downstairs and begged Anna to let them have a bottle from the wine rack that filled the whole wall in the dining room. Mark was a connoisseur of wine, so Harry turned the bottles carefully, so as not to disturb any sediment, until she came across a relatively inexpensive bottle. She'd never forgotten the day Christina had helped herself to a bottle of wine that had turned out to be a very expensive Semillon. Mark had gone crazy when he had discovered the empty bottle in the kitchen.

Returning to her room, the day flew by. The two friends changed into their pyjamas and got into bed. They talked and drank into the early hours of the morning, only stopping when Harry popped down to the kitchen to get them some cheese and biscuits. Harry felt relieved to get everything off her chest, sharing her intimate secrets with her best friend and someone of her own age. Julie had been very understanding, and gave Harry some good advice. They finally fell asleep, tucked up under the patchwork quilt Harry's grandmother had made her for her sixteenth birthday, in Harry's brass framed, double bed.

The following morning Harry was in a much better mood. The dark cloud that had been hanging over her head for the past forty-eight hours had lifted. She was feeling relaxed and rested. Julie and Harry had decided they were going into Cheltenham to open a savings account so that she could transfer the money she had received for her Ski-Summer modelling. They would do some shopping. Harry needed some new clothes to go back to college.

Anna warned Harry over breakfast that they had received several phone calls the previous day from different papers, asking to speak to Harry. The press was still hot on her trail and after her side of the story. Harry decided she would take a chance as she needed to go shopping. She couldn't risk a catalogue clothes order that might not arrive in time for her to wear to college.

The traffic was light and parking spaces above the Regent arcade were plentiful. There were empty spaces everywhere. The coast so far had been clear. They had not been followed and headed straight into Cavendish House to scan the boutiques. There was no set uniform for college. Screening the racks of clothes, Harry soon had an armful of skirts, jeans, blouses, tops, and jumpers. Julie had already been in and got her college clothes the week before, so taking half of Harry's garments from her, they headed for the changing rooms. After an hour trying various combinations, Harry settled on a skin tight, short navy skirt and cardigan. As well as a pair of black- fitted jeans and a pink jumper, she bought a couple of blouses and long-sleeved tops for when the weather changed. Next she needed some high shoes to wear with her skirt. She already had a pair of boots that would be sufficient for the time being to wear with her jeans. By the time they had finished purchasing Harry's clothes the arcade was busy. It was lunchtime and the arcade was filling up with office workers on their breaks.

Heading straight for the shoe shop, Harry knew she would find a well-made pair of shoes that would do. The shop was teaming with people. They were having a sale. Harry browsed the racks of shoes and picked out a couple of pairs she liked. Not wishing to wait for a seat, she tried them on and stood in front of the mirror, waiting for Julie's approval. Julie gave her honest opinion and Harry agreed; the first pair she had tried on would look the best with her skirt. Harry took the shoes up to the checkout and joined the queue to pay while Julie put the second pair of shoes back on the rack for her. The queue moved slowly. Harry was feeling impatient. She had forgotten how infuriating shopping could be. Why were people always changing things, or getting refunds, when you were in a hurry? At last it was Harry's turn to be served.

As the middle-aged assistant swiped Harry's debit card, she looked up. "Are you the girl out of the papers?"

Harry blushed as the crowd of people around the till gawped at her. Without speaking she coyly nodded, signed the receipt, and waited for the shoes to be boxed.

"Are you the skiing girl? Can I have your autograph, please?" A young girl with her mother, waiting to be served, handed Harry a scrap of paper and a pen. Harry quickly scribbled her name on the paper and dotted it with a kiss.

The assistant handed Harry the boxed shoes. By this time a boy, not much younger than Harry, stepped forward and asked for an autograph. In minutes the shop was swamped with people wanting Harry's autograph. Most of them didn't have a clue who she was but that wasn't going to deter them. At last the assistant felt sorry for Harry and asked her if she would like to step out to the back of the shop.

Julie, who had managed to scramble through the crowd, was by her side. Hand in hand, so they wouldn't be parted, they made a quick exit, leaving the shop heaving with people, most of whom had just popped in to see what the commotion was about.

"I'm terribly sorry about that." The assistant was most apologetic as she led them down a corridor lined with multi-coloured shoe and boot boxes. She could see how agitated Harry was. She had had no idea how her one little question would snowball and now felt guilty. "If you like you can go out of the back door and into the alley. It will take you out by the Theatre."

Harry and Julie nodded in gratitude and made their exit. The alley was quite dark and smelt of urine. They followed the rows of wheelie bins and boxes of rubbish that littered the alley, back out into the main street, and came out by the theatre and opposite Cavendish House. Julie caught up with Harry, who was now in a hurry to get back to the car, and was suddenly several paces ahead.

"I can't believe that people could get into such a frenzy. Is this what it was like for you in Spain?"

"Yes, and worse. Pablo and I had to sneak around in dark glasses with caps on most of the time." Harry felt a stabbing pain in her chest and a lump rise in her throat as she spoke his name, remembering how he would take her hand and lead the way.

Wandering casually around Mothercare, trying to look natural, they waited for the lift to arrive before they ventured back out into the arcade. As the lift doors opened Harry sprinted across the arcade, followed by Julie, and dived into the lift. Once they were back in the safety of Julie's mini the two girls collapsed laughing. It had been an adventure for Julie, even if it had been a little scary.

"So much for opening a savings account; I told you last night they won't leave me alone. I just hope it's still safe and press free at the farm. I will just have to get Mum to pay the cheque into my account. It will be easier and I won't have to worry about another trip to town."

A suspicious looking white van was parked just up the road, and opposite the entrance to the farm. Harry had spotted it. Harry crouched down in the front of the mini and Julie threw a jacket over Harry as they drove past it and pulled into the farm.

"I think that the person in the passenger seat of the van was holding a long lens camera. At least, that is what it looked like to me." Julie pulled the jacket off Harry and told her it was safe to sit up. The van was out of view and she had parked right outside the front door of the house. Grabbing her shopping, Harry ran into the house.

"Harry is that you?" Christina came marching through the hall. "The press has been here this morning. Dad told them you were not here and they all left."

"Except one van that's parked in the lane. We just passed it on the way in. Luckily I spotted it and Julie hid me under a jacket so they haven't seen me return."

Julie followed Harry into the kitchen. Harry's head was aching and she needed some paracctamol. Anna had been shopping and the fridge was restocked.

"Would you like a drink, Julie?"

"Yes please, just some chilled water. I am feeling a little dehydrated after last night!"

Harry took two small bottles of chilled water from the fridge and handed one to Julie. Sitting themselves down at the kitchen table, Harry fretted over the prospect of going into hiding for the next few days until everything had cooled down. Julie was very reassuring and said it would soon blow over; they would get fed up and leave. After staying for a sandwich Julie said she would have to go home shortly. She had promised her mother she would help her that afternoon. They'd had decorators in for the past week and the house was in chaos. After finishing her drink she jumped back in the mini and was gone.

Chapter 44

Later that day, Harry bumped into Fred as she sneaked down through the large stone barn to check on Bounty.

Christina had updated Fred on the holiday and he was very sympathetic. He asked her to join him for a catch up and assured Harry he had already checked on Bounty who was grazing happily at the far end of the paddock.

Fred popped back to his flat, the old coach house, which had been converted into a modern flat. It was situated above the tack room and stables and was Fred's home. Minutes later he arrived back with a couple of cold ginger beers. It was nice sitting on the bales in the cool, stone barn. It was good to be away from the house where the phone was constantly ringing, and where Harry was afraid to walk past a window in case she was seen and photographed.

Harry had spent many hours in Fred's company as she had grown up. Fred was only a few years older than Harry, in his early twenties. He had been living at the farm since he was sixteen. He had never talked about his family or where he had come from, he just seemed to appear at the farm one day and had stayed there, initially doing odd jobs, and eventually working full time for Mark.

The afternoon went quickly. Harry was enjoying chatting with Fred. He was a good friend. He always treated Harry as if she was his little sister and felt protective towards her. Fred said he would bring Bounty up to the yard the following morning for Harry to ride. Checking the coast was clear for Harry, he kissed her on the cheek and gave her a reassuring hug before she ran back to the house.

Chapter 45

Grandma had made marvellous progress and was being discharged from the hospital the following day. She had some paralysis in her left arm and leg but had regained her speech and was drinking and eating well.

Fred had kept his promise and had Bounty tacked up and waiting for Harry at six in the morning. The white van had vanished overnight and Harry felt it was early, and therefore safe enough, to go out for a quick ride around the village.

After delivering a sweated-up Bounty back to Fred, having had a short refreshing ride, Harry spent the day helping Anna transform the family games room in to a bedroom and living room suitable for her grandmother to recuperate in.

The twins had been out playing down by the stream. They had returned caked in mud, carrying bunches of buttercups. These they had proudly arranged in various containers around the room to cheer it up. Anna and Harry, delighted with the transformation, set about preparing a nice meal for the family. They would eat when Mark arrived back from the hospital with grandma.

The kitchen smelt of the garlic and rosemary the leg of lamb had been dressed in while it spat, sizzled, and cooked in the middle oven of the Aga. The fresh vegetables were steaming away on the top ring. An apple pie, made with the first Bramleys of the season, was baking in the bottom oven. Christina had been busily setting the large, round, polished table in the dining room. That night they would be eating with the best cutlery and china to celebrate Grandmother's homecoming. Carefully she arranged the place settings out on the starched white cotton cloth. Napkins, placed in silver rings, matched the rich, linen curtains framing the tall windows and the woollen rug fronting fire place. The twins had enough flowers left over for Christina to arrange for the centre of the table. Everything was prepared so, one by one, they disappeared upstairs to wash and change, ready to greet their grandmother and welcome her home.

The car pulled up the drive and stopped outside the front door. Mickey and Sophie raced out to greet their grandmother while Harry and Christina hung back, not wanting to crowd her. Mark took a hospital issued wheelchair from the back of the car and helped his mother into it. She was frail, had lost weight, and seemed very one-sided in her seat. Mark placed her brown leather handbag, that went everywhere with her, on her knee and wheeled her into the house. The girls waited until she was safely manoeuvred into the dining room before they engulfed her with hugs and kisses. Grandmother signalled to her bag and Harry opened the clasp that was now too difficult for her partially paralysed fingers to manage. Harry took out a hanky and wiped her grandmother's watering eyes. The love and attention clearly overwhelmed her.

The hospital had sent out a list of instructions for the medication and care she needed. Mark had arranged a private nurse to start that evening as extra support. A physiotherapist would also be visiting every other day. The rest would be down to the family to provide good food, lots of love, and support.

The meal was delicious. Anna had seated herself next to her mother-in-law and had carefully cut her food up. This she managed to spoon into her mouth with her working hand.

After eating a very small portion and thanking Anna, she made it clear to them how lovely it was to be with them all and how much she appreciated it, but she now felt very tired and wanted to rest.

The nurse had arrived and had been introduced to everyone; she was waiting in the converted games room for Mrs Smyth-Thomas. One by one they got up from the table and filed round to say goodnight to their grandmother before Mark wheeled her off to her new room.

Mark took the twins up to bed while Harry and Christian tiptoed quietly around clearing the table. With the washing up done and dishwasher whining away, it had been a jolly but tense evening, and the older members of the family were feeling the strain. Anna made the girls some hot chocolate to take up to their rooms and thanked them for their help. Before the grandfather clock struck ten, everyone had retired, and the house fell silent.

Chapter 46

After a few days, Grandma had clearly improved a great deal. She had settled in nicely. The physiotherapist, a pretty young lady with fresh new ideas, said she was impressed with her progress; it would not be long before she would start on the leg exercises that would hopefully get her walking again.

Harry had filled her days helping her grandmother with her exercises and reading to her. She also helped Anna prepare all the meals and with the never-ending pile of washing and ironing. It was a welcome distraction for her during the day. At night, however, she was now having difficulty sleeping. Reading until the early hours, every time she put a book down and closed her eyes, Pablo would appear. She could not blank him out. Her heart still ached for him and her body longed for him. She started dreading going to bed.

Julie had been over a few times with fresh gossip and had kept her temporarily distracted from her thoughts of Pablo, as well as from worrying about returning to college.

The dreaded day was approaching; Christina had spent the week shopping and packing, ready to return to university. She wanted to arrive early so she would have the weekend to settle in and party with her university friends before getting down to the hard work of studying for her exams and her final dissertation.

Soon after Christina had left the phone rang. Harry had been avoiding answering it as the press were still waiting for their chance to catch her. Although their calls were decreasing, Harry was taking no chances. Every time they had called, someone would answer the phone and say Harry was staying with friends or she was away. No-one else was around and Grandma was asleep after a strenuous session with her physiotherapist.

Harry worried that the loud ringing echoing around the hall would wake her, so she grabbed the phone up without thinking. "Hello, The Smyth-Thomas residence."

"Oh, hello, is that Christina?" A public, college voice enquiry Harry thought, one of Christina's playmates.

"Oh, no, I am sorry. You have just missed her. Christina has gone back to uni!"

"Is that you, Harry? It's John here. Remember me? I rescued you from the press at Birmingham airport."

Oh great, Harry thought, this is all I need.

"How do you fancy coming over for supper tonight? I know you can't be getting out much because I drove past the other day on my way to the Glasshouse and saw all the press cars and vans camped down the lane. I could come over and pick you up. You could hide while we make our get-away. They would never know where you were going if they spotted you. And I'd be the other side of Newent before they had a chance to get their vehicles started and in gear."

"Um, well," Harry tried desperately to think of an excuse but before she had the chance John spoke again.

"I will not take no for an answer. Don't worry about dressing-up. I'll be over in an hour."

With that the phone went dead, and Harry had no option; she was going out.

Harry rushed up stairs, showered, and changed into a clean pair of jeans, a plain white T-shirt, and her denim jacket. She felt her old nervousness coming back but had no time to stop and think what she'd let herself in for. Her hair was wet and she had to get on if she was going to have her hair dry in time. She certainly wasn't going to make any effort, yet she didn't want to look scruffy. She had been sitting on the floor in Grandma's room teaching her how to wiggle her toes earlier and was covered in dust. No matter how often the house was cleaned, the dust just appeared from nowhere.

The Audi pulled up on the drive-way and crunched to a halt. Harry's stomach was in knots and she was feeling sick. If she could get through the evening it would be a step forward for her. She would make it quite clear she was not interested in any sort of relationship.

John was about to knock on the door just as Harry opened it. He was wearing an old pair of faded jeans, a T-shirt, and a denim jacket also. As they spied each other through the door and saw what the other was wearing, they both smiled. It had broken the ice. John looked a lot younger in his casual clothes. Harry thought he was a bit stiff when she first met him and thought him rather old. Seeing him dressed in jeans knocked years off him.

"Are you ready?" He leant forward and brushed cheeks.

Harry nodded and followed him out to the car carrying a token bottle of red wine, another one she had had to pinch from Mark's collection; she would have to confess and replace them.

"You smell nice."

"Oh, thanks."

"There was no-one out on the road when I pulled in. You are quite safe," he assured her as she seated herself next to him and clipped her seat belt in. "What have you been up to all week?"

Harry began to relax and felt quite at ease, chatting to John about her week.

John's parents' house was a picture of elegance. Driving in through wrought iron, electronic gates, a large white house lay before them. The driveway swung around a pond with a fountain bubbling up in the centre. Lilies, in full flower, floated on the surface. Giant gold fish circled the cascading water.

John lined the car up to the bottom of the steps leading up to the roman-pillared entrance.

Harry got out of the car, swinging her bottle of wine nervously in her hand, and followed John up the short flight of steps and in through the door. The entrance contained a mirrored dresser covered in hats, walking sticks and umbrellas filling its pockets. Four sets of golf clubs leaned neatly against the opposite wall. A set of double doors opened into a large bright hallway. In front of them a mahogany staircase ran straight up to the second floor. Following John past the closed doors leading to various rooms, Harry stepped onto a thick cream, plush, spongy carpet; white walls with family photos lined the way into the kitchen.

"I thought we would just eat in here tonight. My parents are going out and it's a bit daunting sitting in the dining room when there are only two of you."

The kitchen was vast, painted pale yellow with bluebell print curtains and blinds. The floor was blue and white checks tiles. Modern beech units, with stainless steel handles, ran around the entire room. In the centre, a breakfast island surrounded by tall, elegant stools, housed a gas hob with a stainless-steel chimney suspended down from the ceiling. This piped cooking smells and smoke out of the room. Two cocker spaniels lay sleeping in a wicker basket, lined with sheepskin rug, next to the French windows that opened out onto a patio and barbeque area. Harry went over to the dogs and gave them a stroke.

"Aren't they lovely, what are their names?"

"I am too embarrassed to say. Promise you won't laugh if I tell you?"

"Okay, I promise." Harry smiled up at John.

"My parents named them Ant and Dec. Apparently, Grange Hill was one of my favourite programs and they swear I chose the names!"

Harry couldn't help but laugh. Remembering she was still holding a bottle of wine in her hand, she walked back to the breakfast island and handed the bottle to John.

"Thank you, I was beginning to think that was your security blanket." They both laughed and John pointed to one of the stools and Harry sat down. "What can I get you to drink? Would you like wine or would you like a g and t or something else?"

"I don't mind. Whatever you are drinking."

"I like to start the evening with a g and t. Bombay, what do you say to that?" John took two bucket glasses from a shelf and went over to a walk-in pantry with an American fridge in. Half-filling them with ice from an automatic ice machine, he returned with the gin and tonic. "Lemon?"

"Oh, yes please."

John poured their drinks gave them a twizzle and handed one of the glasses to Harry. "Cheers! Here's to a chance meeting." He chinked his glass against Harry's.

Harry smiled back at him and took a sip. God, it was strong; she'd be on her back in no time, she thought. Placing the glass down on the work top, she looked around the kitchen for some hint of what he might be cooking.

John took a wok down from a hook on the ceiling, a selection of vegetables from the fridge, and began chopping. "I thought I'd cook us a chilli, if that is all right with you?"

"Oh yes, that sounds great." Harry felt nervous during the long silences, which John tried to fill in with a systematic guide as to how he liked to cook his chilli.

The door opened and a very sophisticated, middle-aged woman, with blond hair piled up on her head, entered the room. She was dressed in a white, silk trouser-suit with a long jacket. Her eyes roamed over Harry and John noticed and was quick to respond.

"Oh, Harry, this is my mother. Mother, this is Harry."

Harry got down from her stool and leant forward with a greeting kiss.

"Charmed, I am absolutely charmed."

Harry blushed at her response. "I hope she isn't going to join us for a drink, before she leaves," Harry began to worry.

"Come on, darling, or we'll be late." Seconds later a rather well-built, silver-haired man with a distinguished moustache entered the room. "Oh, I say, who do we have here?"

John made the introductions; his father took Harry's hand and kissed it.

Saying their goodbyes, and leaving John instructions as to what time to let the dogs out, the handsome couple left the room.

John looked at Harry and grinned. He could see she had been rather taken aback by his eccentric parents. Handing Harry a plate of freshly cooked chilli, John poured them both a glass of wine and joined Harry at the breakfast bar. The food was great. John could certainly cook a good chilli. When they had both finished their first course, John offered Harry a choice of cheesecake or a lemon sorbet. Harry opted for the lemon sorbet. It was quite a warm evening and the chilli had been a little hot.

The kitchen door flew open again and in walked another tall, blond haired man. He looked very like John, but younger. Harry blushed. She realised this was the guy she quite often saw in Newent. It suddenly clicked. This was why she thought she recognised John when she first met him at the airport; they were so similar to look at, both tall and blond, both had nice tans.

John was quick to introduce her. "James, this is Harry, a friend of mine."

James strutted across the kitchen floor and, in the same manner as his father, took Harry's hand and kissed it. "Don't I know you from somewhere?" His deep blue eyes fixed on Harry's making her feel uncomfortable and look away.

"I think I have seen you in Newent a few times when I have been shopping."

"Oh yes, that's right," James replied as he pulled a stool up to the breakfast bar and helped himself to a glass of wine.

John glared at him but he just ignored his big brother's threatening gaze and started chatting Harry up, asking her where she lived, how she got her gorgeous tan, and if she played any sport. He had just qualified as a games teacher; he played every sport going. Perhaps Harry would have a game of tennis with him sometime. He made a point of saying John would be going back on Sunday but he would be around if Harry got bored and wanted some company.

John was getting quite agitated at this intrusion. There was no way he was going to let his brother interfere with his plans for the evening. He was the one who had found Harry and invited her over. Harry sensed the atmosphere and began to feel uneasy as the two brothers tried to outdo each other.

"Could you tell me where the bathroom is?" Trying to break the tension, Harry thought it best if she left them to it for a little while.

"Oh yes, it's this way. John led her back into the hall and pointed to a door in the middle of the corridor.

While she was in the bathroom she heard raised voices. She waited for a few minutes, studying the prints on the wall that reminded her of a book she once read, call the "Shell Seekers", until she heard a door slam and it went quiet. When she returned to the kitchen James had vanished and the door into the garden was open. John was out in the garden, throwing sticks for the dogs. Harry went out and joined him.

They strolled around the highly fragranced rose beds and colourful, well-stocked borders. The dogs ran ahead yapping and chasing each other. It was dark but the paths were well lit with lanterns. The lawn and flower beds stretched out ahead of them. Harry was enjoying herself; the awkward silences that had hung in the air while they were in the house now filled with the sound of playful, barking dogs. John, being very kind, hadn't mentioned Pablo or asked Harry any questions about their relationship. He hadn't even tried to hold Harry's hand; he was a perfect gentleman. The garden bordered the vineyards of the farm next door. Vines were now a big industry for the local growers, who won awards for the wine they produced. Harry felt a few spots of rain. Holding her hand up, she pointed at the dark sky. Before they had time to move, the thunder rumbled in the distance and lightening lit up the vine covered valley.

Grabbing Harry by the hand to direct her, John shouted, "Quick, this is the shortest route back to the house. Run for it!" The heavens opened and it poured. Running as quickly as they could, trying not to step on the yapping, confused dogs at their feed. They made it to the kitchen just as another louder clap of thunder echoed across the sky. John looked at Harry who stood dripping in the doorway. "I'm so sorry. You look absolutely soaking. Come with me and I'll lend you a dry shirt or something."

"No, it's okay, I'll be fine. Could you just run me home?"

John shook his head. "Not until I've got you into some dry clothes and you've had a warming drink."

Reluctantly Harry followed John up a back stairway, hidden in the corner of the kitchen, and out onto the upstairs landing. This was decorated in the same way as the entrance hall, with light coloured walls plastered in family photos, and the floor covered in the thick cream carpet. He opened the door into a bathroom and, leading the way in, he opened a cupboard and handed Harry a thick, clean, blue towel that matched the nautical design of the bathroom.

"Wait here and I will get you some clothes."

As he vanished down the corridor, Harry shut the door and took her wet things off. The rain had been so heavy that she was soaked right through to her skin. There was a knock at the door. Harry wrapped the towel around her body and went over to open the door.

John was standing holding a sweat shirt and some jogging pants.

"Sorry, these were mine when I was younger, but I have grown out of them. They were all I could find that may possibly fit you."

Harry said they would be fine, and thanked John, who left her to change and said he would quickly change and meet her back down in the kitchen when she was ready. Harry placed the soft, navy, sweatshirt over her head and pulled they light grey joggers up over her slim legs and to her waist. Luckily they had a draw-string belt which Harry pulled as tightly as she could. There was another knock at the door. Before Harry had time to respond, James entered. "Oh sorry, I thought I heard voices but didn't realise you were in here." He grinned, looking Harry up and down.

A likely story, Harry thought as she gestured for him to leave before she collected her things together.

He made no move to leave but instead he came closer to her. "Look, I know my brother is a bit of a bore, but he'll be gone at the weekend. Anytime you want, give me a ring. I could show you a good time."

"Your brother is a perfect gentleman and I've had a lovely evening with him." Harry scooped her things closer to her chest and barged past James to the door.

"Aren't you forgetting something?"

Harry glanced back and James dangled her knickers from his little finger. Harry went to snatch them off him and he raised his hand higher.

"What is the magic word?"

Harry wasn't going to take any crap from this idiot. Kneeing him in the balls, she grabbed her knickers and left him bent over, cupping his privates and groaning.

Down in the kitchen John had poured them a brandy. "Are you all right, you look cold?"

Harry was shaking with anger. She wouldn't tell John what James had said; she could see there was quite a bit of rivalry between them already.

"Yes, I am a bit." Harry drank her brandy and instantly felt it warming her through.

John refilled her glass and watched as she opened her delicate mouth and drank it down.

Feeling comfortable Harry found her voice and started telling John about her relationship with Pablo. Once she started she couldn't stop.

John sat and listened.

Several glasses of brandy later Harry, who was now rather tipsier than she had realised, stood up and said she should be going home. He was a good listener but she felt she'd bored him enough for one night. The room started spinning as Harry veered off in the opposite direction to the door. The last thing she could remember was being sick in the kitchen sink.

Harry woke in a strange bed, in a room she did not recognise. Where was she? As she tried to sit up her head banged. She leant back on the pillow and closed her eyes. Oh God, it was all coming back to her now. She'd got very drunk and told John all about Pablo, and that was the last thing she could remember. Who had put her to bed? Harry moved her leg. She had no clothes on. Someone must have undressed her and put her into bed. Sheer horror filled her thoughts. Opening her eyes again, she noticed daylight peeping through the crack in the curtains. She had to get home. She couldn't face John, not after he'd undressed her and put her to bed. Forcing her reluctant body from the soft, cosy bed, she spotted her clothes, neatly arranged over the chair, in the corner of the room. Creeping gingerly across the floor, she fought her way into them. Her shoes; where were her shoes? Harry fumbled around the room until she'd found her shoes. Spotting the large mirror on the wall she had a quick glance at her face. She didn't look as bad as she was feeling. Without the use of a brush, she ruffled her hair into a bad-hair-day style. Making her way to the door she slowly turned the handle and crept out. There was not a sign of life anywhere. She could see the stairs at the far end of the landing. Walking as quickly and quietly as she could, she crossed the landing and went downstairs. Voices came from the kitchen. Now was her chance. She headed for the front door, unbolted it, and made her get away.

Once she was outside she felt very exposed. Reaching the gate without being seen, she could not work out how to open it. Hearing a car door slam she hid behind a bush and waited for something to happen. An old Jaguar approached the gates that opened automatically. Harry jumped from the bush when the car pulled away and just managed to squeeze through it before it closed. Good, she'd made it. As quickly as she could she marched up the road, staying close to the verge. After she had been walking for about fifteen minutes she heard a car. It started tooting. She ignored it and carried on walking. The car pulled alongside her and stopped. It was John in his Audi.

"What do you think you are doing? Come on get in."

"I am so sorry," Harry mumbled as she climbed into the car. "I felt so embarrassed about last night, I couldn't face you."

"Don't worry, you were fine; just a bit tipsy. Let me at least buy you some breakfast before I take you home."

Harry nodded as she shut the door. "My parents?"

"Don't worry, I phoned your mother last night and said you had a migraine and had gone to have a lie down. When I had checked on you a little later you were asleep so I didn't like to disturb you."

"Thanks, John, you have saved me again."

John drove towards the motorway and stopped at a Little Chef. He bought two full English breakfasts and told Harry to eat it all up; it would make her feel so much better.

Harry tucked in and began to feel brighter. With a little more courage and feeling more with it, Harry asked John what had happened.

He told her that after being sick in the kitchen sink, he and James had carried her up to the bathroom where he sat with her for an hour while she was sick repeatedly. He had held her hair back for her and kept making her take sips of water. He felt very guilty and responsible. When she had finally stopped, but was very weak, he carried her to the bedroom.

"Did you put me into bed?" Harry blushed and looked away as she waited for the response.

"Yes, I did. Once you were in bed and under the covers I helped you remove your clothes, but don't worry, you were covered over and I didn't peep." He traced a cross over his heart. "Then I made sure you were propped on your side before I left you."

"I am so sorry. I feel even more embarrassed now."

"Don't be. You have a fantastic body, not that I saw it. I had to stop myself climbing in next to you and having my wicked way with you. And you clearly wanted to talk about Pablo."

Harry laughed.

"I am just wondering how much I could sell my story for!" This time John laughed at Harry's shocked expression before she realised he was joking. Even in the state Harry had been in she was gorgeous. If he played his cards right there was no reason she wouldn't fancy him. He was quite a good looking bloke and had plenty of money. At the airport the girls were queuing up to go out with him. John paid the bill and drove Harry home.

Once again she thanked him for a lovely supper and for looking after her. She apologised for being such a light weight.

He said it had been a pleasure and, before leaving, he asked if he could see her next time he was home. Harry could not refuse, not after the way she had behaved last night, and he had been very nice so, Harry said he could, and to ring her in a couple of weeks when he was next home. Before Harry got out of the car John leaned over and gave her a polite peck on the cheek.

Chapter 47

The brass alarm clock trilled. Harry sleepily fumbled for the switch to turn it off. She finally found it and turned it off. Lifting her head from her soft, duck down pillow she glanced at the clock. Six thirty a.m. The day had arrived when Harry had to go back to college. She had plenty of time and took a leisurely shower and got ready. Taking her new skirt from the wardrobe she stepped into it and tugged it up over her hips. The short skirt was a perfect fit and hung snugly over her slender hips.

September had been fine so far and the forecast for the week was dry and warm. She wouldn't need to wear tights; her legs were still tanned from the sun. She slipped her new shoes on, showing off her long slender brown legs. Her new blouse fitted perfectly and was finished off by the new cardigan. As she stood back and looked at her outfit in the mirror, she felt quite satisfied with her new clothes. Hair held up in a navy-blue band, she applied a little eye liner and some lip gloss.

Anna knocked on the door and asked if she was going to college by bus or whether she wanted Mark to run her down when he ran the twins to school. Normally they all used the bus but, on the first day of term, Mark had always made a point of driving them directly to the school gates and promised to take Harry to college. Harry declined the offer as Julie had promised to pick her up that day to give her some moral support. Harry placed her pink pencil case, body spray, a hair-brush, and a packet of tissues into her back pack. Securing the buckles, she headed down for breakfast.

The twins were tucking into their boiled eggs, dipping their toasted soldiers into the small, yellow craters and dribbling yoke all over their napkins. Harry helped herself to a bowl of muesli and a glass of fruit juice before joining them at the table. Anna was busily packing apples, crisps, and sandwiches into lunch boxes for the twins. Mark had not yet arrived. He had gone out early with a cup of coffee. His usual task on a Monday morning was to have a meeting with the farm workers and to set them up with their tasks for the week.

Neatly dressed in their grey and blue junior school uniforms, the twins removed their napkins and went in to say goodbye to their grandmother. They couldn't wait to show off their new uniforms and let her see how smart they looked.

Anna took the opportunity of having a quiet chat with Harry. She asked Harry if she was going to be all right. The press had not been seen for a few days so she thought Harry was old news and she could start to relax a little. Harry, knowing Anna had a lot on her mind, what with her grandmother staying with them and the twins to organise, fibbed and said she was fine. She popped in to see her grandmother who was sitting up with a shawl around her shoulders waiting patiently for the nurse to arrive to dress her. Harry's grandmother told her she looked beautiful and to hold her head high, and wished her luck on her first day back at college.

When a horn tooted, Harry peered out of the ivy framed window. Julie had arrived. Julie was also wearing a short skirt, blouse and a v-necked jumper, with her blond hair hanging loosely around her shoulders. Harry got into the battered old mini next to her friend, holding her rucksack on her knee. She clipped her seat belt in place and Julie moved off towards the road.

"Hi, Harry. Are you still feeling nervous?"

"A little. I've got butterflies in my stomach and will be glad when our first day is over."

"You will be fine. You look great. I wonder what our new tutor will be like. Any ideas? Do you think it's someone totally new or one of the old members of staff taking on new responsibilities? What do you think?"

"I don't know, but we will soon find out."

It was only a twenty-minute journey to the college. The green busses were piling down the road through the main college gates, circling the roundabout before parking in their allotted spaces. Julie turned into the end gate and parked in the college car park. The college housed over a thousand pupils. It was well designed and split neatly into various pods. In the main building most of the first year college pupils had their lessons. Joined to the main building by a maze of corridors and internal bridges were the art rooms, the library, the music rooms, sixth form block and the sports centre. A group of girls waited by the door into the tutorial block. It was Jane Smith, Sarah Bates, and friends. They were Harry's and Julie's arch enemies. During their days at college, Jane Smith and Sarah Bates had made life very difficult for Harry and Julie. They were very jealous of the pair of them. Both Harry and Julie were very pretty and had brains. All the boys had always fancied, admired, and made a fuss of them. Both girls had come from different private junior schools, and then the local senior school, which Jane had always resented. She spent her time trying to belittle Harry or Julie whenever she got the opportunity.

Julie linked her arm through Harry's. "Just keep walking and ignore them, Harry. They are bound to make some snide comment."

On cue, as Harry made her way through the group, Jane asked her how Pablo was. Julie tightened her grip on Harry's arm and pulled Harry towards the open door. She kept her moving until they were halfway up the corridor and didn't release her arm or stop until they had reached their lockers.

Well out of ear shot of Jane and friends, Harry turned to Julie. "I don't know if I am going to survive the day."

Julie could see how distressed Harry was and patted her arm. "You'll be fine. Let's go into the student common room and find Russ and Stew; they're always good for a laugh."

Harry placed her backpack into her locker and went on ahead whilst Julie needed to stay and tidy her locker which was still full of her old books from the previous year. Harry thought she couldn't rely on Julie all day. She had to be independent and face everyone and everything the day presented her with. Pushing the double doors to the common room open, everyone went quiet and just stared. Harry had always been a knockout at college but she had been very shy, kept herself to herself, and had concentrated on her work. Today everyone was looking at her in a new light. Not only was she stunning but she was now famous. She'd had a whirlwind romance that had ended in tears, and gained a modelling contract, all during the holidays.

Harry surveyed the room for a friendly face. Stew, like a knight in-shining-armour, looked up from his game of cards and shouted at Harry to join them. Harry's legs felt like lead as she crossed the room in front of everyone's penetrating gaze and quiet whispers. Stew and Russ threw their cards down, indicating to an empty table in the corner of the room. Harry slid onto the bench as Julie appeared and slid in next to her. Stew and Russ mischievously started taking the Mick in their old way. Harry felt relieved her entrance was over and was happy to be amongst old friends.

The buzzer sounded for morning tutorial. Harry, Julie, Stew, and Russ had all been assigned the same tutor for the year, so they headed off together. Arriving at their tutorial they had their first glimpse of their new tutor. A tall man in a Fred Perry T-shirt and jogging bottoms was bent over his desk facing away from them.

"Just come up to the front so I can see you all." He carried on leaning over his desk and reading the register. The four friends made their way to the front of the room and perched on the front four desks. Harry wished the floor would swallow her up when he turned around. It was James, John's brother who had been so beastly to her the night she got drunk. A smirk cracked across his face when he saw Harry. After some moments careful thought, his smile broadened to take the four of them in. He carried on as if he had never met Harry before, introducing himself first, then asking them one by one to spell out their full names and what subjects they were taking. Harry felt herself break out into a cold sweat and the colour rush to her cheeks when he reached her. As she mumbled her name Julie gave her a funny look wondering what the matter was. James handed out their new time tables, followed by a brief lecture on the amount of work that lay ahead of them, and how it was up to them to use their free periods wisely. The buzzer went sounding the end of tutorial and the start of many boring lectures.

Harry made a hasty retreat towards the door but was soon stopped in her tracks and called back.

"Er, Harry, Harry Smyth-Thomas?" He pretended he could not remember her surname and looked down his register. "Can you stay behind for a few moments?" Harry raised her eyebrows at Julie who whispered they'd wait for her by the bridge.

"Now then, Harry, you and I have obviously got off on the wrong foot. Here I am, your tutor. Anything that happened in the past I want you to forget about, and I will keep quiet about the drunken state you were in when I helped John carry you to the bathroom. Do you think you can do that?" Avoiding her angry gaze, his eyes traced the line of her firm bust under her blouse.

"Yes, that's fine by me." Harry turned clutching her cardigan tightly around her chest. She walked from the room glancing back over her shoulder as James ran his eyes up and down her long legs. James smiled. "This is going to make life a little difficult," he thought. He was determined to ask her out. He'd fallen for her big time the night his brother had brought her home. Now he had the added excitement that she was one of his pupils. That gave him a sense of power over her. He could have some fun here.

Harry caught up with her three friends at the bridge.

"What did he want?" Julie quizzed her as she approached them.

"Slimy bastard," Harry muttered. "I'll explain at break time".

Stew and Russ shrugged their shoulders and left for their first lecture.

The rest of the day passed without incident. At lunchtime Julie took them for a drive in her car and parked it by the lake in the centre of the town. They all got out and wandered around the lake, sitting for a while eating lunch and enjoying the autumn sunshine. Chucking their leftover dried-up, vending machine sandwiches to the ducks, while Harry explained in detail about her previous encounter with James, they all vowed they wouldn't leave her alone with him again until she felt safe and that she could trust him. Stew and Russ had a quick cigarette before they had to rush back to college.

During afternoon tutorial Stew and Russ sat at the back of the room chatting and playing cards with Harry and Julie. James called the register then vanished off to prepare for his next games lesson. On the way home from college Julie's car started careering across the road, making a loud clanking noise. Bringing it to a halt, Julie announced the steering felt funny. Opening her window, she leant out and surveyed the car and saw the back tyre was flat. "God, that's all we need." Julie jumped out of the car to take a closer look.

"It's really flat, Harry. I daren't drive it anywhere. I'm going to have to change the tyre here."

Harry rummaged through Julie's makeshift tool kit, looking for a socket to fit the nuts on the wheel, while Julie jacked the car up.

"I'm sorry, Julie I can't find it. Have you ever had to use it before?"

"Only once and that was on the drive at home when my Dad insisted on making me change a tyre before he would let me drive on my own. I bet I never put it back in."

"I didn't bring any change to college. Have you got any in your purse? We could use the phone box up the road to phone Fred. He would come down and help us."

"No, sorry, I only have a note. Don't worry, Harry, I'll walk to the farm on the corner and ask if I can use their phone. You stay here and watch the car. I'll leave the radio on for you." Julie changed into her plimsolls and headed off for the farm. It was only about a quarter of a mile away.

The lane was quiet; they had not seen another car. The sun was high in the sky and still warm. Harry took her cardigan off and threw it into the car. She lifted herself onto the bonnet of the old mini and loosened her collar. Leaning back on her elbows, face pointing towards the sun, she hoped to top her tan up while she waited. Lost deep in her own thoughts and listening to the radio, she never heard the car pull up. Not until a shadow blocked the sun out did she open her eyes.

Standing in front of her was a woman dressed in tatty jeans and a T-shirt, holding a camera up and joyfully snapping away.

Harry jumped up, straightening her skirt as she climbed off the bonnet. "What do you think you are doing?" she said frowning.

A man stepped out from behind the car. "It is Harry, isn't it?"

Harry's voice turned to thunder. "You are from the papers, aren't you? Well, you've got your photo, just leave me alone."

"We just want to know what plans you have for the future. What are doing now?"

"What do you think I'm doing? I've college to finish. Then, who knows?"

"So, you've gone back to your studies. What subjects are you studying?"

"Okay, if I give you some answers will you leave me alone?"

"Sounds good to us." The woman carried on snapping.

Harry put her hand up masking her face. "Surely you've got enough photo's now?" The man nodded to the woman who put the camera down.

"I am in my last year at college studying sports and business studies. I have a horse called Bounty and will be returning to Spain in the winter to do some promotional work modelling ski wear for Señor Cruanos. That's it. Now can you leave me alone."

The man finished scribbling with a broken pencil in his grubby note book. "That's great, thank you for that." The man nodded and handed Harry one of the business cards he'd taken from his wallet.

"Just in case you have another story for us or feel like getting anything off your chest."

"Thanks, but I'm sure I won't be needing it." Harry took the card and tucked it inside her rucksack. The man and the women got back in their car and pulled off just as Julie arrived back.

"Who was that?"

Harry explained what had happened just after Julie left. The two girls laughed as Harry got back on the bonnet of the car, taking up her pose to show Julie just how she had been sitting. She had to ask Julie if she looked respectable or whether you could see her knickers.

Julie killed herself laughing at the picture of Harry sitting on the bonnet of her red car with the top buttons of her blouse undone and her short skirt slightly riding up. "I'd say you've just had a dead sexy picture taken. You'll be lucky if you're not summoned to the Principal's office at college when that hits the papers."

Harry was giggling; she could see the funny side of it and knew she would be quite safe from the press for now. They had their little story. Hopefully she would now be left alone.

"Let's see the card they gave you."

Harry took the card from her rucksack and handed it to Julie.

"They were from The Sun. What a surprise." Julie handed the card back to Harry. Rolling her sleeves up, as she had been unable to get hold of Fred or her own Dad, she set about changing the tyre. Having borrowed what she needed from the farm, and with Harry's help, the tyre was changed in minutes.

Mark and Anna thought she had done the right thing speaking to the reporters, even though they worried about the picture that would also be printed, especially after Harry had described how she was sitting.

Chapter 48

Life returned to normal at the farm and the Smyth-Thomas's were now in a good routine after the chaos they had returned to.

Julie picked Harry up every day that week. They left for college early each morning before the milk man had been. Making a quick detour, they would race down to the shops and scan all the papers to see if there were any pictures of Harry. So far nothing had appeared. The week had been pleasant, despite discovering her teacher for special PE that year was James. James, or "Sir" as she now had to call him, kept his word and other than the occasional moment when Harry would catch his eyes wandering up and down her body, he generally treated her like any other pupil.

On Friday morning Julie parked in her usual spot on the double yellows outside the supermarket while Harry sat in the car, radio blaring away and patiently waiting. Following Julie's movements up and down the paper racks, she noticed Julie hesitating. The next moment Julie picked up a paper and waved it at Harry.

"Oh God, it's in!" Harry's heart started pounding as she patiently bided her time whilst Julie paid for it.

Jumping into the car Julie thrust the paper at Harry and started the engine. On the front page of The Sun was a very suggestive picture of Harry. Her worst fears confirmed, one could see the top of a very shapely thigh showing just a shadow of the black pants Harry had been wearing.

"God, Julie, that women must have been on her knees to have managed to get this shot."

"I know, that's what I thought. Quickly, read what it says. We will be at college in a minute.

You had better hope none of the teachers get their papers until lunch time."

Harry read out the title line. *"Sexy College skier blows out Spanish lover and returns to studies.* This is awful". The heading was worse than the editorial contents. As Harry read on she had a brain wave.

"Julie, you have just given me an idea. You know the shop near the college?" Julie nodded as she weaved in and out of the parked traffic. "All the teachers generally pop in to it for their papers, cigs etc. Drive up there and stop outside."

Julie frowned. She wasn't quite sure what Harry was getting at. Following Harry's instructions, she pulled into the parking area outside the little shop.

"Would you pop in and buy all the copies of The Sun?"

A smile lit up Julie's face. "What a good idea!" It was still quite early so few copies would have been sold, if any. Julie went into the shop and asked the assistant for every copy of The Sun she had and said she was doing a project and needed loads. The assistant said she would have to keep a few back because some had been ordered, before she helped Julie carry the remaining bundle out to the car. The Mini boot squeaked open and the papers were carefully placed on top of the spare wheel.

"Sorry, what did you say you wanted them all for?" Julie repeated her story and told the assistant that they were doing a project on the media and they had been asked to pick up enough copies of The Sun for the whole class.

"Let me know the day before if you want to do this again and I will order extra papers."

Julie thanked her for her help and waited until she was back in the shop before she opened the car door and got in.

"Oh, thanks, Julie, you are a great friend. What would I do without you? I owe you a big favour now. Any time you want some help, just let me know."

"Forget it. That's what friends are for. Now, let's sneak in to college before the busses start filing in and Jane and co arrive."

Once they had reached the car park Harry tucked the paper she had been reading neatly under the car seat before Julie carefully locked the car up and they dashed into college. Stew and Russ were waiting at their usual table in the empty student common room. Arriving early each day they were monitoring the situation too. As Julie and Harry slipped into the seats opposite them, they informed the girls that they had seen the paper. After mischievously congratulating Harry on her sexy pose, they announced that they too had been hard at work. Having been down to the staff room before any teachers had arrived, they'd been able to sneak in and remove the teacher's copy of The Sun from the rest area. They had also removed the library copies.

Harry thanked them very much. She had forgotten the college had papers delivered. At least now she felt she could relax and concentrate on her college work. The chatter continued between the two boys and Julie before Julie noticed how Harry had gone very quiet and asked her to pop into the loo with her. Doors securely closed, she checked there were no other pupils in any of the cubicles and then asked Harry what the matter was.

"If Pablo sees a copy of that he will think I've turned into a tart."

Julie placed her arms around Harry's shaking shoulders as the silent tears began to fall. Rubbing her friend's back she suggested it was time Harry wrote Pablo a letter explaining how she felt.

"You're right, maybe I should write to him. I completely lost my head and just ran, I can see that now. If we had talked I probably wouldn't be feeling like this still. I'll do it at the weekend."

Julie gave Harry a big hug as she tried to reassure her. "I really think it would be for the best."

Harry wiped her tears away as the buzzer went for tutorial.

Julie joined Stew and Russ at the tables in the back of their tutorial. "Look, you two, Sir's got a paper rolled up and tucked into the top of his kitbag. It looks suspiciously like a copy of The Sun to me."

"Damn," Harry cursed, "trust him to read that trash. How can we get his copy off him before he sees my picture?"

Russ kindly volunteered himself and Stew for the task. They headed up to James's desk and placed their rucksacks on the floor. Stew started asking questions about his timetable and, once he had gained James's full attention, Russ bent down and pretended to tie his shoe laces right next to James's bag. Quietly he slipped the paper from the kitbag and into his own. Straightening back up, he joined in the conversation and kept their tutor busy until the buzzer went enabling them to make their escape.

Once outside the room Harry thanked her friends and told them how grateful she was for all they had done for her over the past week. She promised them a good slap up meal at Dr Fosters on Saturday night. Arranging a meeting place for break time, they all split up and headed off in separate directions for the first lecture of the day.

Chapter 49

Pablo had thrown himself into his work. His father had given him the opportunity and backing to open a new snow-boarding shop. He had a three-week deadline to put a plan into place. The first, if all went to plan, was due to be opened in Barcelona in a month. If this turned out to be successful he would start a chain and open one in Paris and another in London, before branching out to the smaller cities across Europe.

Jordi had been very impressed with the hard work Pablo had been doing. His research had proved invaluable. Premises in an upmarket part of Barcelona were under negotiation.

Pablo had only spent twenty four hours in Barcelona looking for premises. He found it heartbreaking returning to the city he had recently been so happy in. Everywhere he went he was haunted by happy memories of the time he had spent with Harry in Barcelona.

Manolo called him up and asked if he fancied going out for a drink. Pablo refused saying he had too much work on. Jordi could see how Pablo was hiding from his emotions by filling all his waking hours with work. Harry's hasty departure had really knocked the stuffing out of him and he had lost his lust for fun. Dark shadows hung under his eyes and he had lost weight.

Having heard the tail end of Pablo's conversation with Manolo, Jordi finally ordered him to take a night off. He made Pablo phone Manolo straight back to say he would join him for a drink.

Manolo arrived half an hour later to pick Pablo up. He had not seen his friend all week and was shocked at his drawn appearance. They headed down the mountain and into Playa. On the short journey Manolo hardly got two words out of Pablo, who had sat very quietly as though preoccupied. The bustling town of two weeks ago was now deserted. Most of the tourists had returned home and only a handful of retired people remained. A lot of the bars, night-clubs and restaurants had closed down for the winter. Security boarding covered most of the shop fronts and bars. It was a winding down period in Northern Spain when most of Catalonians headed to the mountains to get a well-earned rest after the long hectic season. Only a few night-spots frequented by the locals remained open. Parking was no problem. Two weeks ago it would have taken up to an hour to find a parking spot on the main streets. Now Manolo was able to pull up right outside the Dutch owned Captain's Bar and into one of many deserted parking spaces.

Pablo followed Manolo down the steep steps to the familiar basement bar. The dark lit bar, filled with smoke, was packed with locals. Manolo had to fight his way through the lively crowded room to the bar. Pablo followed. Once Manolo managed to get his elbow on the bar, Marc recognised him. Ignoring all the other demanding hands waving empty glasses or bottles in the air for refills, he asked Manolo if they wanted their usual.

Pablo and Manolo had spent many hours drinking with Marc and his partner Dennis during the past winter. They had met on a skiing trip in the Pyrenees. Pablo had introduced Marc to a property developer in Spain who had helped them find the premises for the Captain's Bar a few years before. Marc poured out two large beers and handed them over, refusing to take any payment. Manolo passed one to Pablo. Fighting their way back through the crowd they found a couple of stools at the far side of the room.

The pub was dotted with upright pillars surrounded by high circular tables and tall stools. Most were occupied. Pablo had been lucky to spot a table just being vacated. Once they had sat down, Pablo confessed that this was the first drink he'd had since the night Harry had left. As he drank his chilled beer from the thick frosted glass he began to relax for the first time in a few weeks.

Manolo did not know whether to bring the subject of Harry up and was relieved when Pablo mentioned he had not heard from her. Manolo showed Pablo a postcard he had received from Christina a couple of days after she had returned to university. It briefly mentioned Harry and how she was trying to shut out how hurt she had been over what had happened. She was desperately trying to return to normality although it had been very difficult as the press were still hounding her. After touching on the subject only briefly, Pablo was quick to change the conversation. They talked about the snowboarding industry and of their last winter holiday when they had both learnt to snowboard for the first time. The evening had been very pleasant and Pablo was glad he had been persuaded to go out.

Not intending to have a late night, as they were about to leave a couple of refills arrived on their table. Feeling obliged to stay for another drink, and after a quick chat with Marc and Dennis, who were always great fun and very entertaining, they called it a night. Manolo dropped Pablo back at his parents' villa before returning home where he phoned Christina to catch up on her news and fill her in on Pablo's progress.

The following morning, when Pablo popped into town to check out some stock in one of their shops for his father, he bumped into Conchitta. Having discovered the baby was not Pablo's, she'd had an abortion. Pablo had been appalled. The baby had meant nothing to her. All she had been after had been his name. Unexpectedly confronted by Conchitta, bile rose in his throat. He could not speak to her. Surely she knew by now how much he hated her. Flanked by her two gormless brothers, Pablo could not get away.

She could not help herself. Throwing her arms around him she started kissing him full on the lips. He pushed her away as he tried to move between Conchitta's beefy brothers. They blocked his path allowing Conchitta time to ask if he had seen that day's Costa Brava Fun.

Pablo was not in the mood for this. The kiss almost made him retch. She made his flesh crawl and he could not bear being anywhere near her. He had too much on his mind now with his new business project and was determined she couldn't hurt him anymore. Not replying he turned away, head hanging low. The two brothers, almost feeling sorry for him, stepped aside and let him through. Pablo made for the first shop with its door open. He stumbled in and stared aimlessly around, browsing at the rows of wooden carvings. At last he saw a flustered, outraged Conchitta being comforted by her brothers and disappearing into the shop next door.

He had finished his business in the town so he made a quick exit whilst he had the chance. Curiosity getting the better of him, he went to a newsagents to buy a copy of the paper. It was all over the newsstands; a picture of Harry looking extremely sexy, sitting on a car bonnet in a sexy little outfit. Having snatched up a copy of the paper, he paid for it and made for the security of his car before he dared read it. The picture of Harry sent his heart pounding.

God, he still loved her. This was not a picture he could have imagined Harry posing for. She looked sexy and very raunchy. A deep desire stirred within him, which he thought he had managed to block out. Having read the article accompanying the picture he felt sick. She had obviously got over him. She had returned to England and not given him another thought. When he got home he would write to her and wish her well. Maybe it would put an end to his torment if she thought he too had got over her.

Chapter 50

Harry had been for a long ride in the autumn sun. She had given Bounty the freedom to choose her own path. Riding on auto pilot had given her time to think. She had composed a letter in her mind and decided it was time to put pen to paper. After supper she showered and changed into her PJ's. Feeling comfortable and relaxed she sat down at the old Victorian writing bureau that had once belonged to her grandmother and now occupied the space in front of her window. Writing paper neatly laid out before her, she sucked on the end of her pen, trying to remember the letter she had composed earlier.

The words, once written on paper, did not seem the same. Sheet after sheet was torn from the pad and screwed up in frustration before being tossed into the bin. As the tears of love flowed over Harry's cheeks, she at last put something down on paper:

Pablo

*I am so sorry I left without speaking to you and giving you
a chance to explain. All I could see at the time was I had
given you my heart and you had broken it.*

*Both Christina and my mother explained that you
were not the only one keeping me in the dark. Nevertheless,
I thought we had an understanding and that we were
working together, we were a couple in love and nothing
would come between us. You obviously felt my love for
you was not strong enough. You were unable to confide
in me. This hurt me more than seeing the pictures of you
with Conchitta. These I now know were all part of her
plan and it worked. In the end, you could not trust me
enough to ask for my help so maybe it was a good thing I
left when I did.*

*I am now working hard at College. You may have
seen my picture in the papers. It was not what it seemed.
I hope you knew me well enough to realise I has been set
up and they caught me by surprise.*

*Send my love and good wishes to your family,
especially to Papa of whom I was very fond.*

*Thanks for the wonderful time you gave me. A time I
will always treasure and file in my heart. I hope you have
a good life and that one day you find your soul mate. You
will always be my first true love.*

Harry

That would have to do. It still didn't read the way Harry wanted it to,
but no matter how many times she tried, it would not flow or sound like
it did in her head. Sealing the addressed envelope, having placed a stamp
in the corner, she ran down the stairs and out to the post box before she
had chance to change her mind again.

The little, red post box was situated through the wrought iron gate
leading from the vegetable garden to the road. Harry pushed the letter
through the mouth of the box and, with a feeling of relief, let out a sigh,

thinking 'Chapter over. I wonder if I will ever love again or feel the love and companionship I had. Oh no, I still love Pablo, what have I done?'

Once in bed Harry had a restless night's sleep. Why had she posted the letter? It was a mistake. She should have written that she forgave him and still loved him and asked him if they could meet and talk. It was too late. The letter would have been collected and be half way to Spain by now.

Chapter 51

Julie arrived dressed in white shorts and a blue T-shirt. She sat and waited in the car for Harry, who appeared dressed in a little strappy tennis dress with a Nike tick embroidered onto the back panel, white knickers and plimsolls.

Mark had always drummed into his children that if they went out dressed for a sport they would feel, and play, better. This had always stuck in Harry's mind whenever she played tennis. It seemed to work so she always insisted on wearing her Wimbledon whites.

Joining Julie in the car, they headed off to the local tennis club. The club was privately owned. The fees were expensive but Mark always stated it was part of the girl's education to be taught how to play tennis properly. It was still early morning and the car park was empty. Harry collected their rackets from the locker room and joined Julie out on their favourite court.

There were six courts altogether, five of them lined up on one side of the wooden club-house, and the sixth, on its own, at the side of the club-house offering privacy. This was the court Julie and Harry always liked to play on and had booked. It was surrounded on three sides by a tall conifer hedge, whilst the section in front of the club house was separated off by a low wall and high netting. It was also the court all the club championships were played on.

Julie detected Harry was in a mood the minute they stepped onto the court. Her heart was not in the game. Every time Julie hit a ball Harry would miss the ball completely, stumble, or hit a wild shot.

"Come on, Harry. What's wrong with you? You usually beat me hands-down, but you don't seem to be enjoying it."

Harry apologised and said they should break for a drink. She wasn't in the mood for tennis after all.

As they approached the netting they had the shock of their lives.

James was sitting on the wall by the court all dressed in his tennis whites. He had been watching them. Harry looked extremely sexy with her long legs still tanned from the summer sun, a tiny skirt to her dress showing just a glimpse of the frills covering her firm bottom. It had been quite a turn on every time Harry had bent down to scope up a ball. With a big smirk on his face James greeted the girls and then, turning away from Julie, he challenged Harry to a game.

It was like a red rag to a bull. Harry wanted to wipe the smirk from his face and she was in the mood to do it. She was a natural at all sports she had ever played and tennis was one of her strongest games. He must have thought she was pathetic in her last game. Well, she would show him.

"Would you mind, Julie?" Harry winked at Julie who smiled back knowingly. "Just one set then. That's all I've got time for".

"Fine by me if that's all you're up to."

After tossing his racket in the air, he asked Harry to shout. Harry opted for the smooth side. His racket crashed onto the all-weather surface and landed on the rough side. James chose which end he was going to serve and start the game from. James started off with quite a gentle serve but soon realised Harry had not been playing her best when he had watched her earlier. Harry violently smashed the ball back at James. He soon began to learn that Harry was a strong player. Harry had won the first game to love and it was now her turn to serve. James laughed and shouted he was just giving her a chance. At the start of the second game James had no idea what Harry's serve was like. He stood centre and mid-court, presuming Harry would have a weak serve and just plop the ball over the net. Harry was slender and did not look as though she could put any power behind the ball. He was in for a shock. The first serve came straight at him at such a speed he did not know which way to move. The ball bounced up high and caught him on his chest. The wind knocked out of him he walked back and stood on the base line. Spinning his racket in his hand he did not know what Harry would do next.

Harry aced all her serves, taking the second game. Julie clapped from behind the netting as Harry cheekily took a bow.

James was still pretending to laugh and joke, but he was beginning to get worried. This was not going to be an easy game. He would have to treat Harry as one of the toughest opponents he played with and show her no mercy.

It was Harry's turn to be alarmed. James increased the speed of his serves and, for the next game, Harry had to really concentrate on her return. Panting around the court, beginning to feel completely useless as she sprinted back and forth, James worked the ball left and right. He won the third game.

It was two-one to Harry and time to change ends. As Harry walked around the tennis net James, showing off, ran and jumped over it. Then, turning to Julie, he took a bow.

Julie couldn't help but smile. She had to admire his cheek.

Harry was not to be put off and soon discovered James had a weakness. It was his backhand. She was now back in the game. After that, the games went to the server until, at last, Harry's determination enabled her to break James's serve. She took the set six four. Harry marched off the court to a huge applause from the audience that had gathered to watch the game.

"Now you must buy me a drink. After all, you did win," James pleaded as he tried to keep pace with Harry.

"Sorry, Sir, we've run out of time. We'll have to make it another day," Harry smugly replied as she stepped into the women's locker room, shutting the door behind her.

Julie was ahead of Harry and had made her way to the seats in the changing room. She was crying with laughter. "Harry, you should have seen his face. It was a picture when you served that first ball at him."

"I did! Do you think he is really angry now?"

"No, he'll be fine. He obviously fancies the socks off you and now he has an excuse to challenge you to another game."

The two girls didn't notice James was eavesdropping on the other side of the hedge as they chatted away, while waiting for Julie to unlock her car.

"Are we still on for Dr Fosters tonight, only I told Stew and Russ I'd let them know by lunchtime?"

"Yes, I think I deserve a night out with my three best friends, don't you?"

James listened to their arrangements. This would be his chance; he would go to Dr Fosters and bump into them.

Chapter 52

Dr Fosters was situated in the docks. The docks, built on the River-Severn for importing goods through Gloucester, had cut out the former need for moving goods at Bristol, and had become a thriving port. Then, after the expansion of the railways and the increase in road transportation had led to its decline, the docks had stood dormant for many years until its transformation started in the eighties. The run-down, red brick buildings had been turned into craft shops, yuppie-style flats, restaurants, bars, museums, and other attractions, putting the old mills and Victorian warehouses back to good use.

Julie called for Harry and then picked Stew and Russ up on their way. They all managed to squash into Julie's old mini. It was tight but they made themselves cosy and headed for the city. Stew and Russ were dressed casually in jeans and T-shirts. Harry wore her boyfriend jeans, a little crop top, and denim jacket. With her hair hanging loose she looked stunning. Julie had her hair tied up for a change and wore jeans along with a little slit necked top.

Arriving in Gloucester they found a space suitable for the small car. Julie paid for the parking using the change they scraped together, and they walked along the jetty admiring the colourful barges and a large old ship that had sailed up from Bristol to be used in some period drama currently being filmed in the old docks. It was the ideal place for making films, with the towering mills, warehouses, and many waterways, all of which had been recently renovated back to their former glory. One claim to fame, the popular television series The Onedin Line had been filmed in front of Biddle warehouse.

It was getting dark and, linking arms, they made their way over the bridge. The street lamps illuminated the cobbled pathway leading to Dr Fosters. Harry had made the reservations so led the way through the door. It was an open plan, old warehouse that had been gutted and redesigned to hold a modern, popular, restaurant and bar. Brick walled, with steel girders rising to the roof, a deep oak, wooden bar, lined with bottles, ran from one end of the ground floor to the other and was already crowded. Sawdust lined the floor giving the place a rustic feel. The tables, made of up-turned boats were surrounded by barrels, cleverly turned into stools and seats. In the middle of the floor was a wrought iron staircase running up to the formal restaurant on the first floor.

Harry's fame had preceded her and the staff had been waiting for her arrival. Greeted at the door with, "Would you like drinks at the bar first or do you want to go straight to your table?" Harry turned to her friends who all agreed they were looking forward to a drink.

The waitress led them to one of the upturned boats and, once they were seated, took their orders. The boys both ordered bottled lager; Harry opted for a vodka and Coke while Julie hesitated, worrying about having to drive back later.

"Oh, come on, Julie, this is my treat. We'll call a taxi and you can drink too." Harry smiled and Julie didn't need much persuasion. She too ordered a vodka and Coke. The music was pumping out loudly so they had to shout to be heard.

Heads turned as Harry and Julie excused themselves and walked the entire length of the bar to find the toilet and to check their hair and make-up. They were both naturally very attractive. As they walked back to join their friends, eyes from around the room again followed them.

Stew and Russ sat proudly noticing the disappointment on the other young male's faces as the girls joined them. After several drinks they began getting jolly. Stew and Russ had a good laugh over the tennis story. They had seen Harry in action many times and knew she could wipe the floor with most of her opponents.

When they moved upstairs the music faded into the back ground. Menus were handed around and Harry was feeling hungry. She needed to eat now. The vodka was beginning to have an effect. It was Cajun food.

After briefly scanning the menu they decided on a mixed platter and a giant combo, a couple of large dishes they could all share. Once the food had been ordered along with a couple of bottles of wine, one red and one white, Stew and Russ vanished off for a cigarette.

The wine arrived and Julie and Harry helped themselves to the white wine whilst the boys both went for the red. Trays of sizzling spicy chicken wings, ribs, potato wedges and an assortment of dips arrived through the swing doors from the kitchen and filled the table. It was a very unrefined affair using fingers to eat and napkins to wipe dripping mouths. Several bottles of wine later the evening ended.

Julie went on ahead with the boys to seek out a taxi while Harry settled the bill. The waitress had offered to call them a taxi when they had finished their meal. They all decided they would like to have a stroll around the docks to clear their heads before heading home, so declined the offer.

Having caught the girl's conversation back at the tennis club earlier in the day, Harry had no idea that James had been stalking them all evening.

Outside Dr Fosters he was lying in wait and soon spotted Julie, Stew and Russ, who were now very mellow and quite giggly. "Hi, fancy meeting you three here. Can I join you for a walk?" Not waiting for an answer, he took Julie by the arm, supporting her swaying body, and he began leading the way. Stew and Russ were well gone; they hung back and waited for Harry, giggling as they watched Julie staggering along on James's arm.

When Harry appeared she was shocked to find the two boys on their own. "Where is Julie?"

Trying to suppress their laughter they explained how they had bumped into 'Sir James,' as they had now nicknamed him, and how he and Julie had walked on ahead.

"Oh, poor Julie, quick we must go and find her." Harry was the only one with her wits still about her. Getting between the two boys she took Stew and Russ by the arms and marched into the darkness, finally catching up with Julie who was just getting into James's car.

"Hi, Harry, boys. Look, I can give you all a lift home. Jump in."

It was too late to convince her friends that this was not a clever idea as they piled into the back of the car leaving Harry no option but to follow. "A fine load of friends you've turned out to be," Harry mumbled as she squeezed in next to Stew.

On the way home James was the perfect taxi driver, dropping the two boys off first as they lived the farthest away. Next, he drove Julie to her house and even offered to take her back the following morning to pick her car up. Now he had Harry on her own. Once Julie's door had closed, James asked Harry to move to the front seat so she could direct him to her house.

Harry was very wary but felt she had no choice and clambered over the seats to join James in the front. Once she had safely strapped herself in, James started the car engine and drove on. Harry sat in silence. Feeling extremely tense she found herself gripping the seat with her hands. She could not believe her friends had been so stupid; fancy leaving her in that position. She'd have a few words to say to them in the morning.

James tried in desperation to make polite conversation and got very little response. Harry just gave him brief answers to his questions and managed to end every conversation he started.

After a while Harry began to feel sorry for him. He was trying so hard and being very sweet. Perhaps she should at least be nice to him. In the past, on the odd occasion she had bumped into him in Newent, and before she'd been introduced to him, she had thought he was good looking. It was just unfortunate they had met the way they had. There was a lot of rivalry between the two brothers and this had brought out the worst in him.

At last a frustrated James pulled into the farm. As the car came to a halt, Harry was quick to un-strap her seatbelt.

As she made for the door James hit the central locking. Turning to face Harry he asked her if there was any chance of them starting again. He explained how sorry he was for how he had behaved before. His voice was low, quiet, and pleading.

Harry began to breakdown her personal barrier and melted a little towards him.

"Come on. My name is James, it's so nice to meet you at last." James stuck out his hand as if they were meeting for the first time.

Harry placed her delicate hand in his. "You too. My name is Harry." Introductions over, Harry burst out laughing and James joined in.

"Now, when am I going to be able to challenge you to a return tennis match?"

"Unlock the door and I might give you a date."

James flicked the switch releasing Harry's door. Harry climbed from the car. Leaning her head back in through the open door she said, "How about lunch time on Monday? That's if you're free." With that she slammed the door closed. Swinging her bag over her shoulder, she walked toward the house and did not turn around until she reached her front door. When at last she looked back she gave James a big smile and a quick wave before she went into the house.

James drove off feeling pretty chuffed with himself, happy and relieved that Harry had at last put the past behind them and he could start anew.

Harry went up to bed with a glow around her, relaxed and happy for the first time in weeks. College would no longer be a problem; she could go in feeling comfortable on Monday morning and no longer dread the tutorial sessions.

The next day Julie phoned to apologise for her behaviour the previous evening. She also wanted to check if Harry was okay. She couldn't quite remember what had happened, but she had a bad feeling about something. Much to her relief Harry was fine and in good spirits. She told Julie how the evening had ended. Everything had turned out well. Julie had done her a favour. She and James had made friends and they were going to play tennis on Monday at lunch time.

Julie could not believe her ears. "I thought you hated James."

"Well, let's just say we started off on the wrong foot and now we have made up and have decided it would be better and healthier if we were friends."

"God, Harry! Are you sure you have not had a knock on the head or something?"

"No, I'm fine. I am just going to be his friend and leave it at that. It will make life a lot easier and you have to admit, he is quite cute."

Julie arranged to pick Harry up and take her to college the next morning before hanging up the phone. Later in the day Julie received a call from both Russ and Stew checking everything was okay with Harry and making sure she had got home safely and wasn't cross with them. This had given Julie the opportunity to inform them about Harry and James's newfound friendship.

Chapter 53

It was Monday morning and the weather was terrible. Wind, rain, and hail burst from the skies in-between spells of bright sunshine. The tennis was off.

The atmosphere in tutorial had changed for the better. Tutorial was now a very pleasant social event for them all. James confessed he had only recently qualified as a teacher. This was his first position in a college. He had felt like an outsider when he first started. Having been sent to a private school himself, he found it hard fitting in with both the staff and the pupils. Now he felt he was one of the gang. Instead of the four friends sitting at the back of the room whispering, speaking in code, or playing cards, they now all sat with James, arranging themselves around his desk and having a laugh and a good chat every morning and during afternoon registration.

The weeks had flown past. Harry had settled down and was working harder than ever at college. Her social life revolved around the tennis club, playing tennis whenever the weather was dry enough, or just going for a social drink with her friends when the autumn storms bombarded the county, stripping the leaves from the trees.

John had come home for another long weekend break. At first it had been very awkward for Harry trying to be friends with the two brothers and coping with their continuous rivalry for her attention.

Then, one evening, the atmosphere had changed. Harry had gone up to the tennis club with Julie for a drink whilst John was home. Harry had introduced him to Julie; it was love at first sight. Julie had fallen for John in a big way and John thought Julie was the most beautiful thing he had ever seen. Julie and John made a great couple and often joined Harry and James for a game of doubles, or a social drink. The two brothers were at last getting on well. They had so much in common it was nice to see them laughing together and no longer trying to get one over on the other all the time. Harry found herself in her own company more and more, and finally got around to opening a savings account. She had transferred the money from the Ski-Summer contract. With some of the money she had made she had gone out and invested in a car.

Julie was now spending every moment of the day with John when he was home on leave and, since their relationship had started, John arrived home far more frequently. He would make the trip back from Birmingham at every opportunity, if he had enough hours on the ground, to spend time with Julie. Harry could no longer rely on her friend for company and lifts.

James had, of course, been very good, but Harry did not want to become reliant on him. They spent enough time together and, although Harry enjoyed his company and he was fun to be with, she also found him a bit over protective. He was very quick to get jealous if Harry talked to other boys. James would always give Harry a quick peck on the cheek when they met or parted. When they were together, James would not leave Harry's side. Harry quite often worried James was reading more into their relationship than she was. Harry made sure she never gave him any encouragement or false commitment; after all, he was also a teacher at her college. This had been the inspiration for her to buy a car. She needed to maintain her independence and freedom.

Mark thought it was a great idea. He had made the expedition a family outing and had taken Harry to all the car dealers and show rooms in the area.

Stopping for lunch at the twin's favourite restaurant, "McDougal's", where they all dined out on junk food, and the twins got a special lunch in a box with a free toy in from the latest Disney film.

Lunch over, Mark was beginning to despair; they had already visited most of the car show rooms he could think of. He had one last hope and, on the way home, called in at the Volkswagen garage that had recently opened on the Herefordshire border. Harry had instantly fallen in love with a bright yellow VW beetle convertible parked in the centre of the show room. Mickey and Sophie nick named the car Harry's little duckling. Harry couldn't wait to get behind the wheel, although she had to wait patiently for several days while Mark sorted out a suitable insurance. Harry had insisted on continental cover; she had decided that, when she had to go back to Spain for the Ski-Winter modelling, she would drive to Calais and put the car on the train in France. This she wanted to do to ensure she had her own transport while she was away and could come and go as she pleased.

Once the car had been paid for, the bank transfer had gone through and the insurance had at last been sorted out, Harry was able to go and pick it up.

Luckily it was whilst Julie was at a loss. She suddenly found she was feeling lonely; she had too much time on her hands. John was on a long haul flight roster for a fortnight and Julie was just sitting at home, pining and feeling sorry for herself. Julie had been up to see Harry, who was very excited about her new car and was due to pick it up. Julie offered to drive Harry over to collect her new pride and joy.

Once Harry got her little duckling home, she spent the first week running errands for Anna and Mark, or driving the twins to their various activities. She hardly stepped out of her new toy. If it was raining she just enjoyed feeling cosy and warm, driving around in her Beetle with the radio or her cassette player blasting out her favourite music. When the sun was shining, the top would be neatly folded down. Harry would tuck her flowing hair up into a leather, navy cap and, wearing her new leather jacket, would drive around enjoying the feeling of freedom and the cool fresh air swirling around her face. Sometimes, with just the local radio station for company, she would drive for hours on her own going nowhere. People began to recognise her and would wave at her in her bright yellow car as she travelled around the country lanes.

James was a little put out at first. He could not keep tabs on Harry's movements. In the end he brought her a mobile brick phone; it was yellow to match her car. This he made her promise to carry with her always in case she broke down or was in trouble. He had managed to key in all the numbers of the people he knew jointly with Harry.

Harry was a little irritated at first. She liked the freedom of having her own wheels and it had been refreshing not to have James by her side constantly. When, at last, the novelty began to wear off and Harry stopped polishing her little duckling, Harry became more accessible and started seeing more of James.

Chapter 54

During the second week in December Harry received a letter from Señor Cruanos. The snow had started falling in the Pyrenees and they were hoping to start shooting the Ski-Winter ads in January. Harry had a lot to prepare. She had not been snow skiing for a couple of years so the first thing she did was to sign up for refresher lessons at the local dry ski slope, as instructed by Señor Cruanos. James insisted on taking a refresher course at the same time to keep her company.

Not wishing to hurt James's feelings, Harry had no option but to agree, and she resigned herself to the fact she would have a companion. When the evening finally arrived for their first lesson, James picked Harry up and they arrived at the ski slope together. Gloucester Ski Centre was the premier dry ski slope in the South West. On their arrival they were immediately met by their instructor, a tall man in his late twenties with a distinguished head of thick, light brown hair, a moustache and a beard. He introduced himself as Ryan.

Having explained that they would have the slopes entirely to themselves, as requested by Señor Cruanos, Ryan showed them into a changing room and told them to get ready and meet him outside. He was not quite sure what to make of Harry. He had expected some loud-mouthed model. Harry had surprised him and been very sweet when she had introduced herself. Maybe it was just nerves, he thought, and her true colours would come out on the slopes when she had her first tantrum.

James had been out shopping all day and had spent a fortune on new equipment. Harry made do with the Old Salomon skis, Head Ezone boots, and Rossignol ski poles that she had had for Christmas a few years ago from Anna and Mark. The boots, although a little scratched and worn, were still a perfect fit.

Harry slipped on a few more layers including well-padded joggers for protection against the hard-matting surface should she fall, a yellow padded ski jacket, her old woollen hat, and a scarf to keep her warm. Harry eased on her boots, positioned them carefully in the bindings, and clicked them in. She stood up and bounced around a little checking their fit. James chatted excitedly to Harry as he put his brand new, shiny black boots on and clipped into his skis. Once they were both satisfied with their gear, they slid across the matt flooring to the external door where Ryan was waiting. It was dark and the air was frosty. Harry could see her breath when she spoke.

The main one hundred and sixty metre slope was in darkness and only the lower part of the seventy metre training slope, and nursery area, were floodlit. Ryan explained they would start at the beginning on the nursery slope. This was very short with a gentle slope. Ryan made them practice the snow plough position before sending them side-stepping up the slope until they reached the top. Once at the top of the small slope they had to snow plough back down. Having repeated this exercise several times, Ryan said he was quite satisfied they could both safely stop and that they could move onto the junior slope.

James chatted to Harry and showed his skiing knowledge off, giving her extra instructions every time he thought they were out of Ryan's hearing.

Harry could tell Ryan was no fool and James was getting on his nerves.

Calling them over to the button lift, Ryan briefly instructed them on how to safely mount and ride it up to the next level. He asked James to demonstrate. James slid forward on his skis and waited for a pole to arrive. Looking over his shoulder he waited for it to appear from the rear. As the hanging pole passed his shoulder, James grabbed the pole and sat down on the seat. The seat gave way and James landed on his backside on the floor.

Harry suppressed a giggle and saw the glint of glee in Ryan's bright blue eyes. She hadn't noticed before what lovely eyes he had and couldn't help staring at them.

"That was exactly how not to use the lift. You must not put any pressure on the seat, just slip it between your legs and let it drag you up. You cannot put all your weight onto it. Now, Harry you have a go." As Ryan directed his speech towards Harry, James got to his feet and sheepishly brushed himself down. Ryan thought if Harry messed this up he would see her first tantrum.

Harry stood in line and, as the next pole came around, she reached for it and pulled the seat down between her legs and just let it gently pull her up the slope. With her skies running firmly along the ground, and all her weight being carried on her legs, Harry made it to the next level with ease.

Ryan waited while James had another go and, once he was safely standing next to Harry, Ryan took his turn. They were told to spend the rest of the lesson snow ploughing down and getting used to the lift. Ryan left them to it and told them he would be keeping an eye on them from the cabin.

Harry concentrated hard and put a lot of effort into her snow ploughing. She wanted to get every aspect of her skiing perfected before she headed off to the Pyrenees. It seemed very slow and as if Harry had taken a step backwards, but she was happy to embed the core skills in her memory once again. When at last they were called in, the warmth of the heated clubhouse hit them. As Harry stripped off the extra layers she had been wearing, Ryan poked his head around the door and told them there was a drink waiting for them on the bar.

The bar was styled like a Swiss chalet, with wooden polished floor, panelled walls and a wood-burner glowing in the corner of the room. A stag's head hung over the bar.

"Miss Smyth-Thomas, I have been asked to give you and your friend whatever you would like to drink." A short, stocky, jolly barman, with a balding head and rosy cheeks, waved his hand down the optics hanging behind the bar.

Harry led the way forward. As she reached the bar James, hot on her heels, found her a stool, so she sat down. "That's very sweet. Can I just have a cappuccino please?"

"And you, sir, what can I get you for you?"

"I would like a brandy please."

The drinks arrived very promptly. Harry's arrived in a tall, tankard shaped glass. She asked for a straw to sip her boiling hot, frothy cappuccino through.

James found himself another stool and sat facing Harry. He was enjoying playing with his smooth brandy, rolling it around the goldfish bowl sized crystal glass he had been handed. He was also enjoying the looks he was receiving from envious people when they saw who he was with.

With her skin slightly less tanned now, her eyes were sparkling and her face was glowing after exercising in the crisp night air. She looked radiant and others around the bar could not help but stare at her beauty. Harry and James chatted away until their glasses were drained. It was getting very late and they both had college the next day. It was time to head home. Harry was looking forward to her next lesson. She kept trying to remember what Ryan looked like.

It soon came around. Once again James had insisted on picking her up and driving to the ski slope. Ryan was already waiting for them out by the slopes. "Hello, Harry, James. It is nice to see you both again." Ryan's smooth deep voice was very welcoming. "Before we move on, I thought we'd have half an hour running over what you did in the last lesson. So, if you don't mind, can I see you both snow plough down the nursery slope. Then, using the button lift, make your way half way up the training slope and do the same down it." Holding out his hand he gestured towards the nursery slope.

Harry led the way and, stepping sideways in her skies, slowly made her way to the top of the small slope. Once at the top she waited for James to join her. Counting to three they both snow ploughed down side by side. Harry glanced in Ryan's direction and he nodded his approval before they moved on to the training slope.

"Okay, James, would you like me to lead the way or would you like to go up on the lift first?"

Ryan had warmed to Harry and winked at her as she spoke.

James laughed and stood back while Harry took up her position waiting for the lift to come around. As one came up behind her, Harry was quick to grab hold of it, slide it between her legs, and let it drag her up to the first level of the training slope.

James was a little nervous, not of using the lift, but of making a fool of himself, worried if he should be too heavy-handed when pulling it down between his legs and that it would give way again. This would be disastrously embarrassing for him. He didn't want to land on his bottom as he had during the previous lesson. It was easy for Harry, he thought to himself. She was so light. The lift came around and, much to James's relief, he successfully manoeuvred it into position and arrived on the first level where Harry was waiting for him with a huge grin on her face.

She had sensed his fear and could not help smiling when she saw the look of relief on his face as he dismounted the lift.

Once again, laughing together, they counted to three before pushing off and slowly snow ploughing down the slope to where Ryan was waiting. Once he was satisfied that they had both got the hang of snow ploughing, he went up to the first level with them and demonstrated how to slalom down the slope.

James went first followed by Harry, who traced his tracks and zigzagged down the slope. Ryan was pleased with them both. He left James to it and followed Harry up and down the slope, showing her how to make short, sharper turns. She was such a natural that she did not need much encouragement. It was obvious she had done quite a lot of snow skiing in the past. The time flew by and the lesson ended.

Ryan again offered them both a drink in the bar afterwards but Harry insisted they declined. She had some course work to hand in the next day and, although she had finished it days ago, she just wanted to go back through it and check it over once more. James was a little disappointed. He enjoyed having Harry to himself and didn't get the chance very often these days.

The following few lessons were more enjoyable. Harry learnt new skills using her ski poles and no longer had to snow plough to stop. She was looking increasingly more professional as the lessons progressed. They were now both on the main one hundred and sixty metre slope. This was the only slope that needed to be floodlit. The smaller slopes were no longer of use and remained in total darkness.

The last lesson approached. Harry had received a phone call from Ryan firstly enquiring what relationship she and James had. After Harry explained they were just good friends, Ryan offered to buy her supper in the restaurant after her lesson.

Harry was dreading telling James she was going to have a meal with Ryan and would drive herself. She could not think of a reasonable excuse. Just as she had given up hope and had decided not to hurt James feelings by declining Ryan's offer, James had phoned. He said he had an awful cold and didn't fancy going out into the frosty and chilly evening air. He was very apologetic but she would have to drive herself. He also asked her to give Ryan his apologies.

It was Friday evening. There was no college the next day and Harry took her time getting ready. She normally didn't bother taking makeup or perfume with her when she was having a lesson, but tonight was different. She was going to have a meal with her instructor. She felt very wary but, at the same time, excited at the thought of supper with Ryan after her lesson. She had thought he didn't like her and the phone call had been a complete surprise. Packing her kitbag, she rolled up her favourite black trousers and pink floral top to wear. She placed her perfume, along with her make-up, in the side compartment of her kitbag. Kissing her grandmother goodbye, then telling her mum and dad she would be very late as they were eating after the lesson, she headed off in her little yellow duckling for her final lesson.

Chapter 55

Ryan had not seen Harry's VW before. She had always arrived with James. As she pulled into the car park he hesitated for a few minutes until he was certain it was Harry before he went out and helped her carry her gear into the changing room. Harry explained on the way about James' cold and how he had sent his apologies. Ryan seemed pleased. He was very patient with James despite James' cocky attitude. At least now he would have plenty of time to concentrate on Harry's moves. Harry put on her layers, jacket, boots, and skis, while Ryan waited for her by the door.

It was a bitterly cold evening and Ryan's breath was like smoke in the air as he gave Harry her instructions for the evening. They both headed up on the button lift to the half way marker of the main slope. Harry positioned herself next to Ryan on the slope. He made her feel very safe and protected.

"Okay, Harry, now we must conquer your parallel turns. The key to bringing your skis parallel is ensuring you have your weight in the right place. Most of your weight should be on your downhill, outside foot, then you will stay balanced but also be able to slide your uphill, inside foot parallel to it. Watch me and follow." Gently he pushed himself off, heading to the left side of the slope before turning sharply just as he reached the edge. He then whizzed back towards the opposite side passing Harry.

Harry cut her way stylishly down the slope tracing Ryan's tracks. As Harry skidded to a halt at the bottom of the slope, Ryan smiled proudly at her achievements. "Come on then, Harry. Let's go right from the top a few times. This time you lead so I can watch you."

Harry led the way to the lift and dismounted at the very top of the one hundred and sixty metre dry ski run. Ryan watched her push off and glide down the slope, manoeuvring gracefully with speed. Ryan pushed off and followed her down. He could not fault her movements and she stopped perfectly. He was very pleased with her progress. She had good co-ordination, balance, and flexibility. She was obviously very fit which enabled her to perform a more dynamic range of movements than his usual students. They went up one after the other on the lift, and then came down shadowing or chasing each other until they were exhausted. Finally Ryan said he thought they had done enough and praised Harry for her progress and commitment.

Harry looked radiant. She was breathing heavily from the exercise, chest expanding and contracting. Her cheeks were flushed and glowing; her eyes sparkled.

Thank God his job as a teacher was over. He had never felt like this about a pupil before. She made his heart miss a beat and he was having trouble resisting her.

Ryan left Harry alone in the changing room to get her gear off while he vanished into the office to change.

Harry peeled her salopettes off as quickly as she could. She did not want it to seem like she had taken ages getting ready. She just wanted to appear natural. Popping into the wash room she freshened up and slipped into her black trousers, top and boots. Brushing some tinted lip-gloss onto her full lips and a touch of eyeliner to her shapely eyes, she completed her natural look. On her way back into the changing room she tidied her hair, stuffing everything back into her kitbag, she checked her watch; it had only taken her eight minutes. When she knocked on the office door Ryan greeted her. He had a pair of washed out jeans and a faded T-shirt on.

He looked her up and down as he took her bag off her and placed it securely in the office. Then, locking the door, he turned back to Harry. "You look nice."

"Thanks, I just threw my trousers into my bag to change into as we are having supper." Harry blushed.

"Come with me." Ryan took Harry's delicate hand in his and led her into the bar.

The bar was crowded; it was Friday night and all the locals were in. Bill, the jolly barman, made his way down the bar to Ryan. "What can I get you, Ryan?"

"A couple of gin and tonics." Ryan glanced at Harry who nodded in agreement.

Bill tossed some ice into two glasses, added a twist of lemon, and then splashed the gin in, submerging the ice. Setting a glass down in front of Harry and one in front of Ryan, Bill asked them to indicate how much tonic they wanted.

Harry let the tonic flow. She was not very good on gin these days. It normally went straight to her head, but she was not prepared to admit that to Ryan.

Ryan just let the tonic touch the gin then raised his hand. "Come on, look, there are a couple of empty stools over by the burner. Let's take our drinks over there and sit down. Give me a shout will you, Bill, when they are ready for us in the restaurant." Harry followed Ryan over to the wood-burner and sat down. Ryan pulled his stool in front of Harry's and straddled it.

"I didn't think you would stay and have a meal with me." He looked Harry in the eye and waited for her to respond.

"Why not?" Harry passed the question back to Ryan.

Playing with the lemon in his drink briefly before he looked up into Harry's clear, sparkling eyes, he said, "I thought that James was your boyfriend. Then, when I started to notice how much he showed off in your company, I thought he could not possibly be your boyfriend as he is obviously still trying to win you over. What is he to you really?"

"You will never believe this," Harry blushed. "He is my tutor at college and out of college he's a very good friend."

Ryan laughed. Puzzled, Harry asked him what was so funny. "Poor chap fancies the pants off you and he cannot make a move on you because it's more than his job's worth."

Harry felt slightly sorry for James and a little angry. Is that what most people thought of poor James, that he spent his time trying to impress her? "Okay, then, what was the other reason you thought I would not have a meal with you?"

Slightly embarrassed Ryan looked away and at the wood burner. The reflection of the flames flickered and danced in his eyes as he took his time to answer. "I could not ask you before for the same reason as James. I was your teacher and it was not ethical. I also thought you may think I was too old for you. I am twenty eight and you are what, seventeen or eighteen?" Without waiting for a reply, he continued, "I am at least ten years older than you."

Harry was feeling a lot more confident these days. With every sip of her gin her courage increased.

"We are only having a meal. There is nothing wrong with that."

Bill arrived over and interrupted them saying they were ready for them in the restaurant. The restaurant was very cosy with warm, panelled pine walls. A large open stone fireplace roared away in the centre of the room. Little blue napkins draped over low hanging lights above the individual tables and cast a sliver glow across the diners.

They were led to a table in the corner of the room. Ryan held the chair out for Harry before taking his place opposite her. The tables were laid with blue cloths and decorated with bronze cutlery. Three yellow gerberas smiled from jug in the middle of the table.

Harry removed her yellow linen napkin from her side plate and laid it across her knee.

"I have already ordered for us. I hope you don't mind and you like most foods."

"No, that's fine and yes, I will eat almost anything." Harry smiled up at Ryan. He always spoke very gently to her, as though he was speaking to a child. Harry loved the way he made her feel. Tingles ran down her spine when he spoke; he had such a deep voice.

The starter arrived. Ryan had ordered prawns and a garlic dip. Harry loved both prawns and garlic. Harry picked out a large prawn and, snapping its hard outer-layer off, she dipped the soft, pink fleshy part into the dip before biting a small part off and chewing on it.

Ryan watched as she licked the garlic from her lips. She was sexy even when she ate, he thought, mesmerized by her every move.

Taking their time over the prawns they chatted about skiing. Ryan suggested various aerobic exercises Harry could do to maintain her fitness over the next few days before she headed down to the Pyrenees. Ryan explained how important it was to be aerobically fit to exercise in the thin mountain air. He said there was only one way to achieve this, which was through some sort of programme of exercise that raised the heart rate and kept it there over a period of at least several minutes. He also went on to talk about the anaerobic fitness she needed to have the strength and ability to sustain short bursts of exertion; skiing bumps, short radius turns and schussing all required power as well as stamina. Finally he touched on co-ordination, balance, and flexibility. He thought Harry had all this and would do well.

Finishing their prawns, they washed their fingers in the bowl of warm water and lemon that the waiter had placed on the table. Drying them on their napkins, they had to discard them with the prawn shells and Ryan asked for fresh ones.

They found plenty to talk about and, after finishing off the bottle of white wine that had arrived with their starters, Ryan ordered a bottle of red to eat with the steaks he had ordered for their main course.

The steaks arrived and Ryan's was rare and very bloody. Having never known a woman eat a rare steak, he had ordered Harry a medium done steak that suited Harry down to the ground.

Still sizzling, they were transferred from the wrought iron plate onto two wooden platters that had been placed before them. With the steaks came the traditional big fat chunky chips and a typical English salad consisting of lettuce, tomatoes, grated carrot, onions and small mushrooms.

Harry helped herself to a small portion of chips and loads of lettuce and tomatoes, avoiding the onions. Cutting into her steak it was tender and succulent. She had built up a good appetite out on the dry slopes and the first mouthful was juicy and delicious; it went down beautifully.

The conversation stopped briefly while they tucked into their steaks. As they began to fill up and, after Harry had consumed several more glasses of wine, Ryan asked her what had happened between her and Pablo. He had obviously done his homework.

Harry instantly looked down at her plate. Toying with the chips left on the side of her plate she thought for a moment. She had to swallow hard as a lump formed in the back of her throat before replying. "I'm sorry, Ryan. I really don't want to talk about it."

Ryan had noticed how she had reacted and could see how hurt she was so he apologised for asking and quickly changed the subject.

The time seemed to fly past. The restaurant had emptied. Ryan and Harry made their way back into the bar and were now the only two people remaining.

Ryan kept Harry very entertained for the rest of the evening with stories of his travels. After leaving university he had taken a year out to travel around the world. Finally running out of money, he had ended up becoming a ski instructor in Austria. He had enjoyed a full and fascinating life. He had never married or had a relationship that lasted longer than the time he spent in a single place. Finally he had returned to England; his father had had a terminal illness and his mother had not been able to cope. He had helped nurse his father through his final months. After his father had died, as he was an only child, he felt that he could not leave his mother alone. His parents had been together forever and his mother could not come to terms with his father's death. She had died of a broken heart a few months later and Ryan had stayed on to sort out their affairs. Ryan looked down into his brandy and suddenly looked quite sad.

Harry reached over and patted his hand.

Ryan, looking up into Harry's eyes, placed his free hand over the top of Harry's and gently squeezed it. "I'm fine really. It was a couple of years ago now. I've had plenty of time to get over it." Releasing Harry's hand Ryan got to his feet. The lights around the bar had been turned right down. Bill had covered all the pumps over and had vanished. Glancing down at his watch Ryan checked the time. "It's very late. I don't want you to drive home. You've had quite a lot to drink. Would you like to stay, or shall I call you a taxi?"

Chapter 56

Ryan took Harry by the hand and led her to a door in the corner of the bar. The door had a little sign on it saying PRIVATE. Ryan pushed the door open and made his way up the steps with Harry following him. They arrived on a landing with numerous numbered doors running along either side.

"This is the staff quarters. Everyone else goes clubbing on a Friday night so, other than Bill, I am normally the only one in." Taking a key from his pocket he opened one of the doors. A small clean room with clothes scattered everywhere lay before them. Ryan grabbed a few handfuls of clothes while he apologised for the state of the room, and stuffed them into a cupboard before starting on the unmade bed. The room was fully fitted like a hotel room with TV, video player, radio, a small fridge, and a drinks maker. The walls were also panelled in a soft pine. The thick woollen carpet was blue and spongy to walk on. The curtains and unmade bed were made up in matching blue and white gingham. Ryan indicated to the door on the opposite side of the room. "There is a bathroom through there."

Harry went into the bathroom. It was tiny and compact and contained a ceramic shower, sink and toilet, all neatly arranged to give maximum space. Harry checked herself in the mirror and looked around for a few minutes giving Ryan the time he needed to tidy up his room. When she heard the soft music filtering under the door she went back out to meet Ryan.

"Would you like another drink or a coffee?"

Harry shook her head. The room was so small and the space around the bed was limited. Ryan placed his hands on Harry's slim shoulders. Looking into her eyes and stroking her cheek, he told her how beautiful she was.

For the first time in months Harry felt something stirring inside. This man she had only known for a short space of time made her feel sexy. He made her feel wanted but not in the same way James made her feel. He always tried very hard but Harry never felt anything. Now suddenly she was trembling. Ryan ran his hands down her arms and then pulled her in towards him. Placing his firm lips on top of hers he kissed her roughly. Harry kissed him back with passion, his moustache and beard tickling her face.

Gently he pushed Harry back onto the bed. Lying on top of her Ryan slipped his hand inside her top, resting it on her bosom. Sliding his hand around under her back, he felt for the clasp on her bra, expertly releasing it. Her bra came off. His hands now ran over her bare breasts. Pulling her top up over her head he moved his face down and sucked on her erect nipples, playing with them with his tongue as they hardened. As his lips traced their way back up to her mouth, his hand released the stud at the top of her trousers, and made its way into her lacy pants and over her soft down, searching for the opening. Harry became wetter and hotter as he pushed his finger in and out of her small, tight opening. Breaking for a minute he tore his own T-shirt, and jeans off. He knelt on the floor and rolled her trousers down her slender legs and left them crumpled on the ground. Taking her legs, he hooked them over his shoulders and found her moist opening with his tongue.

Harry felt his moustache and beard tickling against the top of her inner thigh. This was only the second person she had ever been intimate with and she was lost in her own desire for sex. He teased and played with her G spot until Harry had to beg him to enter her. At last he thrust his firm penis inside her, thrusting in and out of her as hard as he could. They climaxed together. Ryan collapsed in a heap on top of Harry. Exhausted, they both slept and remained caught up in each other's arms until the morning.

Ryan woke first, stroking Harry's cheek with his nose, he kissed her.

Harry woke realising where she was and was briefly alarmed.

Ryan's deep voice soon calmed her. "What a wonderful night. You are just so gorgeous." His hand ran once more down her naked body feeling, and admiring, how faultless she was.

Harry felt like she had escaped from reality; she felt distracted and safe for the first time in months. Not wanting her bubble to burst she snuggled up to Ryan, hanging on to every last moment of feeling secure in his arms.

Looking at his watch Ryan announced he had a lesson to deliver at nine. He had to shower and prepare. Reluctantly he rolled over the top of Harry and briefly held his position on her and kissed her on her nose and then lips before leaving the bed.

Harry hugged the quilt around her whilst she waited for him to finish in the shower. He took his time and appeared back in the room smelling fresh and clean. Whilst he dressed in front of her, he switched back into teaching mode and gave Harry some final tips to help her with her skiing. Making himself a coffee he offered one to Harry and placed it on the bedside table for her.

"I have to go, but just help yourself to anything you need. There is some bread and a toaster in the cupboard, fruit over there, and butter and jam in the fridge. Can you lock the room and give the key to Bill for me?" Leaning back over her he gave her a final kiss. "Ring me if you need any help, you still have my number, and come and look me up when you get back." With that, as he made his way to the door, he looked back once more. "I had a great night, Harry. You are so perfect in every way and you will be great on the slopes of the Pyrenees."

Harry lay for a while revisiting the night; she had enjoyed herself. Climbing out of his bed she stepped over the clothes he'd left on the floor from the previous evening and went into the shower room. The only towel she could find was the damp one he had just used. Showering, she started getting feelings of guilt. Had she betrayed Pablo? What would he think of her now? Was she easy? Has she made a big mistake? Oh, my goodness, what had come over her? She decided she wouldn't tell anyone; it was her secret night of passion and she would not share it with anyone, even Julie. More horror; what if Ryan contacted the papers? She could barely think about the consequences. She needed to put it behind her, go home, enjoy Christmas, and think about packing for her trip.

Chapter 57

The farmhouse was bustling with excitement. Mark and the twins had been to get the Christmas tree. The Scots spruce stood twelve feet tall and had been placed in a prominent position in the hallway. Anna was standing on a stepladder decorating the top of the tree. An angel had taken pride of place at the crown of the tree; brightly coloured tinsel swirled round its skirt and white lights twinkled like dancing fairies around its trunk. Icicles and glass baubles dangled from its branches.

The twins sensed Mark and Anna's relief when Harry's car crunched onto the drive and she walked in through the door. "Harry, Harry, look at the tree! Doesn't it look pretty?" Sophie threw her arms around Harry's neck, breaking the tension. Harry dropped to her knees placing the bag containing her clothing on the floor. Sophie placed her arms around Harry's neck and placed a welcoming kiss on her cheek.

"It looks wonderful. Did you two go and choose it with Dad?"

"Yes, we did, and Mickey and I both decided on this one, didn't we,

Dad?" Sophie stood up, proudly looking at the tree. Mickey was carefully searching through the box of decorations, sorting out all the old tin soldiers and clipping them to the branches of the tree.

"How did your last lesson go, darling?" Mark quizzed Harry with a concerned look on his face.

"Oh fine, I feel prepared to hit the slopes now. Do you need any help?" Harry quickly responded changing the subject.

"No, we've just about finished. What are you up to today?"

"I'm going shopping for Christmas presents and to get some of the things I need for my trip. Then I will be all prepared and will be able to help Mum for the next few days and enjoy Christmas. Is Grandma awake?"

"Yes. We've got her a little tree, and your father has been over to pick up her Christmas decorations so she has her own tree in her room. Pop in and see her."

Harry knocked on the door before entering the room.

Grandma was a little more mobile and enjoyed her privacy. "Hello, my dear. Did you have a nice evening?"

"Yes, I did thank you, Grandma." Harry greeted her grandmother with a kiss. "Oh, Grandma, your tree looks lovely. Did you decorate it all by yourself?"

"I certainly did! And I have put some of my cards up over the mantelpiece."

Harry sat down in the Queen Anne chair opposite her grandmother who was seated in front of the glowing fire. She stayed for a while, listening to her grandmother's stories of where and when she had acquired her multi-coloured, ancient, tree decorations. The stories Harry had heard a hundred times before, but she loved each and every story and would never tire of hearing them. Getting to her feet she excused herself and went to her room to change. John was away and Julie would be arriving shortly to go shopping with Harry.

The Regent Arcade was a mass of colour and glistening lights. A giant tree, with a hollowed-out base for the children to hide in, dominated the centre of the arcade. Julie and Harry made their way from shop to shop, studying their lists and ticking off the names of family and friends as they went along. Lists completed, they made their way to the coffee house. Julie could not wait to hear about Harry's evening. Harry had said she would tell her all about it when they had completed their shopping.

As they went through the revolving door of the coffee shop, the aroma overwhelmed them. Harry ordered her favourite, cappuccino with chocolate sprinkled over the top. Julie settled for a regular coffee. Both girls, pleased with their day's work, treated themselves to a couple of Danish pastries. They took two empty seats by the window overlooking the promenade. Harry told Julie all about her meal, what a nice chap Ryan was, and what a great instructor he had been. She omitted to tell Julie how they had spent the night together.

Julie accused Harry of fancying Ryan, an accusation Harry flatly denied. She swore Julie to secrecy and made her promise not to mention the meal to James. She did not want to hurt James' feelings. Harry got away with her little white lie and, after finishing their coffee, Julie went with Harry to get the final bits she needed for her skiing trip.

Once home Harry off loaded her shopping into her bedroom. Mark and Anna were out at a pantomime with the twins, so Harry helped herself to some cheese, biscuits, and a large glass of chilled wine, then went to sit with her grandmother while she ate them. It wasn't long before tiredness overwhelmed her. Leaving her grandmother watching TV, and with her fire stacked up crackling away, Harry went up to bed.

Chapter 58

The days passed in a blur. There was so much to be done in preparation for Christmas, presents to wrap, last minute cards to write and deliver, mince pies to bake, and the Christmas cake to ice and decorate. In the middle of the chaos, Christina arrived home with a new boyfriend, and shocked everyone as they announced their engagement over dinner on Christmas Eve.

Anna, Mark, and Grandma were all thrilled. Harry had met so many of Christina's boyfriends she was unsure how to feel and was reserving judgment. Mark popped the cork on a bottle of Moet and made a toast wishing them a happy future.

Gerard explained that he was a student doctor in his last year of training. He and Christina had recently met at a party and had hit it off straight away. He was tall, dark haired, quite handsome and seemed nice. Christina seemed very happy; she was glowing. It was clear she was enjoying someone else being in charge and she genuinely seemed to be in love. Gerard was a hit with the twins and fitted in well to the Smyth-Thomas family's eccentric life style and seemed very at home straight away.

It was the family tradition on Christmas Eve for everyone to place their presents for each other around the tree. Sophie and Mickey arranged them neatly in individual piles and size order, having a feel and a shake as they went. Even Grandma made it unaided and, with just the use of her stick, came out of her room to place her neatly wrapped parcels, tied up with gold ribbon, under the tree. After dinner and later that evening, Harry helped the twins dig out their old, dusty Santa-sacks from the attic. Sophie's was red and had a picture of a fluffy white rabbit on whilst Mickey's had a white bear. After overseeing their baths and giving them supper, Harry took them up to their rooms to hang their Santa sacks expectantly on the end of their beds. They were making such a racket that Anna had to send Mark up to take over and calm them down. She also needed Harry's help in the kitchen.

Mark sat on Sophie's bed with Mickey on his knee and tried quietening them down by reading them the Twelfth Night, during which they slowly calmed, engrossed in the Christmas story and listening to Mark's soothing voice. Once they were quite settled Mark let them back down stairs briefly to leave a glass of whiskey and a mince pie for Santa, and a carrot for Rudolf by the fireplace, before tucking them in and kissing them goodnight. When Mark was sure he could no longer hear them and they were at last silent and sleeping, he joined Fred, who always joined them for the Christmas celebrations, and invited Gerard to accompany them for their pre-Christmas drink at their local. This had become another Christmas Eve tradition, with hot, freshly-baked mince pies and mulled wine served to all the locals.

Christina and Harry spent the evening in the kitchen helping Anna prepare the vegetables, stuffing, potatoes, and little sausages wrapped in bacon, for the feast on Christmas Day. They had the radio on listening to Christmas hits of the past and enjoyed a glass of wine whilst they prepared the food. When everything was organised and the men, merrily singing carols, returned from the pub, it was almost midnight.

Harry crept upstairs, avoiding the creaking floorboards as she passed the twins' rooms, making her way along the landing to her own room. She had received a rather thick Christmas card in the post earlier that day. Her heart had leapt when she had seen the Spanish post mark on the envelope. She had hidden it away, not wanting to open it in front of her family and hoping they would forget about its arrival and not question her about what was in it or who was is from. She had sneaked it up to her room and blocked it out of her mind for the day. She decided it was time to look. Sitting cross-legged on her bed, in her warm, fleecy, tartan pyjamas, her heart racing, she smelt the envelope. There was a faint aroma of aftershave. It seemed very familiar and it didn't take Harry long to confirm her suspicions and realise it was Pablo's aftershave as she opened the envelope and pulled out a card. On the front was a picture of a dove; the symbol of peace. A small package fell out and slid onto her lap. Harry read the card over and over to herself, imagining hearing his voice saying the words, whilst closing her eyes and seeing his handsome face.

Harry

You will always be my English Rose. My feelings for you have not changed. This belongs to you, keep it safe.

Love forever
Pablo x

On opening the small, tightly wrapped package, a ring fell out. It was the engagement ring Pablo had bought for Harry. Choking back the tears, Harry placed the ring on her finger. It still fitted perfectly. What did he mean? The symbol of peace; was he sending her a message and letting her know, after all these months, that he still cared for her, that he still loved her?

Harry placed the card on the bedside table before curling up in her bed. What would he think if he knew she had spent the night with Ryan? Would he hate her? Weeping quietly into her pillow, wracked with guilt, she cried herself to sleep.

Chapter 59

Christmas morning arrived with shrieks and excited screams echoing around from the twins' rooms and waking the whole household. Harry looked at her clock. It was only 6. She put on her dressing gown and joined the rest of the family gathering around Mark and Anna's king sized bed.

Mickey and Sophie sat in the centre of the bed between Anna and Mark, with their Santa sacks spewing their contents onto the feather down duvet. Toys, sweets, and games were plucked from their sacks. After being briefly studied and admired, Harry and Christina neatly stacked them, in two piles, on the blanket box at the end of the bed. When the last gift left by Father Christmas had been opened, Harry helped the twins carry their presents back to their rooms.

Breakfast was a hurried affair; Church started on the dot of nine and time was creeping on. Any late arrivals would not get a seat and would remain standing for the entire service. All the pews would be overflowing as Catholics from around the area arrived for the Christmas celebration and to do their duty before they could fully indulge in the merriment.

Grandma remained at the farm, waiting for the nurse to arrive to help her wash and dress in her Christmas Day outfit, a green velvet dress with a fur collar which she had sent Anna to collect from her house a few days before.

Mass was a drawn-out affair; the twins were quite agitated and ready for Father Murphy to dish out Holy Communion so they could get home to the pile of presents waiting for them under the Christmas tree. At last he said the words they had been waiting for, "The Mass is over, go in Peace." Sophie and Mickey were like coiled springs bouncing over the pews, trying to drag Anna and Mark away as they shook hands with the congregation, wishing them a merry Christmas and accepting their good wishes to take back to Grandma.

Within half an hour of getting home the parcels had been opened. The once proud tree that had dominated the hallway for the past week was surrounded by a sea of torn paper.

Harry concealed her sadness wishing she could turn the clock back, wishing she hadn't slept with Ryan, wishing she hadn't run away and had given Pablo the chance to explain. Was it all too late now? She needed to put it out of her mind. Harry thanked her parents for the sheepskin lined snow boots they had given her, Christina for her woolly hat and scarf, and her grandmother, who had presented her with a pearl necklace that she had worn on special occasions and to dances when she had been a young lady. She briefly left the bedlam to take her gifts up to her room before getting a bin bag and clearing up the discarded and torn wrapping, checking for guarantees and receipts as she went.

Gerard had been a Godsend and went off to entertain and help the twins set up their Playstation, and to teach them how to play Mario, whilst Mark lit the fire to warm the dining room and chose some bottles of wine from his collection to complement the dinner.

Anna and Christina helped Grandma into the kitchen and sat her in the warm, comfortable chair next to the Aga where she watched them whilst they stirred, tested, and tasted the food. Grandma was happy watching all the activities with a glass of sweet sherry in her hand.

When the turkey had finished cooking and had adequate time to rest, Mark transferred it to the huge serving plate and Fred helped him carry the huge bird into the dining room and planted it at the head of the table for Mark to carve. Sprouts, peas, carrots, cauliflower, mash and roast potatoes, pigs in blankets and stuffing were placed into heated serving dishes. Beautifully displayed, they were trooped in and placed around the table.

The dining room looked like a Christmas card with holly and ivy draped around the antique mirrors. All the silver candelabras had been polished and were gleaming. With the candles lit they were placed around the room. The best crystal glasses glistened down the table along with the silver cutlery creating individual place settings. Mark carved the turkey onto hot plates and passed them around. Once everyone had been served, their plates overflowing, Grandma said Grace, and everyone pulled their crackers, put on their party hats, and tucked in to the feast.

Half way through the main course Gerard made a toast to Anna and the girls for the wonderful food being served and which had been cooked to perfection. Anna blushed but appreciated the compliment.

Once the main course had been devoured Christina and Harry carried the empty plates out to the kitchen and stacked them straight into the dishwasher. Mark took the pudding from the bubbling saucepan on the Aga. He then carefully prized the Christmas pudding out of the bowl and onto a heat proof plate. Pouring a very generous portion of brandy over the rich fruit mixture, he struck a match and set the pudding alight. Harry ran ahead of him, opening doors and turning off the lights as Mark entered the candle-lit dining room, with curtains drawn, and the blue flames dancing around the pudding. A chorus of "We wish you a merry Christmas," rang around the table before the brandy burnt out, and Mark started serving everyone a wedge of pudding. Crowned with brandy butter it was soon consumed and only a few crumbs remained on the serving dish. With everyone full to bursting the evening was spent in the lounge, sitting around the roaring fire, playing games. Even Grandma had a stab at charades; she performed a very entertaining "Last of The Summer Wine," from her chair, which Gerard got straight away, gaining more brownie points and going up in Grandma's estimation.

Sophie, exhausted by her busy day, had fallen asleep on Mark's knee and was the first to be taken up to her room. Not long after Sophie had dropped off, Mickey started to flag, so Mark helped him up to his room and into bed. He returned with night caps of brandy for the remaining family before they followed suit and, one by one, headed up to their rooms.

Christmas week flew by. Friends and relatives dropped in for drinks. Mark and Anna went out a few times to dinner with friends and to parties. Christina and Gerard, with Mark's permission, had a change of plan and decided they would marry the following summer. They spent the week drawing up a wedding list and laying down plans for the big day. Harry made the most of her free time, packing for her trip or exercising. The rest of the time she spent playing with the twins or taking advantage of the mild Christmas weather to go out riding.

Chapter 60

It was New Year's Eve. Harry was going to the tennis club with James where they were going to meet up with John and Julie and see the New Year in. Harry, who was normally quite organised, hadn't planned what she should wear until she stepped out of the shower, and then she started to panic. It was ages since she'd had to dress up. It was a dinner dance and Harry decided she should try to dress for the occasion. Dripping water all over the floor, she ran to her bedroom with only a towel wrapped around her. Pulling open her wardrobe door she surveyed the contents and her choices. Fingering through her dresses, she came across the beautiful dress she had worn to the Ski-Summer launch. Pablo had bought this for her and it was the most beautiful garment in her wardrobe, in fact, the most beautiful dress she had ever possessed. She couldn't wear it. It had been purchased for a special occasion by a lovely person. A lump rose in her throat so she pushed the dress to the back of the wardrobe and moved down the rack of clothes. She had bought a long, silk, navy dress, just in case there was a finishing dinner after the Ski-Winter filming had been completed. She could wear that. No! She suddenly remembered that she had already packed it, and it had taken her hours to carefully wrap it in tissue and to pack it, avoiding creasing it. Her little black dress sprang out at her. This had always been a lifesaver. She checked it for creases or marks. It was fine. When she arrived downstairs, Anna said she was a picture.

James was due at any moment so she grabbed her long, mohair coat before peeping in on her grandmother to say goodnight. "Give me a twirl, darling?"

Harry turned around and around, laughing as her grandmother told her how beautiful she looked.

"You know dear, you do remind me of your mother. She was a very beautiful young woman. All the boys used to give her the eye, even though she was with your father."

Harry kissed her grandmother goodbye and wished her a happy New Year as James pulled onto the drive.

Harry met him at the door and gave him a kiss on his cheek in greeting. James looked very handsome in his tuxedo. Complimenting Harry on her outfit, he helped her into her coat, then took her by the arm and led her to the car.

The car park at the tennis club was already heaving. James parked in front of several cars, blocking them in. No-one would be driving home that night and, if they did need to get their cars out, they could always come and find him. They all knew his car and he would put his keys behind the bar with the registration number as a precaution.

The function room was specially decorated for the party with burgundy and gold balloons suspended from the ceiling in large nets. Mistletoe was displayed over every light fixture and doorway. In the dining area the small tables had all been joined up to make several rows of long tables. These were set with gleaming cutlery, shining glasses, and paper burgundy napkins. The tennis club had gone to town for the New Year's party. Party poppers and streamers, arranged in clusters on the tables, were being popped and exploded around the room as people found their places. The bar was crowded. John and Julie had arrived just before Harry and James. John had already wedged himself into a gap and was getting them all drinks. James joined him to help carry the glasses and some champagne, while Julie and Harry found their names indicating their place settings. The table had been arranged following a boy-girl pattern. Drinking their champagne, Julie and Harry caught up on news of their families and Christmas.

Bottles of red and white wine had been placed intermittently down the table. The first course arrived from the kitchen and waiting staff wandered up and down enquiring as to whom had ordered pâté, soup, or prawn cocktails. As soon as the starter had been consumed the plates were whipped away and the main course arrived, another roast with a choice of vegetables and all the trimmings. Once again, as soon as it had been eaten, the plates were taken and the puddings arrived, the waiting staff hovering up and down the tables trying to track down who had ordered Christmas pudding, Sorbet, or Chocolate Cheesecake. Coffees followed the puddings, then it was time for a toast. The president of the tennis club had been introduced and he made a brief toast to all the members, old and new, and wished everyone a happy New Year.

There was a brief pause in the celebrations as tables were cleared and the room was rearranged. The DJ took to the stage and "Let Me entertain you." by Robbie Williams boomed from the speakers and everyone took to the floor.

It was a wild night. John and James kept the drinks flowing and Harry and Julie, well charged and inhibitions lost, joined a group of their friends, dancing and letting themselves go. The time flew past and it wasn't long before the DJ started the countdown to midnight. Everyone linked arms. The clock struck twelve, the balloons were released from the netting above the crowded floor, and Harry found herself sandwiched between James on her left and Julie on her right. Auld Lang Syne chimed out and, as it ended, kisses were traded between friends with a few intimate, deeper exchanges taking place fuelled by the alcohol. The crowd moved around kissing everyone in their path and wishing them a happy New Year. Harry found herself kissing total strangers as well as people she knew, all the time hoping she had not offended James by breaking off his over-friendly, lingering kiss.

When she finally caught up with him, the DJ snapped into action with "Sweet Caroline," followed by "High Ho Silver lining," before he switched the pace down and played "When You're in Love with A Beautiful Women."

James pulled Harry in close for a slow dance. Harry could feel his pelvis getting closer and closer to hers. His hands had moved down over her bottom. Just as Harry thought she could feel him becoming aroused the song finished.

Breaking free, she said she could do with another drink and led the way towards the bar. On reaching the bar she was whisked back to the dance floor by Alex, the club champion. He was tall, dark, unattached, and quite a playboy. A few dirty looks were shot in Harry's direction from the other single girls as they took to the floor. She was relieved to escape from James and give him a chance to cool down. The DJ played the last song of the night and the lights were turned up.

Alex asked Harry if he could see her again. Harry explained that she was going away for a few weeks so he should ask her again when she returned. Alex took Harry's number and gave her a gentle kiss on the cheek before saying goodnight.

Harry searched the emptying room for a glimpse of James but could not see him anywhere. She headed out to the cloakroom to find her coat. Julie had beaten her to it and had collected both their coats.

"Have you seen James anywhere?"

"He went outside and said he would wait for you in the taxi."

"Was he in a bad mood?"

"I must admit he didn't seem very happy."

"Oh dear, Julie what am I to do? Do you think he'll make a scene? You know what he's like when he's had a few drinks. He goes one way or the other."

"He'll be fine. He can't do anything if we are all in the taxi with you, can he? I'll make sure we drop you first."

Julie and Harry linked arms and stepped out into the frosty night air together.

James sat sulking in the back of the taxi as John had taken the front seat.

Harry sat beside James and whispered into his ear, "I hope you are not sulking, James."

James took her hand and whispered back, "No, just wishing our circumstances were different." He slid his arm around Harry's shoulder. "Don't worry, it's not your fault. I understand how you feel. I just find it hard to accept."

Pleased that he wasn't angry with her, Harry snuggled into his shoulder. John and Julie quickly broke out in a chorus of "Show me the way to go home," and they all joined in.

Once they arrived at the farm James got out of the car with Harry and walked her to the door. He apologised for his bad mood.

Harry said she understood and was not upset or cross with him. Stopping by the front door Harry leaned forward and gave James a reassuring peck on the lips and thanked him for a lovely evening, telling him that she would catch up with him on her return from the Pyrenees and before they were due back at college.

Chapter 61

After an emotional goodbye the Smyth-Thomas' waved Harry off in her loaded-up, yellow car. Harry drove to Dover and took the Pride of Calais across the Channel to France. The ferry crossing had been smooth and without any delays and Harry had made it to the train without any hitches. She had phoned her family when she had settled for the night and would sleep until she reached Narbonne with only a few hours of driving ahead of her. The train rattled along slowing as it passed through various stations. The chugging had lulled her to sleep and, thank God, no-one else entered her couchette; she had not had to share the bunks with anyone else.

What a beautiful winter's day, Harry thought as she drove off the train. It was too nice to be driving with the top up. It was gorgeous with the sun low in the sky, so she put her sunglasses on. She felt she wanted to make the most of the sunshine and fresh air after being cooped up on the train all night; she needed to freshen up and feel the breeze on her face.

There had been no fallout from her night with Ryan. He had sweetly phoned her the night before she left and wished her good luck.

As soon as Harry had the chance she pulled off the motorway onto the old roads and found somewhere to stop. Getting out of the car, she stretched her arms and legs while inhaling the fresh clean air. It took a few minutes to put the top down on her little yellow duckling. Taking her jacket from the back seat she put it on and turned the collar up. Twisting her long hair up into her cap, she sat back in the car and checked her face in the mirror. The night on the train had taken its toll. She was looking tired. Reaching for her makeup bag to touch her face up and apply some pink lip-gloss, she instantly felt better and ready to face Señor Cruanos. Feeling happier with the crisp air flowing around her face, the wind blowing the cobwebs away and the sun shining down from the clear blue sky, Harry drove on. With her new hero, Robbie Williams, blasting out of her cassette player, she only had a short journey left. Following the map with the address Señor Cruanos had sent her, she headed up the mountain road. As she climbed higher traces of the white stuff started appearing in patches, and soon the snow lay like a feathery eiderdown on the ground, sparkling in the sunlight. Stopping briefly to admire a small mountain stream framed with icicle shaped stalagmites and stalactites, the fresh clear spring water winding its way down the valley, Harry checked the final instructions on a map. The road wound up and up until the mountain top touched the skyline. In all she had eleven sharp bends to negotiate. At last she spotted the small town of Pas de la Casa below her. It was a typical mountain town. A rather large sixteenth century church, cut out of the rocks, stood towering over the storybook picture that lay before her. After pausing momentarily to marvel at the clock tower, she set off down through the narrow streets lined on either side by small whitewashed houses with their shuttered windows.

A few quaint little shops, a bar, a coffee shop and a restaurant, formed a square around a snow-blanketed park at the centre of the town. Some children were building a snowman in the square while others towed their sledges along the slush-covered cobbled street towards the edge of town. Men and women bustled around seeing to their daily chores stopping only briefly to stare at Harry's little yellow duckling as she drove through. It was an unusual sight, a pretty young girl driving a bright yellow car with the top down in the middle of winter.

At the edge of the town Harry came to a halt at some crossroads.

Checking once again on her map, she rooted around in her bag to find the address of the Chateau. Taking a right turn she was confronted with a fingerpost sign pointing in the direction of the Chateau. She was on the final part of her journey. The road twisted back up towards the mountain top. As Harry turned a sharp bend in the road she could see the old Chateau that had been recently converted into a hotel ahead of her. Driving between the stone pillars leading up the long drive to the Chateau, Harry suddenly felt very nervous and wished she was not alone. Taking several deep breaths, she tried to relax and calm herself down as she made her way slowly along the lengthy drive, walled by snow where it had been recently cleared. The lawns on either side of the drive were still thick with snow and the small moat in front of the beautiful old chateau was frozen solid. It looked like a picture postcard.

The Chateau itself looked like something out of a fairy tale with tall, spiral towers at each end. Sky blue shutters opened out from every window. A huge set of stone steps lead the way up to an oversized wooden, studded door. Several Porsches, Mercedes, a Rolls Royce, and a few Jeeps sat motionless either side of the steps. Harry picked out a parking space between a black Porsche and a black BMW soft-top and pulled in. Before making her way to the door she put the top back up on her car. As she started sorting out her luggage the front door opened.

Up on the second floor Pablo had been admiring the view as the yellow VW came up the drive. The driver looked stunning. A young girl wearing a blue jacket, matching cap and sunglasses stopped and got out of the car. Pablo watched as she daintily glided around the car, releasing clips and putting the top back up. She seemed familiar. He could not take his eyes off her and watched with intense curiosity as she took several bags from the car. His uncle arrived down the steps and wandered over to the car. Pablo could not believe his eyes when the young woman removed her sunglasses. His heart missed a beat as he instantly recognised her. It was Harry. He had thought he would be gone before she arrived although he had been wondering when she would turn up.

Her beautiful face smiling up at Señor Cruanos, Harry placed her hands on his shoulders as he leant forward and kissed her on both cheeks.

A porter, dressed in navy with gold trim on his jacket, appeared to carry Harry's bags. Waiting for Señor Cruanos to take the lead, he followed several paces behind. Señor Cruanos took Harry by the arm and led the way. The porter, trailing behind, struggled with Harry's heavy matching luggage.

A deep churning stirred in Pablo's stomach. He felt excited and sick at the same time. He had come to supervise the arrival of all the ski outfits and equipment. He had thought they were not starting the filming until next week. That was what he had been told. Had he been set up? What should he do? Pack quickly and go home? What would Harry do if she knew he was there? Would she want to leave? Thinking quickly, he realised there was still too much for him to do. He would have to stay for a couple of days. He would keep a low profile and stay out of her way. From then on he would eat in his room or down in the kitchens. The Cruanos crew had taken the hotel, and all its staff, over for the duration so it wouldn't be that difficult.

Señor Cruanos took Harry straight to her room. This was situated on the second floor. Once inside he kissed her again on her cheeks and left her with an itinerary to study and to settle in.

Harry's room was huge with doors leading out to a balcony that overlooked the snow-covered hills which ran in carved out slopes and finally halted at the back of the hotel. Harry could hear the chair lift and spotted it as it reared up through the pine trees to the left of the hotel.

The room was decked out with pink, velour-covered, luxurious furniture. A large four poster bed with pink satin sheets stood against the back wall of the room. The furniture was all matching and made from the same rosewood as that from which the framework of the bed had been crafted. A leather suite was casually arranged around French doors that led to the balcony. There was a wide screen TV in one corner of the room. In the other corner was a mini-bar and coffee making facilities. Harry opened the door leading to the en-suite. A sunken bath with a Jacuzzi covered half of the room. A shower unit, toilet and sink, made of matching porcelain, took up the rest of the space. The floor was carpeted in a thick, cream pile that ran right through from the bedroom and right around the sunken bath. The walls were tiled in ceramics and displayed a picture of a naked women feeding doves by a fountain.

Señor Cruanos had told Harry to relax for the rest of the morning. He would send for her so they could lunch together in the dining room while he ran over her schedule for the next few days. He had also left her with a layout of the chateau to study and get her bearings.

Harry helped herself to a cup of coffee that she sipped slowly, enjoying the rich flavour as she unpacked her clothes and hung them in the wardrobe. Heading into the bathroom with her large case of toiletries, she arranged everything in order around the bath and sink, making it look as homely as possible. Thinking of home, she suddenly remembered she'd promised to phone her parents the minute she arrived. Finding her brick mobile in her bag she discovered she had left it on for the last twenty four hours; the battery was flat. Finding a socket, she fitted her adapter to it and left her mobile on charge. She would ring as soon as it had enough charge later.

The time flew by as she arranged and rearranged her things around the room making it as cosy as possible.

There was a knock at the door. Harry opened the door to a porter who informed her it was time for lunch. Harry left what she was doing to follow the porter along the light, airy corridor with its plush carpet and old portraits staring out from the walls. They descended the stairs to the hall where she had first entered the building. Crossing the entrance hall she saw walls lined with books from floor to ceiling. It was set out like an old-fashioned library with its scattering of leather arm chairs and occasional tables. They passed the reception desk and entered the dining room through swing doors.

"Harry, my dear, you are looking very well, in fact, you look radiant."

Harry thanked Señor Cruanos and took the seat offered her between him and Armando, whom Harry recognised from S'Agaro. Armando got to his feet and kissed Harry on both cheeks. Once Harry was seated, a light lunch of salad and a selection of cold meats was served. All the time they ate Señor Cruanos handed Harry copies of each day's activities, running through what was required of her. By the end of the meal the table was littered in papers. Nothing else was required of Harry that day so she was free to go out and explore. She was now under strict instructions that, should she leave the Chateau, she would be assigned a bodyguard. It would not take the press long now to realise she was there and to stir the locals up. He thought it would not be safe for her to venture beyond the gates of the Chateau alone. Harry was quite happy with all the arrangements. If everything went well and the weather held, it would only take a few days or a week tops. She had two weeks at the Chateau but, if everything had been completed, Señor Cruanos saw no reason Harry could not leave a week earlier, unless she wished to stay and enjoying the skiing and relax. After being introduced to the film crew and a couple of photographers, Harry left Señor Cruanos. They seemed a friendly bunch and all spoke broken or perfect English.

Harry returned to her room and, after reading all her instructions again, she phoned her parents. Mark was out but Anna was very relieved to hear her voice. They spoke only briefly as Anna had just loaded the twins into the car to take them shopping when she heard the phone ring.

Harry decided she would go for a walk around the Chateau and changed into her sheepskin lined boots and her matching sheepskin light brown jacket, and headed out of the Chateau. The building was huge. At the side of the Chateau was a walled area; Harry could just make out an antique grape crusher and various other wine making stonework, all covered in snow.

"Do you mind if I join you?"

Harry, startled for a moment, turned around and was face to face with Fabien, one of the film crew she had met earlier.

"No, of course not, I'm only exploring the grounds."

Fabien was fair-haired and looked more Swedish than Spanish. He had a tall, slim frame, golden skin and blue eyes. "It is a very beautiful place. Do you think, yes?"

"Oh, I think it is. I've never stayed in the Pyrenees before and the town I passed through on the way here was very sweet." Harry smiled at him as he caught up with her.

"Maybe one night, when you have not had a very hard day, I could take you into the town for a look around."

"I would like that." Harry looked at the ground as she answered, suddenly feeling shy with this man she had only just met.

"Come, I have already explored every part of the grounds, let me show you the frozen fountains in the kitchen gardens." Fabien cocked his arm and waited for Harry to link hers before setting off in the direction of the kitchen gardens. As they walked along Fabien pointed out which directions the ski slopes were in. He explained the layout of the run that they would be using to do most of the filming. He described the beautiful pine forest that they had chosen to do some of the still shots in. Harry felt relaxed in Fabien's company and was relieved to have instantly found a friend. He had a natural gift of knowing the right thing to say and making Harry feel at ease in his company.

The kitchen garden was laid out in neat rows. Although everything was covered in snow it was well designed and still used to its full potential.

The fountain was the centre point of the garden. Just as Fabien had promised the fountain had frozen solid and stood to attention with only a few droplets of water dripping from the chrysanthemum head onto the frozen ring below. They wandered on around the Chateau through frosted archways, across blanketed lawns of snow, and back around to the front of the building.

"Would you like to go in now or would you like to walk around the lake?"

Harry checked her watch. Dinner was going to be served at eight. She still had hours to kill. "I would love to walk around the lake."

Fabien carried on talking. He was very sweet and never once asked Harry personal questions but waited for her to volunteer any information she wanted to share.

At the far side of the lake was a steep bank. Fabien ran down it and waited for Harry at the bottom. Harry gingerly made her way down the steep slope, only to slip half way down and glide the last few yards on her bum. Fabien burst out laughing as he helped Harry to her feet. She was covered in snow.

Brushing herself off and feeling a little humiliated, she scooped a huge ball of snow into her hand and hurled it at Fabien, who instantly retaliated. All hell broke out as they chased each other round, running in and out of the snow-covered arches beyond the lake, throwing snowballs backwards and forwards, pushing each other into drifts. When Fabien and Harry were both plastered in snow they called a truce, walking back to the hotel together, laughing at the sight of each other like a couple of children. Fabien decided they should go in via the back entrance where no one would see them, and sneak up to their rooms via the back stairs, used normally only by the hotel staff. Harry agreed and tiptoed up the stairs quietly trying to suppress her laughter. Once they reached the main landing they parted company and ran for their rooms.

Harry filled the bath while stripping off her wet clothes and hanging them neatly around the radiators in the room to dry. After a long, relaxing bubble bath Harry put a denim skirt and a pale blue cashmere jumper on. Comfortable and clean she stretched out on her bed to relax with her book until dinner.

Pablo arrived back from the cabin where he had been sorting out the skiing equipment for the next day's shoot. He had already seen his uncle and expressed his concerns over seeing Harry. He did not know how she would react, whether she would want to see him, or whether she would storm out. His uncle had agreed. Harry should not know about his presence until the filming had finished. Pablo would keep his distance and only watch the girl he still loved from afar.

The film crew surrounded the long oval dining table. As Harry stepped through the door the room briefly fell silent, broken only by the tall grandfather clock in the corner of the dining room as it struck eight. Harry nervously scanned the table for somewhere to sit. Fabien stood up and waved across the room. He had kept her a place. Grateful that she had made such a thoughtful friend, Harry went over, kissed him on both cheeks in greeting, and then sat down between Fabien and a pretty, dark-haired young woman who introduced herself as Rosa. Rosa was the make-up artist on the set and would be taking charge of Harry's face and hair.

Rosa studied Harry for a moment.

"You are as beautiful as I have been told, and even more so than your photo's give you credit for."

Harry blushed and thanked Rosa.

Everyone relaxed and chatted freely as the meal, a piping hot goulash with warm rolls, and several bottles of the Chateau red wine, was served. It was delicious. Everyone was extremely pleasant; the ice had been broken. Everybody made a point of speaking in English so as not to exclude Harry. Fabien told them all about their snowball fight and had the whole table in rapturous laughter when he described how Harry had slid down the bank on her bottom then had appeared out of the snow looking like the abominable snow-women.

A selection of cheeses, fruit, and coffee, completed the meal. Harry felt like one of the crew. The dinner had been a success and served its purpose of team bonding. Harry declined the offer of a drink with them all in the bar and headed off for an early night. She had to be on the slopes for seven. That meant leaving the Chateau at five-thirty a.m. It would be an early start and she was feeling exhausted after her journey the previous night in the couchette and her first day.

Pablo had a narrow escape as he saw Harry disappearing down the corridor and into her room. Leaving his room for the first time that evening he popped down to the bar for a night cap. Having said his hellos, he ordered a brandy. He then isolated himself from the rest of the crew, sitting in the corner of the room, having picked up the daily paper to read while he tried to relax with his large, warming drink.

It was difficult for him to concentrate on the paper or relax as the chatter from the bar drifted over. Harry was the main topic of conversation. He listened for a while until a couple of the crew started placing bets on who would bed her first. Disgusted at their immaturity and, finding it difficult to refrain from shouting at them all she was once his girl and far too good for the likes of them, he knocked back his brandy and headed back to his room for an early night.

Chapter 62

Harry had a good night's sleep. Feeling refreshed and ready for action, she dived out of bed when her alarm clock went off at the unsocial hour of five a.m. After a quick shower she slipped into her jeans, whilst cautiously sipping on a scolding hot cup of coffee she had just poured, and then made her way down to the main entrance hall where they were all to meet.

Everyone ticked off Armando's check list, their names called out like he was taking the school register. Each was issued with a walkie-talkie for the duration of the filming before the crew piled into various jeeps, with snow chains clamped around their tyres, that had miraculously appeared overnight.

Harry was escorted to the shoot by Armando in his BMW. Harry could not enjoy the scenery as it was still very dark; she could only follow the rear lights of the convoy of vehicles they were following. It was a short ten minute journey to the cabins they had hired next to the slopes. Once inside the cabin chaos broke out as orders were barked around at the various staff. Harry was taken into a bedroom that had been converted into a dressing room. A rack of Salopettes and jackets lined one wall. A shelf covered in hats, gloves, goggles, and various "Ski-Winter" accessories lined a couple of other shelves. Boots in assorted colours covered a portion of the wooden floor.

Rosa picked out a scarlet outfit for Harry to try. It fitted perfectly, hugging Harry's trim figure. Next, she sat Harry down and applied her makeup, picking out a scarlet lipstick to match the outfit. Harry's look was almost complete. Once she had finished a member of the ski equipment team, whom Harry had not yet met, came into the room with some scales.

His name was Pierre and he was French. Very sweetly he apologised to Harry but he needed to know her weight and height so he could get the correct DIN setting for her bindings. Harry jumped onto the scales. Once her weight had been noted several pairs of different shades of boots and bindings were brought in for her to try. Harry found the most comfortable fitting black ones she could and put them on. The bindings adjusted to the correct settings, Harry was almost ready.

Señor Cruanos wanted Harry's hair up for some of the shots then down for others. The red all-in-one suit was very retro and needed to be worn for some sophisticated shots, so Rosa had been instructed to place Harry's hair up.

Once Harry had her jacket on she followed Armando out of the cabin. The dark night sky had vanished and the sun was climbing slowly up behind the mountains and positioning itself in the sky. It was to be another fine day. Armando helped Harry over to the empty single man chairlift where he followed her up to the level she was to ski down from.

It was a skiing area integrated in spectacular natural countryside, with a total of three pistes covering ten kilometres of skiing in the very heart of the beautiful natural valley. Pine trees formed a thick woodland either side of the slope, the perfect back drop for filming.

Feeling a little queasy, Harry had a mixture of excitement and nerves as the cable bumped jerkily up to the waiting film crew. The film crew, along with a couple of photographers, had been positioned at various points on the run. When Harry came into view cameras started rolling, shooting her arrival and every movement she made on the chair.

Once off Harry was handed a set of red poles to match her outfit.

She was positioned on the slope while rolls of stills were taken as she got ready to ski off. Another skier joined her. She had been briefed to follow him down the slope. He knew the positions of the cameras and which way to lead Harry for the best shots. Harry had been told to ski down slowly the first time and to always ensure she smiled when she was in shot. They could speed the film up later if necessary.

Harry dug her poles into the deep virgin powder and pushed off. Grateful for someone to follow, she kept a safe distance back and slalomed gracefully down the slope, remembering her instructions from Ryan, making perfect turns at the appropriate places. Halfway down the slope, and much to her disappointment, her leader pulled off the slope and stopped.

This was an induction, so she too had been instructed to follow him off and stop. Rosa was waiting to touch up her make-up. After a brief rest, make-up checked and lipstick reapplied, she was off again.

The lower slope was not as steep and a lot slower. Trying to follow directly in her leader's tracks, Harry hoped to gain more speed as she traced his tracks in and out of the pine trees. She was really enjoying herself and it showed. She skied like a professional. At every bend was a camera waiting for her, the crew urging her on as she flew past, as well as shouting encouraging compliments. The bottom of the run was in sight. Harry wanted to make the perfect finish. She skied straight down, finishing the run with a fabulous quick stop, throwing a sprinkling of snow up at the cameras. Señor Cruanos was waiting. He had been in radio contact with his crew and had been monitoring her progress as she made her descent. Removing her goggles, bubbling with excitement, Harry beamed at Señor Cruanos and gave him a big hug. "Oh, that was great. When can I go again from a higher starting point?"

"Are you sure you are not too tired? Maybe you should have a drink first."

Harry assured him she was fine.

Señor Cruanos surveyed the slopes. They were still very empty with just the odd lonesome early skier out enjoying the fresh powder. "Okay, go quickly and change, my dear. We may have time for one more run but from the same point. There is not enough time to go higher."

Harry released her boots from the skis with her poles, stepped out of them, and was helped back into the cabin. Like a grand prix pit stop, two dressers waiting, her boots were taken off her feet with great speed.

Rosa miraculously appeared and helped Harry change into a baby blue set of Salopettes and a matching jacket. Removing her scarlet lipstick, she replaced it with a pale blue, trendy shade one from their own "Sunblock" range of cosmetics. Removing the pins from her hair, it was brushed out leaving it flowing down her back. White leather ski boots replaced the glossy black ones and Harry was back up the slope in no time.

This time Harry knew the layout of the slope and let her leader go well ahead before she pushed off. Harry looked good in the baby blue outfit. The goggles had been replaced by a pair of modern, blue-tinted sunglasses, specially designed with anti-snow glare for skiing in. Harry flew down the slope slowing only where the cameras were situated. Reaching the end of the run she felt full of life, very excited and still eager to carry on.

She turned to Señor Cruanos with a pleading look to go again on her face.

Señor Cruanos' stern face broke into a big smile as he shook his head saying no more that morning.

Harry had changed into her jeans and, with the team, headed back to the chateau where they were greeted with the smell of hot chocolate and croissants that were being served for breakfast in the dining room. After stuffing their hungry faces, Harry and the crew were straight back to work. This time Harry had to pose in several different ski outfits in the grounds of the chateau. The conference room downstairs was being used as a store room for more of the equipment, as well as a changing and make-up room for Rosa to use.

The sky was blue and made a perfect back drop for the new Ski-Winter range Harry had to model.

Pablo had made his own way up to the slopes in the morning and discreetly placed himself with some of the crew. He had been as impressed with Harry's snow skiing as he had her water skiing. As he had previously thought, she was a natural all-rounder at everything she did. His sleeping heart had been woken and his love for her was overwhelming. Watching her posing in the grounds of the Chateau from his bedroom was almost too much for him. His body was now aching with desire for her. How could he hold out until the filming had ended? What if she wouldn't even speak to him? He had managed to blank her out temporarily but now here she was again taking up every waking moment in his thoughts.

That night Harry joined the rest of the crew in the bar for a few drinks before going back to her room to spend some time reading before she slept. Pablo slipped quietly out of the Chateau and into town looking for some company to distract him from his thoughts.

Chapter 63

The next day the weather was equally beautiful. With another overnight dusting of fresh snow, it was perfect weather for skiing and textbook weather for filming. Harry was dressed in a black ski suit, with black boots, a black fur hat, and a very luminous pink lipstick. Her hair was left loose, flowing down her back. Filming was to be very "James Bond" in style. This time she was instructed to ski down from the higher slopes. They wanted to get some distant shots as well as some close-ups.

Once again Pablo had followed the crew up to the slopes and had positioned himself on the terrace of a bar halfway down the slope. From there he could follow Harry's every move.

Harry posed for the usual shots at the top of the slope before pushing off and following her leader's tracks, carving a path down the slope. There was also a crew following her descent of the slope, all on skies, with special miniature cameras attached to their bodies or helmets.

Señor Cruanos had said that, if the filming went smoothly, he thought they would have enough footage to make a few good adverts. With today's modern technology they could change the colour of the ski suits back at the portable studio and superimpose different hats and hair styles etcetera on to what they already had.

The first part of the course was quite tricky. After the fresh snowfall overnight it was very powdery. Harry zigzagged in and out of the trees, being greeted at every beauty spot by a waving film crew. The wind rushed past her face as she sped down the slope. A cluster of log cabins and a bar caught her eye as she approached the halfway marker. It looked a perfect place to stop for lunch if the weather held and she had the opportunity to enjoy some skiing on her own. Taking a little detour, and leaving her leader's tracks, she headed towards the bar decking for a closer look. As she whizzed past someone caught her eye. "I'm sure I know that man. God! He looks familiar." Temporarily distracted she almost lost her footing and began to wobble towards the boundary marker. The crew behind her slowed down and held their breath as they watched. Harry managed to gain control and made a sharp turn, avoiding a tree, before bringing herself to an abrupt halt. The crew pulled up behind her.

Fabien skied up to her side. "You okay? You seemed to lose the leader's tracks and get a little wobbly then."

"Oh, I'm fine. I just thought for a moment I saw someone I knew, and it distracted me. Did you see the man sitting alone on the terrace of the bar back there?"

"Ah, you mean Señor Cruanos's nephew."

"Pablo. Pablo is here?"

"Yes. Have you not met him yet? He keeps himself very much to himself. He is in charge of all the skiing equipment."

Harry was totally shaken. Pablo was here and he hadn't even bothered to let her know. What did the note mean at Christmas then? Doesn't he even want to be my friend?

"Come on, Harry, let's get this over with and then maybe I could take you skiing. We could have some fun."

Harry turned to the rest of the crew who were anxiously waiting a few yards away. "I'm fine, honestly. Let's go." Harry looked for the leader's tracks and pushed off. She knew she had to concentrate on the job in hand and forget about Pablo. He obviously was no longer interested in her.

She finished the rest of the course without a hitch and was soon back at the Chateau, pacing the floor of her room, wondering what she should do.

After lunch the afternoon was hers. The film crew and Señor Cruanos were going to look at the footage and stills to see if they had enough to work with, so Harry had the whole afternoon to herself.

Wanting to clear her head she asked for permission to go for a drive. Señor Cruanos had given his permission but had insisted Hugo go with her to give her some protection. Harry declined the offer and said she would just go for a walk in the grounds instead. She needed some time alone; she was feeling a little tired. Señor Cruanos said he understood and left her.

Chapter 64

Where was Pablo? Was he staying in the hotel? She headed down to the bar to find Fabien. Maybe he would know where she could find Pablo. The bar was empty. Next she tried the conference room. Perhaps Rosa would know where she could find Fabien and Pablo.

"Hi, Rosa." Rosa looked up from where she was working and smiled. "Have you seen Fabien anywhere?"

"Fabien is with the crew and Señor Cruanos running through the footage now, and I think he will be busy all afternoon. Can I help you at all?"

"Well, actually I was looking for Pablo, the nephew of Señor Cruanos. Do you know him?"

"Yes, I know Pablo. He is a very nice, quiet man. He's always alone and stays away from the rest of the crew."

"Would you know where I could find him?"

"I'm sorry, Harry. We were all told Señor Pablo was not to be disturbed while he was here and anyway, I would not know where to begin to look."

At that moment Harry glanced out of the window and saw someone who looked like Pablo getting into one of the jeeps.

"Thanks," she shouted back to Rosa as she hastily shut the door then raced up to her room where she grabbed her car keys and jacket. She was out on the drive and in her car before anyone had time to stop her.

Rosa heard a car door slam and glanced out of the window as Harry, alone, headed off down the drive. Having heard Harry's instructions that she was not to leave the grounds alone, Rosa thought she should report the matter to Señor Cruanos straight away. Not wanting to alarm any of the other members of the crew, Rosa made her way from room to room, opening doors, searching for Señor Cruanos. First, she found Fabien. Walking quietly over to him she asked him if he could spare a moment.

Fabien, seeing the anxious look on Rosa's face, stepped out of the room closing the door behind them. "What's wrong, Rosa?"

"It is Harry. She came to the conference room about ten minutes ago looking for you and asking about where she could find Pablo. I said you were busy and I did not know where Pablo was. The next minute I saw her take off down the drive in that little yellow car of hers. She was alone, no security with her! What should I do? She was told she was not to leave the hotel grounds without a bodyguard once the filming had started."

"Don't worry. I'll take one of the jeeps and go look for her. I have my walkie-talkie with me. If I am not back by seven-thirty with her you had better inform Señor Cruanos." Fabien checked with his colleague that he could manage on his own for a few hours, then excused himself. Jumping into another one of the jeeps he made his way down the twisting road towards Pas de las Casa. Driving down the main street, scouring every side road, he searched for Harry's car, stopping on occasions to ask the locals if they had seen the yellow VW pass through.

Harry had set off like a bat out of hell and had finally caught sight of the jeep. The jeep was headed in the opposite direction from the town and towards the ski slopes. The jeep ground to a halt right outside the cabin. As Harry flew in and parked next to the jeep, she glanced over and saw the cabin door just shut. Getting out of her car she made her way up the steps and tried the door. The door was unlocked. Hesitating momentarily and taking a deep breath, she carefully opened the door. Tiptoeing in she could hear movement in the far room. Suddenly overcome by emotions, tears streaming down her face she tapped on the door. "Pablo is that you in there?" The door opened. Much to Harry's disappointment it was not Pablo, it was Luis, one of the film crew.

"Oh! I am so sorry." Harry backed away, not quite knowing what to do or say, wiping the tears from her face.

"Are you okay?" Luis went to slip his arm around Harry's shoulder.

Harry stepped back and quickly regained her composure. "I had something in my eye. I was actually looking for Pablo."

Luis stepped back from the doorway, revealing the empty room, and indicated for Harry to look around the room. "As you can see, I am alone."

Harry, feeling very stupid, glanced into the room. No-one else was there. It must have been Luis she had followed from the Chateau.

"Hey, you look upset. Why don't you come for a ski with me?" Harry tried to think of an excuse.

Luis patted her arm in a comforting way. "Come on, it will be fun. No cameras, just a good ski".

"Okay," Harry nodded. "I had better pop back to the Chateau and let someone know where I am."

Luis pointed to a phone in the room and punched in the number then handed the phone to Harry.

"Hello, this is Harry. Could I speak to Rosa please?" There was a brief pause. Harry could hear the clatter of shoes on the wooden floor back at the Chateau.

"Harry! Where are you? I have been so worried."

"It is okay, Rosa. I am at the cabin. I'm just going to go for a ski with Luis. Will you let anyone know if I'm missed?"

"Are you sure you are okay?"

"Honestly, Rosa, I'm fine. I'll be back later."

Luis left Harry alone to change while he sorted out some skies and poles. Harry changed quickly and arrived out in the baby blue Salopettes she had worn on the first day. Her hair was tied up in a knot and tucked into a matching, pale blue, knitted ski hat.

"Hey, you look great. Shall we go?"

Harry followed Luis out of the cabin and waited at the bottom of the steps while he locked up. They stepped onto the hardened icy track of compressed snow, skies over their shoulders and poles in hand, and headed over towards the chair lift. Taking a seat, they sat side by side on a bench near to the lift and tightened their boots before they put their skies on and took the chair to the top of the slope.

Back at the Chateau Rosa had managed to contact Fabien and tell him not to worry; Harry was skiing with Luis. Fabien, very relieved, returned to the Chateau and got straight back to work. He was worried; Luis had a bad reputation with women and Harry seemed very young and naive. Still, there was nothing he could do about it so, the best thing for him, was to get stuck into his work and block it out of his mind.

Luis let Harry ski on ahead so he could follow and watch her body in the fitted salopettes, gracefully twisting and turning down the slope.

Pablo had finished his work for the day and decided he ought to find Harry. He had a feeling she had recognised him when she had been skiing earlier, and this had caused her to lose concentration, which was when she nearly skied into the boundary fencing. It had worried him all afternoon. He needed to see her; it was time.

Señor Cruanos had confided in his nephew. He had been very pleased with the results of the film editing and only needed to use Harry for a few more stills. These could all be done at the Chateau if the weather turned against them.

Pablo went to Harry's room and, at first, knocked quietly on the door. He then knocked louder.

There was no answer so he went down to the conference room to see if Rosa knew where she was. Rosa apologised and explained what had happened earlier. Pablo thanked her then stormed out of the Chateau. He was very angry. Luis was one of the crew members who had a bet on that he would be the one to bed Harry.

Pablo drove to the cabin at such speed that at one point he almost skidded off the road on some snow that had blown across it. It was getting late; the sky was beginning to darken. Storms were forecast that night and the last thing Pablo wanted was for Harry to be driving back to the Chateau alone along the narrow icy road.

Half way down the slope Luis caught up with Harry and suggested they stopped and had something to drink at the bar before they completed the lower part of the run. Harry was enjoying the skiing so much she took some persuasion. Finally she agreed she would stop for one drink. Removing their skies they planted them into the snow and hung their poles between their skies then, gripping the iron safety railing, climbed the slippery wooden steps to the bar terrace. Harry headed into the bar to find the toilet. When she returned Luis was sitting looking over the slopes with a couple of double brandies.

"I don't think I should drink one of those when I still have to ski down and drive. It will go straight to my head."

"Don't worry, Luis is here. I will take care of you and make sure you get back safely." He smiled as he placed one of the glasses in Harry's hand. "Smoke?" Luis pulled a packet of Marlboro Lights from his inside jacket pocket and offered one to Harry.

"Well, I don't normally." Harry took a sip of brandy and felt it burn as it trickled down her throat and into her stomach warming her instantly.

"Go on, there's no-one around to see you."

Harry was beginning to thaw as the alcohol kicked in. "Okay." She nodded and slid one from the packet. Luis flipped his zippo into action and lit it. Harry inhaled and began to cough straight away. She hadn't had a cigarette in months.

Luis pretended not to notice. All he was concerned about was winning his bet; he had quite a lot of money running on this one. Once the first double was finished another appeared. Harry was feeling fairly, mellow. Luis chatted about the film crew and how he had come to work in the industry. Time seemed to fly past.

Harry suddenly realised how dark it was getting and that all the ski lifts had stopped for the night. Getting to her feet, she giggled. "We had better go. Dinner will be served and we'll miss it." She wobbled towards the steps.

Luis left some money on the table and rushed to help Harry down the steps.

"I think the brandy has gone straight to my head. I hope I can still ski."

"Come on, let me put your skies on for you." Luis took Harry's small hand in his as she placed her boot into the ski. Once he'd got both her feet securely in the bindings, he dropped a pole and took Harry's hand, leading her onto the run. "Now, just stay behind me. Take your time and follow my tracks."

Harry could just make out the deeper tracks in the snow and pushed off not waiting for Luis.

"Wait for me, Harry," Luis pleaded as he groped around in the snow for his missing ski pole. By the time, he found it Harry was out of sight.

Skiing back and forth Harry made her way carefully down the slope. She could hear Luis in the distance shouting for her to wait. This made her giggle and so she pushed on, the fresh air cooling her flushed cheeks and sobering her up as she inhaled and filled her lungs. On the last bend she slid slowly into the trees and hid, trying not to laugh as a very cross Luis raced past. Creeping out, she pushed off again.

At the bottom of the slope Luis was frantic. Where had the little minx got to? The next moment Harry flew in behind him and startled him. Luis got such a shock as he swung round that he lost his balance and he fell over, his legs all tangled up with skies and poles.

Harry burst out laughing. Taking his skis off Luis grabbed a huge pile of snow and began chasing Harry with it. Laughing and shrieking, she desperately tried to get her skis off so she could make a run for it, but Luis was too quick. He covered her from head to toe in snow. This time they were both laughing and collapsed in a heap on the ground.

Chapter 65

Pablo heard voices and the commotion outside. He had been sitting in the cabin for over an hour waiting for Harry, worrying about Harry in the hands of Luis, worrying about the darkness and Harry still being out on the slopes, angry at himself for not letting Harry know he was there.

He opened the door throwing a beam of light across the ground, his eyes focusing on Harry and Luis rolling around in the snow.

The light startling them both, Luis and Harry dropped their handfuls of snow and looked up to the open doorway of the cabin. Harry knew it was Pablo straight away. She sat motionless unable to speak. Luis recognised Pablo. He had always resented him. Luis had come from a broken home himself and had none of the family love, or the security of the bank account, Pablo had been born into. He also knew that Pablo and Harry had once been an item.

"Come and join us, Señor Pablo. We are having fun, aren't we, Harry?"

Harry was still speechless. Her body would not move; her mouth wide open she tried to call out Pablo's name but nothing happened.

"You're late for dinner," Pablo hissed back at Luis as he headed for his car.

Harry had at last managed to struggle to her feet. Picking her skis up and finding her voice, she shouted after Pablo. It was too late. Pablo was already spinning his car around in the car park and heading for the exit.

Luis tried to make small talk while Harry snatched up her clothes from the cabin.

"I've got to get back and speak to Pablo. Explain nothing is going on between you and me."

Luis didn't try to stop her; he would have his chance with Harry yet.

Once back at the Chateau Harry looked for Pablo's car. It was not there. She would have to speak to him later, explain and tell him nothing was going on. No-one would ever take his place.

Dinner had been served and was being cleared away when Harry entered the dining room.

Fabien was quick to spot her; she looked wretched. "I've done you a plate of food. It is in the kitchen. You go up to your room and change. I'll make you a tray and bring it up to you."

"Thanks, Fabien that was really sweet of you."

Harry had a shower and changed into some dry clothes. She was seated on her bed drying her hair when Fabien knocked on the door. Harry let him in.

"I have things to do so I can't stay and talk but I'll meet you down in the bar in an hour. You look like you could do with someone to talk to." Leaving the tray on the bed he kissed Harry gently on the cheek. He could tell she was very upset.

Fabien got into one of the jeeps and headed into town. He needed to find Pablo. It was time Pablo and Harry got together for a chat. Pablo had been moody since Harry's arrival. It was obvious he still had very strong feelings for her. As for Harry, Fabien had known, the minute he'd noticed her spot Pablo on the terrace of the little bar, when she had nearly lost her footings, that she loved him. He would have to be quick. He had told Harry he would meet her in the bar in an hour. Firstly, he drove to the coffee shop in Pas de la Cassa. He knew Pablo sometimes went there for a drink. He made some enquiries; no-one had seen Pablo. Some of the locals who knew Pablo suggested he should try Manuel's bar. Fabien got back in his car and drove over to the village square. Sure enough, Pablo's jeep was parked right outside the front door. Fabien went into the dark, crowded bar and looked around. Just as he turned to leave a voice he recognised called to him.

"Hey, Fabien! Come and join me for a drink."

Fabien looked across the room in the direction of the voice. Pablo was sitting with a couple of girls surrounded by empty whisky glasses and a bottle of Champagne. Crossing the wooden floor of the small bar in three strides Fabien helped Pablo to his feet. "Come on, I've got someone back at the Chateau who wants to talk to you."

Pablo was not capable of putting one foot in front of the other and happily let Fabien support him up from his chair and struggle out to his car. Fabien strapped him safely in. Checking on his watch, the hour was nearly up. He had to get Pablo back and sobered up before he could take him to meet and talk to Harry. Getting his walkie-talkie out of his jacket pocket he tried Rosa. Fortunately she had hers turned on and he quickly filled her in. Rosa was very willing to help. Wishing Fabien luck, she said she would keep Harry in the bar as long as necessary.

Chapter 66

Harry was already sitting on one side of the fireplace, cradling a glass of wine, when Rosa found her.

"Hello, Harry, do you mind if I sit with you?" Harry looked around the room. There was a handful of the film crew at the bar so far and no sign of Fabien.

"Sorry, Rosa, Fabien was joining me for a drink, but please do." Harry patted the empty seat. Harry liked Rosa a great deal and didn't want to refuse her.

"Okay, great. I'll just have a quick drink with you while you are waiting." Rosa headed for the bar and ordered a bottle of wine just as Luis walked in. Rosa saw Luis scan the room and his eyes instantly fell on Harry. Without waiting to pay she snatched up the bottle of wine and glass that had been placed in front of her and headed back to the empty seat next to Harry.

Checking her watch every few minutes, Harry could not understand what had happened to Fabien and was pleased Rosa had joined her. Fabien must have had too much to do. Harry, relieved she had some company, began to get stuck into the wine.

Rosa kept pace to prevent Harry from drinking the entire bottle herself. Eventually Rosa heard her walkie-talkie crackle. It must be Fabien. She made an excuse that she needed the bathroom and told Harry to keep her seat. Fabien was outside the Chateau with Pablo and needed help.

Fabien struggled in through the doors with Pablo who was well and truly out of it.

"What are we going to do with you? Harry's sat in there waiting for you!"

"Let us just get him into the kitchen and get some coffee into him." Rosa could see how much Fabien was struggling and took hold of Pablo's other-arm. When they got to the kitchen the door was locked; the kitchen had been closed for the night.

"You go to reception and get the key. I'll go around through the dining room and see if I can open the door from the other side."

Carefully, they propped Pablo against the wall before heading in different directions. Luis had seized his chance jumping straight into the chair Rosa had just vacated. "Tell me, Harry, how did you enjoy our little roll around in the snow?"

"Luis, we were just having a bit of fun. Please don't read anything into it. I am not interested."

Pablo began to come to and found himself alone and a little confused. Deciding he wanted another drink he staggered in the direction of the bar.

"Come on, Harry, you know Pablo is no longer interested in you. If he was why has he kept himself hidden away and managed to avoid you the whole time you have been here?"

Harry began to think, "Maybe Luis is right. Did he just send me the ring at Christmas as a keepsake? Maybe he just wanted closure."

As Pablo entered the bar he spotted Luis perched on the edge of the chair next to Harry. Catching the end of Luis's speech was like a red rag to a bull. Staggering across the room he launched himself in Luis's direction. "Who said I am no longer interested?" Pablo growled as he threw a punch straight at Luis but lost his balance.

Harry jumped to her feet and, as Pablo fell to the floor, she went down on her knees next to him. As the tears rolled down her cheeks she gently lifted Pablo's head and cradled it onto her knee.

"Pablo, are you okay? Speak to me, Pablo." She pleaded with him but he was out cold.

Fabien and Rosa had heard the commotion and rushed into the bar to see what was going on. Fabien pushed past all the crew who were now standing and had gathered around to watch the action. He spotted Pablo unconscious on the floor. Quickly he shouted to Hugo, one of the crew, to take Pablo's other arm and help get him up to his room.

Receiving no sympathy from anyone, Luis made a hasty retreat from the room, nursing his bloody nose.

Harry ran ahead, asking which way it was to Pablo's room so she could open the door. Once she had reached the upstairs landing, Fabien told her to stop. She was almost opposite her own room.

"That's the one, there."

Harry tried the door. It was locked. "Has he got his key in his pocket?"

Fabien paused momentarily while Rosa felt down the outsides of Pablo's pockets. Looking up at Harry she shook her head.

"Okay, look, my room is there. Let's just put him on my bed." Harry crossed the corridor and unlocked the door into her room. She removed the tray with her empty dinner plate from her bed. Struggling for breath, whilst carrying Pablo's full weight, Fabien and Hugo made it into the room. At last they reached the bed and gently lowered Pablo onto the pillows Harry had arranged.

Chapter 67

Sitting on the side of the bed Fabien began to examine Pablo, firstly taking a good look in Pablo's eyes to check his pupil reaction and then looking in Pablo's mouth and taking his pulse. "I took a basic course in paramedics last summer when I was unemployed. I know just the basics and I am sure Pablo will be fine. He has drunk too much alcohol on an empty stomach and he just needs to sleep it off. In the morning, he will have a very bad head. Maybe a little concussion too where he bumped his head when he fell, but nothing to worry about."

Rosa, who had been standing quietly watching Harry's concerned face, stepped forward and placed her arm around Harry. "Would you like me to stay in here with you for the night?"

"Oh no, don't worry, I will be fine."

"I will be just down the corridor in room number twenty-six if you want me." Rosa placed her arm briefly around Harry's slim waist and gave her a quick squeeze and waited for Fabien to finish.

Fabien got to his feet. Rubbing Harry gently on her arm he asked if she wanted any more help. Harry shook her head and said she would be fine. Leaning forward he gently kissed Harry on both cheeks. They left Harry alone with Pablo, closing the bedroom door behind them.

Harry sat on the side of the bed and looked at Pablo. His face looked as gorgeous as ever. She still loved him. She couldn't help herself. After a while she thought she ought to make him more comfortable. "I'm just going to make you a little comfier, Pablo." Harry spoke like a nurse to her patient explaining, as she went along, what she was doing. "I'm going to take some of your clothes off, okay?" Not expecting an answer, Harry carried on undoing the laces on his brown leather Italian boots. She wriggled them loose before removing them. Next she took his socks off his feet. Unbuckling his belt, she unzipped his jeans and, with a struggle, managed to get them over his bottom, revealing his white boxer shorts. "You are still so sexy, Pablo." Harry spoke quietly to him while she striped off his clothes. Removing his jacket, she left him looking cosier in his T-shirt and boxers. "Oh, Pablo! I could kiss you all over. I just wish I knew how you felt about me." Harry pulled the thick duvet up over Pablo's body leaving him exposed from the chest upwards. She then manipulated his arms from under the quilt and laid them gently on top. "There you go." She stood back and took a long, hard look at the man she still loved, and blinked back the tears of relief. She was at last with the man she had missed so much, even though Pablo lay motionless. "I'll just pop into the bathroom and put my PJ's on." Harry vanished into the bathroom and climbed into her PJ's before washing her face and brushing her teeth.

Tiptoeing around the bed she turned the bedside light on and the main light off. Then gently she slid into bed next to Pablo, thinking if she felt him stir she would quickly get out of bed and sit in the chair next to it. She didn't want him to know she had crept in to the bed and slept next to him all night. That is exactly what Conchitta had done that fateful night.

Chapter 68

"I hope you don't mind, Pablo, if I just pinch a quick kiss while you are sleeping? If you don't still love me when you wake up, it may be the last kiss I ever have." Resting on her elbow, studying the face she so loved, she gently traced a line softly around his face with her fingers. "Pablo, I do love you so much. Why did I ever run away?" Leaning forward she kissed him gently on the forehead and slowly down his nose until her soft, warm lips rested on his.

Pablo's arms shot around her body holding her tightly. "Do you know how long I have been waiting for this moment?"

Harry got such a shock that she nearly screamed. Fighting with all her strength Harry tried to struggle free. "You bastard, Pablo! How long have you been awake for?" Wriggling, and thumping him on the chest, Harry fought to get away.

"Come on, Harry. Now I have you here I will never let you go again, so let us talk."

Pablo could not stop Harry struggling so, tightening his arms around her body, he moved his hands to the back of her head and held her delicate face firmly, preventing her turning away from him. He swung over the top of Harry, pinning her down with the full weight of his body. Now he was on top, he forced his lips onto hers. Kissing her forcefully at first with no response, he then kissed her gently and more tenderly.

Slowly the memories came flooding back. Harry could smell his familiar aftershave. The weight of his body on hers felt natural. His lips were warm and memorable. She loved this man. She could not deny or resist him anymore. Her body surrendered and her lips began to respond. Pablo's tongue pushed its way through Harry's lips and into her mouth.

Feeling Harry's muscles relax, he loosened her one arm and slipped his hand under her PJ top and up around her back, feeling her soft, warm, naked skin. Once Harry had totally succumbed, her body no longer stiff and fighting, Pablo knew she was once again his English Rose. In his soft Spanish accent, he spoke. "Did you mean what you said? Do you still love me?"

Harry looked up into his dark, sparkling eyes, holding his gaze as she answered. "Of course I do." Pablo brushed his nose against her smooth cheek then gave her a long lingering kiss.

"Did you mean what you said, Pablo? Are you still interested in me?"

"Interested in you? Yes! Love you? Yes! Want to marry you and spend the rest of my life with you? Yes! And this time I will not let you go."

Harry wrapped both her arms around Pablo and held him close and whispered in his ear, "This time I'm not going anywhere."

The End

.

Lightning Source UK Ltd.
Milton Keynes UK
UKHW012024091118
332085UK00001B/157/P